Cigerets, Guns & Beer

Phillip T. Stephens

Fiction
Literary Fiction
Suspense
Mystery

ISBN: 978-0-9858285-4-7

Phillip T. Stephens
Too Bright Girls Publications
Austin, TX
toobrightgirls@gmail.com

Cover design includes
Sonoran Moonrise, Photo by Lisa Langell
Burned Can, Photo by Maurice Boere
Courtesy of freeimages.com

Too Bright Girls is a family publisher.
Not accepting submissions or queries.
Follow Phillip on Twitter *@stephens_pt*

Books by Phillip T. Stephens

Raising Hell

The Worst Noel

Prologue

The wind nudged his back. Get up. Move on.

Dodd kneeled on the rise above the arroyo—one leg on the knee, the other on the heel —chewing a blade of grass and studying the horizon. He was dressed for Texas in August: white T-shirt, blue jeans and boots. With his sandy hair and flat stomach he looked like any one of the old boys who sprouted across the landscape.

The highway stretched for miles in both directions. The land looked deserted by God, modern civilization, any sign of creature comfort. Heat waves rolled off the asphalt as thick as a fog bank. A hawk and a buzzard circled warily, as though deciding whether to fight over the same morsel or wait for the other to die first. The sky looked as white as the sun, no clouds, not the slightest blue tint, nothing to indicate the day would get anything but hotter.

To his right he could see a fifteen-acre farm, untended and years before gone to seed. Below the farm, a small branch of the Pecos River meandered slowly by, as though hopelessly separated from the main stream. Any fish would be buried in the mud at the bottom, hoping the river above them didn't evaporate in the afternoon sun.

The town, what little of it there was, could be seen a few miles south.

He wondered if this is what physicists referred to as an event horizon.

He knew he should get back in the car and drive. An easy decision—four steps and back into the car.

He just couldn't make it. The attraction to the town seemed irresistible.

He thought to ask for a sign. He didn't particularly believe in signs. From God, from the universe, it didn't matter. But if he were ever to ask for a sign, now would be the time. If the wind stopped, he would stop. If it kept blowing, he would keep going. He tossed a handful of dirt into the air. The wind kept blowing. West to I-10; to Santa Fe.

"Praise the Lord," he whispered to himself.

Dodd returned to his Mustang. His back seat carried his luggage because his trunk was filled with books. His suit bag was draped over the passenger seat. He twisted the ignition. The starter choked and died. The gas gauge lifted only slightly, to just above empty. He pushed open the door and climbed back out to look underneath the gas tank. A gasoline puddle crept from underneath his car toward his foot. He cursed under his breath.

Which is why he would stop for gas and find himself caught between two maniacs with guns.

Dodd had crossed the event horizon threshold. No pulling out.

It reminded him of a class on mythology he took in prison. The teacher said the most important lesson taught by myths is this: even the Gods can't argue with fate.

Monday Afternoon

Chapter 1

The sign dominated the town, right where Preacher said it would be, spelled exactly the way Preacher said it would be. As big as Texas. Sixty-foot high red neon letters over painted yellow letters: "CIGERETS GUNS & BEER." Underneath the sign read: "One Stop Shopping."

All that for a gas station, for Christ's sake.

Preacher would describe that sign in loving detail even though he hadn't seen it for thirteen years. The sign that marked Sweet Water Falls, a sign visible from any curve of I-10 for miles in either direction.

He lifted the pump handle and rattled his keys while the gas gurgled into his Mustang, a vintage '65 metallic blue convertible he found blocks behind an elderly couples' house. Like him, their son did time in Huntsville but he wasn't due for parole until 1992 and hadn't written or called since he went inside. They were glad to let it go for five hundred and it cost him another six to get it back to factory condition.

Dodd figured he could find an overnight mechanic in Ft. Stockton. He just hoped the fuel wasn't leaking too fast to keep him from getting there.

He studied the storefront while the gallons ticked off. Dust bunnies and handwritten promotions littered the large windows:

"Cigerets: Two free cartons with any Smith & Wesson. You're choice Camals or Marlbros." Dodd guessed that spelling wasn't covered in the local high school.

"Six & Six special–six pack and six packs of Winstons $6." Wouldn't that be the Six-Six-Six special? Dodd wondered.

He counted the cents as they ticked off the gas pump, slower and slower. After five dollars, the counter slowed down to eternity. When the pump trigger tripped, he racked up the handle and crossed the dusty concrete to the store.

Eight dollars and fifty-seven cents. Dodd still couldn't get over it. Before prison gas was twenty-seven cents a gallon, and it went down to twelve when the stations went to war. Cigarettes sold for thirty-five cents a pack. While he did his time, the Arabs proved they could be greedier than Gulf Oil. Now that he'd finished parole, a gallon and a pack of cigarettes both went for more than a dollar. A four hundred percent increase in less than ten years.

He glanced at his reflection in the doorway. The American Flag tattoo rippled on the muscle under his t-shirt sleeve. His thick blonde hair was furrowed by the wind through his open car window and his mutton chop sideburns were growing shaggy.

As soon as he opened the door, Dodd wanted to walk back to his car. A hyper cedar chopper with a ski mask and grease on his collar aimed a double-barreled shotgun right at his stomach. The kid wore a knee length trench coat, soiled at the cuffs and hem. His mask couldn't conceal the fact that he wasn't more than sixteen.

The clerk behind the counter stood with his hands in the air, which caused his shirt to stretch even tighter across his belly than it would have other wise. A clerk in his late fifties, maybe even sixties. Wearing a suit. What kind of clerk wore a suit in the middle of the summer?

Dodd stopped with the door still open. Talk about your déjà vu, he thought to himself. He tried to focus all of his patience and knowledge into the moment. He knew far too well that even backing away could trigger a bloodbath.

"Stop. Right there!" the cedar chopper shouted.

For a moment Dodd heard nothing but the air conditioner and his beating heart. The refrigerated air blew past him like a northeaster, but the chill in his bones came from someplace entirely different.

The kid was built like a broomstick, not much wider than the double-barreled shotgun that shook in his hand. His high-water jeans cuffs fell just short of ankles so skinny they seemed to disappear into his high tops. Dodd figured he was still wearing jeans from before his last growth spurt.

"I'm rooted to the spot." Dodd said. He pronounced each word evenly and calmly to avoid spooking the kid. In prison, Preacher stressed over and over that panic killed you quicker than the guy with the weapon.

Dodd nodded to the shotgun. "That thing can get you killed."

"Shut up. Just shut up," the kid said, waving the barrel erratically.

"You ever done time?" Dodd continued. He resisted adding the word "son" at the end of the question. He didn't want to set him off. He took a breath and walked to the counter. He measured each step, breathing silently and concentrated to keep his hands from shaking. He reached carefully for a pack of Marlboros.

"Shut up and stay right there, or I'll blow you all over the cash register," the kid shouted. Now Dodd knew he probably wouldn't.

Dodd flipped a cigarette into his mouth. "You might want to think about it while you still have a chance of getting off with probation. Meat like you, I know some pretty big bucks on the inside who'll be trying you out for pussy within the week. You want to stay cherry, you need to sink a knife deep into one of them in the shower, and hope he stays down. Otherwise they'll be after more than your ass. Once that happens, you have to make allies with the grease balls or the Nazis. They won't cut you, but you're stuck with them for life. Of course, they may not keep you alive if you piss the wrong inmate off. They'll just make sure somebody else goes down if you do."

"I could shoot you," the kid said. His pupils were so large Dodd imagined he'd go blind in moonlight.

"Your bed and your crapper are behind bars. Every shit, every piss you take, you take in full view of everybody else. You jerk off, they know it all the way down the cell block. No seats on those cold metal crappers either. You have to squat above the things to keep the crabs off, and usually that doesn't work. Put that gun away now, you get off with a little county time, maybe even probation. You still have it when the cops get here, you'll be locked up for a long time to come."

The thief shook his head. "I'm warning you."

"Shut up and have a cigarette." Dodd tossed the packet. The kid reached instinctively for the cigarettes. Dodd crossed the floor and twisted the shotgun out of his arms.

The kid fell back against a display of luminescent tortilla chips. He tried to balance against the cardboard Bandito shooting chili peppers from his pistol and almost pulled the entire display to the floor. Dodd turned to the redneck behind the counter. "When you call the sheriff, make sure to tell him the kid's already given himself up so no one rushes in here and starts a shootout."

He spotted a nine-millimeter Glock in the clerk's hand. The clerk couldn't decide whether to aim at the boy or at Dodd, but his hand trembled so hard Dodd figured he'd shoot out a window before he actually hit his target. Dodd laid the shotgun on the counter and took the Glock in the same move.

"Where did you get this?" he asked.

"I'm the owner. Ralph Meeker." He offered Dodd his hand. Dodd didn't take his offer. Meeker was one of those rail thin old-timers that sprouted across the Texas landscape like carcinomas. In spite of spindly legs and arms, his belly stuck out like a basketball over his silver belt buckle. His eyebrows were so white and thin they disappeared in the afternoon light. His cracked leather skin peeked out from a polyester suit spotted with alcohol and coffee stains. He wore his jacket open because it wouldn't close over his belly. Only his ostrich boots looked polished. His watch was a Rolex, not the kind of watch Dodd associated with West Texas couture.

Dodd laid the Glock next to the shotgun and flattened his palm over both. Meeker frowned. "I keep that under the counter in case we get robbed. I woulda got him in a couple of minutes."

"Next time, keep it locked up in the gun display. The blast from the shotgun was more likely to get you than your bullet was to hit him. Even if either of you could aim straight." He turned to steady the kid. "And you need to take that stupid ski mask off."

The kid pulled the wool cap from over his head. His hair stuck out in several places, clearly unwashed for several days. His face hadn't seen any soap either, although it was hard to tell which pigment was dirt and which was freckle. His teeth gapped in the middle. Half of one tooth was broken off, another looked like it would fall out any day.

"You know him?" Dodd asked Meeker.

"Never seen him," Meeker said. He reached for the Glock. "Let me shoot him now."

Dodd slapped Meeker's hand down. "You shoot him, it'll be a murder rap."

Meeker growled. "I could do you both."

"Christ. Buy a tank of gas, save a man's life, this is the thanks I get." Dodd held out the clip.

"How'd you get that out of my gun?" Meeker asked, flipping the handle over to see the empty chamber.

The kid said, almost at the same time, "How'd you know I wouldn't shoot you?"

"I met a lot of guys like you in Huntsville, kid. Land there for five-to-eight, never figure out how you got there."

Meeker held out his hand for the clip. Dodd slipped it under his belt. "Let's just wait here for the sheriff."

Meeker shrugged and laid the gun under the counter, out of sight but close to his hand. "You got a name, stranger?"

"Dodd."

"That your first name or your last name?"

"First name."

Meeker fired his own cigarette with a plastic butane lighter. A Pall Mall King with no filter. "What's your last name?"

"Dodd. And I don't know why I bothered to save your life. Those cigarettes will kill you."

Chapter 2

The sheriff slammed open both glass doors and stepped through them with a long-barreled .44 magnum in each hand. He said nothing, scanning the entire scene carefully as though he expected to find himself at the OK Corral.

Dodd knew that real city cops–the kind who might have to blow away a crack head brandishing a Saturday night special at any moment–never carried guns as big as the sheriff's. Magnums seemed to be popular with rural cops whose only firefights involved deer or the occasional drunk with a squirrel gun.

The sheriff lowered his massive body to one knee and aimed the magnum at Dodd's forehead. Before he could open his mouth, Dodd said, "You must be Sheriff Meeker."

"Get your hand in the air, you son-of-a-bitch," the sheriff said.

Dodd raised both hands, pointing one thumb toward the kid. "He's your perpetrator. Not me."

"And how did you know my name?"

"Maybe it's the family resemblance, Joe Bob," Ralph said.

Joe Bob might have been five years younger than Ralph, but his shirt stretched at the same buttons. More, in fact. Joe Bob was Ralph's bonus-sized edition. His shoulders were broader than a Grizzly Bear and his arms and legs heavy with muscles that had broken down years before. He sported a ridge of white hair that circled his bald crown. His eyes and brows were hidden behind aviator shades.

Dodd figured him for a cop who wanted to make sure no one could fail to see he was a cop. He wore a blue uniform with epaulets and a dozen insignias stitched to the pockets and sleeves. His navy trousers disappeared at the knees into jet-black jackboots. Most men with massive stomachs let them fall over their belts. The sheriff let his belt stretch across his belly to emphasize his nine-inch diameter chrome badge belt buckle. Not just a badge, but an embossed silver badge rising from a gold state of Texas riding on a three inch leather belt with badges carved all the way around. He sported a second badge on the holster. These only complemented his official gold badge, which was so heavy it pulled his pocket away from his shirt. His legs were as skinny as his brother's, and barely seemed to support his swagger. Dodd was surprised he didn't see any grenades clipped to his belt.

"Who are you kidding, buster? That kid wouldn't stand a chance against my brother."

Ralph held up the shotgun. "He got the drop on me, Joe Bob. Things were looking dicey when Dodd here interrupted us."

Joe Bob stood up, but didn't holster his weapon. "I find that hard to believe." His expression of doubt was more an expression of scorn, as though someone had told him they'd just seen Elvis back from the dead and buying women's lingerie.

His cellmate Preacher described the Meekers often. He described Ralph as the crooked one, more precisely, "a twisted and bent mother fucker, like a joint you been carrying in your back pocket." In Preacher's storyline, Ralph was the bad brother. Joe Bob was outright dangerous. "Same twisted joint, only this motherfucker filled with unstable dynamite. Rub it the wrong way, gonna be half your ass blown across the county line."

"He had a bead on your brother, sheriff," Dodd interrupted. "It looked like your brother was going to leave the store on a stretcher." He looked over at the kid who was huddled against the back wall next to the self-serve Slurpee machine.

"Now ain't that a damn shame," the sheriff said, taking the shotgun. He draped it across one elbow and took a gander down the barrel. A large wad of tobacco bulged in and out of his cheek as he chewed.

"You'd a thought so if it was you," Ralph said.

The sheriff laid the gun back on the corner and unclipped his handcuffs from his belt. "I guess I'm gonna have to haul you in, son."

The boy's eyes grew wild and he backed into a Copenhagen display. He pointed a finger toward Dodd. "He said I wouldn't go to jail if I turned myself in."

"He lied," the sheriff said, twisting the boy around and cuffing his hands to his belt.

"I said you might not go to prison, son," Dodd reminded him. "The county lock-up will be bad enough."

"That sucks," the kid said, spitting on the floor.

The sheriff slapped him across his left cheek and nose. "You son-of-a-bitch. You rob my brother's store and you figure to get off?"

Dodd grabbed the sheriff's wrist before he could slap the kid again. "Hey, it's not like we have a hardened criminal here. He gave himself up before anyone got hurt. Isn't that right, Mr. Meeker?"

Ralph drummed his fingers on the counter as though he had to carefully consider his answer.

The sheriff pulled his wrist away from Dodd and rested it on his gun belt against a row of shiny shells. "You don't have to answer this guy's questions, Ralph. It's your store and our town."

Ralph, however, glanced up to the ceiling and admitted, "Okay, maybe the kid had that shotgun and maybe Dodd here convinced him to turn it over before you showed up. I'm not saying for sure that's what happened, but you could interpret it that way. Maybe."

The sheriff lifted his hand to slap the kid again, and made a fist instead. "Ralph," he said, "I'm conducting the investigation here. I told you that you don't have to answer his questions.

Besides, how do you know these two ain't in it together? Maybe he waited outside until the runt here had things under control." He stared at his brother as though willing him to corroborate his version of the crime.

Dodd cleared his throat. "I hate to point this out, Sheriff, but you do have the shotgun and your brother still has all the money."

"Shut up," the sheriff said. "I was talking to my brother. I can bring you up on charges for grabbing my wrist the way it is. Understand?" He gave Dodd the cop look, the one that said "If I didn't have my shades on, my eyeballs would burn you blind."

Dodd glanced to Ralph. "How about a little help here?"

Ralph continued to stare at the ceiling, as though counting the tiles. "Joe Bob, the kid did have the gun, he did aim it at me, and Dodd here did take it away from him. Okay. Maybe I'm beginning to remember it exactly the way Dodd here does. I just lost focus for a minute. I don't know what came over me."

"Probably too much Jack Daniels in your coffee mug," the sheriff growled. "Probably got caught reaching for your bottle instead of your fucking gun." The kid started looking around the store, and Meeker yanked him by his handcuffs. "Where's that little shit Wetzel anyway? I never seen you work the counter before."

Ralph popped open the cash register and counted the cash as though it might have ended up in the thief's pocket anyway. "Called in sick for the third day in a row. Couldn't get anyone in to replace him. You'd think kids'd line up for work. No better opportunities in this town; we pay close to minimum wage."

Joe Bob looked Dodd up and down, carefully, as though sizing up a side of meat. "I guess I ought to thank you," he added, without a trace of sincerity. "Come by my office tomorrow and give me your statement."

Dodd shook his head. "I'm just passing through, sheriff. I need to be in Santa Fe by tomorrow. The kid's in custody, you have his gun, and your brother can testify."

Joe Bob holstered his gun and gave another tug on the boy's handcuffs. He pulled a fat cigar from his shirt pocket. "Son," he said, tearing off the wrapper with his teeth even as he spoke, "you look like you've done time, so you know how this works. I take your ID and confirm that you did time. Guy looks like you, I'd figure you for armed robbery."

"You're right, but they went easy on me since my gun wasn't loaded." Dodd glanced around the store looking for cavalry that would never arrive. "Look, Sheriff, I finished parole. I'm not looking for any more trouble. I just want to find a garage for my car and get moving."

"Follow me out to the car, at least." The sheriff lifted the would-be thief roughly under the shoulder and hustled him out of the store. Dodd and Ralph followed them into the harsh afternoon sunlight. They waited patiently while the sheriff wrestled his prisoner into the back of his cruiser.

"You don't have to be so fucking rough," the kid protested; his first words since the sheriff slapped the cuffs on his wrists.

Joe Bob whacked the kid on the shoulders with his nightstick. "Shut up. Kids and prisoners's supposed to be seen, not heard. You're both."

"Nice car, sheriff." Dodd said, wincing with the blow.

The sheriff shut the back door, windows rolled up, and leaned his elbow across the roof. He grinned back. "Thank you, son." He patted the paint job. "It's my pride and joy. I bought it brand new twenty-two years ago."

"With the township's money," Ralph added. Joe Bob passed a look that made Dodd think he might just lay in on his brother with the nightstick.

The cruiser was a 1958 Thunderbird, metallic blue and white, with the county sheriff's star stenciled onto the driver's door and sporting the largest rack of lights and sirens Dodd had ever seen.

"I imagine the lights didn't come with the car."

Joe Bob grinned. "Upgraded the package four times since I bought the car, but I only rebuilt the engine once. Two hundred and thirty thousand miles." He spit a large piece of his cigar onto the asphalt. "Now let's go over your options. You can stick around town and give me a statement in the morning, or I can arrest you on suspicion and hold you over night. Either way you give me a statement."

"Why can't I follow you to your office and give you a statement right now?"

Joe Bob pulled his cigar from his teeth and inspected the frayed tip. He rotated his wrist to reveal his Rolex, and pointed at the dial with the cigar. "Son, my shift is over in half an hour and I don't intend to work late tonight filling out reports. Besides, if your car needs work, you're probably not leaving town for a couple of days. Takes that long for our mechanic to sober up."

"All the more reason to be moving on, Sheriff. I was hoping a mechanic in Ft. Stockton could work on it overnight."

Meeker pretended not to hear him. "Maybe my brother here will spot you the cost of a night at the hotel up the road. You did save his bacon after all."

Dodd looked at his own watch, unable to read the sheriff's watch in the afternoon glare. "It's barely three o'clock. Isn't that early for a shift change?"

The light blue ice around Meeker's eyes shifted to a deeply enraged purple.

His brother stepped between them. "Joe Bob, how long would it take to take Dodd's statement?"

"The Astros play the Dodgers at three-thirty. Ryan against Sutton, and I hate the Dodgers. How do you think I'd feel if Ryan pitched a no-hitter in the heat of their only pennant race ever, and I was at the office taking his statement?"

"Can't you buy one of those video cassette recorders? Charge it to your office?" Dodd asked.

Joe Bob spit another piece of his cigar. "You might want to consider how likely I am to go easy on the kid if you don't stick around to testify he turned himself in. I mean, I didn't see him do it, did I? And Ralph here has been known to forget what he saw after a couple of drinks. Ain't that right, Ralph?"

Ralph glanced through the window into the back seat to take a last look at the kid. "You're a rat bastard, Joe Bob. You always been a rat bastard. I'll put Dodd here up at the hotel. But I'm sending the bill to the county."

The sheriff opened his driver's door and slid into the car. "Why don't you do that, Ralph?"

The cruiser pulled into reverse and spun out of the parking lot like a top, spraying loose gravel across the gas pumps and their knees.

Dodd: "Who would've thought? The Astros in a pennant race."

Meeker: "Most folks around here root for the Red Raiders."

"That's football."

"Far as I'm concerned, that's all there is, son." He seemed to wobble on his feet, as though he needed a bourbon fix. "Better watch yourself. Joe Bob's an ornery bastard. Not to mention being a rat bastard; a rat bastard in a town full of rat bastards. You might be better off taking your car to Fort Stockton and forgetting about the kid. If your car can make it that far."

He nodded to Dodd's Mustang, which had already leaked a river of gasoline onto the concrete. It streamed toward the nearest drain, and looked to be developing a current.

Dodd patted his pocket for his cigarettes again. He thought to himself that he might stay quit if he could avoid these stressful situations.

"You just quit smoking, didn't you?" Meeker added. "That explains a lot."

Dodd didn't want to go there. He hated talking about smoking. Non-smokers whined about smokers, rudeness and side stream smoke. Smokers whined about fascism and personal freedom and felt compelled to light up to prove they wouldn't be intimidated.

"Look, I can pay for my own hotel."

Meeker looked down and realized he was still holding the shotgun. "No, I owe you one. I would a shot that kid." He turned to look at Dodd. "You really been to prison? The stuff you told that boy true?"

"I didn't tell him the half of it. You know what really gets to you when you're inside?"

"I never exactly thought about it."

"Boredom. After a month you're bored out of your skull. A year and you want to crawl up the bars and rip them out of the cement. Sometimes you want to pick a fight just to make something happen. But you can't tell that to a sixteen year old grease ball with a shotgun in his hand."

Meeker ran his finger over a nick in his gas pump left by the sheriff's gravel spray. "So what did you do? To keep from being bored, I mean?"

"I became a lawyer."

Chapter 3

Dodd studied the highway from his hotel window. Bright orange flares of sunlight broke through the orange and magenta clouds on the horizon. He thought about walking to the lobby for a pack of cigarettes, and immediately began to think of all the mornings he had had to kick-start his lungs to breathe. This ritual, and this ritual alone, kept him from dropping his money into a cigarette machine.

Earlier that afternoon they left Dodd's Mustang at the town's auto dealership. Bill Todd's Auto Emporium, an emporium that consisted of an air-conditioned Airstream trailer, one Caddy, one Camaro, a Buick, Escort. K-Car and an Imperial parked under an overhang (all of them last year's models), and a dozen used cars, most covered with dust, a few of which looked as though they might be hiding rust on the undercarriage and probably sawdust in the transmissions.

The sign on the garage said the mechanic would be back in 30 minutes. After waiting forty-five, they spent the next hour trying to track him down, even though the town was six blocks long and extended for two blocks in either direction. All that remained was open land, barbed wire and road. Dodd thought that when the wind kicked up it would carry off generations of topsoil and shallow weeds.

They found Jim Bob Tucker hidden in his trailer with a Forty and a nine-inch black and white TV. Dodd wondered if everyone in Sweet Water Falls had three names.

Tucker looked like a rat on a hunger strike. His face was thinner than his rail-thin body, his nose preceded his face by a good six inches and his eyes never stayed focused for more than a second. He smelled of cigar smoke and engine oil, the same engine oil he probably used to keep his hair in place.

It took another hour to pry Tucker away from the baseball game, and, after the drive back to the auto lot repair shop, another hour for him to tinker underneath Dodd's car, and yet another for him to announce that it would take three or four days to get a new fuel line from a parts store in Ft. Stockton. By that time it was after seven.

"It's a forty-minute drive," Dodd complained.

"How're you gonna get there?" the mechanic countered. Since Tucker had uncoupled the original fuel line, and parts even Dodd didn't recognize surrounded his car, Dodd didn't see much point in arguing.

"You can trade it in for a new car," Tucker said. "Be on the road before noon. Mr. Todd will give you a hell of a deal."

Dodd had passed. Even if he would consider abandoning a vintage Mustang, having seen the selection waiting for him outside, he'd rather risk the drive with a front seat filled with leaking gas cans.

Now that he was alone in his room, he missed the excitement of the garage.

The hotel sign, turned on about half an hour before, glowed in the drifting sunset; red neon on yellow painted letters proclaiming: "Stickett Inn. Where the stars shine at night."

How many horny high school kids shared a chuckle about that name, Dodd wondered. "The stars at night" evidently referred to the flocking on the ceiling, luminous glitter mixed in with the pea green linseed oil paint. If he threw the light switch and closed the curtains, the glitter sparkled for at least fifteen minutes.

He stared at the highway until the last red flares of sunlight disappeared behind the pavement and the hills. He left his curtains open and wandered to the lobby with an ice bucket. He stopped at a pay phone to place a collect call to Joel Burns of Lockhart, Bacon and Burns in Sante Fe. "I figured you'd still be in your office. It looks like I'm gonna be tied up in Texas for another day or two. How long is the job open?"

"It's not as though we're looking for another associate. I'm taking you on as a favor."

"I thought you liked my work."

"I like the fact that you're a meticulous, unscrupulous, cold-hearted bastard who never misses a trick."

"What's the difference?"

"Look, Dodd, take your time. Just because you had to leave the public defender's office, doesn't mean you have to jump at the first offer you get."

"I'm broke."

"Never a problem for a lawyer. Every crack in the sidewalk represents a large settlement, and you get thirty percent."

"I don't think this town is modern enough for sidewalks."

Dodd hung up and started back to his room, but returned to the pay phone and stood beside it for a moment or two. He dropped a quarter to place another collect call, this time to Houston. "Guess where I am? Sweet Water Falls. Surprised or what?"

The receiver was silent for several seconds. "I thought you weren't going to call."

"I wasn't. Then I wondered if you reconsidered."

The whiskey voice on the other end sighed. "It's in both our best interest."

"Maybe I just wanted to hear your voice."

"Well I don't think it's good idea, okay? And for god's sake don't call collect."

He rang off and returned to his room, stopping to fill his ice bucket and buy a can of RC cola.

His room barely fit the double bed, bed table, easy chair and television. One arm of the armchair was tucked under the rim of the table, inches away from the television resting on the peeling Formica surface. The sign outside the hotel advertised free cable, but the free cable dangled from the wall because the TV didn't have a co-axial connection. Dodd could find only three channels, two of them UHF channels featuring "I Love Lucy."

He dropped several ice cubes into a dusty glass and poured the RC. He stood at the window and studied the neon sign to Meeker's store, glowing red and yellow letters, like an infection spreading into the night sky.

"That sign be quintessential Texas," Preacher once said to him, his teeth large and yellow. "Big, bright and gaudy. A total lack of taste or even consideration for what little taste others who live here picked up when they be living somewhere else."

"Quintessential" was Preacher's newest word. "The task I be setting for myself?" he told Dodd on another occasion, "Learn one new white word a week. So that when I finally earn my release you white folks be saying, 'He sure talks good for a nigger, don't he? He has 'diction' and 'vocabulary.'"

Preacher never actually believed he would earn his release. He was serving a life sentence for a series of armed robberies he pulled off with a partner in 1967, and his first parole hearing wouldn't be scheduled until sometime in the nineties. In most cities he would have pulled down fifteen years for his effort, but he made the mistake of robbing stores in Sweet Water Falls.

Dodd asked him how he got his name. The answer? "Cause that's what I would a been if I wasn't so good at stealing." Dodd pointed out he couldn't be too good if they were sharing a cell.

Dodd loved Preacher's stories about Sweet Water Falls, about the weeks he spent working for Ralph Meeker, digging for a UFO; about Joe Bob Meeker strutting around with his big guns and his blue and white T-Bird; about the half-dozen churches on the main street only a block or two from a hotel that turned over occupants by the hour; about businessmen who never bothered to conceal their weapons; about the rich banker whose wife slept with every one in sight and whose arguments with her—when she did come home—woke the entire county.

He twisted the on knob to the black and white TV and draped himself across the bed. The lone network affiliate featured the Republican National Convention and Ronald Reagan trying to convince the country that they could cut taxes, double military expenses and still get rid of the budget deficit. And every redneck, rubberneck, oil rigger and lumberjack seemed to be buying it.

The biggest laugh was all those born again Christians selling out their Baptist President Jimmy Carter for this wax work dummy with throwaway lines. Wasn't there a line in the Bible about worshipping graven images?

He watched the commentators stumble over themselves not to laugh at the thought of Reagan as Presidential candidate. He must have been the only guy that could make Gerald Ford look Presidential. Finally Dodd slammed off the television and slammed the door to the room as he left. He wanted a beer and a pack of cigarettes. He settled for dinner and a glass of tea.

Chapter 4

The hotel diner matched his room; adobe walls and southwestern tile floors. The floor might have been laid sometime before the Korean war. Grease and cigarette smoke streaked the windows, which didn't matter because all Dodd could see along the highway were the hotel lights and the sign "Cigerets, Guns and Beer" flickering on and off a mile down the road. Dodd figured Sweet Water Falls could last well into the twenty-second century and never have a problem with urban sprawl.

The walls were painted pink and the tables were set up at random, four chairs to a table, across the room. Every table had a paper napkin dispenser and a glass ashtray with the Stickett Inn logo glazed across the bottom.

He asked his waitress to remove the ashtray. She gave him a puzzled look, as though it never occurred to her that someone might not want to eat in front of a small pile of Camel butts.

A western style bar ran the length of the far wall, with a Coors promotional mirror running the length of the wall behind it, the reflection making the shabby diner look twice as shabby. The bartender wiped the counter whenever he wasn't serving drinks, which, considering there were only two customers besides Dodd, was most of the time.

The waitress dropped his order in front of him, a large portion chicken fried steak with home fries smothered in grease, greasy gravy, and even more grease. The iceberg lettuce salad, the lettuce wilted and brown, came with cheese and red onion sprinkled sparsely across a watery ranch dressing. His iced tea came in a sweating red plastic glass.

"Eat hearty," the waitress said. Her name plate said "Hazel." She looked to be in her late forties; one of those aging country women with no meat on their bones, bouffant, whiskey voice and the strong scent of cigarette smoke and Chanel. Dodd thought a woman named Hazel should be pleasant and slightly overweight, like Shirley Booth on TV.

He would have settled for pleasant.

"Aren't you gonna try it?" she said.

Dodd held up his hand to hold her off, and contemplated a small piece of his steak on the tip of his fork for at least a minute before biting down. He chewed for a minute, and swallowed, having no place better to put it.

"How is it?" she asked.

"Better than prison."

"I should hope so," she said and left in a huff. Dodd figured she was easily offended, or else she made him for a light tipper.

Once he was free of Hazel's watchful eye, Dodd realized how hungry he was and began to carve into his steak. He shoveled a forkful of steak and gravy into his mouth.

Before he could chew, the door opened and a young woman in her early twenties swept into the room. She ordered a Tom Collins then arranged herself at one of the tables facing the bar.

Her legs stretched for miles. The longest legs he'd ever seen. No, longer than that. They swept out from under the table like spun glass, and then curved back at her knees, sweeping under her seat so that she could wrap her ankles around the chair's back legs. In that moment he envisioned her ankles wrapped around his neck, those long legs intertwined like ivy.

Her hair flowed over her shoulders, as long as her legs—a dark chestnut color that shined in the dim lights of the bar. Every few minutes or so, she tossed her hair. He could catch the highlights dancing from one wave to another. She wore a flannel shirt, jeans and Tony Lamas. The shirt fell loosely around her body, the jeans molded her legs. In spite of her clothes, Dodd knew there was nothing redneck about her.

Dodd watched her take a long pull from her drink and light a Virginia Slim. She opened her mouth in a perfect circle to let a smoke ring float away, the way her legs flowed under the table, in long, lean brush strokes. She sat like that while he finished his dinner, totally unaware of him, taking an occasional long pull on her Collins and crafting smoke rings to drift into the already hazy atmosphere around the bar.

The waitress dropped his ticket onto his plate, the grease soaking into the paper. "Who is she?" he asked.

"Mary Beth Rafferty," she said. She dragged out the name, mustering as much contempt as she could. "Her daddy owns the bank. She'd be the town whore if she charged anybody."

The meal was $3.75. Dodd laid a five over the ticket. His fortunes were looking up for the fist time today. He laid another five on top of the first one. "Why don't you send her another Collins and keep the change?"

The waitress cleared her throat, making it clear that he may have been a better tipper than she expected but he made up for it by being a lout. In spite of her disapproval, she palmed the bills and delivered the highball. The girl turned around to look at him for the first time, then collected her drink to join him at his table.

She nodded toward his tea. "Aren't you going to join me?"

"Gave it up. Always got me into trouble."

She smiled around the rim of her Collins. "What kind of trouble?"

"Last time it was five to eight for armed robbery."

She put her glass on the table and took a practiced drag at her cigarette. "You're the guy that broke up that robbery this afternoon, aren't you?"

"That was me."

"Here's to you," she said, holding out her glass.

He tipped his tea to her. "Word gets around fast."

"Faster than you think. Nobody reads the local paper cause everybody knows everything within an hour or two anyway."

"I've been in this place half an hour and I already know that your father owns the local bank."

She blushed. "That's Hazel, the waitress. I bet she told you I'm the town tramp too."

"She didn't say it quite so politely."

She ground her cigarette out into his plate. "See, that's what I mean about this town. You not only get the news but the editorials. In a town this small you have to find something to pass the time. Me, I surf."

"Where do you find the water?"

"Some people surf on water. I surf on bedsprings. Do you surf?"

"Any time I get the chance."

"Well then I guess I better introduce myself. My name's Mary Beth."

"My name's Dodd."

"Is that your first or your last name?"

"Both."

"Well, Dodd. I hope your name's the only thing short about you."

Chapter 5

Dodd studied Mary Beth's leg in the moonlight. It crept out from beneath his sheet and wrapped around his thigh. She draped her arm across his chest and her hair tickled his chin.

Dodd enjoyed having her leg draped around his. He especially enjoyed the way she could wrap one leg behind his neck and one behind his buttocks and pull him deeper into her with both. And the way she panted, "Go, go, go team" over and over again.

"I bet you were a cheerleader," he said earlier, after some particularly vocal cheers. She leaned over him to light a cigarette.

"Kilgore Rangerette. Captain of the team. If you can't get your legs up into the air and show your cunt to every panting alumnus, you don't even get an audition. Do you like my cunt?"

"It would inspire Georgia O'Keeffe."

"Who's Georgia O'Keeffe? A lesbian?"

"She painted flowers that look like cunts."

She giggled and balanced the ashtray on his stomach. "No wonder nobody every heard of her." She ran her fingers up his chest. "You don't sound like an ex-con."

"Trust me, honey. I spent five years inside and three on parole."

"But you sound so educated. Ex-cons don't talk about flowers and paintings. I'm sure they think about cunts all the time, but never as a flower."

He laughed. "I educated myself inside. Got my law degree, in fact."

"You can do that?"

"Not a very good one. Mine was from a correspondence school."

"So you're a," she paused before she said the word, "lawyer?"

"Right now I'm between jobs. None of the law firms wanted to hire me after I got out. Who wants a guy who spent time on the inside when you've got these law review grads in suits knocking at your door? My own lawyer, Joel Burns, ran the public defender's office. He hired me as a clerk until I passed the bar, then he let me serve out my parole working for him."

"So what happened? I mean, something must have happened or you wouldn't be between jobs, right?"

"Joel went into private practice with his father-in-law in Sante Fe. The guy that took Joel's job was a pencil pusher. As long as I was on parole it was good PR for me to be in the office. You know, parolee makes good as public defender. Once as I finished parole, however, they couldn't find room for me in the budget. Joel offered to hire me as an associate in Sante Fe, that's where I'm heading now."

She crushed out her cigarette and rolled over onto her back, using his stomach for a pillow. "Good story, Dodd. Is it true?"

"Why would I lie about something like that?"

"You're a man. You don't know how to tell the truth."

"Then why bother asking?"

"It's a bad habit. Like men." She pulled another cigarette from a gold embroidered case. She offered it to him and he shook his head.

He let her lay there with the back of her head on his navel, hair splayed in every direction, blowing smoke straight up to the little luminescent sparkles in the ceiling that had long ago ceased to sparkle even in the moonlight. He stroked her hair and watched the smoke erupt like a geyser from her lips before breaking apart and curling toward the ceiling.

Being with her, lying on his back with her head on his belly, watching her smoke, made him want a cigarette more than he could have imagined.

"How come you slept with me?" he asked her.

"You think I shouldn't have?"

He stroked her hair again. "No, that's not what I meant. But I'm not that used to buying women a drink and ending up in bed with them twenty minutes later."

"You never bought a woman a drink and ended up in bed?"

"I handed a woman a drink at a party about a year ago, and we ended up in bed. But that was several hours later, after the party. And she was old enough to be your mother."

She reached her free hand over to stroke his chest. "Poor dear. You must have been desperate."

"No, she was pretty good looking. A lot like you. Just older. You seem easier to get along with."

She took a long pull on her cigarette and let the smoke tumble from her mouth, cascading out in a cloud that floated to the ceiling. "My mom lives in Houston most of the time. You'd think there'd be other things to do besides sleep with someone. Not like here. Boredom and sex tend to be bosom buddies in my experience."

He let her answer lie for a minute and stared out his window, waiting for a cloud to cross the face of the moon.

"You're daddy owns the bank. Or so I was told. Surely you can find plenty of entertainment."

She laughed. "All the more reason to fuck you, honey. Piss the old man off. Truth is, you're cute, you're smart and you been to jail. I can't say I ever had the opportunity to sleep with all three in the same man before. Now I find you're a lawyer, hell, in my old man's eyes that makes you a criminal two times over."

She handed her cigarette to him and he crushed it out.

"I guess I should tell you the whole truth," she admitted, lifting herself up onto her elbows and resting her chin in her hands. "You being named Dodd and all, kind of makes you the biggest trophy a girl can snare in this town. Been to jail, been a lawyer, maybe you being a Dodd. Hell, that kind of makes you a sixteen-point buck to the bad girls of Sweet Water Falls."

"Am I missing something?"

She reached across him for another cigarette, finessing it from the pack with her long pale fingernails. He tried to suppress a picture of her at fifty, hacking up phlegm and trying to mount some bony cowboy while puffing her way through an orgasm. "See, there used to be a family of bank robbers named Dodd. Back in the forties. They were notorious. Shot down my grandfather during the hold up. They escaped in their pickup truck, but Sheriff Meeker tracked them down to Sweet Water Canyon. There was a big gun battle. One got away and got shot down by Texas Rangers. They stole a half million dollars and none of it was ever recovered."

"Is this local legend or is it true?"

"The truck's still down in the gorge if you want to see it. Bullet holes and all. Probably the only real excitement in this town in forty years, except for the flying saucer."

"The flying saucer?"

"Before the bank robbery." This time she opened her mouth and released a perfect circle that floated over her head like a halo in the moonlight from the window. "Crashed outside of town. Everybody in town remembers it but me because I wasn't born yet. Anyway, after the robbery, Daddy took over the bank and got control of the Dodd farm and sold it to the Meekers. They've been looking for the half million ever since, but they never found it. Some folks think my old man forced the Dodds off their farm cause of the flying saucer, but he'd never care. He only wants something if it's green and has a president's picture on it. Hell, mama says we should just give cash for his birthday, the bigger the bill the better. That's why I always give him cologne."

Dodd took her cigarette from her finger and crushed it out. "You've had too many of those already."

"Maybe so," she admitted, and settled her cheek in on his breast.

Dodd knew the story well. Preacher made the same connection the day they became cellmates. "Knew a whole family named Dodd back home. Three brothers robbed a bank, two ended up dead and the third one disappeared with the money. You even look like them."

Dodd pulled a thin strand of Mary Beth's hair through his fingers. It looked like silk in the dim light of the room. "What does this farm have to do with a flying saucer?"

"I thought I made that clear. The flying saucer's supposed to have crashed on the Dodd farm."

"Doesn't that strike you as a little improbable? The same family that has a flying saucer crash on their land robs a bank within the year?"

She pushed herself up on her elbows again and gave him a nasty glare. "Which part don't you believe?"

Dodd knocked a cigarette out of the pack to appease her, even though his nose and chest were starting to feel puffy. "If I had to choose, I'd say I had a little bit easier time believing the part about the bank robbery."

"Well, there really was a flying saucer. You can ask anybody in town. Except for the skeptics, of course. Just like Roswell, New Mexico a couple a years before. Poisoned all their crops. The government came in and took away the pieces. Mama used to tell me stories about this big streak of light in the night sky and this explosion out near the farm. The next day she saw the government trucks with the men in the silver suits inside, driving out the highway to the Dodd farm, setting up roadblocks for miles to keep folks away. But they didn't get all of it. So the story goes. Then the land was, like, radioactive or something. According to some folks, that's why the Dodds robbed the bank. 'Cause they went broke 'cause of the flying saucer. Other folks think the Meekers set them up so Ralph could get control of their land and find the flying saucer himself."

"Not to mention the half million dollars."

This time she ran the smoke through her nostrils. "I beg your pardon?"

"I thought you said the Meekers wanted the half million dollars?"

"Well, yeh, that too. But that was after the robbery. Some people think the Meekers wanted the farm before the robbery. To find where the flying saucer was hidden."

"You people take acid in your spare time?"

She giggled. "Honey, we don't take acid in West Texas. We drink. I'm not saying any of this is true." Even as she said this, he could tell she believed every word of it. "There's other stories about that land. But it's a fact that the government sent all these trucks out to the Dodd farm back in 1949, and I do know the Meekers hired a crew to dig up all the land on the farm when I was a little girl. No one never found a thing, but, whether it's a flying saucer or a half million dollars, my old man broods about it all the time."

Dodd laughed, and ran his hands across her breasts, tweaking each nipple in turn. "Imagine that."

"Anyway, one of the Dodd brothers had a son would be your age now. My old man thinks that would be you. He thinks your father told you where the stolen money is and you came back to claim it for yourself. What do you think of that?"

"Did your old man send you on a fishing expedition?"

"Dodd, honey, my old man thinks I should still be a virgin waiting to be a blushing bride. He'd shoot you if he knew we were surfing the bedsprings. If I were you I'd be paranoid about that, and not about my being a spy."

"Mary Beth, I'm back on the road as soon as I give my statement to the sheriff. If I hadn't ruptured my fuel line, I'd be in New Mexico and trying to pick up some waitress in a hotel over there."

"Good thing you stopped, isn't it? Cause I'm a better piece of ass than anything you're going to find in New Mexico. Or any where else in Texas. That's for sure."

He tweaked a nipple again. "That is for sure, sweetheart."

Of course, Preacher had told him the stories many times over. Preacher's brother Alvin got him a job on a work crew with twelve other black laborers digging up the old Dodd farm. They dug up the entire property looking for a flying saucer, and when they failed to find it, they dug the farm up again. Preacher didn't believe the UFO story for a minute. He thought they were digging for money.

"Imagine that," he said as he watched her chest swell with the shallow breathing of sleep.

Chapter 6

It didn't take long for Dodd to walk from his hotel to the sheriff's office. The sheriff, J.P.'s office, mayor's office and town jail were hobbled together in one adobe structure painted dark rust red like West Texas mud. The structure resembled half the commercial buildings in town. Even half the houses seemed to be made of white or pink adobe, with log roofs and cactus gardens.

Dodd figured one architect came through and designed every structure facing the highway and then left laughing and with his bank account bloated.

The only differences between this adobe building and the others blighting the horizon were the dome rising from the roof, the oblong driveway that circled from the highway to the front doors of the building, and the sign: "Towship of Sweet Water Falls Administrative Complex." The sign was made from hand carved individual rosewood letters fastened to the adobe wall, letters that cascaded lopsidedly over the frame of the double door leading into the complex.

Dodd wondered if the same guy made the "towship" sign and the "Cigerets" sign on Meeker's store.

The semi-open breezeway connecting the offices was abandoned and only the sheriff's office seemed to be open. The door opened directly to a view of the town's two cells where he spotted his would-be armed robber. The deputy offered Dodd a cup of coffee so thick he suspected he could roll it out on a baking sheet and cut it into cookie dough.

Dodd pulled a chair in front of the cell. "They treating you all right, kid?"

The boy sat hunched against the cell wall, his knees under his chin, his arm wrapped around his knees. He still wore his coat and sweat ringed his t-shirt collar in several gray layers. Dodd thought he looked like a beat-up Raggedy Andy doll—button eyes, sewn on mouth, hair strung out at the side of his head.

"What's your name?"

"What do you care now that I'm in jail?" He rubbed his nose with his coat sleeve.

"You're not in prison. Not yet. Trust me, this is a vacation in comparison. Now what's your name?"

"His name's Bobby Wayne Bathwater. He's from Tanglewood, about fifteen miles down I-10," a voice boomed out from behind Dodd. Dodd turned to see Joe Bob Meeker standing just inside the open door, mirrored shades posed on his nose, his body silhouetted by the morning sun from the skylight.

"Boatright," the boy sniffled. "It's Boatright."

Meeker ignored him. "I ran a trace on you, Dodd. You did eight for armed robbery, and another year in Sabine County for DWI before that. Born criminal."

"There's two sides to that question, sheriff."

Ralph Meeker appeared at his brother's shoulder, and pushed him aside to get into the tiny office. "Joe Bob, you're a born asshole. You ain't the only one wanting to get in out of the sun, but you stick your fat ass inside the door as though the world ends with it."

"You got in just fine," the sheriff said. "Didn't take your breath away to get past me or nothing. 'Sides, it's my office and my ass, and I can park it where I want to."

Dodd looked at his watch. "Sheriff, I really need to get on the road. Can we get this over with?"

Joe Bob pulled a cigar from his shirt pocket and bit off the tip. "So why don't the two of you sit down so I can get your statements? Then we can get this kid sentenced when the Justice of the Peace comes in later this morning."

"Why do you say shit like that?" Ralph complained. "'We'll consult with the mayor,' or 'we'll wait until the JP holds court,' when I'm the goddam JP and I'm the goddam mayor and I'm sitting right here in front of you."

Dodd stretched his neck back slightly to access the situation. "You're the JP and the mayor?"

Ralph tossed his question off with a nod. "You bet I am. But Joe Bob has to get all official. 'We'll bring that up before the mayor at the next town council meeting,' instead of saying 'What you think of this, Ralph?'"

Dodd shook his head. "My point is that there might be a conflict of interest when the judge hearing the case is also the guy pressing charges."

Ralph threw his hands up in the air as though one of them had, finally, seen the light. "Exactly. We can take care of things right here and now, and get on with our day."

Dodd reached over and eased down Ralph's hand. "Aren't we skipping a step or two here?"

Joe Bob eased into the high backed leather chair behind a chrome and Formica desk that dwarfed any other piece of furniture or equipment in the room. He rolled his chair back to the wall to make room for his formidable girth. He beckoned to his deputy, who brought two folding chairs.

"What're we missing, son?" He beckoned for Dodd to sit.

"Don't you have to convict him first?"

Joe Bob grinned as though Dodd delivered the punch line to a particularly amusing joke. He opened his desk drawer and removed a Copenhagen tin. Dodd could see another dozen shrink-wrapped in a roll and a handful of loose tins as well. He stretched his lip and dropped at least two pinches at the base of his gum. Dodd expected to see him pitch the cigar, but he continued to chew on that as well.

"Seems to me I did forget that part, Dodd. I wonder how I could have done that?" He handed his pen to his deputy. "Carl Ray, why don't you take their statements?"

"Sure, Joe Bob," the deputy said. He placed a cup of coffee onto a typing table and shifted the typewriter until one side straddled the edge to make a small space for his legal pad. Dodd figured the deputy to be forty, blonde, probably a former high school fullback, going nowhere in his current job and weary of waiting for Joe Bob to retire or die so he could take over the reins.

Ralph gave his statement first, describing how he came in to work the counter—in spite of his numerous duties as realtor, business manager and town mayor—because his usual clerk Wally Wetzel, the lazy son-of-a-bitch, called in sick for the second good fishing day in a row, and then the kid named Bobby Wayne walked into the store and pulled a shotgun out from under his trench coat.

Dodd's mind started to drift when Ralph began to embellish the story, adding a sequence in which he pulled his Glock on the kid just before Dodd showed up, creating a Mexican stand off.

Dodd scanned the jail to see how Sheriff Meeker spent his days. After the sheriff's desk, the next largest piece of furniture in the room was a gun rack displaying more than two dozen shotguns and rifles. A gold plaque bolted to the ammunition drawer read: "Weapons donated to the county, courtesy of Ralph Meeker, Meeker's Corner Store."

A portrait of Dwight Eisenhower rested on the wall behind Meeker's desk. The radio dispatch unit faced the desk, maybe three feet behind Dodd's chair. According to a blue display board with white letters, three deputies served the county, one on a twelve hour shift from seven am to seven pm, and the other two staggered to make sure two deputies were on duty from six until midnight. The three of them evidently shared the single typing table/desk the deputy was using now.

"So you're the hero that saved my bother's ass," the sheriff interrupted Dodd's reverie.

Dodd raised his eyebrows. "Or saved the kid's ass, depending on whose version of the story you listen to."

"So tell me your version."

Dodd recited what happened as best he could remember. He edited his account just enough to imply that he didn't see Meeker holding the Glock rather than stating for a fact that Meeker didn't bring out the Glock until after the kid had given Dodd the shotgun.

Joe Bob nodded to his deputy as he wrote everything down on a legal pad. When Dodd was finished talking, he announced. "Well, that wraps it up. Type that up so these two boys can sign it and be on their way."

The deputy lifted the legal pad and moved the typewriter back into the center of the table. He began to peck away, one key at a time, balancing the legal pad next to the machine. He pulled the carriage return arm slowly, so that it echoed a long zip and a loud ping at irregular intervals, reaching up to keep the legal pad from falling as the carriage slammed back to the left hand margin. Joe Bob's eye twitched with every ping.

"So what are you going to do?" Dodd asked. "The boy did turn himself in."

Joe Bob leaned toward Dodd on his elbows, making it clear that he didn't tolerate suggestions from ex-cons. "Bathwater over there committed armed robbery. He needs to do time."

"Christ, sheriff, he's too young to do time. Get him started now and he'll be robbing gas stations for the rest of his life."

Joe Bob leaned back in his chair, added a third pinch of snuff, and said, "So what do you think I should do about it?"

"Give the kid probation and find him a job."

Ralph dropped his foot. "Now wait one goddam minute. That kid tried to rob me. Why should I drop the charges?"

Dodd leaned into Ralph's face. Ralph pulled away instinctively. "Send that kid up, all you get back is an adult who doesn't know anything but how to rob gas stations, steal cars and whatever other skills the cons teach him. Your tax dollars'll pay his room and board for the rest of his life. Find the kid a job, make him report to you once a week for a year. If he still fucks up, drop the dime on him."

Joe Bob spit a dark black goober into his trashcan. Dodd wasn't sure if it was snuff, cigar, or a piece of his lung. "Jail'd do that kid a lot more good than a job. Hard labor changes your thinking."

"I've been there, sheriff. You haven't. Believe me, jail will fuck that kid up for life. He doesn't have what it takes to make it on the inside and come out straight in the head. The only thinking that changes is that they convince themselves they'll be too smart to get caught next time. You know why? Because they spend all their time inside with guys who give them tips on how not to get caught the next time and they're all too stupid too realize no one on the inside is an expert on how not to get caught."

"I can handle myself in prison," Bobby Wayne yelled from his cell. Dodd had forgotten the kid could hear everything they said.

"See what I mean, sheriff? That kid's too stupid to know what he's in for. Look at him. You know who's tough enough and who's not, and that kid's not tough enough for six months in county."

Ralph pulled a pack of Camels from his shirt pocket and unwrapped the cellophane. "He is awful young, Joe Bob. Did you get hold of his parents?"

"His father said I should drop him down a hole and fill it in behind him. Wouldn't even come to bail the kid out."

"See there?" Dodd said. "The kid needs a chance. Maybe there's some Christian family around that could take him in, he could pay them a small rent while he works off his probation."

Ralph leaned over his brother's desk. "He may have a point, Joe Bob. That kid can't be more than fifteen years old."

"I'm seventeen. Got my driver's license," Bobby shouted.

The deputy hit the carriage return arm twice, producing two grating zips and two sharp pings and knocking the legal pad into his lap.

Joe Bob slammed his fist down on his desk. "Goddam it, Carl Ray, type that goddam thing later."

"You told me to type it quick so these two gentlemen can sign it."

"Well then why the hell haven't you finished?" Joe Bob turned back to face Dodd and his brother. "What next, Ralph? You gonna vote for the peanut farmer?"

"We're Democrats, Joe Bob. Can't be Texan and not be a Democrat."

"You know as well as I do that the only reason that kid surrendered is 'cause you could have blown a hole the size of Amarillo through his chest and Dodd here let him back out without looking chicken. Dodd here doesn't show up, that kid's a blood spot on the wall. No way that's turning yourself in."

Ralph stared at Joe Bob, as though debating whether to include him on the secret.

"Goddam it, Meeker, tell him what really happened," Dodd prompted.

"Tell me what?" Joe Bob demanded, staring at Ralph while dangling his cigar at a seven o'clock position. For a minute Dodd thought he was about to witness a shoot-out.

"Okay, maybe I exaggerated. A little. Maybe I didn't have a gun on the kid when Dodd showed up. Maybe he just gave up when Dodd talked some sense into his head and I just panicked and picked up my gun after he turned himself in. I can't remember exactly. It was all confusing. But maybe that's what happened."

"He didn't have no gun, sheriff. Not till I gave mine up. That's the truth," Bobby Wayne called through the bars.

A vein in Joe Bob's neck began to bulge, swelling a deep purple. "You shut up," he called over his shoulder. Then he faced down his brother. "You better not be changing your story now that it's all typed up," he growled.

"Don't worry, Joe Bob," Carl Ray said. "I only got a paragraph typed."

Dodd thought the sheriff would to pop that vein and kill the deputy with a speeding blast of blood. He shifted his chair to the right to avoid any possible spray.

"Why don't you let me talk to the boy for a minute, sheriff?" Dodd offered. "See if we can work something out?"

Ralph nodded with him. "Can't send a kid that young to prison, Joe Bob. No telling what the niggers'll do to him in there."

Joe Bob rolled his eyes. "I can't believe I'm in a room full of bleeding hearts and one of them is the one that got held at gun point. My own fucking brother, for Christ's sake." He waved his hand in dismissal. "Go ahead, just trample over the fucking law. And excuse me if I have to barf in my little trash can here." He dropped another black goober to punctuate.

"Carl Ray," he waved to his deputy, "let Dodd into the cell."

Carl Ray muttered under his breath as he got up from the typewriter, pulled the keys out of Joe Bob's desk drawer and beckoned Dodd to follow.

Bobby Wayne pushed himself as far back against the wall of his cell as he could without actually becoming part of it. Dodd sat beside him anyway, not more than a foot away. "I know you've been listening to the whole conversation. Tell me what to do next."

"I can take prison," Bobby Wayne insisted, not looking up from his arms. "You don't have to stick your fucking neck out for me."

"You didn't think so yesterday afternoon. Otherwise you'd've kept the gun."

"I ain't going home."

"Fine. I'll have the sheriff contact child welfare services. Or else some good Christian family in one of the local churches could put you up. Hell, there're a dozen churches to every family in these small towns anyway."

"Don't put me with no Christians. Prison's a hell of a lot better than Christians."

Dodd patted him on the shoulder. "How about you work for Meeker to pay back any damages? I'm sure you'll find a better job in a month or two. How old are you?"

"Seventeen."

"Try again."

"The sheriff's got my ID. You can check it."

Dodd laughed. "Okay, I'll take you at your word. But look; no one in their right mind is going to let you walk. You take

Meeker's job, then the sheriff has to release you on your own recognizance. Then you get yourself a public defender, plead out and you can get off with a couple of years probation."

"What good is probation? Don't that mean I have to stick around this shit hole?" He wiped his nose on his coat sleeve again.

Dodd threw up his hands. "Jesus Christ, did God give one brain to the whole county? With probation, if you stay clean, you walk clean. You don't play ball and Meeker will bury you in Huntsville for at least four years. Then another three on parole where you have to kiss a P.O.'s ass and just about everybody else can get in your business. This shit hole smells sweet compared to the shit hole in Huntsville. There's guys there that're never getting out, so they'll be looking for meat like you. Understand? Ready to cut a shank out of your bed spring and melt it into a toothbrush? Ready to slip it to a three hundred pound lifer with a hard on for your ass? Before he gets his razor blade under your throat and wrestles you face down into your bunk?"

For the first time, Bobby Wayne looked directly at Dodd. "Can I get my own apartment?"

"You still don't get it, do you? You do two years under the county's watchful eye and then you can do anything you want. Buy a car, get laid, maybe even tie one on every once in a while. Two years living with Christians is still better than four years with a three hundred pound lifer's dick up your ass."

"Can I get a good job? I mean, I don't want to pump gas or nothing."

Dodd shook his head and pushed himself from the mattress. "You win, Joe Bob. Send this little shit to Huntsville before I kill him myself."

The kid jumped off his bunk and grabbed Dodd's elbow. "I'll pump gas, mister. I'll do anything you say."

It took Dodd half and hour to work out terms. Joe Bob agreed to release Bobby Wayne into Ralph's care. Meeker would hire the kid at two-fifty an hour for six months, and then raise him to minimum wage if he was satisfying the terms of his probation. Dodd even persuaded Meeker to put the kid up at the Stickett Inn, which Bobby would pay back out of his salary, until he found a place to stay.

"God damn well better find one by the end of the week," Ralph muttered as they shook hands on the deal.

"If that kid even sniffs the wrong way at somebody's cash register, he's going to Huntsville," Joe Bob said wiping his hand on his shirt sleeve.

"Joe Bob, if that kid fucks up, you can call me and I'll come back, kick his ass and drag him to Huntsville by a belt loop." Dodd glanced over at Bobby Wayne to make sure he understood. Bobby wouldn't even look his way, which he took to be the teenagers' time honored signal of acquiescence.

Chapter 7

That afternoon Dodd checked Bobby Wayne into a room with a television and an ice bucket. Before he could settle into his own room, Ralph Meeker dropped by and offered Dodd a drink at the hotel bar.

Dodd ordered coffee. Meeker ordered a double shot of Jack Daniels. "Thanks for helping the kid out," Dodd said.

"We didn't discuss my terms," said Meeker. "If I'm going to hire that kid, I'm going to hire you to be my business manager."

"I've got a job, Ralph."

"Look, Dodd, I'm pushing sixty-five, and I'll never get richer than I am right now. I own the gas station, the Ben Franklin, the dry goods store, the pharmacy, the insurance agency, the real estate agency and a lot of land. Joe Bob's partner with me on most of them, but some of them I own outright. I want you to manage everything for me. Twenty thousand a year."

Dodd stirred his coffee, amazed at how quickly the cream had disappeared into the oily depths. He wondered if Texans confused coffee with oil once you passed the Permian Basin. "I've been inside, Ralph. Cons don't make good management material."

"Your style is guns, not embezzlement. Besides, you strike me as the kind of fellow who never wants to go back. Not too many jail birds earn their law degrees inside."

Dodd's coffee attacked his throat like shale sludge.

Meeker took his coffee and glanced at the cup. "Wanda Louise," he shouted to the waitress, "when did you make this coffee?"

"How the hell should I remember?" the waitress snapped back.

"How many times do I have to tell you to make a new pot every half hour?"

The waitress stormed the bar and snatched the cup back without looking at either of them.

"That might be one of the reasons nobody tips you," he called behind her. He returned his attention to Dodd. "I own the hotel too," he added. "How about it? I'll go twenty-two, and raise you to twenty-five in six months if you do a good job. I already got a bookkeeper, so you don't have to do no numbers. Just keep an eye on my businesses and keep my employees in line. Twenty-three thousand, and I'll pick up your health insurance. It's worth it to have my own lawyer on call."

"It took me three times to pass the bar."

"Well, you still passed it quicker than anybody else I know. There's this lawyer, Red Ferguson in Pecos, he took the exam every year until he was thirty-five. We usually only get local boys and guys who washed out practicing in the city."

Dodd watched the waitress scoop twenty-seven tablespoons into the basket for a ten cup pot of coffee. He doubted she even counted. "I don't know, Ralph. Anything does go wrong, everybody will point the finger at me."

"That's gonna happen anywhere you go, boy. I figured you'd be smart enough to figure that out by now."

The coffee maker began to sputter as Wanda Louise added the water. "Twenty-five now, plus health insurance. Thirty in six-months if I make the grade. If I don't get the raise, I want two month's severance. Two weeks off at Christmas and two weeks off in August. Plus two days at Thanksgiving, and don't forget Easter, the fourth of July, Labor Day and Memorial Day."

Ralph leaned over the counter and pulled the Jack Daniels bottle out to refill his glass. "I ain't that desperate."

"I didn't come to you with the offer."

Meeker downed his shot and poured another. He seemed so good at drinking that Dodd wondered how long his liver would last. "Okay. How about this? Instead of the vacation time, I have a vacant property on a large piece of land I'll let you live in rent-free for a year, and a low-interest mortgage if you stay."

"What if I settle for twenty-four thousand, the vacation, the house and the insurance, and wait a year for my raise instead of six months?"

Meeker studied his drink. He lifted it up into the light over the bar and turned it around to see the colors change. Dodd couldn't picture Meeker as a man who would ever take the time to think about a decision. "I can do that."

He offered Dodd his hand.

"How'm I going to get around town until my car's fixed?"

Dodd thought Meeker would spit his tongue out with his words. "God damn to hell, you don't give a nickel do you?" Before Dodd could answer. "I'll get you something to drive until your car's fixed. But don't expect a goddam Cadillac."

Dodd offered his hand. "We have a deal."

"But you got to put up that boy in the bargain."

Dodd took his hand back.

"Can't imagine I'll find a family willing to take him in," Ralph added. "Not around here. Probably end up in Huntsville no matter what I do."

"You're a hard-nosed negotiator, Ralph," Dodd said.

"Ain't no soft deals in this shit hole," Meeker replied.

Chapter 8

Dodd walked Bobby Wayne to the Five and Dime. He bought the boy two pairs of jeans and two work shirts with snaps, all four items so old they would probably show the shelf folds for as long as Bobby wore them. After forking over twenty-two dollars for the ensemble, he took Bobby to the town barber shop and thumbed through a two-year-old issue of Playboy while the barber butchered Bobby's hair past redemption. The two of them barely spoke. When they were done, he dropped Bobby at his room, keeping the key.

"That's not going to keep me here," Bobby said. He showed Dodd how the door opened from the inside.

"It will keep you from getting back in later," Dodd said, demonstrating the automatic lock.

"So what am I gonna do for the rest of the night?" Bobby Wayne complained, a reasonable complaint given that it was only four in the afternoon.

Dodd pulled his cash from his side pocket and peeled off a ten. "Buy dinner and watch TV. You'll survive."

"Why don't you keep your cash in your wallet like everyone else?" Bobby asked him, eyeing him with a level of suspicion Dodd had only seen in small town residents.

Dodd pressed the money into Bobby's hand. "It makes it harder to lift. You feel a hand in your side pocket where you don't always feel it in your back pocket."

Bobby looked at the bill as though not sure whether to thank Dodd or ask for more. Finally he decided. "Could you loan me enough for a hooker? There's this chunky girl, Ronda May, she'll do it for fifteen."

"I gave you ten. And that's for dinner."

"She'll do a blow job for five."

Dodd snatched the money back. "You're too young for whores. Wait'll you're old and desperate. Why don't you try reading?"

"Like a book?"

"You've never read one?"

"I skipped that part in school." Dodd started to make a wise crack, but Bobby Wayne cut him off. "Why do you think I got held back two times?"

"I didn't know you got held back two times," Dodd said, but the news hardly surprised him.

Bobby barged on. "Besides I don't see a hell of a lot of books around here." He lifted the dog-eared TV Guide on the dresser to prove his point.

Dodd took the boy to the magazine rack in the hotel lobby. The offering wasn't much better than the TV Guide. He saw a Ft. Stockton newspaper, *True Western, Field and Stream, Guns and Ammo,* and an Archie comics digest. "Don't you have any books?" he asked the desk clerk.

"If you want a book, there's a library in Fort Stockton," the clerk said, not lifting his head from the game show on his tiny black and white television.

"How about the *Guns and Ammo?*" Bobby suggested.

"I guess you're stuck with TV," Dodd answered.

He decided it would be safer to hold onto his money and buy Bobby's dinner for him. When the waitress served their chicken fried steak, Dodd wasn't sure if he was treating the kid to the dinner or inflicting it on him.

Bobby didn't seem to mind. He plowed through his meal. While he chewed he told Dodd all about life with his father, Frank Boatright, Jr., an oil-rigger on a disability pension, drinking himself to death and using Bobby Wayne for target practice when his beer cans were empty.

"Where's your mom?" Dodd asked, waving away the cigarette smoke that crowded its way through the restaurant. Tonight was "2-4-1" steak night, and the restaurant was packed wall-to-wall with skinny rednecks sporting boot-cut jeans, hefty wives with jellyroll chins, and screaming children. Every one of them smoked, even the children.

Hazel had replaced Wanda Louise for the evening waitress shift and her fuse seemed exceptionally short. Part of her temper could have been all those high tipping customers yelling at her between drags on their cigarettes. Part of it could have been the other waitress on duty that night, the fat one sitting behind the counter and ignoring the customers, smoking her own cigarette and tapping her feet to the Tanya Tucker tunes on the jukebox.

Bobby cut a piece of steak with his knife and stuck the knife in his mouth with the meat dangling from the tip. "Mom met this vacuum cleaner guy, and took off. It's hard to blame her. The old man made her work two shifts a day at this fast food joint in Ft. Stockton. It's called the Pig Palace. They use pork instead of beef. You'd like it."

Bobby pushed his steak around the plate while he chewed. "They's in Montana now. Mom said they'd send for me when they got settled in, but it's been two years so I guess they ain't settled in yet."

Dodd asked Hazel to refill their iced teas and leave the ticket. She looked at him like he was asking her to break her back on the table, then carry the weight of the world on her mangled spine.

"Last week, the old man tells me it's time to start paying rent. Three hundred a month. Well I'm in tenth grade cause they held me back a year, two actually. But I told you that. So I'm working part time at a gas station out the highway, I got twice that much saved up, but after two months, I don't make enough to cover it.

"I figure he's bluffing so I keep my money, but when I come home last Friday night, he locks me out. Throws my clothes all over the front yard, not that I had that many. I can go over to a friend's, but his old man makes it clear I ain't staying there more than a week."

"So you figured you'd take your savings, rob Meeker, and live high off the hog until when? Next month when the money runs out?"

"I never really thought past robbing the store. Not having a car or nothing. Had to hitchhike to work. But everybody knows Meeker rakes in a bundle everyday from all the highway traffic. And, see, usually this other guy works the store. He's kinda an asshole so I figured he would be a pushover. Instead here's the owner hisself, who I guess the whole county knows has shot all these robbers back in the forties, and then you show up, and I guess I knew I was fucked from the word go."

Dodd didn't comment, but waited patiently while the Hazel collected their plates and laid out the runny peach cobbler that came with the meal. The scent of Chanel and stale Winstons almost overpowered him.

Bobby held his cobbler at his chin and shoveled it into his mouth.

"So how about yourself, Mr. Dodd? How'd you end up in prison?"

Dodd cleared his throat. "It's a long story, Bobby. Let's just say I didn't grow up with your advantages."

Chapter 9

Dodd made sure Bobby was settled in his room and not likely to wander from the fold. He bought an RC Cola and took it with him to the pay phone to call Joel Burns.

"I suppose you're going to tell me you won't be here tomorrow either," Burns sighed at the other end.

"I picked up some baggage I didn't anticipate."

He could hear Joel clucking his tongue. "Care to explain?"

"A client. Armed robbery. Teen going on twelve. A ten watt bulb."

"Kind of like you were when your case came across my desk?"

"I was never that dim, Joel. Just ignorant."

"Keep telling yourself."

"I got him released into custody. Found out after the fact they'll only release him into my custody. It may take a couple of weeks to pawn him off on someone more responsible."

"It's hard to imagine you'd go soft on a kid. What happened to the cold-hearted bastard I hired?"

"This kid would never make it in the joint."

Joel didn't answer for several seconds. "You don't have an altruistic bone in your body. You've got a deal cooking."

"It's not what you think, Joel. Trust me."

"Dodd, whenever I hear the words 'trust me,' I start watching my back." He rang off.

Dodd spent the next half hour under the shower. He toweled off and pulled on his blue jeans. He tried to arrange himself in the hotel armchair so he could read his Zane Gray novel comfortably and still reach his drink without pulling a muscle.

He decided his task was impossible after fidgeting and trying different positions for half an hour. He climbed onto his bed, propped his pillows against the headboard, draped his legs over the bedspread, popped on the snap on his jeans to let his stomach breathe. Just as he settled in, somebody banged on the door.

He crossed the threadbare carpet to the red metal door, twisted back the bolt lock and pulled the door open. Joe Bob Meeker stood in the hallway staring at him through his mirrored aviator shades. Or so Dodd assumed. Since he'd never seen Meeker with the glasses off, he wasn't sure the man actually had eyes.

Meeker dangled a set of keys from his finger.

"My brother was going to give you these, but I said I'd do it. I guess you got a truck in the deal as well."

A truck. Dodd should have known. Probably standard transmission with an AM radio. He shoved his hands in his pocket. "It's a loaner until my car's fixed."

Meeker glanced at Dodd's waistline. "You queer or something?"

"Excuse me?"

"Isn't that what you queer fellows do? Leave your trouser button unsnapped so you'll know who you are?"

Dodd didn't bother to look, and made no move to fasten it. "I guess that's something only queer guys would know about."

Meeker chewed his cigar for a moment. "Think you're a comedian too, do you?"

Dodd stepped back from the door and gestured for the sheriff to come in. Meeker surveyed the room in a single take. "What you got to drink?"

"RC and water. Mostly water."

Meeker squeezed his enormous bulk between the two armrests of Dodd's chair. For a minute Dodd thought the arms would break off, but the chair managed to hold him. Joe Bob fished through his shirt pocket for his snuff and carefully placed a large pinch in his cheek.

"A man should have more than soda pop to offer his guests. A man should have more than that period."

Dodd sat down on the bed, swinging his right ankle under his left knee. "I don't drink."

"A man as rough as you. Did hard time. Can't tell me you don't drink." Meeker began to fiddle with Dodd's empty pop can, jiggling the bottom on the small table.

Dodd reached over and took the can. He pitched it across the room and into the small wastebasket by the dresser. "Sheriff, I figure if I want to stay out of jail I need to do two things. First, I need to quit doing things without thinking, and booze makes me do things without thinking. Second, I need to cut down on my expenses so I won't need to go robbing gas stations to pay my bills. I figure a half-pint and two packs of cigarettes a day over a year costs me close to two thousand dollars. That's more than I would get robbing a gas station, so I kinda gave up everything."

Joe Bob sat silently for several minutes, aviator shades frozen on his nose, twirling the keys on a ring around one fat finger. "That's the stupidest thing I ever heard."

Dodd took a sip from his glass. "So are you going to give me those keys or do you want to keep talking about the queer and stupid things you don't like about me?"

Joe Bob threw the keys into the air, forcing Dodd to catch them with his glass. He pulled them out of the drink and wiped them on the bedspread. Joe Bob pulled a piece of paper from his shirt pocket and flattened it on the table. "This here's a map to your new lodging. Kind of makes me think Ralph's going senile, giving you a job, and a car, and a place to stay."

"I hope you're expressing concern as his brother because I'm not sure this is an issue for the law."

Joe Bob grabbed his pants leg and pulled it up to cross his leg at the knee. "Me and Ralph's kind of partners on a lot of his business, and I don't like the thought of no ex-con running our business."

Dodd leaned over the bed, offering the keys back to the sheriff. "Suits me. I'll be gone in the morning."

The sheriff didn't move.

Dodd laughed. "This is a nice incestuous set-up you boys have. One brother's the JP. The other's the sheriff. Both on the town council. Somebody complains about a business deal, you run them out of town, the judge rules in your favor, or the council rezones their property."

Traces of purple creeped past Meeker's collar and up his neck. "I been thinking," he said.

Dodd almost recommended the sheriff not work too hard at it, but he held his tongue.

"I been thinking that maybe you're related to them other Dodds what used to live here."

"What other Dodds?"

"The one's got killed in the bank robbery. In forty nine. "

"I guess I missed one, Joe Bob. Clue me in."

Joe Bob added another pinch to the little knot under his lip. Dodd marveled at his ability to simultaneously chew a cigar and snuff but not fall over from nicotine poisoning. "They're famous. One being shot down by the Texas Rangers in Llano in 1951. Walking out of a theater just like Dillinger. Took rounds from three different Rangers at once. Those Dodds."

"I thought you said they were killed in a bank robbery."

"You being funny?"

Dodd slipped his glass back on the table, a few inches from Joe Bob's elbow. "I heard of Dillinger. I heard of Bonnie and Clyde. I heard of Sam Bass and the James Brothers. I never heard of a family named Dodd. Except for mine, of course. But none of us were bank robbers."

Joe Bob slammed his fist on the table, rattling the ice at the bottom of the glass. "I don't like you fucking with me, boy."

Dodd slipped his legs over the edge of the bed and drew his face in close to the sheriff's. "I'm going to go get another RC Cola. You want me to bring something back?"

Meeker leaned forward to meet him, leveling his glasses with Dodd's eyes. "You can get yourself another soda pop when I'm done with you. Now I want you to swear to me you never heard of the fucking Dodds. The Dodds that robbed the bank here thirty years ago. Got away with half a million dollars. Those Dodds."

"My answer isn't going to change, Joe Bob. It's no. At least not before I showed up in town yesterday and every one that learns my name asks if I'm related to the Dodd brothers that robbed a bank thirty years ago."

"And why should I believe you?"

Dodd threw up his hands. "Run a background check on me, for God's sake."

The slight blush to Meeker's cheeks told Dodd that he already had. And Dodd had come up clean. Well, clean except for the jail term.

He put his hand on Meeker's shoulder. "Look, Joe Bob, just between you and me, I'm black. Just very light skinned." This was a bald faced lie. Dodd just wanted to see what Meeker would do.

Meeker slapped Dodd's hand away, just as Dodd expected him to.

"I can't imagine many black folks living in Sweet Water Falls in the forties. In fact, the population looks pretty white now."

Meeker took a moment to chew the thought over. "You know, people always suspected the Dodds had a nigger in the woodpile. Considering everything."

"Our whole woodpile is black, although my father did accuse my mother of sleeping with a white boy when he was too drunk to hold his temper. Me? I always figured that, coming from the plantations, every family had a cracker in the watermelon patch."

Joe Bob growled, "I don't know if you're fucking with me or telling me the truth. But if you are part nigger, which I highly doubt, you ought not be telling people." He drummed his fingers on the desk. His knuckles were thick and hairy, his nails chewed to the quick. "I do know you're an ex-con working for my brother and that means I'm gonna be on your ass like a fly on shit. You got that? You take a piss, I'm gonna know it. You get laid, I'm gonna know it. You stray from the straight and narrow by more than an inch and you're fucked and so is that teenage friend of yours. Are we clear?"

Dodd stood, and stared down at Meeker. "Sheriff, I finished parole. You can't hold me; you can't threaten me. What you just said constitutes harassment. And let me remind you. I don't have a lawyer, I am a lawyer." Joe Bob struggled to pull himself up from the chair. Dodd used the time to open his door. "Share your concerns with your brother because they don't mean shit to me."

The two of them stared at each other, nose to nose, until a bead of sweat formed between Joe Bob's eyebrows and dripped down his nose to drop to the carpet between them. "I got your number," he said finally. He jabbed Dodd's shoulder with his finger.

Dodd lifted Meeker under the armpit with a move the Huntsville guards often used, and steered him to the door. Meeker was too shocked to resist. "Of course you do, it's right here on the door. Twenty Two." Before Joe Bob could respond, he shut the door in his face.

Dodd leaned his back against the door and breathed deeply. He earned a lot of bad karma during that exchange—West Texas karma.

Guys on the inside talked about West Texas karma all the time. West Texas karma could leave you dead and weighted down in a river somewhere. Only the sheriff wasn't going to spend a lot of time investigating because he probably weighted you down himself.

It was the worst kind of karma.

Worse than walking into a soul food restaurant with a bald head white power t-shirt. Worse than ordering drinks on the house for twelve-steppers celebrating their one-year chips. Worse than wearing a Longhorn t-shirt in Norman, Oklahoma the day before the game and shouting out "Sooners" like a hog call.

That kind of karma.

Chapter 10

The truck Meeker loaned Dodd was about as far from a Cadillac as a vehicle could get. A 1946 Ford pickup with the engine exposed, no tailgate and the bed half rusted. If there were ever tread on the tires it had worn off sometime before the Korean War. Dodd had been right about no FM radio; there was no radio at all. There was no handle to raise the window on the passenger door, but that didn't matter because the window was duct-taped in place. There was no door handle on the passenger door either.

"You actually paid for this?" Bobby Wayne said when he emerged from the hotel. His clothes were packed in the bag from the dry goods store.

"It's a loaner," Dodd said.

"Can you loan it back?"

"We can walk everywhere until my car's fixed," Dodd said.

Bobby poked his finger through a hole in the cowl. It was covered with rust and grease when he removed it. "We may end up walking anyway." He wiped his finger off on his jeans. "Makes me really look forward to your new digs."

They stopped at Tucker's to unload Dodd's trunk. Bobby Wayne leaned against the fender as Dodd transferred the contents to the floor of the cab, the only surface he thought they might not fall through. "You got a lot of books," Bobby said.

"Had to do something while I was inside. Got tired of beating off after the first six months." He tossed Bobby Wayne's clothes next to his suit bag.

"How could you ever get tired of beating off?" Bobby Wayne wondered.

Dodd realized the truck needed more work than his Mustang after passing through the first, and only, stoplight in town. The starter strained to turn the engine over. One of the valves stuck. He had to double clutch every gear and use the toe of his boot to lift the clutch from the floor of the cab. Oil smoke followed the truck for several blocks. The sealed window raised the temperature in the cab, and exhaust leaks made it even hotter. The shocks were so worn the slightest bump knocked Dodd's backbone into his jaw.

Bobby tried to lean his elbow against the taped window, but every bump knocked him clear. "Your car was in worse shape than this?"

"I should have just headed to New Mexico with the front seat full of gas cans."

Their new lodgings stood in the middle of fifteen acres of land, the same fifteen acres he'd studied from the highway two days earlier. The land had been plowed under so many times the grass refused to take root. Row after row of dirt turned onto row after row of dirt. The first rain would wash it all into one giant mudslide. The road wasn't much better–dirt that hadn't been plowed.

Even though the paint had peeled away from the weathered wood frame years before, the house looked solid and the windows intact. A wooden porch ran the length of two sides and a power line ran to a transformer behind the house.

An aging barn and silo stood back from the house, in far worse condition. They looked like they had been torn apart piece by piece in anything but systematic order. Half of the buildings were little more than frame.

"Welcome to the Hilton," Dodd griped.

He had to lift the front door from the ground and push with both hands to get the handle to turn. When he finally got the door open a wash of musk and mildew hit him in the face.

They dropped their bags inside the door to inventory the property. The kitchen/living room was nothing more than a stove, a sink and cupboards against the far wall. A chipped Formica table and three chairs provided the only furniture. One of the chairs, its back leg missing, lay stacked on the table. Three bedrooms were visible from the living room. One sported a canvas camp bed; another a set of box springs with a mattress. The third was empty. The lights dangled by a wire from the ceiling, one to a room, each swinging an unshielded thirty-watt bulb in the slight breeze through the front door.

"Where's the bathroom?" Bobby Wayne asked.

Dodd didn't need to guess. "You know what an outhouse is?"

"I heard of them," Bobby Wayne said, in a defensive manner that made it clear he hadn't.

"You'll figure it out when you have to go bad enough," Dodd said. "You can have the room to the left." No sense in giving the kid the good bed.

Bobby Wayne walked into his room and dropped his rucksack to the floor. "Where do I hang my clothes?" he called through the door.

"We'll hang a rope across your room," Dodd answered, studying the four bare walls in his own room. He finally understood why people had wardrobes in the old days. "Or keep them folded in that bag of yours."

At least the room had windows on both sides, he told himself. The room faced to the north and west, another advantage over Bobby's room that he would appreciate on weekend mornings. The view onto plowed-up dirt and an occasional mesquite tree still standing would be the same from both rooms.

He found Bobby Wayne in the kitchen, rubbing the grime off a window with his sleeve. "How could anyone live like this?"

"Don't kid yourself. During the great depression, this would have been a luxury."

"Was that before or after World War II?"

Dodd studied his face to see if he was serious. It scared him to realize Bobby was. "After," Dodd said. "Just before the Vietnam war." He walked through the back door and out onto the tiny step porch.

"I heard of that," Bobby Wayne called after him, following Dodd out onto the porch. "Where's the bathroom?" Dodd pointed to the narrow wooden stall thirty yards back from the house.

"That's the outhouse."

"Why's it so far away?"

"Take a shit when you're stomach's fucked up, on a day when the wind's blowing in from the gorge. You'll figure it out."

"Why don't you just flush?"

Dodd laughed. "I met this guy from this little town called Llano. Bought a hotel that was built in 1888. Renovated in the forties and not since. Had all the luxuries of this place. There wasn't enough electricity to have a light on in every room, no air conditioning, one bath for twelve rooms. He spent six thousand dollars to bring it to code and left it alone other than that. People who wanted a swimming pool could take a path to this narrow creek and had to beat the ants off their clothes before walking back. He calls it The Dabbs Railroad Hotel, advertises it as 'The ultimate rustic experience,' and charges fifty dollars a night. He almost never has a vacancy."

"No kidding?"

"No kidding."

"Do we take our showers in that thing too?"

"Let's look at the stove," Dodd said.

Dodd loved the stove, the one thing of value in the house, probably because it was too heavy to move—an old brushed-steel wood-burning stove with a bread warmer and hot water steamer in the back. "They don't make these anymore," he told Bobby

Wayne and showed him the wide-variety of compartments to bake, boil or warm food.

While Dodd was lifting a lid to show Bobby a soup well, Bobby said, "I don't know if I ought to tell you this."

"Don't tell me anything you don't feel comfortable with." Dodd pulled open the wood bin to show where they could load coal or split logs. "You stack your fire wood in here, see. Then the stove keeps the house warm all day long."

"Look, I figure, if it was up to that bastard Meeker I'd be headed to prison right now. You're the only one who really helped me get out."

Dodd shut the door, and stood up, leaning against the stove. "You figured right."

"Well, Mr. Meeker told me not to tell you this, but he's paying me fifty extra a week to tell him if I find you looking around the property."

"Oh really?"

"You know, digging holes, looking under boards? Shit like that? Pretty weird, huh?"

"Well then, the first thing you better tell him is how I just finished looking through the stove."

Bobby Wayne seemed taken aback by Dodd's comment, and then he broke into a smile. "Yeh. I guess I better."

"Don't worry," Dodd promised him. "Things will get even weirder over the next couple of weeks. May as well make a few extra bucks while you can."

Chapter 11

Unpacking consisted of little more than hanging his suit bag from the top of a windowsill, and plugging his alarm clock into the wall by his bed. He hoped there was enough current to keep it running. After changing into one of his suits he stepped back into the kitchen.

Bobby's face looked like he licked a sour jalapeño sucker. "What kind of suit is that?"

Dodd glanced down and brushed his lapels. He had no idea how much the suit, a Brookes Brothers gray pin-stripe, cost. It was one of two given by a woman as a present for passing the bar. A woman who, as he reflected back on his situation, probably thought of the gift as upgrading her property.

"Is there a problem?"

"Got no yokes, no vent, no boot cut in the legs. Nobody in their right mind'd wear something like that. Hope you didn't pay more than ten bucks."

"Do you see me wearing boots, Bobby?"

Bobby glanced down to his polished black Oxfords. "Damn, you were wearing boots this morning. What's wrong with you?

You think this is the city? And what is your suit made of? It's all fuzzy. It don't shine like it's s'posed to."

"It's a wool blend, Bobby."

"You're going to be hot as hell in the middle of summer if you don't wear something polyester."

Dodd debated explaining the finer facts of fabrics to his unwanted ward, but decided against it. How could you explain clothing to someone who dressed for work in Levis and Keds?

He dropped Bobby off at Meeker's Corner Store at ten.

"You want me to go in with you?" he asked.

"Naw, I can handle myself," Bobby assured him.

"Remember," he told the boy. "You're not robbing this place anymore, you're working there. It's a job, and the truth is there's nothing worse in this world than working a job."

Bobby nodded in agreement, but Dodd could tell he wasn't clear on the details. So Dodd draped his arm over the car seat and explained. "Now listen to me. How a job works is this. You spend all day sucking up to some asshole with half the talent you have."

Bobby crossed his arms and said, "That sucks."

Dodd rapped the top of his head. "This isn't a joke, son. Now you can't just suck up, you have to pretend you enjoy sucking up. That's the most important part. Because if they don't think you enjoy sucking up, then they do everything in their power to find ways to make you suck up more. Once that happens, you're going to spend the rest of your life working under some asshole with half your talent, or robbing stores again, and you know where that got you."

Bobby looked at his feet, and mumbled, "I got you."

"There is a good side to this, Bobby. If you pretend you really enjoy sucking up, then sooner or later they'll forget you're sucking up and think of you as one of them, and promote you. Then you get to be an asshole all day long while some poor Joe with twice your talent sucks up to you. Do you see how this works, kid?"

Bobby turned to catch Dodd's eye. "I appreciate all this help, sir. I can see you're preparing me for a long, successful future."

Dodd turned the engine over, and pushed him out the door. "You've got the idea already."

Dodd made sure Bobby pushed his way through the gas station door before he left. He drove through the town, trying to assess the lay of the land. Most of the businesses faced the highway, marked by a street sign proclaiming "South Main." Three blocks later, at the center of town, the street sign changed to "North Main."

Just in case tourists became lost, a big sign by the courthouse/jail announced: "Welcome to the downtown shopping district of beautiful Sweet Water Falls."

Dodd shook his head. The downtown shopping district didn't even contain a town square, just a five block strip with the courthouse, the post office/bus station, an auto dealer, a real estate agency owned by Meeker, an insurance agency, also owned by Meeker, a Western Auto and Sears catalogue outlet (in the same building), a Ben Franklin, dry goods store and pharmacy, all three owned by Meeker, a feed store, five churches, a restaurant called the Paris Cafe and the Stickett Inn hotel. The First Bank of Sweet Water Falls dominated them all, by far the largest building in town, perhaps in the county.

Traffic was heavy this morning. Dodd counted at least seven pickup trucks.

He parked his pickup between a Lincoln Continental and a Dodge Ram in the five-car lot that served the realty office, dry goods store and Sears/Western Auto. He lifted the parking brake but the handle offered no resistance. Great, he thought to himself.

The realty office looked like a mobile home cut in half. Since Meeker's insurance agency looked just like it, Dodd suspected Meeker had done exactly that. The lobby barely fit the receptionist's desk and a coffee table, much less the receptionist. When he opened the door, he found her, a woman with Joe Bob's girth and humor, typing up a deed while grinding a cigarette out into an ashtray that spilled butts out onto her desktop calendar and over onto the floor.

Dodd couldn't imagine anyone buying property in Sweet Water Falls, but he figured that wasn't something his job would require him to worry about.

"He's in the back," she said, not even looking up from her typewriter. She pecked at the keys, one at a time, and Dodd guessed she didn't want to look up and lose track of them.

He squeezed between her desk and the wall and knocked on Meeker's door. It opened into an office twice the size of the reception area, but still barely large enough to fit two people.

Ralph sat in front of an ancient roll-top desk next to a half-full bottle of Jim Beam and a coffee cup. He wore his vest unbuttoned and appeared to be halfway through his newspaper and bourbon. He held out his hand, not even bothering to get up. "Glad you made it, Dodd. I was just sitting here trying to think how I could best use you."

Dodd took the upright wooden chair Meeker offered to him, the only other chair in the office. Ralph pushed the door shut with his foot, shoved aside his newspaper and found a second mug somewhere inside one of the cubbyholes in his desk. He blew into it, producing a large cloud of dust, and filled it halfway to the top with Jim Beam before offering it to Dodd.

Dodd held up his hand. "I don't drink, Ralph."

Ralph took back the mug, studied it for a second and then emptied it into his own. "All the more for me."

"Joe Bob came by my hotel room last night. Thinks I'm related to some bank robbers that used to live around here."

Ralph balanced his mug between his fingers and leaned back in his chair. "Now why would he do that?"

"He's your brother."

Ralph put his mug down and rose from his chair, beckoning for Dodd to join him. "Never you mind. Joe Bob? He's a suspicious man, but I have controlling interest in the business. Do a good job and I'll guarantee Joe Bob'll forget there ever were any other Dodds in this town."

Dodd followed Ralph into his outer office. "Betty, I'm taking Dodd here on a tour of the Meeker Empire."

"More like a back lot than an empire," she mumbled. Ralph stopped in front of her desk and glared at her. "Fine with me," she said, still not looking up from her typing. "As long as he doesn't think he can boss me around."

Ralph led Dodd back out into the parking lot, across a small grass island and into the dry goods store.

The dry goods store featured coarse wool horse blankets, a wide variety of crackers, dog biscuits and feed grains, plaid shirts with diamond and square-shaped rhinestone snaps, and hats that rose a good eighteen inches from their brims—the brims sweeping way back from the crowns which swept back from a peak in the front to a point about two inches lower at the back. Each hat sported a tiny feather, sticking from the headband. Dodd even spotted several suits on the rack, all brown or blue polyester, with shoulder yokes and slanted side vents. Just like Bobby Wayne thought a suit should look.

The store clerk, a crusty old man who looked like he was about to bowl over and die from cancer, kept a cup full of straw under the counter so he could pull out a new piece to chew on every twenty minutes or so. He called Meeker's attention to his newest shipment of hats.

"Goddam it, Hank, couldn't you sell the other hats before you order new ones?"

"Gotta keep up with the times, Ralph," the old man mumbled around his piece of straw.

"Don't you have a plain old cowboy hat?" Dodd asked. "You know, something with a smaller crown and a soft brim that I can roll into a curve I like?"

"Why would you want that?" the old man mumbled around his straw. "Ladies won't go for that. They want a big hat, tells 'em you're packing, if you know what I mean."

"I thought that's what socks were for," Dodd said, holding one of the hats in front of him and trying to picture it on his head without laughing out loud.

"Before you go mouthing off, Hank," Meeker said, "this isn't a customer. This is Dodd Dodd. I hired him to manage all my businesses for me. From now on, you'll be handing the cash over to him at the end of the day."

Hank leaned over the counter, twirling his straw between his teeth.

"Dodd? Dodd? Didn't you and Joe Bob kill all the Dodds a couple a years back?"

"More like the Truman administration, Hank," Ralph sighed, rolling his eyes.

"Different Dodds," Dodd said, offering him has hand.

"You coulda hired me," Hank complained. "I bet I'd be cheaper than some out-of-towner."

"Just let Hank know when you want to pick up the bank deposit," Ralph said to Dodd, ignoring his store manager. "He'll be more than glad to cooperate."

"Like hell I will," Hank announced, but Ralph was already pulling Dodd by the elbow back out into the parking lot. The two men climbed into Meeker's Lincoln to drive three buildings over to Ralph's insurance agency to meet Bill Angerman, Ralph's insurance salesman. Angerman, who wore his blond hair in a flat top that made his baldness all the more obvious, shook Dodd's hand with a death grip and assured him he was on the team, all the way, ready to run, block or pass.

"Class quarterback?" Dodd asked as they climbed back into the Lincoln.

"Tailback and defensive tackle. Class of 65. They won the state championship in seven-man-football."

"Seven man football," Dodd said, kicking a couple of Daniels empties back under the seat. "What kind of football is that?"

"The kind that gets you recruited by junior colleges," Ralph told him, pulling a half-full bottle from somewhere inside his door and pouring it into a coffee cup he kept on the dashboard. "He broke his ankle in the second game of his freshman year, but he would have flunked out anyway."

In the time it took Ralph to pour his drink, they arrived at their next destination, Meeker's Feed and Forage, which was three buildings further down and around the corner.

Over the next hour, Ralph chauffeured Dodd to the pharmacy, even though it was across the street from the feed store, across the highway to the corner store and back up the highway to the veterinarian's office, which stood directly across the highway from the Dry Goods store.

Fred Waspergas managed the feed store. His twin brother Harvey owned the independent grocery directly across the street. The Waspergas brothers stood at well over six feet, with thick shoulders and red hair. Fred paid more attention to his tobacco cup than Dodd. When the introduction was finished he spat in the cup and mentioned that Ralph might have thought about giving him a raise before he added someone to the payroll.

Jack Withersmith, the veterinarian, proved quite a surprise. A tall man, no more than twenty-five, he seemed to be the only person in Sweet Water Falls Dodd met who wasn't under twenty or over forty. He greeted Dodd with a handshake while trying to hold down a piglet for an injection.

"Belongs to Job Hodkins," Withersmith explained. "He'll run up several hundred in bills and then give me the pig." Ralph introduced Dodd and Withersmith said, "You mean, I've got two bosses now?"

"He won't interfere with your business, he'll just collect the money," Ralph assured him.

"Man doesn't know a pig's ear from a pig's rear," Withersmith complained.

"Actually, I do," Dodd said, "but I'll defer to you if we disagree."

Back in the Continental Dodd asked, "Don't veterinarians usually work for themselves?"

"I loaned him the money for vet school at A&M," Ralph admitted.

"At what? Eighteen percent?"

"Twenty," Ralph confessed.

"Jesus, Ralph, I've known loan sharks friendlier than you."

As far as Dodd was concerned, however, the prize for store manager went to Wally Wetzel, who couldn't be found when they arrived at Meeker's Corner Store. "Are you here by yourself?" Ralph shouted to Bobby Wayne, who stood at the back of the store loading beer into the cooler.

"Wally said he had to collect a poker debt from a friend of his in Pecos," Bobby said.

"I suppose he took his gas money from the cash register before he left."

Bobby shrugged. "I think so."

"Some manager," Dodd said as they walked to the parking lot.

"He's just the shift manager. My midnight guy's more reliable," Ralph said, unlocking his car door.

"That makes me feel better," Dodd said.

"His father is an investor at the bank," Ralph explained, but illuminated Dodd no further. Dodd assumed anyone in town would know what that would mean.

They reached the township administrative complex by eleven. Ralph led him across the narrow lobby to an oak door with a smoked glass window at the far end of the building.

They stopped at the mayor's office and Ralph sorted through his keys. Dodd glanced across the lobby to the JP's office, which looked exactly the same except for the words "Honorable Justice of the Peace" above the door.

Ralph tried a key in the lock and pulled it out again, shaking his head. Dodd glanced at the dome, a papier mậché and mud structure badly patched into the ceiling and supported by little more than a wood beam. The dome had no skylight to let illuminate the building, which Dodd always thought was the point of a dome. Dark brown stains surrounded the neon light fixtures and crept across the seam where the dome and roof came together. Dodd imagined that most of the rain ended up in the lobby and might even conspire with the shoddy wiring to electrocute someone.

Ralph tried another key.

"I like your dome," Dodd said.

"Isn't it great?" Ralph said, twisting the key, and forcing the door with his knee. "I insisted that the architect add it. Quite distinctive." He pulled the key off his chain and handed it to Dodd. "This office is your main responsibility."

The mayor's office looked like a breakfast nook made even smaller by the sixteen-inch-deep oak bookcases lining the walls and the six foot oak desk buried under loose papers and manila file folders. Two leather armchairs fit awkwardly between the desk and the door, leaving little room for Meeker to squeeze around his desk.

"Don't you have a secretary?" Dodd asked, trying to tally the number of folders he would have to sort through.

"Of course I do. Mrs. Brazwell. You met her back at my company offices. The township only pays her a part time salary and I need her full time."

"What if someone needs to contact this office?"

"It's not as though they don't know where to find me." Ralph opened the bottom desk drawer and removed a quart of Jim Beam. He poured a healthy dose into yet another dusty coffee mug. "This is the fuel of local government," he added, tipping his cup toward Dodd.

Dodd ran his finger through the dust on top of the folders. "How long since you've actually been in this office?"

He leaned back and took a sip of his whiskey, smacking his lips before answering. "We're kind a loose about things. Except for Joe Bob."

Dodd nodded his head even though Ralph hadn't answered his question.

Ralph nodded back with approval. They were men now, communicating like men. "From ten to noon, or thereabouts, I want you to be at this office, taking care of any mayoral business that doesn't require my personal attention, which is pretty much everything. Anything I need to see? You should leave on top of my desk for when I get a chance to drop by."

"You don't want me to drop it by the realty office?"

Ralph refilled his mug. "No need. I get by when I need to." He patted a stack of files that probably began piling up during the Eisenhower administration.

"Now you don't need be to back in the office at one. When lunch is over you swing by the stores to collect deposits. Except for Withersmith. You just need to collect his interest and rent checks at the beginning of the month."

Ralph stopped to take another sip from his mug and gather his thoughts. Dodd figured it must be getting harder and harder for him to gather those thoughts given the amount of Jim Beam he put away in the last hour.

"The one thing that's important is getting all the deposits to the bank by two-thirty because Rafferty likes to close for business at three. He's a real son-of-a-bitch about that. Why he can't just take off himself and let his employees run the bank is beyond me, but he's got to be there all the time watching them. After you make that deposit, hang out with the boys at the Paris Cafe. Listen to the conversations. Get a feel for the town."

"Most bosses would call that goofing off," Dodd suggested.

"Call it surveillance," Ralph said, rolling his cup in his hands. "You'd be surprised at the profit you can turn from an innocent conversation."

He tucked his whiskey back in its drawer and took Dodd to the courtroom, which was little bigger than his office. All sheetrock and no windows, the room was lighted by two neon fixtures running the length of the ceiling. Meeker's bench sat against the back wall, along with an empty typing table. Two small tables sat in front of the bench, surrounded by half a dozen straight-backed wooden chairs.

"Where's your court reporter's equipment?" Dodd asked.

"Hell, we couldn't afford one of those. I just bring Mrs. Brazwell over to write everything down in shorthand."

Dodd couldn't believe how easy the job sounded. Show up at ten, catch lunch at twelve, cruise the town for an hour after lunch and make a bank deposit by two-thirty. How hard could that be?

He recalled his own lecture to Bobby Wayne about work, and somewhere, at the back of his mind, Dodd began to suspect he was being set up. But try as he might, he couldn't see the angle. He would have to play his cards until he could cash in or he saw a hand that he should fold on.

"The town council meets every Friday night." Ralph locked the door and handed Dodd that key as well. "It's the last thing we do before the week comes to a close. No one is welcome but the council right now, but as people get used to you I'll expect you to start attending. To make sure we both heard things the way I heard them."

"You don't always see eye-to-eye on the issues?"

"We all three gotta agree on everything we pass. Problem is, after we all agree to it, even when we wrote it down, some of us,

I won't say who, can't always remember what we meant by what we agreed to. You get my drift?"

That was the main reason lawyers stayed in business, Dodd thought. But it never stopped people from complaining about lawyers.

"Now this Friday is one of the few Fridays of the year we don't meet. The others being Thanksgiving, and Christmas. This weekend's the barbecue. A man can't do business when he's looking forward to all that brisket and beer."

"A barbecue? Like the town barbecue?"

"No, like the bank president's barbecue. Could feed all them Biafran babies for a year, only we eat it all in a night. But don't get your juices flowing, cause you gotta be invited by either Rafferty or his misses."

"How about the daughter?"

Ralph paused and studied Dodd carefully. "How the hell did you know about Mary Beth?" Before Dodd could answer he shook his head sadly and said, "No. Jesus Christ. I don't want to know. I should a known. Just don't tell me."

Chapter 12

The First Bank of Sweet Water Falls was modeled after a Victorian church, built from large stone blocks with massive oak doors and stained glass windows. The Bank even sported a small bell tower that resembled a steeple.

The bank's somber elegance and beauty, not to say sheer ostentatiousness, stood in stark contrast to the five churches on the same street, each erected within two buildings of the next, each little more than frame building with whitewashed walls, none of them capable of squeezing in more than three dozen people at a time. The churches proclaimed themselves to be, in order, "First Baptist Church of Sweet Water Falls," "First Church of Christ of Sweet Water Falls," "First Christian Church of Sweet Water Falls," the slightly smaller "Bedrock Baptist Church of Sweet Water Falls," and, smallest of all, the "Bible Believing Bedrock Baptist Church of Sweet Water Falls."

The fact that the town sported five different churches on its main street didn't surprise Dodd. He knew how fractious small town religious folk could be. What struck him the most was the fact that, at different times of the day, every single one of those tiny churches would fall under the bank's shadow.

Ralph guided Dodd into a quietly decorated lobby with marble floors, marble columns and marble counters. Six teller windows ran from the front of the bank to the back, five of them displaying the sign, "Please use another window." The sixth seemed to be unoccupied. Three desks sat on the other side of the lobby, slightly behind the reception desk. Each desk had its own nameplate and title, "Loan Officer," "Savings Officer," and "Checking Officer." Only the reception desk was occupied.

The vault door stood on prominent display at the back of the bank, an enormous chrome and steel door with three different time locks. Stairs at the side of the vault climbed to a second floor that boasted little more than a small suite of offices and a balcony walkway around the lobby.

"What do you think?" Meeker asked, nudging Dodd in the ribs.

"I think they're all dressed up with no place to go."

"Don't kid yourself. Rafferty spent a good chunk of change to bring a former IRS executive over as the bank's CFO. Those two have cooked some sweet deals with Midland and Odessa wildcatters and ranchers to bring in tons of oil and cattle money from the Permian Basin."

"Is Mal in, Marla?" Meeker asked the receptionist.

In stark contrast to Meeker's assistant Mrs. Brazwell, Marla was a knock-out. Dodd felt lust for her swelling inside the minute she looked up from her typewriter where she had been pecking, like Mrs. Brazwell, one key at a time. She tossed a long mane of red hair over her shoulders and smiled to reveal a row of perfect white teeth. Her pale blue dress managed to emphasize her round D-cup breasts and nineteen-inch waist.

"Well now, I'll just have to check, won't I, Mr. Mayor?" She continued to smile while she pushed six or seven buttons on the intercom, trying to connect.

Finally a woman's voice answered, "Yes?"

"Mom, Mayor Meeker is here to see Mal."

Within a minute a door opened at the far corner of the room and a mature model of Marla crossed the lobby to greet them. Dodd had heard the receptionist call her mom, but he still did a double take to see the tall woman with her own large bosom and nineteen inch waist in a sharply angled business suit. The only differences between the two women were the hints of gray in the mother's pageboy and the hint that the mother started drinking on the sly years ago, while the daughter still drank because she thought it was fun.

The woman nodded to Meeker. "You don't need to announce yourself, Ralph."

"I wanted to introduce everybody to my new assistant. Dodd, this is Rhonda and Marla Mayfield, the two women who run the finances of the town."

"You're the fella that busted up the robbery in the mayor's store," Marla said, her face showing the sudden light of recognition.

"Do you have a first name, Mr. Dodd?" Rhonda interrupted her, pushing the familiarity to the side. Dodd's personality thermometer told him the girl was fairly warm but the mother would take a long time to thaw.

"Dodd," Meeker burst in. Dodd could tell he'd been waiting all afternoon to spring that on someone.

"My middle name's Dodd too," Dodd added. "I think my father read Catch-22 before I was born."

Rhonda dropped his hand as though suddenly tired of the conversation. "I'm afraid I don't read much at all, Mr. Dodd." She pronounced "at all" like one word "atoll."

"No, D period D. My initials."

She sighed. "Why don't you two gentlemen go right on in?"

Meeker steered them up the stairs to Rafferty's office. In the background he could hear Rhonda chastising her daughter: "Marla, dear, when we are here in the bank, you do not refer to me as 'Mom.' We've discussed this before."

"Yes, mom," the younger woman sighed.

Rafferty's office was an armchair sportsman's dream. The walls were solid oak, the desk and furniture oak and leather. Two gun racks on the wall displayed a variety of antique rifles, from carbines to flintlocks. His trophies included a fourteen point buck, a bear head and a ram with black, wraparound horns. Dodd's shoes sank three inches into the plush chocolate carpet. Only a small corner window and a tiny desk lamp lit the room.

Rafferty didn't bother to rise, address them, or even offer a chair. He studied a legal document while Meeker and Dodd seated themselves. Even though he easily stood at six feet, the ornate back of his leather chair towered over him, and he sat at his desk with his sleeves rolled to the elbow and his jacket folded over the top of a filing cabinet.

Dodd figured the man was Meeker's age, but his body showed no signs of it. His hair, while slightly gray, was thicker than his carpet, his arms sported healthy muscles, and any wrinkles faded in the dim light of the room. A slight pair of reading glasses in thin wire frames seemed to be his only concession to age.

Dodd couldn't see a sign of any ashtrays or tobacco in the office. He took a deep breath and enjoyed the fresh air.

Finally Rafferty initialed the bottom of the last page and turned the document over. "What can I do for you, Ralph?"

"I just wanted you to meet my new property manager, D.D. Dodd."

Dodd leaned forward to offer Rafferty his hand, but Rafferty leaned back in his chair and crossed his fingers in front of him like a church house. He pressed his lips together in a forced smile. "Your reputation precedes you."

"Which one? Ex-convict, or hero who broke up a robbery?"

Rafferty closed his eyes as though he had already lost patience with the conversation. "I keep tabs on everyone in this town. I keep tabs on everyone because it's good for business. I, myself, don't think I would have hired a man convicted of armed robbery to manage my business. Too many opportunities to divert businesses resources."

"Different skill set. And since I don't think Ralph would send me to a seminar on embezzlement, I'd have to learn those new skills like any other first-time manager."

Rafferty folded his fingers over his knuckles and rapped them against his chin. Dodd couldn't tell in the dim light, but he thought the man's eyes had begun to cloud, if only slightly.

"He got a law degree in prison, Mal. That should count for something. And Joe Bob talked to his parole officer, and the parole officer told him that Dodd was a model parolee. Never missed an appointment, never missed a day of work at his job, never gave him the slightest reason to write a negative report. He said the man never wants to see the other side of prison again."

"It's the truth," Dodd added. "Never again."

"Where did he work while he was on parole?" Dodd noticed that Rafferty addressed the question to Meeker and not to him.

"I was a law clerk for a public defender's office," Dodd answered anyway.

"He said Dodd was a hard worker and a good law clerk. Best he'd ever had," Meeker added.

"Then why isn't Mr. Dodd still gainfully employed?"

Meeker started to answer, but Dodd jumped in. "Once I passed the bar, I became a political liability." He tried to hold Rafferty's eyes, but they slipped away in another direction while still staring straight at him.

Dodd had seen that look before. In prison, in the yard, when a prisoner decided another prisoner should die but hadn't gotten around to killing him yet. That prisoner would give the condemned man the same look, staring at him but focused elsewhere, talking to him and keeping his attention while a buddy came from behind with a shank.

Meeker interjected, "I talked to Dodd's supervisor and it was pretty much the way Dodd here describes it."

"Mal," Dodd said, making it clear he understood Rafferty didn't think they should be on a first name basis. "I'm curious. Do you always make it a habit to interview prospective employees your friends have already hired?"

Rafferty leaned forward, propping his elbows on his desk, his hands still clinched together. He focused completely on Dodd now, with the look of a killer about to slip the shank face-on. "Let me explain something. In some towns Meeker might have the right to hire whoever he wants to run his business. But it isn't true in Sweet Water Falls. That's because everything that happens in this town affects everything else that happens."

Dodd was tempted to point out that was true in other towns as well. But prison taught him when he was about to step over a fatal line, and he knew any further comment would be that step.

Rafferty pulled a deck of cards from his desk drawer. By the way Meeker shifted in his chair and rolled his eyes toward the open window, Dodd knew he'd seen this demonstration many times before.

Rafferty lay four cards down in a square, corner to corner. "This is the town," he said. Then he built a house from three cards on top of the four-card foundation. "This is the bank." He added a second wing to the bank and built another story on top of that. Then he built four three-card houses at each corner of the foundation.

"When the bank grows, the town grows," he said. When he finished the little card city on his desk, he sat back and intertwined his fingers again. "What's good for the bank is good for the town. Understand?"

Dodd kept his eyes level with Rafferty's.

"The other side of the coin, Mr. Dodd, is that what's bad for the town is bad for the bank. And it doesn't take much." He tugged slightly at one corner of one of the foundation cards. The bank fell first, knocking down the card houses as it fell.

Rafferty leaned forward. "Anyone who works in this town works for me. It doesn't matter who hires you. And if you fuck with your employer, you fuck with me and then you better be fucking careful or you could bring the entire weight of this bank down on top of your head. Do you understand?"

Dodd understood perfectly. He didn't have to cross the line. Rafferty had already pulled him across it. In prison, once you crossed that line, whether you wanted to or not, you couldn't retreat. You had to make a move right then or you'd be dead before the week was over.

"Do you mind if I smoke?"

Rafferty's neck snapped back, just a fraction of an inch.

"A cigarette. Do you mind if I smoke?" Dodd pretended to fish through his jacket pocket for cigarettes.

"I don't allow smoking in this office, Mr. Dodd."

"You could have fooled me. You were blowing enough of it out your ass." Before Rafferty could regain his composure, Dodd stood up, and leaned over Rafferty's desk, his palms flat on Rafferty's appointment schedule.

"You don't own this town and you don't own this bank. The people who deposit their money own you. Before you say something that really pisses me off, you better remember that I'm Meeker's manager now, and that if I don't like doing business with you I can recommend that he shift his account to another bank. Out of town. A bank that would probably improve his return. So you better think about how much capital you'd lose, how much less you could loan and how much less interest you'd be earning before you talk to my employer like that again."

Dodd straightened and brushed off his sleeves. "It's been pleasant, but Mr. Meeker and I have other appointments."

Before Rafferty could answer, Dodd lifted Meeker by the shoulder and steered him from the room. They passed Rhonda Mayfield who stood in the doorway with several files close to her chest. She passed her boss an alarmed look.

Had she been listening? It was almost as though she wanted to shelter him from a foreign influence. Then it dawned on Dodd that she was sleeping with him.

Of course. She was sleeping with him. What else was there to do after work in a town this small?

"That went well," Meeker sighed. "I've never seen Mal so pissed."

Dodd continued to steer him toward the stairs.

"I pissed off bigger guys than him in prison. That guy's name is really Mal?"

"No, his real name is Marion. But he never let anyone call him that. Even when we were kids."

Dodd looked back to see Rhonda watching them from Rafferty's doorway. He winked at her.

"I can't imagine why he wouldn't let you call him Marion."

Chapter 13

It didn't take Dodd long to figure out no one in Sweet Water Falls conducted business in their offices. After they left the bank, Meeker led him down Main Street to the Paris Cafe, a smoky diner even smaller than the restaurant in Stickett Inn. There he found himself in the company of two dozen men, all sitting around square tables smoking, drinking coffee, playing dominos and making business deals—most of which consisted of bets on upcoming Southwest Conference football games.

Dodd experienced pack behavior almost every day in prison, but this newest breed of pack animal surprised him. As Meeker introduced him around, each new acquaintance mumbled something unintelligible around his cigarette, squeezed Dodd's hand and immediately turned back to a conversation or game of dominos.

Five men in identical black suits sat around a table at the far wall. Each had a Bible spread before him. Each Bible had almost every verse underlined with handwritten notes filling the margins. One of the men drank coffee, two drank tea and two drank water while they consumed identical plates of chicken and dumplings and jammed bony fingers in each other's faces. Each wore a crew cut (although two were so bald it was hard to tell). "I beg to differ, brother Malachai," Dodd heard one say, with a heated vibrato voice. "The book of Proverbs clearly implores us to..."

Before Dodd could hear the end of the sentence, Meeker took him by the arm and guided him further into the room. "That's the town's ecumenical council, if a rat pack of Baptists and Church of Christers can be considered ecumenical. Their leader is the Right Reverend Malachai Spears." He nodded to the baldest and thinnest. "By virtue of the fact that the First Baptist Church has the largest congregation. They all have biblical names." He gently nodded as he listed them. "Ezekial Scruggs, Nathaniel Williams, Matthew Marks, he gets double bonus points, and Peter St. John, who gets triple bonus points only he has the smallest congregation. Once you acknowledge one of them, they think you opened the door for them to save your soul. So make sure to change course as soon as you see one walking toward you."

"Hey, Ralph," shouted a middle-aged entrepreneur in a green plaid western shirt and a blue pin-striped suit. "You boys gonna discuss my property option at Friday Night's council meeting?"

Ralph smiled. "You know damn well we don't meet the week of the barbecue. But we'll get to it." Then he mumbled to Dodd under his breath, "He's been trying to get us to annex some of his land so he can write it off. Got about thirty too many acres to support his herd. He starts asking me two days before every meeting, even though he knows we're gonna do flat nothing."

Meeker smiled at a portly businessman in a polyester double breasted leisure suit, something Dodd had never before seen anywhere. They wrestled each other's wrists and slapped each other on the sides of their arms. "Good to see you, Jasper."

"You too, you old lard ass," Jasper growled.

As they squeezed between two tables, Dodd whispered, "Hasn't anyone taken him aside and killed him for wearing that suit?"

"His wife takes sewing lessons in Ft. Stockton. All the wives do. Only material they use is polyester. Sooner or later every married man in town puts on one of those god awful suits or he won't get any pussy for a month."

At first Dodd thought he was joking, but he quickly realized the man was deadly serious.

"Not much business in this town?" he asked as they settled in at one of the tables. "Or does every one just come to the cafe?"

An old boy sitting just behind Dodd leaned in his direction. "Bill Todd." He thrust his hand toward Dodd like a sword. "They's two kinds a business in this town, son. Business with customers and business with other businessmen. Business with customers is as busy as any other town but we hire help for that. Business with businessmen goes on every day right here where your butt's parked."

Meeker settled into his seat and nodded to the waitress. "Todd here owns the GM, Ford and Chrysler dealerships where we left your car."

"That explains why it isn't getting fixed," Dodd grumbled.

Dodd glanced out the window and saw Marla Mayfield drive past, easily faster than the speed limit and touching up her hair. He shook his head and turned his attention back to the men in the cafe.

"Say," Todd said, raking the dominos on his table into a pile, "What kind a car do you drive?"

"Sixty-five Mustang," Dodd said.

"Shit, son, you should drive by. I could fix you up with a Caddy for less than two hundred a month."

What part of the left my car at your garage did you not hear, Dodd wondered. He shook his head, "It's a '65 convertible, Bill. The original pony car. Guys who ride stallions don't trade for Cadillacs."

Todd started to sweat slightly about the forehead, as though he were negotiating a high pressure deal. Dodd wondered how he made any sales at all. "But you're a business man now." Dodd could tell that he was working up to a pitch. "A business man should drive something that reflects the town he does business with."

"Bill," Dodd said, remembering the choice selection waiting for him at the Emporium, "this is the west. About as close to the wild west as it gets. Only three cars speak the west to me. The Camaro, the Thunderbird and the Mustang. I think the sheriff would piss in the boots of anyone who dared to drive another Thunderbird, and why the hell would trade a Mustang for a Camaro?"

Todd snorted air through his nose. Dodd wasn't sure if he was laughing or suffering from asthma. "Well you know where to find me. West as the crow flies."

Ralph yelled across the room. "Goddam it, Elna. Two cups of coffee and two cigars." Dodd recognized Elna as same waitress who sat out the dinner rush at the Stickett Inn the night before. Elna remained behind the counter, smoking a cigarette and ignoring Meeker completely. Meeker confided under his breath, "Elna used to be a lot hotter when she was younger. So we don't push her too hard or she'll go reminding our wives how hot she was and exactly who she was hot with."

Todd plunged ahead with his sales pitch as though he hadn't been interrupted. "Understand, Dodd, that in the city most businessmen are lucky to sign off on two deals a week and they have to call all over creation, drive all over creation, set up meetings with people they don't know all over creation, and leave butt tracks all over creation to sign off on those two deals. We do a deal every week or two and stay right here at the Paris to do it. On top of that, the chances of a deal going bust aren't as good cause who wants to have a deal go belly up with the men you got to eat with every day? So you tell me. Who does business better, city boys or us?"

"I wasn't criticizing. Just observing." Dodd said.

Meeker slapped his shoulder. "The boy can't help it. He thinks city. He'll get over it."

Dodd glanced through the window again, this time catching a glimpse of Rafferty driving past in a red Cadillac Seville with faux wood-paneling, touching up his hair in the rearview and headed in the same direction as his receptionist.

Elna laid two tin cups of thick black coffee in front of them, and tossed their cigars by the saucers. She rubbed her breast against Dodd's ear as she backed away and he jerked back himself, just in time to see her wink.

"She does that to all the boys," Meeker laughed, peeling the cellophane away from his cigar. "Elna was always meaty, but when she was younger it was well-packed and well-distributed. She'd walk down Main Street and all the younger boy's peckers would try to pop right out of their jeans. Come Saturday night, the boys would line up all the way down the street with a ten spot in their hand to thrash around with Elna there. I thrashed with her a few times myself."

Todd snorted and broke in again. He had most of the dominos laid out in front of him. "Hell, Ralph," he snorted again, "As I recall you was always the first one in line."

A bald fellow in his fifties, with a shirt open at the belly just like Meeker's, joined in, "Then he'd hit up the rest of us in line for the ten dollars to pay her." Meeker introduced him as Del Rayburn, owner of the "Suds-N-Duds, the county laundry and dry cleaning emporium."

Dodd took a sip of his coffee, and nearly dropped the cup. "Don't like the coffee, son?" Ralph asked.

Dodd's face was still contorted into a grimace, but he couldn't straighten it out. "This is worse than the crap at the hotel."

The men around him laughed. "That's cowboy coffee," Rayburn told him. "Elna comes in at five in the morning, before the cook even gets here. She throws two cans of grounds in a five gallon boiler and leaves it on the burner all day long. If it starts to get low, she just pours another can into the mix."

"Kind a makes you shit straight," another ole boy laughed.

"You'll get used to it," Ralph said. "It's part of the cost of doing business in our fair city."

Dodd closed his eyes and took another sip of coffee. On this one they were wrong. He would never get used to the coffee.

He picked up Bobby later that afternoon and they drove to the dry goods store for groceries. They indiscriminately loaded a hand basket with lunch meat, saltines, Cream of Wheat, oatmeal, bread, cheese and beans.

At the counter Bobby reached across to grab a pack of Marlboros. Dodd slapped his hand. "Don't start that shit. It's bad for you."

"You're not my old man."

"Damn straight. I'm a better fucking influence."

"I've smoked before."

"Not around me."

"Fine," Bobby said, and slipped a pack into the basket anyway. "I'll buy it with my own damn money and smoke it when you're off being a manager."

"You don't have any money."

"I'll pay you back."

Dodd counted out his cash to Hank. Bobby lowered his voice. "You're right about bosses wanting you to suck up. My assistant manager must need me to suck real hard because he's got a cork shoved so far up his ass he'll never pull it out."

"Don't talk that way in my store, son," the clerk said.

"He's ignorant," Dodd said. "His mama dropped him on his head when he was born and now he cusses in church and takes his bible to the whore house."

"Fuck you, Dodd," Bobby muttered under his breath.

As Dodd drove them to the homestead Bobby picked up his complaints about the shift manager. "The guy's name is Wally Wetzel but I call him Weasel. He sits in the storeroom all day reading dirty magazines Meeker keeps for the customers. Me, I have to keep the store stocked, measure the gas, sweep the floors, change the coffee and wait on customers. All at the same time."

Dodd resisted the impulse to make some comment about how hard poor Bobby must be working.

But Bobby wasn't through. "When a friend comes in, he comes out and waits on them himself, ringing up half what they buy. Then he pockets half what they give him."

That interested Dodd. "What else does he do?"

"He plays with the guns. He unlocks the display and pretends to shoot them all day long. And he can't add. When he was showing me how to do inventory he counted eight cans as six and seven cartons of Winstons as five. In fact, he did that several times. When I told him he was wrong he just asked me who the manager was anyway."

"Bobby," Dodd told him, shaking his head. "There's a lesson you better learn now cause it isn't pleasant any time you learn it. When you sit anywhere underneath the guy on the top, the shit flows down in your direction."

Bobby didn't say anything for another two or three miles. Then he laid his elbow on the window and his chin on his elbow. "Hey, Dodd," he said. "Do you think we could get a TV?"

Chapter 14

That evening Dodd fried potatoes and eggs and toast in the same cast iron skillet. Bobby complained that eggs were breakfast food. Then he complained how boring life was out on this godforsaken stretch of land. Finally Dodd gave him the keys to the truck.

He made Bobby promise to remember he was on probation, which meant to look for fun in the opposite direction of Sweet Water Falls. Bobby Wayne swore on his mother's grave and immediately tore down the highway with the pedal to the floor. Of course, pedal to the floor on that truck wouldn't reach the speed limit. More likely, the engine would die or drop onto the pavement.

Dodd shook his head in despair, thought of himself at that age and despaired even more. Finally he dragged his chair out onto the porch to read and watch the sunset.

He'd read every Jim Thompson and Zane Gray book at least three times in prison. He even had two or three copies of some because paperbacks liked to fall apart. He would buy a new one, with all the pages in place, and then not have the heart to throw out the old one.

When he thought he should read something else he waded through Plato's *Republic*, Machiavelli, *Moby Dick* and *The Grapes of Wrath*. He still had them beside his law books. Mostly he just read Jim Thompson and Zane Gray. It was like steering in familiar territory.

He tipped his chair back against the house and dipped into *Riders of the Purple Sage*. He got to the part where Venters finds Surprise Valley. He really liked the book, especially the Oldrings, who turned out to be who they weren't supposed to be. And Bess Oldring, the masked rider, who wasn't who anyone thought she was.

But his mind wouldn't settle on the page and he kept putting the book in his lap and leaning his chair against the wall so he could watch the sun sink down into the western mountains.

A cloud of dust at the turn off from the highway told him he had a visitor. He watched suspiciously as a red Toyota pick-up approached the house. The truck pulled up sideways in front of his porch, kicking gravel from under its wheels. It swerved into place with its passenger door facing him, and Mary Beth Rafferty climbed out. She rested her elbows and her six pack on the roof.

"Wha'cha doing?"

"Not drinking."

She looked down at her six-pack and then slipped it back into the truck. "Oh, yeh, I forgot. You're a tea sip."

"Teetotaler. A tea sip is what Aggies call Longhorn fans. And I'm not teetotaler either. I'm a former drunk."

"Well, sorry." She didn't seem too sorry. "I've got a bucket of chicken and some soda pop in here too. How would you like to drive down to Sweet Water Gorge?"

"We can have just as much fun here. The kid's gone. Probably for most of the night."

She wrinkled her eyes in disgust. "What kind of fun can you have in a dump like this? You don't even have a TV."

He stood and laid his book on the chair. "Sweet Water Gorge it is then."

Mary Beth slipped behind the steering wheel and leaned over to pop his door lock. He had to pull his knees to his neck to squeeze into the small cab. "I'd think with your old man's money, you could afford something a little roomier than this," he said. He rolled down the window so his right arm would fit.

"I don't need any more room," she smiled, "I'm not a big dumb gangly-legged man." She threw the car into reverse before the ignition turned over, swerving away from his cabin in a wide curve and covering his front porch with gravel and dirt. Instead of turning back toward the highway, she cut a path across the fields behind his house.

"I guess we're taking the back way," he said.

She cycled through the gears, wrist and clutch in rhythm. "You guessed right."

Driving through the field in fourth gear caused the truck to leap and jump over small mounds of dirt and rock, lifting off each new obstacle with a loud thump and a roar of the transmission. "Is this a steeplechase?" he asked.

"Be a man, Dodd. You don't expect me to drive on a limp and a crawl, do you?"

She slammed down the brake and hard cranked her steering wheel to the left, bringing the car even with the gorge wall and kicking yet more dirt and gravel, this time into empty space and down into the gorge.

"Isn't this a little out of the way?" Dodd said, opening his door and making sure he could find enough ground to put his foot down safely.

"Why else would I come out here? Sure as shit can't fuck you out in the open with people around." She leaped out of the cab and hefted a blanket and backpack from the truck bed.

Dodd stared at the drop off, which was only inches from his toes. "And we're going to do this here beside the truck or are we going to find some way down in the gorge?"

"Jail sure turned you into a pussy. Of course, we're going down into the gorge. There's a path around here somewhere. Besides, there's something down there I want you to see." She joined him at the drop off. "Give me a second to spot the trail."

Dodd inched his way to the front of the truck, keeping his hands on the roof and hood for balance. Mary Beth craned her neck then thrust her finger down and to the left, "There it is."

She dropped into the gorge, hopping down the rocks and jogging back and forth between outcrops until she disappeared from sight about twenty feet below. Dodd took a deep breath and jumped down to the first rock, navigating each rock and outcrop in succession, trying to remember where he had seen Mary Beth put her feet down only minutes before.

Mary Beth took to the trail like jack rabbit. Dodd felt like a hippopotamus, slipping off rocks, twisting his ankle, bruising his elbow, and generally banging his body against rocks along the canyon wall. Twice his foot missed one of the rocks and he tumbled several feet before he could catch himself.

About half way down he spotted Mary Beth, another thirty feet down the river with her hands on her hips and her lips spread wide with amusement. "I guess all that time sitting on your butt behind bars ruined you for the wilderness."

Dodd leaped to a small ledge and decided to slide the rest of the way. He dusted his ass when he finally reached the bottom. "I hope we're going back a different way because I don't think I can slide upward."

She grabbed a belt loop and pulled him to her, running her tongue around the inside of his mouth. "You want to get up bad enough, you'll figure out a way." She turned and disappeared behind a bush before he could catch his breath.

Dodd brushed off his ass one more time, invoked the name of Jesus and his sweet mother, then Jesus' mother's sweet mother, and pushed his way through the bushes in her general direction. A few yards further the river split around a small island, maybe ten yards wide and forty yards long, then the river twisted off to the west.

Mary Beth jumped the river, crossed the delta, and leaped to the far wall. "You are so slow, Dodd," she said, "I can't believe you were ever a Boy Scout."

"I wasn't," he shouted back. In the waning light he could just make out the stones she used to cross and tried to keep his balance as he made his way across to the island. When he finally looked up, she'd already disappeared around another corner.

He cursed silently and waded into the water on the far side, no longer worried about getting his feet wet so much as catching up with her. He slipped a couple of times in the mud on the far bank, and even got his hand muddy trying to steady himself as he climbed out.

He spotted her twenty yards further down, standing before a series of shallow rapids and pointing to a rusting wreck leaning at an off angle against several boulders. A Ford pick-up, a forty-eight or forty-nine, paint long ago rusted away, glass broken out, and the doors, tailgate, hood and rear fenders gone. No doubt scavenged by kids needing to fix up their own wrecks.

She slipped her hand into his. "You know what that is?"

"I'm sure you're going to tell me."

"That's the Dodd pick-up. It's been lying here since 1949. You can still see some of the bullet holes where the Meeker brothers shot it to pieces. You want to look closer?"

"I'd rather settle in right here on the bank with you and explore your own rustic charms."

She thumped his cheek with her finger and said, "Silly. You need a little more morbid curiosity in your life." She slipped her sandals into one hand and lit off again, hopping over the rocks to the other side.

"I suppose you're going to show me all the blood stains, too," he called behind her.

"Of course," she laughed back, balancing on one leg at a time while she pulled her sandals back on. "What's a little blood to a man who's been in prison?"

A lot, Dodd thought to himself, but waded back into the water.

"You'll have a better time of it barefoot," she giggled.

Dodd ignored her and stepped onto the first wet stone. He realized immediately that she was right, but struggled on anyway until he fell onto his ass in the water. He fought to keep his feet under him as he got back up. She laughed the whole time, smug country girl with hands braced at her hips, accentuating her narrow waist.

Even as he cursed her, he felt an emotion similar to love swelling near his waist.

It took several minutes to cross the narrow rapids, one yard at a time, steady surfaces difficult to find in the diminishing light. Finally, when he felt his feet planted on soft ground again, he asked, "Wouldn't it have made more sense to do this on the weekend, some morning when we would be getting more daylight instead of less?"

"The better to grope you with, my dear," she said, reaching around to tweak his ass. "My, your butt did get wet, didn't it?"

"Show me this wreck," he told her.

She led him by the hand to the rocks. The driver's side was caved in, the firewall buckled and engine block pushed back into the cab. "Were they killed on impact?" Dodd asked.

"You should know, being family and all."

"Humor me."

"Legend is they all survived. The sheriff shot Zel Dodd as he tried to get out of the car, and the other two disappeared. People think they had a hideout somewhere around here with the flying saucer and the money. But you probably know more about that than me."

"You seem determined to bring little green men into this," he said.

She ignored him. "The Texas Rangers shot the oldest brother Zane outside a movie theater in Llano." She pronounced it "Lano" with an "l" and long "a." "I think that's near about Austin. But they never caught the middle brother Zack. He just disappeared off the face of the earth. Can you imagine that?"

Dodd poked his finger through a rusted hole in the cowl, just in front of the steering column. He looked into the cab and imagined what it must have felt like to be caught between the driver's seat and the steering wheel at the end of a sixty-foot drop.

"He's your daddy, isn't he? You being about the right age and all. Now I can tell the girls I got laid by a bank robber's baby boy."

"Why would anyone think the money's still hidden?"

"No one ever found it."

Dodd crossed to the passenger side and poked his head inside. No human artifacts remained; the glove compartment was cleaned out and the upholstery rotted away.

"Wouldn't you think the money would be with the brother that got away?"

Mary Beth huffed, "You don't have to interrogate me. I wasn't one of them. I'm just showing you all this because I thought you'd be interested. Now I'm beginning to regret it."

"That's tough because you got me interested." He found several rusted holes in the wall of the truck bed. They could have been bullet holes before the rust started eating everything away. "And you still haven't answered my question. Why wouldn't the third brother have the money?"

Mary Beth pursed her lips, and then stopped to think about his question. "Well, that kinda does make sense. I guess nobody ever thought about that. Flying saucers and hidden money's a lot more fun to think about."

Dodd interrupted her. "If they buried the money, it would have disintegrated by now. Nothing but wood pulp and dirt."

"Aren't you mister buzz kill? Maybe they wrapped it in something before they hid it. Left it in a trunk."

Dodd shook his head. "Trust me, when you've got cops behind you and they're shooting to kill, you don't have time to wrap it. If they left it, they left it with the hopes of coming back in a year or two. The one that got away made it back and the money's gone, or he didn't and the money's gone to dirt. Either way it's still gone."

"Gone with the wind," she added.

He stared at her and wiped his hands off on his trousers. "Something like that."

She frowned. "You know what I meant. Gone to dirt, the wind catches dust and dirt up. The movie...."

He put his finger to her lips then kissed her. "I know what you meant." He circled the truck, looking up the wall of the gorge to the cliff where the truck fell down from.

"You sure it was the driver they shot and not one of the other brothers?"

"When I was a kid, we'd come down and check this out. It was a great town scandal. For the longest time you could see the blood stains on that rock over there. Where they shot Zel."

"By the time you were a kid, wouldn't the rain have washed the blood away?"

She stuck her tongue at him. "Maybe we imagined it."

Dodd followed her gaze to a large rock perhaps twenty-five feet further down the bank. "What side of the rock was the blood on?"

"This one, facing the water."

"Was there any blood between here and the rock?"

"Wouldn't the rain have washed it away?" Sarcasm saturated her voice.

Dodd studied the distances. "He would have been bleeding when he climbed out of the cab. That collision would've done serious damage. He'd barely be able to walk. They probably carried him. And there would've been a lot of blood."

"Oh, now you're interested."

Dodd shook his finger at her. "Blame yourself, not me. But I smell bullshit."

"Why would anybody lie about what happened?"

"After a few months in prison you get to know the smell of bullshit better than any other smell cause there's so much of it around. Most of the bullshit didn't come from the cons, it came from the wardens, the guards and the suits. They didn't even need to bullshit; they just did it because that's what they did."

He looked up. The sun was hidden behind the ledge on the western rim of the gorge. Mary Beth was lost in shadows. "Why did the car run off the road and over that ledge?"

"How should I know?"

Dodd marched back over to stare her down face to face again, pointing his finger up to the ledge. "Isn't that how the story goes? Along with the flying saucer and money? What was happening up on the road that caused them to drive over the ledge?"

"Well, everybody knows that. Meeker and his brother were chasing them. They must have shot a tire out because the car skidded over the side."

"What time of day was this?"

"Evening. Like now. But winter."

"So the Meekers were shooting down into the canyon with very little visibility and they still managed to kill the driver? How did they get him from up there when he was behind this rock out of their line of fire?"

"I always thought they were down here in the gorge."

"The Meekers?"

"Well, yeh, because Joe Bob is supposed to have killed Zel with his shotgun. There was supposed to be this big shoot out down here in the gorge, and the sheriff shot Zel right there, but the other two got away."

Dodd scratched his head, and studied the scenery in what little light was left. "Okay then, answer this for me. I can see how the Dodds got down here quickly. Their truck fell from the road. But how did the Meekers get into the gorge without giving the three of them plenty of time to get away? That ridge is straight down from the top to the river floor. I don't see any way down."

Mary Beth laid her hand on his shoulder. "They just came down, that's all."

"It took us twenty minutes. Is there another way down? A faster way?"

She looked down to the ground, and then turned to examine the wreck again herself. "That's the only way I ever knew about."

"You can't tell me that in the twenty or twenty-five minutes it would have taken for the Meekers to park their car and scramble down that death trap you call a trail that all three Dodds wouldn't have managed to get themselves a few miles further down the river. Even if two were carrying one between them. Not unless the driver was too injured to move. Or dead already."

She leaned her head on his shoulder, and slipped her hand into his pant pocket. "It was a long time ago. Can't we talk about something else now?"

"We can talk about something else now, but the story you just told me seems to defy the laws of physics and nature. Meeker and his brother either shot at the Dodds from up there on the ledge, or those boys had plenty of time to get away."

She reached into his trousers and into the front of his boxers. "Now I want to bring up something else." She pulled his cock out through the opening, rubbing it against her fingers and his jeans. His body cooperated, but his mind was elsewhere.

It wasn't elsewhere very long.

Chapter 15

"Let me tell you bout Joe Bob Meeker," Preacher told him, sitting three feet away and smoking one of Dodd's Camels. "That boy's nothing but cantankerous." He pronounced "cantankerous" like two words, stretching out the "a" in "can" and then running off the last three syllables all at once.

"He be one of the meanest law men I ever had the bad luck to run into. I mean, they be mean as a lot, them small town Texas rednecks with they mirror shades and bad ass night sticks and shit. Joe Bob? He bout be the worse ever fuck with the Preacher."

Dodd was tempted to smile at Preacher's crack about the shades. The late afternoon sunlight could barely find a way though the bars and dirt on the cell's single window, yet Preacher sat against the wall, looking away from the light, sporting his own pair of "bad ass shades."

"I got me fined personal, five hundred dollars for drunk driver bull shit bout five years before I went inside. I had me maybe one can of malt liquor, and no one can of malt liquor be making nobody drunk."

Dodd lit his own Camel. He still thought he could quit smoking by cutting back on a cigarette here or there. It would take another couple of years and several hundred packs to convince him he couldn't quit by cutting back. "You were telling me about the Meekers?" he interrupted.

"Don't be distracting me, brother. I be passing on wisdom here. My cousin Blackburn, he be pulled over for drunk driving? Splashes mud all over Meeker's Thunderbird? No good for a day's work after that; just sit on his porch, be talking to everybody be coming by and nobody if they be coming by too. Poor wife, she want to leave him, everybody say, 'Gracie how can you be leaving that poor nigger on that porch by hisself, can't take care hisself? You need some action, go find some buck in town and ride the pony all night long, but you marry that boy so you be staying with him. Shit, my brother Alvin, he be sending Gracie money to take care of Blackburn and be sending me money inside. I don't know how that boy feed his own family."

"So how come you be talking like city niggers with the Ebonics and all?" Dodd asked. "I thought you were from West Texas where everybody says 'we all' and 'y'all' and 'ain't and shit?"

"Don't be getting all tight ass white on me, my brother. Man be talking like a man gotta talk. And I be talking bout my poor brother Alvin got to feed us all."

Preacher's brother Alvin was fairly prosperous, but Preacher loved hyperbole and digression. A C.P.A. with a knack for making the books appear to show things they really didn't show, Alvin was as popular with white clients as with his black ones. Alvin did time of his own for a little piece of creative accounting commissioned by the town council of Sweet Water Falls, covering up the diversion of town revenues to subsidize business ventures put together by the Meekers and Mal Rafferty.

When auditors forced the council to find a scapegoat, Alvin willingly went up for his employers, and found himself even more gainfully employed—although no longer licensed—when he finished his sentence. Dodd figured Alvin must be the best dishonest accountant in West Texas. Otherwise white businessmen wouldn't have given two shits about what happened to him once he went to jail.

Preacher glanced at his cigarette and realized he'd smoked it down to the filter, which was glowing pale red. "Got to quit smoking these things. They be the red man's revenge on all you white boys but they be killing black folks too." He dropped it to the floor and ground it out with his foot.

"But I be telling you about that mother fucker Joe Bob Meeker." He said it like a question.

Dodd shrugged and tapped another cigarette out of the pack. Preacher leaned into the coal of Dodd's cigarette to light it.

"That boy be meanness and more meanness all rolled up into one fat mother fucker of meanness. When his fat brother Ralph be hiring some brothers to dig up some farmland, Joe Bob decided that he should be the overseer. We all be sleeping in tents outside the old farmhouse where them Dodd's was supposed to live? Wasn't no human being living in that house, much less a white boy, but they told us niggers to sleep in tents outside anyway. Paid us four dollars a day and told us we best dig up all fifteen acres in two weeks, yes they did.

"Every morning, Joe Bob be driving up to the tents in his police car with a bucket of coffee and a blanket full a biscuits. We got fifteen minutes to get us biscuits and coffee and then he follow us out to whatever part of the farm we be working that day. We walk, he be driving behind us, maybe a mile an hour, in his fancy ass Thunderbird. He see some young blood he don't think be carrying the weight, he make that poor mother fucker get in the trunk and shut him in. He be lying in that trunk in hundred degree weather for a hour or two depending on how mad Joe Bob be that morning."

"What were you digging for?"

Preacher laughed and blew two thick streams of smoke through his nose. He leaned into the wall and laughed again.

"Ain't that the joke though, brother? Nothing. Fucking no account nothing. We dig one end of that farm to the other and we be finding nothing and then Meeker lay off half the crew and make the rest of us be digging back to the other side again.

Nothing. A dollar a day to twenty strong bloods to dig up fifteen acres of property and damn if we don't be digging up nothing."

"What makes you think you weren't breaking up the soil? Turning it over so they could plant crops?"

"I can tell you was never no farm boy. We wasn't digging to lay down crops, they had us looking for something, and I swear to God when we done worked our way back to where we started and still never found nothing, I thought Joe Bob be going to shoot us right then and there."

Dodd slipped a fingernail down the side of the package and peeled the cellophane away. He wasn't sure why. On the inside he simply did things.

"What were you looking for?"

"Nothing, man. Flat out, mother fucking nothing. I told you that."

"I don't mean what did you find. I meant, what were you supposed to be looking for?"

Preacher tossed the newest butt to the floor and ground that one out as well. A perfectly good coffee can only half-filled with butts sat next to the toilet, which, Dodd thought, would also dispose of the cigarette just fine. Preacher preferred the floor.

"Oh, that? Why didn't you say so? Well, rumor be those Dodd boys stole a half million dollars, so my thinking be, the Meekers be thinking the Dodds left it on their farm. See, mean and smart, they ain't the same thing. Joe Bob may be mean, but he got to know those Dodd boys won't be skipping town and leave they money behind. That's just stuff and nonsense. No, the Meekers be looking for something else." He lit yet another cigarette. Dodd was tempted to see how many were left in his pack, but he resisted the temptation. You didn't disrespect Preacher in the middle of a story.

"The flying saucer." Dodd wanted to roll his eyes, but he knew that would disrespect the preacher.

"Exactly. The flying saucer. Somebody done one fine job of hiding that thing cause we never saw hide nor hair of it."

"Come on," Dodd protested. "You're the most street-wise guy I know. You can't believe there was any flying saucer."

Preacher flicked the cigarette at Dodd. Dodd barely ducked it, thinking what a waste of a good cigarette it was. "Fool. You ask anybody in that town if there be a flying saucer landing there way back when you be knee high to a grass hopper and they tell you they be seeing it land themselves. Even Alvin, he don't truck with no nonsense, him being a fine Christian man, unlike myself, and he be telling you there be a flying saucer hidden in Sweet Water Falls. You trust the preacher, brother Dodd. The preacher knows."

Dodd leaned over to grab the cigarette then rose to stretch. Preacher studied him to see what he would do with it. He flicked it into the toilet. "You are one crazy bastard, Preacher."

"Well, you be believing what you got to believe and I believe what's right. You be taking them cigarettes with you or what?"

Dodd studied the preacher as he sat against the wall, a narrow shaft of diminishing sunlight casting a halo on the wall around his head. He still wore his shades even though the room was almost dark. Dodd shook his head and tossed the man his cigarettes. Then the sunlight broke through their cell window.

Dodd wasn't sure if the sun woke him—blasting its way through the glass window into his bedroom—or the sense that he was getting into water too deep to swim in safely. Whatever woke him, he worked his arm out from under Mary Beth's neck slowly and delicately, as though he might break it if he twisted too hard.

The bed sheet slipped down to her waist. She continued to sleep, cheek on his pillow, one arm tossed over her shoulder and the other draped across her navel. Her breasts swelled as she breathed, revealing the splendor and glory of a God who cares deeply about the universe and the beauty therein.

Dodd tiptoed across the bare wood floor and into the kitchen. He found the coffee pot already boiling on the stove, grounds settled to the bottom of the pan. Bobby sat at the table with a plate of grits and a juice glass full of black and oily coffee.

A larger serving plate waited for Dodd in the middle of the table, filled with grits and surrounded by butter and trimmings.

"I bet she's a fine piece of ass," Bobby whispered, and added an exaggerated wink.

"That's nothing you're old enough to know about," Dodd said in his regular voice. He ladled the black brew into a chipped mug. He really missed civilized coffee.

He sat beside Bobby, wishing the boy was on a newspaper delivery route. "How do you know, anyway? Were you watching us sleeping in there?"

"The door was open."

"Not when I went to sleep it wasn't." He spooned a lump of grits from the serving plate and into a cereal bowl.

Bobby grinned. "It must have popped open somehow." He pantomimed the shape and size of Mary Beth's breasts.

Dodd reached across the table and cuffed him gently across the temple. "A woman has a right to her privacy."

He cut a wedge of butter with his spoon and stirred it into his grits along with two spoonfuls of brown sugar. "Needs milk to thin it," he said after tasting a mouthful.

"Maybe we should get a refrigerator," Bobby suggested.

"It would fry every wire in the house," Dodd said. "But I can probably get a cooler."

"Some preacher came by last night, and left you all this," Bobby said, pushing a stack of Biblical literature and tracts across the table. "I told him my daddy don't let me talk to strangers, but if he'd talk to you personal I was sure you'd be grateful."

Dodd spread the stack out on the table, glancing at titles like, "Air Conditioning Can't Stop the Heat From Hell," and "The Devil Wants Your Soul. Why Are You Selling It So Cheap?"

Dodd pushed the literature aside. "Next time he comes by tell him I'm Jehovah's Witness and I'd be glad to bring an elder along to the appointment."

"You're Jehovah's Witness?" Bobby yelped.

Dodd didn't bother to answer.

"Where can I wash up around here?" Mary Beth asked from behind him. "You know, tend to womanly things?"

He turned around in his chair, leaning his elbow across the back to look at her. She stood in the door, naked except for the bed sheet wrapped loosely around her, and standing on tiptoe with one foot crossed behind the other ankle.

"It's out back," he said. "A bucket with a chain. There's a ladder you can climb to fill the bucket. About ten feet from the well."

She ran her fingers through her hair, letting the sheet drift an inch or so down the swell of her breasts. Dodd could tell Bobby was enjoying this and Mary Beth was letting him enjoy it. "There's no running water?"

Dodd shook his head.

She cast a glance in the direction of her midriff and then rearranged the sheet ever so slightly, covering herself for the most part but showing the briefest flash of flesh. "You boys. What is it with you? Don't like air conditioning; don't like the amenities of a civilized home. You like to hang out in the bushes and howl with the wolves, scratching your balls and telling obnoxious jokes the whole night long."

Dodd took his plate to the sink and shoveled his scraps into a milk carton. "You're welcome to hold off on your shower and catch a ride into town with me."

"My truck is parked outside, silly."

Dodd rinsed off the plate and leaned it against the side of the sink. He wiped his hands off on his boxer shorts and said, "When do you want to get together again?"

She glanced away to check her nails, letting the bed sheet slip again. "My calendar isn't exactly empty, Dodd. I'm a busy girl, you know."

He walked past her into the bedroom, dropping his shorts in two steps and slipping into a pair of yellow rubber thongs. "Excuse me," he said. "I'm going outside to shower. You can join me if you want and save water."

"You don't want to discuss this further?" she pouted.

Then he stopped in front of her, looking down at her as she framed the doorway. "I know you're a busy girl, Mary Beth. All those social engagements. We'll get together again when you're ready."

He leaned down to kiss her, moving her to his side and slipping past her in the process.

"How about Friday night?" she said. She pursed her lips together as she said it, bringing her eyebrows together at the same time. Dodd wondered if it was an offer or a demand.

"Fine. Friday night it is."

He stepped outside and walked to the shower, his thongs flip-flopping against the dirt. He filled a bucket from the well and climbed the ladder to pour it into the shower bucket. The wood almost snapped. He'd have to replace it before he took another shower.

Dodd pulled the chain to splash water over him, and poured a handful of dish soap into his palm. He'd lathered his head and shoulders when Mary Beth appeared before him, bare feet in the mud and sheet slipping down around her waist and shoulders.

"I'll cook you dinner."

"You can cook?"

She tucked her face under his chin. "Then you can cook."

"I haven't been paid yet."

She grabbed him by the neck and pulled him down to kiss her, letting the bed sheet slip down into the water and the mud. "I'll buy the food and you can cook it." Then she pulled him down into the mud with her, somehow maneuvering his backside into the puddle while she climbed on top.

He pushed himself up onto his elbows. "I have to go to work," he reminded her.

"Meeker's a drunk. He never shows up before noon." She reached between the two of them and eased his cock inside with her fingers.

"Bobby's watching through the window, for Christ's sake."

She put her finger across his lips to shut him up. The smell of her drifted up from her finger. "The boy's going to have to learn sooner or later, Dodd." Then covered his mouth with hers.

Chapter 16

Mal Rafferty was waiting for Dodd outside the mayor's office. "Don't you believe in civilized office hours? I'd hope you'd be more conscientious at this stage of your career."

Dodd jiggled the skeleton key in the lock. He didn't want to turn too hard for fear of breaking the brittle shaft. Finally the tumblers clicked and the door opened. "Take that up with Mary Beth. She thinks she has equal claims on my time."

Rafferty slammed the door behind them. "Are you inferring that you've been intimate with my daughter?"

Dodd draped his jacket over the chair and sat down behind the small oak desk. He opened a random drawer and pretended to scan the contents. "I'm not inferring anything. If I wanted you to think that I was sleeping with your daughter, I would be implying. The truth is I'm not implying, either." He closed the drawer, propped his elbows on the desk and leaned his chin into his hands. "Now what can I do for you?"

Rafferty opened his mouth to answer, but before he could say a word, Dodd gestured to the leather armchair sitting just to the left of the desk. "Have a seat."

Rafferty glanced back and forth between Dodd and the chair, as though trying to decide whether or not Dodd had been insubordinate. Finally he dropped into the chair.

"You haven't answered my question."

"Yes, I have. You asked me if I was inferring that I slept with your daughter and I said, no, I'm not inferring that I slept with your daughter. You are."

Rafferty pursed his lips and then spoke without moving them. "Are you sleeping with my daughter?" His voice growled like a Rottweiler.

"No," Dodd said. "Now how can I help you?"

Rafferty refused to answer, choosing instead to stare at Dodd as though he had drawn a chalk line on the floor in front of the desk and dared Rafferty to cross it. Then he seemed to reconsider, and worked a smile across his face.

"I just wanted to apologize for so flagrantly expressing my reservations about your employment yesterday. This is a conservative, peaceful town, and we don't always welcome strangers with the courtesy we should." When he finished his speech, he waited for Dodd to answer.

"Your apology accepted." Dodd said. Rafferty waited for more, and when Dodd offered no more, he shifted his position in the chair and crossed his knee.

Then he cleared his throat.

"Ah, since it appears you will be moving in the more influential circles of our township, I suppose I should invite you to the barbecue my wife and I are throwing at my house Saturday evening."

Dodd nodded his head and smiled. Then he added, "Let me check my calendar."

Rafferty flushed a deep red as Dodd shuffled files aside to look for Meeker's appointment book. When he found it, he flipped through the pages as though studying them carefully. Nothing had been written in it. In fact, the appointment book was for 1977. But Dodd calmly studied several dates and finally said. "Seems my schedule's clear. I'd be delighted." He rose to shake Rafferty's hand. "I'll bring the beer."

He picked up the top file on his desk and began to browse it, much as he had seen Rafferty do the day before.

"We can do this the hard way, Dodd," Rafferty said.

"Do what the hard way?" Dodd didn't look up from the file.

Rafferty leaned across the desk. "I know your daddy told you where that money is, boy. Folks have been digging up Sweet Water Falls for thirty years looking. But that money's mine. Your family stole it from my bank, and killed my daddy when they did."

Dodd flipped a page and ran his finger slowly down the next. "My family's from Louisiana. I'm the first Dodd who made it this far west."

Rafferty drummed his fingers on the desk. "The truth is, my daddy and I didn't get along, and it's been a lot of years since your family put that bullet in his back. So I can let bygones be bygones. But that don't make the money any less mine."

Dodd finally looked up from the file. "You people are the most focused goddam lot I have ever done business with. On the inside I knew inmates who were so obsessed they wouldn't turn loose of the smallest grievance or fantasy. Didn't matter when you'd see them, they'd be fixed on that one damn thing. 'How you doing Charlie?' you'd ask one, and every day he'd say, 'Mother fucking guard snitched some my cigarettes.' Or he'd say, 'That fucking Otis, he don't quit looking to stab me in the back, I'm gonna cut him some day.' None of them were as fixated as you people are."

Dodd reached into Meeker's drink drawer for the Beam and poured three fingers into Meeker's mug. "Here you go," he said, nudging it across the desk. "You need this a lot more than the mayor does."

Rafferty stared silently. Dodd thought he could see a vein about to pop behind his eyebrow.

"I don't drink," Dodd added. "This is for you."

"You have the arrogance of a man who is way above your station."

"Like I could cough up money I never heard of before I drove through this little fly speck on God's big map of Texas." Dodd leaned his elbows on his desk and leaned his body across.

"Let's be honest. There is no money, is there? This whole Dodd brothers business is a scam from the word go, isn't it?"

Rafferty pushed the cup back in Dodd's direction. "You seem to be the one that's been drinking."

"It's the lawyer in me. I look for more than one explanation to the same set of facts." He took the cup over to the small window, opened it, and pitched the whiskey into the hawthorn bush crowding outside. Then he leaned against the sill.

"In just two days, I hear dozens of stories about these dead bank robbers and money that was never recovered, and at first I think maybe those boys did bury that money somewhere. But then I hear other stories about how those same brothers had something valuable on their property and after those boys were dead, the Meekers ended up with the deed to their farm. So I'm thinking maybe they didn't steal any money at all; you and the Meekers wanted an excuse to blow their brains out and take control of the land."

He let the cup drop onto the desk and sat back down, bringing Rafferty's gaze with him. "I'm staying on that land right now, and I can't for the life of me imagine why you'd want fifteen acres of the most useless dirt in creation. Which makes me even more curious. Makes me wonder what bodies are really buried on that farm. Literally and metaphorically."

Rafferty stood and gathered his briefcase. "Your family took my money, Dodd. You know where it is and I want it back." He made a dramatic exit and slammed the door behind him.

Dodd crossed the room and opened the door. "Hey, Mal," he called, "think about this...." Rafferty had already crossed the narrow lobby and was backing through the courthouse doors.

Joe Bob Meeker stuck his head through his office door.

"You think about this too, Joe Bob. If I had this money you're so convinced I have, I'd've taken it by now. You think I would stick around drinking the most god-awful coffee in the world and jawing with you people? I'd be wrapped in the arms of some skinny Mexican girl on the Pacific Coast watching her drink the tequila I swore off and nibbling on her earlobe. So maybe you should consider the possibility that you've got the wrong Dodd and you're just wasting your breath trying to make me out to be the right one."

"I will see you Saturday, Mr. Dodd," Rafferty said. He gave a sharp look at Joe Bob, which told Dodd they might not be cooperating on this. "But you need to think things through because I can be very generous to those who are generous with me and very spiteful to those who hold things back."

When he disappeared through the door, Joe Bob laughed and spit a loogie onto the rough stone floor. "You don't fool me with that wrong Dodd act, son. I never knowed a con that could tell the truth."

Dodd laughed. "Oh, I get it. I was in jail so I must be lying." He slapped his forehead. "How about this? You're right, Joe Bob, Zane Dodd was my father. Does that make you happy?"

Meeker let a slow grin creep across his jowls and toed some of the rough edges of the floor. "I knew we'd cut through the crap sooner or later, Dodd."

"Yeh, well the problem now is that I'm a con. And you never knew a con who could tell the truth. So if I just said I'm one of those Dodds, but I'm a con can't tell the truth, where does that leave you?"

Joe Bob leveled his eyes with Dodd's from all the way across the lobby. "Wait a minute...," he growled.

"I have work to do," Dodd said, and shut his door.

It took Dodd thirty minutes to clear Meeker's desk, but only ten to be amazed at how little effort the mayor expended on a very easy job. Most of the paper work consisted of nothing more than requests for information. They originally had been called over the phone to Mrs. Brazwell, who typed them and had them forwarded through the mail to the mayor's office where they sat on the desk waiting for someone to respond.

On the other hand, Dodd was amazed to find half a dozen confidential letters and memos sitting out, without files, on top of his desk. One letter, signed by a W.W. Wetzel and addressed to both Meekers and Mal Rafferty, discussed private donations from a lobbying effort to build a harness racing track west of town. The letter also listed potential donors to a campaign to legalize gambling in the state, and, more importantly, a list of state senators and legislators who could use financial help on their campaigns who might lend a sympathetic ear.

Another letter, from Rafferty to Ralph, involved dummy oil rigs that could provide tax write-offs to businessmen and speculators. The letter included a list of bank depositors, including the same Wetzel who wrote the racetrack letter. Dodd wondered if this Wetzel was related to the kid who worked for Meeker. If a reporter got it under his bonnet to write an expose of the Meekers and Rafferty, all he had to do was walk in and take the evidence off Meeker's desk.

Of course, Sweet Water Falls didn't have a newspaper, much less reporters, but that didn't mean the town lacked for busybodies and snoops.

Dodd skimmed through the remaining paperwork. Half had to do with the JP's office, half of what remained consisted of resolutions passed by the town council—of which Meeker was a member—that did not require his signature, half of what remained after that (perhaps a dozen letters) actually required Meeker's attention as mayor, and half of that was time sensitive correspondence whose urgency had expired weeks, if not months, before.

He collected the dozen requests that weren't out of date, and called Mrs. Brazwell for any information she could help with. When it became quite clear that she knew the answer to every one of them he asked, "Why didn't you just give these people answers over the phone?"

"Because they were calls to the mayor's office."

"And aren't you the mayor's secretary?"

Silence. Then, "Yes."

"Then pick up these letters at lunch and call all of these people with answers this afternoon."

She cleared her throat and slammed her phone down. Dodd had no idea whether or not she would do it, but he figured he could drop the letters on her desk personally if she didn't get them by the end of the week.

He slipped the half-dozen current letters that still required Meeker's attention into a file he would give to Meeker personally. If it wasn't for this half hour's worth of paperwork, which Mrs. Brazwell had simply let collect on Meeker's desk, Dodd would have been able to concentrate on his real job as manager which was, in essence, to do nothing.

Dodd checked his watch. Eleven fifteen. He left the mayor's door open and let himself into the courtroom to see if he could do anything in there. He checked the shelves, the bench, the tables and found nothing but dust.

He locked the courtroom and walked over to Joe Bob's office. Joe Bob sat on his desk with one cheek hanging dangerously over the edge while he jawed with his deputy. Dodd knocked lightly at the door.

Joe Bob turned around, pushing a wad of something unimaginable to the back of his cheek. He studied Dodd from head to foot as though the two of them had never met. "You got a problem?"

"I can't find any of the court files or docket records. In fact I can't seem to find any record of any legal proceedings past or pending."

The walnut sized wad in Joe Bob's cheek shifted back and forth. "You mean the files of cases what been here and gone?"

Dodd didn't even bother to answer.

Joe Bob motioned for his deputy to go back to whatever work he'd been doing. "Didn't take you long to figure out that my brother don't keep no records."

"He keeps records all right. lots of them. And keeps track of them very badly. That's why I was surprised when I couldn't find any court records."

Joe Bob stood up and hitched his pants. "You may be smarter'n I thought. See, I keep all the court records on account of Ralph would die under all that paper work if he wasn't so busy drinking himself to death first. I don't care what he does as mayor, but I got to see the court records too, so I don't let him near 'em." Joe Bob crossed the room and laid his hand on top of a fireproof file cabinet. "They's all in here. Which one did you need to see?"

"None, Joe Bob. I was just curious to know why I couldn't find them."

"Well, if you need any, you ask me or you ask Carl Ray here and we'll work together with you." Dodd translated this to mean they would stand over his shoulder whenever he wanted a peek at the records.

Back in his office, he checked his watch again. Eleven forty-five. He began to wonder how many people in the town simply rolled over and died from boredom every year. He called the realty office to talk to Meeker.

"He left for lunch about half an hour ago," Mrs. Brazwell informed him. Dodd saw no reason not to follow that example so he locked up the office. Joe Bob yelled, "Taking off for lunch a little early aren't you?" Dodd ignored him and stepped onto the street.

The sun began to bake him half a block down the road and his jacket, in spite of the blend, made an excellent convection oven. Dodd couldn't imagine how all those old boys kept from melting under multiple layers of polyester. They probably even wore polyester underwear.

He removed the jacket and tie, draping them over his arm.

He spotted one of the five right reverends walking toward him on the sidewalk. The one named after two Gospels. The preacher smiled to acknowledge that he'd caught Dodd's eye, and hastened his step in Dodd's direction. Dodd immediately turned toward the bank, and bumped into Rafferty's secretary, Rhonda Mayfield. "Going to lunch?" he asked.

She nodded, looking at her watch.

He pulled her to the edge of the sidewalk, trying to look as though he was conducting official business and letting the disappointed minister walk by.

"Do they let women in the Paris?" he asked. "Looked like a solid ole boy crowd to me."

"I make my lunch at home. I live around the corner." He thought she was going to say more, but she started to glance around instead, jangling her car key with her hand.

"See you around," Dodd dismissed himself. He stepped away, but she put her hand on his arm. "You're attached to my boss' daughter, aren't you?"

He laughed. "Well, ma'am, we've been seeing each other, but I couldn't exactly call it attached."

She touched her hair for a second and Dodd took that second to admire her again. She wore a pale silk, blue warp-around blouse that hid the bosom he remembered so well from the day before. The tucked blouse funneled her trim waist into a dark blue skirt. Dodd figured her for the late thirties, maybe pushing forty. Her clothes looked nice but the shoes and purse were showing signs of wear, as though she had a nice feel for fashion but couldn't afford to buy anything with it.

She kept her hand on his arm. "Why don't you let me make you lunch sometime? You may find you need some home cooking to help you recover from the grease and fat those boys pack in at the Paris."

"Why, ma'am, I'll certainly take that under consideration," he told her, hoping that her offer was nothing more than polite conversation, or that she would at least realize his answer most certainly fell in that category.

Unfortunately, common courtesy didn't seem to be Rhonda's strong suit. "How about Sunday?" she suggested. "Maybe Sunday evening after church. I could serve some cold ham sandwiches and lemonade."

Dodd pulled back gently. "Ma'am, I don't want to be unsociable, but I don't think I can make it." He looked into her eyes and could see she was distressed to hear his answer. "Maybe you could call me next week," he hedged.

"Is there a phone out at that farm?" she asked.

Dodd tried to figure her out. Yesterday he had her pegged as a closet lush, sleeping in Rafferty's bed. He almost thought she believed him to be a threat to her boss. Today her eyes were clear and she seemed interested in meeting him.

"Mrs. Mayfield, let me be honest," he said, leaning over to speak softly and still be heard. "I spend time with Mary Beth Rafferty because I know she doesn't expect me to wait around for her to call back. Not unless she wants to make me jealous.

But the invitation I received from you, well, that's a different kind of invitation altogether."

She glanced back into the bank and then touched his cheek. "Dodd, I know that I'm more like the Blanche du Bois at Elysian Fields than the exciting young creature she must have been when she taught art to young men exploring the virtues of their bodies. But the truth is that it is I who am extending a kindness to strangers. I have a picture of your uncle Zel. You look just like him. I also have something you might want to see."

Dodd didn't know how to answer her. Finally he took her hand and said, "My family is a whole different line of Dodds. If you see a resemblance, it's purely accidental. I'm not saying I wouldn't love the pleasure of your company, but I just can't make it Sunday night."

He watched her climb into her car and realized that a ham sandwich and the pleasure of her company might make for a perfect Sunday evening. Maybe next time he would think twice about the invitation.

At the Paris he found Meeker surrounded at his table by four other old boys discussing the Oilers' chances after Earl Campbell failed to get them to the Super Bowl three years in a row. Dodd took a seat at a table near the rear and ordered chicken and dumplings with lima beans and corn bread.

Elna poured his coffee and Dodd opened an abandoned copy of the Fort Stockton paper to see what was happening in the world outside. Before he could take in the headline, Bill Todd, the car dealer, dropped into the chair beside him.

"That's a fine Mustang you drive," he said, pointing to his empty coffee cup for Elna to fill. "I got a chance to look it over in my garage. What is it? A sixty-six?"

Todd's polyester leisure suit was lima bean green. Unlike the Meekers and many of their friends, Todd hadn't developed the hard basketball belly; he just ran slightly pudgy, especially in the hands and fingers.

Dodd sipped of his coffee and shuddered. “Sixty-five. Number 13 off the assembly line. You can actually find the vin number. That’s why I got it so cheap. No one wanted it because it was so unlucky.” He wondered if life in a town this small was spent rehearsing the same conversation. Endless variations on a theme.

Todd tried to absorb Dodd’s answer, and finally realized it was a joke. Or hoped it was a joke. He screwed his face into a grin and said, “Say, stranger, we can use men with a sense of humor around here. But what I was thinking....”

Dodd interrupted him, “Say, Bill, what I was thinking was, didn’t we have this conversation yesterday? What kind of car did I drive? A 65 Mustang convertible. Would I be interested in a Caddy for two hundred a month? Or was I just seeing into the future to when we’d have this conversation today?”

Todd shook his finger in Dodd’s face. “Never expect to shake loose a good salesman with a single rebuff. Now I was thinking, you mentioned yesterday that you thought the 65 Mustang was a fine and classic car. It just happens that I have a 66 Mustang on my lot, standard transmission but with eighty thousand original miles. Great car for attracting young women, if you get my drift.”

“I never needed a car to get laid, Bill. Is that something you can see a doctor about?”

Todd blushed and swallowed.

Fred Jaspar chuckled and slapped Todd on the shoulder. “Bill’s problem’s worse. He could troll for women with a Jaguar XKE and come up with his nets empty.”

Harry Waspergas joined in from the table at Todd’s elbow. “His wife left him for a Kerby vacuum salesman driving a Volkswagon. And he’s still wearing that godawful green suit she sewed him.” Waspergas held his Pinochle hand against his chest.

Todd screwed his face on straight. “It was a figure of speech. I just thought you wouldn’t forgive me for holding back a bargain like that.”

“Actually, Bill,” Dodd said, “I can’t imagine getting laid across bucket seats.”

"So I was thinking," Todd plowed on, as though Dodd had said nothing, "maybe I could let you have that Mustang for forty a month. No down payment. If you decide after six months it's not for you, bring it in, we'll work something else out."

Dodd wondered how the man got all those words out without having to stop for air. "Now why would you offer me a deal like that?"

Todd winked and then leaned in to whisper. "Because I know you're not flush now, but if you were to come into money somehow, well, I'd hope you'd remember who your friends are."

"Speak louder, Bill," Jasper crowed. "We want to study your technique."

"Come into money?" Dodd said, not lowering his voice. "You mean like the money the Dodd's stole from the bank?"

Todd looked around to see who was listening. By now it seemed to be the whole restaurant. "Go on, Bill," Pat Pullman nodded to him from the table behind Jaspar's back. "Lay your cards out on the table."

Todd looked down at his plate. "Well, yes. If that's all there was to find." Todd may have been looking at his plate, but everyone else was looking at Dodd to see how he would answer. The dining room suddenly seemed about half the size it had seemed when he first sat down at the table.

Dodd glanced up at Elna, who held his plate out in front of her shoulder and then dropped it straight down onto his table. It clattered down in front of him without spilling a single drop of gravy. He was about to tell Todd where he could shove his Mustang, when he thought it might not be a bad idea at that. "Sure, Bill," he said. "Why don't I drop by your lot this afternoon?"

Todd wrapped Dodd's right hand between the pudgy fingers of both of his. "You won't regret this partner. I'm gong to fix you up with a honey of a car."

Dodd sat through lunch until one-thirty waiting for any of the patrons to leave for work. No one did. After he cleaned his plate and his third cup of coffee, Dodd wandered down to Meeker's Corner Store to check in on Bobby and to collect the receipts. He thought about driving, but decided it would be hotter in the truck than in the sun.

He left his jacket off, wanting to ditch his shirt for a cotton T-shirt, and carried it over his arm when he pushed his way through the door. Wally Wetzel, the assistant manager sat next to the register, eating a can of pork and beans, chewing Beechnut tobacco, smoking a cigarette and reading a Hustler Magazine.

Dodd spotted Bobby in the back of the store putting out cans and pricing them. Bobby started to wave, but Dodd shook his head. He strolled to the counter.

"Wha'd'you want?" Wetzel asked through a mouthful of beans and Beechnut.

Dodd studied Wally's acne scarred face and his "Eat the Rich" T-shirt with cigarettes rolled in one sleeve. The kid had no idea who he was, and Dodd decided to do a little manager-employee role playing.

"Marlboros please."

"Boatright, you've got a customer," Wetzel bellowed, even though the cigarettes were two-feet behind him. Bobby put down his pricing gun and hustled to the front. "Give this man some Marlboros."

Bobby pulled a pack of cigarettes from the wall display and handed them to Dodd. Dodd signaled for him to keep his mouth shut. "Ring them up, idiot," Wetzel yelled. He confided to Dodd, "New kid. Kind of slow." With that he returned to his Hustler and never gave Dodd another thought.

"Don't you wait on customers?"

Wetzel slammed the cover of his magazine flat. "I get a commission on guns. You buying a gun?"

Dodd shook his head, "No."

"Then the kid can help you."

"How about the store receipts?" Dodd asked.

"What about 'em?" Wetzel snapped, popping his gum and refusing to look up from his Hustler.

"Hand them over, please."

Wetzel sneered. "Shit, buddy, there's already been robbery this week. I busted it up pretty good all on my own. Not a scratch on me. So unless you got a big gun in your pocket, you can fuck off."

Dodd didn't know whether to slap the kid or fire him on the spot.

"He's the new boss," Bobby said.

Now Wetzel looked up, tapping the ash of his cigarette onto the floor behind the counter. "I never seen him."

"You can call Meeker. Interrupt his lunch," Dodd said. "You'll still have to hand over the bank bag."

Dodd fully expected the kid to call Meeker, which is exactly what he should have done. Instead, Wetzel grabbed the leather bag from under the counter, opened the register and stuffed it with handfuls of bills and change. Dodd couldn't tell exactly, but he figured Wetzel had shoved close to fifteen hundred dollars in the bag. He couldn't imagine the store earning that much cash in a town that small.

"Aren't you going to count it?" Dodd said.

"Ain't ya gonna to have to count it at the bank?"

Dodd scratched his head. "What if I were to pocket three or four hundred and tell Meeker that's all you gave me?"

Wetzel laughed as though Dodd was even stupider than he'd thought before. "Nothing in writing. Your word against mine."

Dodd tried another track. "Let me ask you this. Why didn't you put most of this cash in the safe? Wouldn't that make sense given the robbery you say you busted up the other day?"

Wetzel laughed again. "I didn't say I busted it up. I did bust it up. And you got all the money right there don't you? What's the problem?"

Wetzel pushed the bag toward Dodd and knocked the can of pork and beans across the Hustler magazine. "Did you pay for that?" Dodd asked.

Wetzel shook his head in disbelief. "I'm gonna put it back in the rack. Besides, ain't you ever heard of fringe benefits or nothing?"

Dodd hefted the bag. Bobby was trying very hard not to laugh. Dodd had to admit, there was something funny about meeting someone who made Bobby look savvy. "Think there might be any college in your future, son?"

Wetzel seemed taken aback, as though Dodd had just asked the stupidest question it was possible for a stupid person to ask. "What good would that do me?"

"I can't imagine it'd do you any good at all."

Wetzel beamed. "See, now you got the picture," he said.

"Nice meeting you, son," Dodd said. "It's been illuminating."

"Well, I'm glad you figured out how things work around here," Wetzel sneered.

Bobby opened the door for Dodd, trying to hide a laugh. Wetzel didn't even try to hide it when he snorted, "Suck up."

Dodd had no problems collecting the receipts from the Ben Franklin, Dry Good Store and realty offices. Each bag waited for him, open and with receipts inside for him to check against the totals. Even Mrs. Brazwell was reasonably polite, telling him nothing more than, "You know I could a run this to the bank just like I used to and saved Ralph all that money he's paying you."

Dodd told her she was more than welcome to continue, but she insisted, "No, that's fine. You do it."

Inside the bank, Dodd waited for the bank teller to tally up the receipts. He couldn't help but notice Rafferty sitting on Marla Mayfield's desk, one cheek style like Sheriff Meeker. Her giggles and blushes made him think back to the afternoon before when he saw both of them driving out of town in the general direction of Fort Stockton.

Dodd wondered if the bank president was slipping it to mother and daughter at the same time. The more Dodd thought about it, the more sense it made. Dodd had been in town long enough to realize that Rafferty would be the alpha dog. That meant he would have his pick of any female in heat. Dodd just wondered if the mother knew about the daughter, and he somehow doubted it.

He took the bank statements with him back to the realty office. He found Meeker in his office, alone and working on a cup of Jack Daniels.

Dodd dropped the bank statements on his desk. "What do I with these?"

"Give them to Mrs. Brazwell," Meeker said. Then he changed his mind, opened up his desk drawer and scooped the papers inside. "We can do that later. How did your first day go?"

"It's an easy job. Except for resisting the temptation to kill that kid you have running your gas station."

Meeker waved him away. "I know he's an asshole. But what do you expect me to do about it?"

"Fire the little shit head. He's incompetent, he has a bad attitude and he's stealing from you. Did you know he spilled a can of beans on a Hustler magazine then put it back on the rack to sell?"

Meeker lowered his voice. "You think that's bad? Mrs. Brazwell once brought in a copy of Hustler she found in the store bathroom. The pages were all stuck together."

"What did you do about it?"

"I asked her what she was doing going through my Hustlers." He lowered his voice even more, "She's that way. You know?"

"I mean what did you do about Wetzel? He's lazy, he's ripping you off and he insults your customers."

Meeker opened up his drawer and poured another finger or two into his cup. "His old man owns half the wells between here and the Permian Basin and he banks it all here. Hell, he sits on the bank's board of directors. If I let that kid go, he and Rafferty would make my life hell. Well, not unless he did something so stupid even his old man wouldn't blame me. But I can't imagine what that would be."

So the two Wetzel's were related after all. Dodd decided not to mention the confidential correspondence on Meeker's desk. Instead he said, "Short-changing you and bad-mouthing customers isn't reason enough?"

"Well, I mentioned it to W.W. and he told me that just proves the boy's cut out for upper management."

"Ralph, do you ever think about retiring and moving to the city?"

Ralph belted down about half the liquor in his cup. "No thanks. I enjoy living in small towns where normal people live."

Dodd looked out the window at the vast expanse of sand and mesquite stretching out to the gorge. A roadrunner touched down, decided the sand was too hot to walk on, and darted away. "How did you like your office when you got there this afternoon?" he asked.

Meeker followed his gaze to the sand and mesquite outside. "I didn't even think to go. Was there a reason to?"

Dodd didn't bother to answer. The more he thought about it, the more he doubted there was.

Chapter 17

On his way back to town hall, Dodd stopped by the Auto Emporium to see how his car was coming. He found it sitting outside, untouched, with two or three other cars. The garage door was up, so he walked inside. He found Tucker sleeping under a pile of Buckhorn empties. Tucker smelled of motor oil, beer and piss.

Dodd kicked him in the ribs, far more gently than he wanted. "What's happening with my car?"

It took Tucker several minutes to focus. Even longer to recognize Dodd. He pushed himself up on one elbow and lit a half Marlboro he found in his lap. "Part's not in."

"Did you order it?"

Tucker squeezed his face together in a futile gesture of concentration. "I think so. I mean, hell, fucking yes. What's your problem? Todd loaned you a truck."

"The truck is a piece of shit."

"It's not like he's charging you for it."

Dodd kicked his ankle. "Tomorrow. Even if you have to drive to Pecos for the fuel line. Or didn't Ralph tell you, I'm your boss now?"

Tucker dug through the empties for a bottle with beer in it. "I don't work for Meeker. I work for Mr. Todd."

"Everyone works for Meeker. Or Rafferty. If you don't owe paper to the bank, Todd does. One call from me, you'll wish you fixed it yesterday."

"Didn't take you long to become part of the problem," Tucker mumbled.

Dodd could barely find a gear as he drove back to his office. When he pulled up at town hall, the truck dieseled so badly that the clutch disengaged then fell onto the pavement and bounced underneath the transmission with a clatter. Dodd slammed the door when he climbed out, and the passenger window broke free of the duct tape and fell into the door. He heard the glass shatter as it hit the frame. He would have kicked the truck but he was afraid to knock loose a fender, or blow out a tire, or, who could know, jam the axel into the transmission.

After he delivered the store receipts to the bank the next afternoon, he walked to the auto emporium dangling the truck keys on his finger and prepared to kick some Tucker ass. Instead he found his Mustang waiting for him outside the Airstream trailer that served as Todd's office. Dodd knocked on the door and stepped inside.

The trailer coughed out dust and stale cigarette smoke when Todd opened the door. The air conditioner rattled against the window frame, blowing air like a turbine exhaust but keeping the room cool. Barely.

Dodd sat across from Todd's cramped desk, studying the reports, charts and calendars that covered the walls. He caught sight of a six-year-old sales tax permit notice peering half way out from behind a three-year-old Sports Illustrated calendar.

Todd pulled the keys to the Mustang from a pegboard and slapped them on the desk in front of Dodd. He appeared nervous, his shirt stained under the armpits and across the back.

"How much?"

Todd snorted nervously. "On the house. Turns out Tucker just had to reconnect the fuel line."

Dodd slammed his fist on the desk. "I could have been on the road two days ago?"

"That's why it's on the house."

"And I spent time behind bars," Dodd sighed.

"Mr. Dodd. I can't rob you the way your family robbed the town bank." Todd's attempt at a smile fell flatter than his joke. But it seemed as though he had something else on his mind.

Dodd drummed his fingers on Todd's ancient TI desk calculator. "I'm not one of those Dodds, Bill."

Dodd glanced out the window. Marla Mayfield drove past in the same direction he'd seen her driving two days before, and easily going thirty miles over the speed limit. Her hair trailed in the wind behind her like fine threads of silk.

Todd rolled the pens on his desk under his fingers. "Rafferty and the Meekers have a lock on this town. No one's been able to unseat them since they took power in the fifties. Not that it was different before then. Rafferty's old man ran the bank and the council. That's before your brothers killed him robbing the bank."

Dodd motioned for Todd to continue. He was more interested in Marla Mayfield disappearing down the highway. He thought he knew who he would see next.

"Meeker was a deputy then, but he and his brother ended shooting it out with the Dodds while the sheriff was across town canoodling with Rafferty Senior's wife. The scandal allowed Rafferty and the Meekers to oust the sheriff, the rest of the town council and take control."

The air conditioner clicked off. Suddenly the room fell so silent Dodd could hear the paper rustle as it settled back into place.

Todd's neck pulsed. He reminded Dodd of a man in desperate need of a drink, a cigarette, a fix, or maybe a hasty escape. "Every resolution the council passes, every law Meeker signs benefits those three and cuts the rest of us out of the action. You don't think I could sell a bunch of them Jap Hondas and Toyotas out here? People use so much gas going from town to town they go broke keeping their big American cars fed. I could make a mint selling those Jap cars, but the council passed a resolution refusing to zone a foreign car dealership in this town. You ask anyone who runs a business that doesn't belong to the bank or the Meekers, the ordinances of Sweet Water Falls are written to keep the profits trickling up to them."

"Everyone?"

Without the air conditioning, the temperature in the room began to rise. A slight pool of sweat gathered at Todd's hairline.

"You know who used to own the Ben Franklin? Bobby Ray Parker. He lives in Marfa now. Ten years ago, when Bobby Ray started running specials to compete with Ralph's dry good store, the town council voted to rezone his property residential. Three-zip. Bobby Ray appealed to everyone he could think of. Nothing doing. So he sold the store to Meeker for the value of his inventory. Next council meeting? Re-rezoned the lot commercial. Three-zip. Meeker got the realty company from Haywood Smith because the bank called in two notes even though Haywood was current on both. Ralph agreed to make the loans good, ended up in real estate."

Todd paused and stared out the window. The air conditioner clicked back in, not a moment to soon. His shirt was soaked through as though he'd spent hours in the sun, or under torture. "Used to be two gas stations. One at each end of town. Jimmy Carl Hargass. Rafferty floated Meeker a capital loan so he could undersell Jimmy Carl by half. Didn't matter how low Jimmy Carl went. And this was when them Arabs was holding up gas lines all over the country. Jimmy Carl said to hell with it, sold it to Meeker, who tore it to the ground. Then he raised his gas to a buck forty a gallon until he paid off that loan."

Dodd let out a low whistle. "So why stick around?"

Todd laughed. "Cause they don't want a car lot I can barely make a living at. They leave the handful marginally profitable businesses to the rest of us. Hell, I clear twelve grand a year after taxes, my home's paid off and my wife remarried so no alimony or child support. Football paid my kid's college. I could do worse selling and moving. But if they thought I were about to make a real profit...." He sliced his throat with his finger. He studied his thumbs for a second or two.

"That's why I'm doing you this favor with your car."

"That and the fact that it just needs a fuel line." Dodd added.

"Well, I took one from the 66 Mustang. It ain't going anywhere. Besides, everybody knows you're here to take the Meekers down. That's why Ralph keeps you close to his chest."

Dodd leaned back into his chair, nearly bumping his head into a small sales chart. "Just what do you think is waiting on that farm?"

"No one knows for sure. Ain't that funny? Best guess? The bank money. It wasn't never recovered."

Dodd suppressed a laugh. "Not a flying saucer?"

The air conditioner cut out again and Todd fiddled with the thermostat. "I don't go in for that kind of nonsense. What'd you do with a flying saucer? Sell it to the government? Hell, you and I both know they'd take it away and leave you empty-handed. It's money. Isn't it? Level with me."

Dodd decided it was time to leave. "I hate to tell you, Bill, but I'm really not one of those Dodds." He offered Todd his hand.

He jangled the Mustang keys and headed toward the door. Todd looked like a beaten man, a man who just realized the wife headed down the sidewalk with her new beau had cleaned out his bank accounts as well.

He turned over the Mustang ignition and then stepped out to look under the car for fuel leaks. Todd watched him from the door of the Airstream, praying perhaps that he didn't find anything else to fix.

Rafferty drove past the lot in his Seville, heading in the same direction he'd been heading on Wednesday afternoon. He had the look of a man with a mission.

Dodd climbed back into the Mustang and reset the rear and sideview mirrors which Tucker had misaligned. He checked the radio and the stations were reset. The odometer had logged another 150 miles which made Dodd suspect Tucker fixed the car a couple of days before and had been joy riding in the evenings. Since he would be following Rafferty he took the time to pull up the top, and then he pulled onto the highway.

He caught sight of Rafferty's Seville three miles past the farm and dropped back to a comfortable distance, letting cars pass between them, but always making sure he could see Rafferty's tail lights. He opened it up and realized the timing was off. Not badly, not enough to screw up the engine, but enough to make the engine cough instead of purr.

Bad enough Tucker had driven his car around, but the bastard couldn't even put it together right, and he would have to drive it the weekend before he could get it back in the shop.

He turned on the radio hoping to hear something besides Country/Western or Gospel. He failed miserably. He draped his right arm out the window, desperately wishing for a cigarette. He thought quitting smoking would be easy. Staying off the booze was easier.

Rafferty's Seville turned into the Old West Inn on the outskirts of Fort Stockton, a nondescript roadside motel that might just as well have been named "Generic Lodge." The rooms were laid out in two strips with the swimming pool and vending machines nestled behind the office on an island between them.

Rafferty pulled behind the first row of rooms so that his car couldn't be seen from the highway. Dodd followed him into the lot, but parked on the highway side so that Rafferty wouldn't spot him. He waited for fifteen minutes, to give Rafferty plenty of time to check into his room then walked to the pool side of the building to investigate.

Rafferty's Seville was parked next to Marla Mayfield's tiny blue Colt, as though their cars were snuggling in the parking lot while the couple snuggled inside. Dodd expected no less. He left his sunglasses on and bought a coke so he could sit by the pool and wait to see what happened next.

Marla emerged from the hotel room after an hour and a half. She stopped just outside the door to touch up her hair and check the button of her blouse. Dodd didn't know why she wanted to touch up her hair, it had a nice tousled look. In fact, watching her climb into her car, swinging both of her clean brown legs up and into the driver's seat at the same time, showing off just a glimpse of the bottoms of her thighs, Dodd wanted to cross the parking lot and strike up a conversation.

Dodd fully expected to see Rafferty climb into his car and follow her back to town. Instead, he emerged from his room with a towel and a glass of scotch in his hand, wearing shades and a bikini swimsuit that rolled down slightly under a belly that was only now beginning to give way to his age.

Well, Dodd thought, sex can keep you trim.

When Dodd realized, Rafferty intended to use the pool, he rose from the deck chair and slipped through the back gate. He loitered next to the soda machine, with quarters in hand, while Rafferty swam laps for fifteen minutes, toweled off and returned to his room.

Dodd settled back into the deck chair to see what would happen next. He wasn't surprised when Rhonda pulled into the spot where daughter Marla had been only a half hour before. She slipped carefully from her Buick Regal, keeping both knees together and toes pointed down. She glanced around nervously before sprinting to Rafferty's room. Funny, Dodd thought, these two had probably been carrying on much longer than Rafferty and Marla, but Rhonda seemed more nervous about being caught.

Rafferty met her at the door and pulled her into the room by the waist. When the door slammed shut, Dodd figured he'd seen enough. He crossed the parking lot to the front office and asked the clerk if there was a coffee machine.

The clerk looked older than granite, with a bleached skull and tiny mustache. His nostrils, teeth and fingers were stained deep yellow from years of tobacco abuse. He wore a threadbare checked polyester shirt with diamond buttons and kept one eye on a game show fading in and out on his black and white portable.

He pointed Dodd toward a pot on a side table next to the door. Beside the pot were a dozen Styrofoam cups and two-dozen half-opened creamer and sugar packets. The coffee barely dribbled its way from the spigot to his cup, but Dodd didn't mind because he didn't want coffee anyway. A large southwestern print filled the wall: coyotes and cow skulls under a cloudless sky. Dodd thought that would certainly attract tourists to Texas.

He returned to the desk. "I'm down the way from this guy with a red Seville. I've seen two different women go into his room and it doesn't look like they're baby-sitting. A sweet young thing, and the other one loaded but old enough to be her mother."

The clerk nodded, a canine tooth missing. "He leases that room permanently. Doesn't want anybody else to use it. Drives in at least three afternoons a week. Most often the two gals you saw, but occasionally he brings in a Mexican or a hooker. He knocked up my maid a few years back. She wanted workman's comp." His laugh sounded like a coyote's bark. "Like she was working when those legs were flailing. I only hire grandmas after that."

"Imagine that," Dodd whistled.

"The best part?" the clerk cackled, nudging him with his elbow. "The young one really is the daughter. And you want to hear the best part?" Dodd thought he'd just been told the best part. "Both of them work for him."

"What a racket," Dodd said.

"You said it," the clerk said. The look in the clerk's eyes said he only wished he could carry on with a mother and daughter. By Dodd's way of thinking, one regular woman was beginning to feel like one too many.

That night Dodd sat at the Stickett Inn bar with a glass of water, tapping the truck keys on the counter. The jukebox glared "Your Cheating Heart" and the bass lines almost bounced the beer glasses on the tables. Rednecks crowded the tables, ankles wrapped around ankles, wrists through wrists and fingers through fingers. Everyone wore a ten gallon hat, male and female.

The cigarette smoke was so thick Dodd thought he would choke. He could barely see until the overhead fan occasionally cleared a path through the haze. He'd always though non-smokers were whiners to complain about side stream smoke. Now he though they should have complained even more. He glanced at the door and checked his watch.

Hazel appeared in front of him, wiping a glass that looked like it would never be clean. "Sure you don't want a drink?"

"Don't drink."

"Expecting company?" She reached under the counter and picked up a lit cigarette. He couldn't imagine why. There was plenty of smoke to inhale already.

Dodd took a last look at the door and his watch. He'd been waiting ninety minutes. "Doesn't look like it, does it?" he said.

Hazel rolled her eyes. It's not as though she didn't warn him his first night in town.

Chapter 18

Dodd woke alone on Saturday morning. He hadn't been able to locate Mary Beth the night before, which didn't exactly surprise him, but it didn't exactly please him either.

He boiled a pan of water, patiently straining it into a cup through two tablespoons of coffee on a folded paper towel. He thought about buying a percolator, but knew he would forget by mid-morning.

Sure enough, by the time he reached the Ft. Stockton library, the percolator was as far from his mind as Mary Beth Rafferty. He was glad to be back behind the wheel of his Mustang, top down, wind in his hair, although he couldn't help but listen for loose bolts and drain pans that might fall to the pavement because Tucker neglected to properly attach them.

He stopped at the library checkout counter and asked for copies of the local papers printed during the time of the Sweet Water shoot out.

The clerk, dressed entirely in black with men's black steel-toed work shoes, black stockings, black nail polish and black eye-liner, took him to the microfilm viewers in the back of the library. Dodd figured her for a university student waiting for classes to start. Not just waiting, in fact, but desperate to flee.

She showed him how to thread the viewer and scroll through the pages. The bluish reverse image made it difficult to focus. "If you need anything else," she told him, "I'm Dee Dee."

"I'll be sure to ask for you personally," Dodd said, spinning through the first few issues of the Fort Stockton paper. As though they were any one else on duty to ask.

He caught the first story halfway through the Wednesday edition for April 13, 1949. "Meteor Crashes in Sweet Water Falls." The story reported several accounts of a meteor sighting as far away as Marfa. Most of the accounts agreed the meteor crashed just west of the town. The story returned in the Friday edition on the second page, headlined: "Flying Saucer Rumors Rampant."

The story ran underneath a picture showing a roadblock with a soldier staring down a civilian with a camera.

The gist of this story was that an object from outer space, originally thought to be a meteor, crashed into farmland belonging to Zane and Elizabeth Dodd of Sweet Water Falls. Dodd's younger brother Zel reported the crash landing to the US Army. Zel received a medical discharge from the Army after his last post in Roswell, New Mexico in 1947.

The Army crews arrived Thursday, some reported to be in radiation gear, and barricaded the Dodd farm from curious spectators. For most of Thursday and Friday, rumors circulated the community that a flying saucer had crashed on the Dodd farm. The story added that another flying saucer was rumored to have crashed in Roswell while Zel Dodd was stationed there, further fueling rumors.

The Sunday edition pushed the story to the front page: "Army Evacuates Sweet Water Falls," with a subhead claiming, "Balloon once again fools civilians watching skies."

This time the picture showed an army officer holding up pieces of plywood and tinfoil beside the road to the Dodd farm. The lead paragraph proclaimed, "US Lt. Colonel Tom Fitzpatrick told reporters Friday that a mysterious object, previously believed to be a meteor, was nothing more than a weather balloon that had strayed from its intended path."

The next paragraph added, "As happened at Roswell, New Mexico in 1947, a weather balloon blown off course confused a number of witnesses, including Zel Dodd, a former army officer who is claimed to have reported a UFO crash. Dodd refused to comment.

"Col. Fitzpatrick, when questioned about the coincidence of Dodd being involved in both incidents, told reporters 'It's easy to tell the difference. One's made of foil and the other's supposed to be from outer space.'"

The story reiterated Friday's account, including Zel Dodd's medical discharge following the Roswell incident. The story added that Fitzpatrick's announcement didn't quell the rumors, and cited deputy Joe Bob Meeker, who served at Roswell with Dodd. "Zel wasn't the only one who never bought the balloon story. One of my buddies saw the alien bodies when they was delivered to Wright Patterson. The army ain't going to send all these trucks out here for a weather balloon if they weren't sure it's not a weather balloon."

The story disappeared for two weeks. Then Dodd found a follow up on the back page reporting that the rumors hadn't died down since the army pulled out of Sweet Water Falls. The story repeated Meeker's quote about the alien bodies and added new rumors, including one that the wreckage contained an unknown metal the army wanted for weapons research. Yet another rumor claimed the army hauled away most of an alien spacecraft, but that other pieces had never been recovered and were still waiting to be found on the Dodd farm.

Dodd smiled to himself. Rumors become legends of the grail, and legends of the grail make men greedy.

Another story in the same issue caught Dodd's eye. The headline read, "Sweet Water Businessman Withdraws Election Bid." Ralph Meeker, owner of Meeker's Dry Goods in Sweet Water Falls, withdrew his candidacy for the Sweet Water Falls town council when the three-man council consisting of Mayor Marion Rafferty, Sr., Sheriff Tom Hargess and Justice of the Peace Wilfred Whatley agreed to change the zoning of recently purchased property from farmland to commercial.

According to the story, Meeker wanted to build Meeker's Friendly Gas Stop, a gas station and small-scale grocery store on the eastern edge of town, but the property's zoning kept him from doing so. After the council denied his zoning change request on three different occasions, Meeker declared his candidacy for Whately's seat, which would be up for election in the first week of November.

The article added that with Meeker no longer running against him, Whately would be re-elected to his seventh three year term on the town council.

Well, well, well, Dodd thought to himself, business as usual in Sweet Water Falls. The Meekers threw the bums out and became the bums themselves.

He scrolled forward to the December 26 issue. The first thing that leaped out at him was a half page picture of the Ford pick-up in the gorge behind the farm. The Meeker brothers stood on each side of the wreck, brandishing shotguns. The headlines read: "Christmas Eve Blood Bath in Sweet Water Falls."

The story read:

> Deputy sheriff Joe Bob Meeker and brother Ralph stopped one of the most daring robberies in West Texas history just west of the tiny township of Sweet Water Falls. At ten p.m. on Christmas Eve, when the town's children were being tucked into bed to wait for Santa Claus, three bankrupt and desperate farmers broke into the town bank, where they made away with one half million dollars and ruthlessly gunned down bank president and town mayor Marion Rafferty, Sr.
>
> Zel Dodd was killed in a cross-fire from the deputies guns, but his two brothers Zane and Zack got away with most of the money. The Texas Rangers have posted the Dodds on their most-wanted list and begun a statewide manhunt for the killers.
>
> Town sheriff, Tom Hargess, was drinking and dancing at a Christmas party thrown by the wife of Mayor Marion Rafferty Sr. during

the robbery. Off-duty deputy Meeker drove past the bank and noticed a light was on in Rafferty's office. Entering the bank to see if the mayor was okay, he found Rafferty face down and shot in the back, with the vault doors wide open.

Meeker tried to alert the sheriff, who told the deputy to handle the case himself. Hargess later claimed Meeker merely called and told him 'there has been a little trouble at the bank.' Whatever happened, Meeker asked his brother Ralph, an on-call deputy, to help.

Having heard rumors that three Dodd brothers, who worked a farm on the western end of town, were having financial difficulties, the Meekers decided to investigate that lead first. They encountered the Dodd brothers in their pick-up truck on the west end of town. When the Meekers tried to pull the brothers over, the desperadoes opened fire.

A high-speed chase and gun battle ensued, but lasted only minutes, ending when the Dodd pick-up truck swerved off the road and tumbled into Sweet Water Gorge, a small branch of the Pecos River. Abandoning the safety of their car, the deputy and his brother followed the bandits into the gorge where they engaged them in gunfire, killing the youngest on the spot.

The two remaining brothers collected the body and the money and disappeared into the many trees and bends of the river. Zel Dodd's body was recovered several miles further downstream, along with twenty-five thousand dollars taken from the bank, but the other two brothers managed to elude capture.

While the final tally from the bank robbery has yet to be made, Marion Rafferty, Jr., the mayor's son and newly appointed bank president, estimates bank losses to exceed five hundred thousand dollars. 'Depositors can rest easy,' Rafferty said. 'The bank was federally insured and accounts will be paid in full.'

> Texas Rangers claim that Rafferty, Sr., was shot with a .38 caliber long-barrel bullet. The weapon wasn't recovered after the gun battle although two shotguns were.

Dodd scrolled through the rest of the film to pick up the last few threads of the story, but he could easily project what happened over the next year. Mal Rafferty replaced his father at the bank, and eventually as mayor. Sheriff Hargess, who was happily drinking and dancing (and maybe more) during the robbery, lost the next election to hero/deputy Joe Bob Meeker. Ralph took his seat on the triumvirate soon after. Rafferty resigned as mayor at the end of his interim term, and Ralph assumed the dual position of mayor and justice of the peace.

As far as Dodd was concerned there was no question what happened that night. Regardless of what crashed into the Dodd farm, regardless of how much money they took from the bank, the demise of the Dodds launched the political careers of the current town council and made them rich men in the process.

He asked Dee Dee to show him how to make photocopies from the film viewer. She offered to give him a tour of some of the library's less public locations. "Dee Dee," he told her, "I think you might be better off at college coffee houses filled with angst and self-recrimination."

"Maybe," she said. "But, mister, I think you could graduate me to a whole new level of self-awareness." She stood in the library doorway watching wistfully as he stashed the photocopies beneath the driver's seat springs. After the stories he'd heard and reading those articles, he decided he couldn't be too paranoid. He waved and backed out of the lot, wondering if maybe his departure wasn't a little too hasty.

Chapter 19

All his life, Dodd heard stories about the Marfa lights. No one who told him about the lights had ever seen them, they heard stories themselves. But even the people who told him about the lights without ever seeing the lights assured him it was worth the trip out west and that they intended to make the trip themselves one day.

Dodd passed the city limits sign. He began to wonder about those lights. Were they like ball lightning? Were they like the aurora borealis? Did they even exist? None of these questions would be answered today since Dodd was in town for the afternoon, when the lights didn't come out, and had to be back in Sweet Water Falls for Rafferty's barbecue that night, well before they would.

He found Alvin Rawlings' two-story shotgun-style house sitting back from a county road at the south end of town. The house was freshly painted. The front porch was hidden from the road by trees and a vegetable garden ran to the side. Rawlings sat in an easy chair, dressed in work clothes, beer in hand and watching a tiny television propped on the railing.

Peach, pear and fig trees shaded the yard. Dodd got the sense that Alvin had done well for himself before he retired.

Rawlings rose from his chair as soon as Dodd climbed out of his car. “I was wondering when you’d show up.” Dodd shook Rawling’s hand and turned down the offer of a beer.

“I never said I was coming.”

“Runt said you’d be coming.”

“Runt” was Alvin’s name for his younger brother Preacher. As far as Dodd knew, no one else was allowed to call Preacher by that name. Alvin was actually Preacher’s half-brother, twenty years older. He insisted he was wiser by twice that many years. He was a retired former CPA, at least that’s how he referred to himself, working odd jobs to bring in extra money while his brother was serving a life sentence with little chance of parole.

“My plans took a different turn. I’m working for Ralph Meeker.”

“That’s a turn I never expected.”

“He made me an offer I couldn’t refuse.”

Rawlings rubbed his chin. He hadn’t shaved in several days but the white stubble against his cocoa skin made him look distinguished. Dodd rubbed his sideburns absent-mindedly. He thought he might skip shaving if he were retired. “According to Runt, ain’t no offer you can refuse. Can’t say ‘no’ to nobody. That’s how he talked you into this shit.” Rawlings moved some seed catalogues from a weather beaten couch, then turned down the baseball game on TV.

Alvin looked nothing like Preacher, in fact he looked more like a Kodiak Bear. Just under six feet with a thick neck and barrel chest, all he needed was a coat of black fur. Alvin served in the Korean War and a dozen years in Harlem after his discharge. Preacher said he ran a black market operation in the Army and did books for a gang connected with the Nation of Islam. He fled to Texas after Malcolm X’s assassination. Alvin never mentioned it, but then it wasn’t the kind of past a Black man in Texas would draw attention to.

Whatever he did in New York, he must have been good at it because he had a long list of white clients with shady connections in a couple of years. Enough shady clients to land a five-year sentence for accounting fraud. That was when he "officially" retired as a CPA.

"Reggie's on," he said. "Yankees, Indians. Tommy John pitching. Yankees're going win another World Series, wait and see. Randolph on base, Reggie knocks him in. He's gonna hit forty again this year."

"Leave it up a little," Dodd said. "Maybe they'll broadcast the Astros' scores."

"Astros? How about 'earth bounds?' Ryan's a five hundred pitcher, and Joe Morgan's just too damn old. He and Rose should of stayed with the Big Red Machine. Wait and see. They always fold in August. Nobody's going to beat the Yankees this year, and the Dodgers will whip Philadelphia in the playoffs, Pete Rose be damned. That's going to be the World Series. Dodgers, Yankees, just like 77 and 78."

"I just wanted to hear the scores," Dodd said.

Alvin rolled his eyes, mocking every black comic relief character in old time movies. "Score don't count, blood. You gotta root for the winner. Rooting for the Astros and working for the Meeker brothers, you're just setting yourself up for disappointment."

Dodd changed the subject. Baseball was a sport he followed to make conversation. Baseball wasn't even a real sport in Texas. Texans worshipped football: high school football, Southwest Conference football and the Cowboys in that order. Even the Oilers were Johnny-Come-Latelys.

"I didn't plan to stay. I got a fuel line leak."

"Why'd Meeker hire you? Have you given that a minute's thought? More to the point, why'd he hire someone named Dodd?"

Both of them stopped the conversation to watch the instant replay of a Jackson home run into the right field seats at Municipal Stadium. Three runs scored to put the Yankees up by one. The camera zoomed in on Len Baker kicking the pitcher's mound in disgust.

"Say what you want," Alvin said, "that boy's the straw that stirs the drink. If you white folks weren't so white, you'd see it too. And how did you get from a gas leak to working for Meeker?"

"I stopped at the gas station to fill up, hoping to make it to a town with a mechanic. Walked in on a robbery. I talked the kid into surrendering if Joe Bob didn't press charges. Then I had to stick around in case Joe Bob charged him anyway. That's how I got hired."

"On the spot?"

Dodd nodded. "Who'd've thought?"

Alvin pitched his empty Budweiser can across the porch. It rolled around the garbage can rim and fell in for a perfect two-pointer. "Which gets us back to the question. Why's that boy going to want to hire you, your name being Dodd and all?"

"Probably to keep an eye on me."

Alvin peeled back another ring tab. "And why's he need to keep an eye on you if you're leaving town anyway? You ask yourself that?"

Dodd propped his feet up on the porch wall. "He's setting me up for something. I just haven't figured out what."

Alvin shook his head and took a long pull of the beer. "So what're you going to do?"

"I haven't decided."

Alvin laughed and opened another can of beer. He didn't offer one to Dodd. He didn't have the white folk's need to keep offering beer to an alcoholic just to be polite. "You better decide in a hurry because those boys will eat you alive." He leaned over to turn up the volume for a commercial with Reggie Jackson. "Damn, that boy can hit."

Dodd turned the volume down. "Preacher told me I could count on your help."

"He's in jail and I'm out here. I don't see how he's got much claim on my time."

"I can cut ten years off his sentence. He could be out in three even if the crap shoot in Sweet Water Falls comes up snake eyes. May not mean much to you, but I bet it means a whole lot to him. More to the point, you promised to help with the legal expenses. Besides, think of all the fun you'll have."

Alvin crossed to the far end of his porch to pee. He walked back, shaking his leg and muttering, "What makes you think I won't forget those expenses anyway? Besides, I told that boy to finish high school like I did, take some college, and get himself a job. A boy that talked that nigger talk like he does wasn't going to get nowhere in the white man's world. Bad enough growing up here. In the joint, he be talkin' like Oakland gangstas. Ebonics my ass."

"And what lingo did you talk in New York, hanging with Malcolm? I bet you weren't nearly this white until you needed to hide under camouflage in Texas. You should have done the time, Alvin, not Preacher. It was your deal," Dodd reminded him.

Alvin chuckled from the bottom of his throat. "I did five years Federal for what they call white collar crime. When I came out, I had more clients than I did before I went in. Just make less money and they pay me under the table. Runt come out, he'll be expecting me to support him." He chuckled again. "Behave like a nigger and you end up with the rest of the niggers in Huntsville."

Dodd shook his head. It was amazing how people simply tuned out the words they didn't want to hear. "He was your bag man, Alvin. The Meekers snookered both of you."

Joe Charboneau teed off Tommy John on the first pitch of the inning to tie the game up at three all. "There he be," Alvin mocked. "The great white hope. Five years from now, no one will remember him."

"Are you going to help me or not?"

Even as he asked the question, Alvin perked up, peering out toward the country road where a car was approaching. "Course I'm going to help you, man. I told Runt I'd help you, and I take care of my own. But I don't want to fuck with the Meekers. Talk's one thing. Getting down to it's another. You understand?"

Dodd nodded.

A Fairlane pulled into the driveway, past Dodd's car and next to the house. Alvin said, "Excuse me for a minute," and hopped down the porch steps. Dodd would have sworn the old man danced his way down to the driveway and around the car to help a young black woman climb out, a young black woman at least thirty years younger. Dodd swore under his breath that she was one of the finest looking women he'd ever seen, slightly thick wasted, but firm breasted with narrow trim legs. Large curls of black hair cascaded past her bronze neck. A heart shaped face with small lips and a straight long nose framed by large chocolate eyes. He could have slid down that nose and flung himself onto those lips before losing himself forever into her mouth.

Even from the porch Dodd caught the scent of sandalwood and almonds.

Alvin helped the woman out of the car, then danced to the trunk to scoop up two large bags of groceries. He followed her up the porch steps and came to an abrupt halt behind her when she stopped to stare at Dodd. "Wanda," Alvin announced over her shoulder, "This's Dodd, Runt's lawyer. You remember, the new one took over his case about three years ago? I told you he might be dropping in in the next few weeks, and sure enough, here he is. Dodd, this is my wife, Wanda."

Dodd offered his hand, but Wanda didn't take it. She turned her neck and said, "I warned you not to do no favors for that jail bird." She refused to even glance Dodd's way as she stormed through the front door.

Alvin stared at the shut door and then said to Dodd. "She's a might temperamental. You might even say she's prejudiced. That's cause she's still young. But she keeps me hard and she keeps me on my toes, so I bust my ass to keep her happy."

Alvin followed Dodd through the front door into a comfortable house with a large living room. A fabric couch, a Lazy Boy and a glass coffee table faced a console color TV with built in stereo. Pictures of Jesus and James Brown hung side-by-side over floral print wallpaper. Accounting books, cookbooks and old issues of Jet and the Sporting News cluttered the bookshelves. An overhead fan and a cross-breeze from the large windows cooled the house. The breeze couldn't entirely blow out the scent of fatback and greens.

"Why don't you watch your game in here where it's cool?" Dodd asked.

"Cause it's an outdoor game. I never liked to watch it in a dome and I don't like to watch it in my house."

Dodd followed Alvin down the long hall that set off the bathroom, a large storage closet and stairs to the second floor. It opened up into the kitchen and dining room. Wanda stood in front of the open refrigerator, waiting for Alvin to unload the groceries.

"By God, she's a peach," Alvin said, and dropped the grocery bags onto their oak dinette.

"I ain't no yellow peach, you old Black bastard," she chided him, grabbing shrink-wrapped packages of ribs, chicken and lean ground beef to stack into the freezer. "I be a plum. A dark black plum with sweet skin and sweeter flesh underneath. You could suck on me all day and never get enough."

Dodd could imagine how right she was.

Alvin juggled two heads of iceberg lettuce and a half-dozen tomatoes to the fridge. "She's not kidding," he agreed. "Wanda, you are the sugar to perk up a dying man's coffee."

Wanda turned to Dodd. "You gone to help this old man with the groceries, or are you just here to get his ass landed back in jail?"

Dodd pulled a few boxes of macaroni and hamburger helper out of the bag. "Where do I put these?"

"In the cabinet, fool." Wanda didn't bother to mention which of the half dozen cabinets she might be referring to. He found the right pair on the third try, and returned for the bread and donuts. The three of them packed the groceries away in five minutes.

"Maybe you could be trained to be useful," she admitted. She set out a pot of water with a half-dozen tea bags to brew. Alvin turned on the TV on the kitchen counter. The Yankees retook the lead 4-3 after Oscar Gamble doubled in Rick Cerone.

"Ain't no Munson," Alvin grumbled as Cerone crossed the plate.

Wanda shook her head. "You never liked Munson. Now he's dead, he's all that?" She turned to Dodd. "All he do is bad mouth them players. If they ain't Reggie Jackson, they ain't worth watching. Nigger can't throw, can't field, can't do nothing but hit home runs and sell candy bars, but my man thinks he's the whole game of baseball." Before Dodd could answer, she turned back to Alvin. "Why you watch, you don't like any of the players?"

Dodd realized, as she turned away, that she had finally acknowledged him as human being, if only for a second.

"Show some respect," Alvin pouted. "Just cause I say Cerone ain't no Munson, don't mean I liked Munson. Neither of 'em Campenella and I watched him play at Ebbetts Field."

Wanda filled three highball glasses with ice, dropped half a lime in each, and poured ice tea from a large pitcher. She laid the three glasses on the table and sat down, beckoning the two men to join her. They both drew up chairs to face her.

"What you want my man to do?" she asked.

"Right now, just sit behind the counter of a gas station and collect people's money. Do some books. He'll add fourteen thousand a year to his retirement."

"That's chump change. The Meekers stole three times that that from Alvin."

"We ain't doing this for the money, baby," Alvin said to her.

"Then we ain't doing it at all. Not less there's money in it."

"I don't know anything about money," said Dodd. "We're just doing a favor for Preacher. A little payback."

"Bull shit," she said. "You wouldn't drive all this way to get some poor nigger out of jail. You got something planned and I want my Alvin to get his cut of it."

Alvin leaned over and patted her hand. "Listen, baby, the key to everything that's about to happen is what Dodd here does know and what Dodd doesn't know. And nobody, not even us, knows what that is. See? They think he's related to the Dodds that robbed that bank. They think there's a half million dollars out there somewhere and they think Dodd knows where it is. They think there's a flying saucer out there somewhere too and they think Dodd knows where it is. But Dodd could be some cracker with the same last name in the wrong place at the wrong time. They don't know for sure."

She looked at Dodd suspiciously. "Are you?"

Alvin took her hand in his and stroked it with a big bear like paw. "I don't know, baby. You don't know. It's better if we don't know."

She sipped her tea and studied both men, shifting her eyes back and forth between each one. "So what do we get?"

"No matter what happens, Wanda baby, Runt gets out of jail a few years sooner. The legal work's mostly done, the appeals are already being considered. We help Dodd, he tears up the bill even if his end of the deal goes bust. Sure, he's got his angle figured out. But it's his angle, not ours. We got to let him work his angle and get what we can get for ourselves. We start getting selfish and nobody gets anything."

Wanda rolled her glass between her fingers, and sighed. "So how are you going to get Alvin this store job?"

Dodd lifted his glass to toast them both. He was glad he wouldn't have to go this alone. "Well, first of all, I'm going to have to rob it."

Chapter 20

Dodd surveyed the Rafferty estate and decided the architect spent too many evenings fantasizing about Scarlett O'Hara. The house resembled two plantation manors married at a forty-five degree angle. Both fell away from an entrance hall faced with Grecian columns and a terraced circular veranda, then disappeared into the horizon. The six oak doors suggested an entrance hall larger than most ballrooms.

Several hundred yards from the house he could see picnic tables overflowing with end-to-end rednecks. Rednecks with crew cuts, flat tops and razor cuts; with thick necks and thick shoulders, turkey necks and narrow chests; wearing hats with wide brims, rolled brims and brims that swept from front to back in a full crest accented with small peacock fathers in the hat bands; wearing lizard boots, alligator boots, and boots from made from plain old Acme brand cowhide. And those were the women.

A valet asked for the keys to his car. Dodd recognized him as one of the bank tellers. He wore a white dinner jacket two sizes two big, most likely a rental. Dodd passed the valet a couple of dollars and the valet grinned. "You're not from around here are you?"

"First tip today?" Dodd asked.

"First tip," the valet said.

"I'm surprised the Raffertys would spring for a valet."

"You think they're paying me?" the valet said. "I'm still on salary at the bank. And I'm not really here to valet so much as keep the yokels from pissing on his lawn."

A high school student picked up Dodd in a golf cart and jockeyed him to the picnic. Three other golf carts sat idle next to the first row of parked cars, their jockeys sharing a cigarette. Dodd figured he must be a late arrival. The little cart cruised down a gravel path, kicking up bits of rock in every direction. "You should a got here already," the driver told him. "They already kilt half the kegs."

Dodd was temped to tell the kid he had, in fact, got here already, but decided the kid might then need him to explain.

No one farmed the Rafferty property. It stretched over thirty or forty acres, grassy and fallow. A dozen horse stalls lined a large parade ring between the house and the picnic tables. A tiny four rafter grandstand sat on the other side of the ring, supporting a handful of spectators who watched a woman in uniform parade her horse around the ring.

A trim woman who looked to be in her late thirties stood between the grandstand and the parade ring, calling instructions to the rider. Her voice was lost in the roar of drinkers staking out their territory beside the row of kegs, spilling beer on the ground and laughing harshly, occasionally wandering off to refill their plates before reclaiming their places in the keg line. If it weren't for the slight touch of frost in her hair and a few extra sun tan lines, the caller would have been a ringer for Mary Beth Rafferty.

Two Chicanos stood at each side of the barbecue pit, sweating beside the dull red coals and turning a hog over the embers, a hog so large it could pull the truck bed off a three quarter ton pick up. Both grinned and nodded their heads when passers-by made relatively tasteless jokes such as, "Don't stand too close to those flames. Grease fires are hard to put out." Dodd figured they didn't speak English or were immune to this kind of nonsense. The Chicanos he knew at Huntsville would have slipped their shivs between the wise asses' ribs before they could finish the word "grease."

Nonetheless, the entire scene impressed Dodd. He'd envisioned the population of Sweet Water Falls as small. In the dozens. This crowd was closer to two hundred. The five right reverends circled the picnic tables like hawks looking for helpless souls who got separated from the crowd. The picnickers, in turn, tried to dodge their impending salvation and balance their beer and barbecue at the same time.

The smaller crowd watching the riders sat with their drinks, mostly cocktails, traded comments as each new rider passed by. A few others floated around in small pockets of two to four people, drinks in hand and standing near their cars, wandering around the stables, playing horseshoes or croquet, or simply walking past the house and shaking their heads at the size.

The heaping plates of ribs and sausage began to look too good to resist. Dodd slipped in line behind a three-hundred pound farmer who watched carefully as the butcher layered slab upon slab upon even more slabs of sizzling, grease-dripping ribs. "Why don't you make two trips, Harlan?" the butcher asked. "There's plenty of ribs to go round."

"I am making two trips," Harlan insisted. He stood his ground until two or three-dozen baby back ribs seemed ready to fold the plate down the middle and topple the pile into the dirt. He glanced coldly at Dodd and carried his plate off to a picnic table, one hand balancing the plate from underneath, the other hand securing the ribs from above.

The butcher watched him walk off, holding his carving fork at his waist. "To watch him eat, you'd never know that man has a hundred acres himself. The beef probably came from his cattle."

"Maybe he thinks Rafferty short changed him and wants to get his money's worth." Dodd meant it as a joke.

"Sounds like you done business with Rafferty." He tucked a tong under his arm and held out a hand. "Name's Will Gaylord.

Own a rib house outside Fort Stockton. I'm catering this affair. Of course, Rafferty wants a volume discount on top of a second discount because he supplied the beef."

"Why didn't you let him hire someone else?"

"He holds my mortgage and business note. Kind of puts me in a bind, doesn't it? I cooked for four hundred people and I'll be lucky if he pays me two grand. That includes the beer. Barely enough to break even."

"What's the hog for?" Dodd asked.

"Mostly show, but this crowd'll eat that too," Gaylord said. "Then they'll think of Rafferty as their benefactor when he gouges them the rest of the year."

Dodd asked for two links and two ribs. Gaylord obliged and poured a thick brown sugar, hickory smoke and mustard sauce over the meats. "You're the guy the Meekers hired to run their business affairs. Real strange stories people tell about you. Some folks say you're a lawyer, some say you was in jail."

"Both. But people like me better if they only know the jail part."

"Well Joe Bob still hasn't paid me for the county-wide law enforcement dinner I catered last April. Could you look into it maybe?"

"What did Joe Bob say when you asked him?"

"He asked if my equipment was up to code. I got the message. I just was hoping against hope that maybe you had his ear."

Dodd waved his barbecue under his nose, savoring the scent of burnt flesh and brown sugar. "Be glad he didn't pay you. And that you're outside his jurisdiction. Knowing Joe Bob, he'd hire someone to break into your restaurant and steal it back and smash a few tables to make his point."

Gaylord spit into the grass. He looked at Dodd with the eyes of a cow waiting for the slaughterhouse. "You learn the ropes quick."

Dodd stepped back to let the man behind him in the line shovel seconds on to an already red and runny paper plate.

This farmer weighed even more than Harlan. He couldn't have been more than five three and his overalls gapped open at the side, with thick rolls of belly pushing their way out to check the weather. He stacked the ribs and sausages so high onto his plate he could barely hold them in place, a practice that Dodd was beginning to believe must be local custom. He trotted over to catch up with Dodd.

"Look forward to this event all year. Sweat my ass from June on to lose thirty or forty pounds and then I pig out on Rafferty's tab. Gain it all back in one night."

Dodd shuddered to think of how much meat that man must pack into his stomach to gain thirty pounds in a single night.

The farmer stuck his own meaty paw out to shake. Dodd winced as he tried to juggle his plate and accept the farmer's sticky, sauce-covered grip with his free hand. "Will Ellerd. Old man's Carroll Ellerd. That's spelled with two r's and two l's so nobody won't think he's a girl."

Dodd tried to wipe the sauce discreetly off his hand by running it down the back of his jeans. "That's real interesting, friend."

The farmer ripped the meat from a thick rib with his teeth and continued to talk even as he pulled the meat into his mouth with his tongue: "Naw, you don't get it. My old man, he was friends with your old man. He asked me if I see you would I send you his way. He don't walk good no more so we set up his wheelchair over where he can see them girls on the horses. Then my wife an I leaves him alone for the rest of the night. You should meet my wife too, but I imagine she's back in the chow line again. That girl's got a hell of an appetite."

"Sorry to tell you," Dodd interrupted, "but my family's not from anywhere near here. All those rumors about me and any other Dodds are just rumors."

Ellerd winked, smothering his eye in a landslide of flesh. "The old man's got hunting pictures with you boys in them, well not you, you boys, but your uncles and your old man, those you boys. You got the cheekbones and the jaw. Mama changed your diapers. Old man let you hold his beer can rings. You gotta be too young to remember him an all, but he sure as shit do remember you."

The sudden silence caught Dodd by surprise since he hadn't been able to pry an opening into the conversation until just that second. In fact, Ellerd only stopped talking when there was nothing left in his mouth left to chew.

"My family's from Louisiana. Any resemblance is purely coincidental."

Now that it was time to talk again, Ellerd devoured another rib. "Mum's the word. I won't tell nobody. Promise. But my old man's really lonely for company. And you'll like watching them girls ride. Their titties bouncing with them horses and all. Makes me wish I was the saddle and they was riding up on my horn." He winked at Dodd twice. Dodd couldn't believe two eyelids that fat could move that fast.

"You bet, Will. I'll talk to your old man."

Ellerd pointed his meatless rib at Dodd. "See, you're being all agreeable now. You'll take a shine to my old man. He's all agreeable too."

"I'll keep my eye out for him," Dodd promised. He made a hasty exit to the iced tea table before he could get trapped in further conversation.

The woman serving tea surveyed him from boot tip to hairline. "You're too pretty to be from round here," she said. She was a tiny woman in her fifties with grey hair and jerky skin. With limbs like twigs and not even five feet tall, she looked like the wind would carry her away with the rest of the tumbleweeds. Her voice sounded like jeep tires on gravel, the kind of voice earned with late nights drinking rye whiskey, chain smoking and singing with the band at the top of her voice.

"I was thinking the same myself, ma'am," he said. He took the Styrofoam cup from her, and she ran her finger along his. Dodd wondered what it was with the local women. Was there Spanish fly in the well water or did the husbands spend too many nights with the cows?

He slipped away as deftly as he could and took a sip of tea. He almost choked. He didn't know why Texans poured more sugar in their iced tea than water, but this was no exception. Maybe they did it to give the Baptists an excuse to drink beer.

He juggled his plastic glass and food all the way to the grandstand. He spotted Ellerd's father sitting in a wheel chair on the east side. Dodd slipped around to the west side, and sat on the ledge. He arranged his plate and napkins on his lap, his tea at his feet where he could conveniently forget it, and relaxed to watch the riders.

The ring was arranged in an oval. Two judges sat in a small trailer at the west end and riders entered from the east. A series of letters circled the rim and the woman calling instructions would refer to them. "Free walk to H, circle to M, controlled trot with rise to C."

Dodd had an easy time recognizing the current rider underneath the helmet and jacket. Those were definitely Mary Beth Rafferty's legs straddling the horse's ribs. She wore a trim yellow English riding jacket with white pants and knee high riding boots. As the horse trotted, she rose up and down in her saddle without using reins, telling the horse what to do with her body and her motions.

She finished her routine in the center of the ring. She and her horse, a black Arabian with a braided mane, bowed in a salute to the judges, then turned and trotted to the eastern exit. Everyone stood up to clap, and Dodd dropped his plate down to join the applause. A new rider entered the ring, and the crowd fell silent immediately.

The rider pulled off her cap and let her red hair cascade across her shoulders. Marla Mayfield. From the crowd's reaction, Dodd figured there must be serious competition between the two girls. It certainly would be hard to give Marla a warm reception when most of the audience owed their livelihood to Mary Beth's old man and yet they cheered her anyway.

Marla guided her pinto into the center of the ring to salute the judges. Her red jacket matched the red-brown in the pinto's colors perfectly, and her white piping accented the jacket as his white patches accented his coat. Her legs seemed to be sculpted to fit her boots.

Dodd, who knew nothing about horses, could tell that Marla could outride Mary Beth blindfolded, backward and strapped to the bottom of her horse. Mary Beth executed every move precisely, but Marla and her horse read each other's minds, switching from one task to the other effortlessly.

"That bitch," someone said at his shoulder. The woman who said it spoke under her breath, lips pursed, so only Dodd could hear. He glanced up to see Mary Beth standing at his shoulder.

"She seems quite graceful." He immediately knew it was the wrong thing to say.

"She's a cunt," Mary Beth insisted, slightly louder this time. "She must have paid six hundred for that outfit. Where does she get that kind of money? Probably letting some oil man with oily skin ride high in her saddle. She probably had to hang the dollars on the laundry line until all the oil dripped off."

Dodd decided this would be a good topic to dance away from. "Is that your mother calling the routines?"

Mary Beth crossed her arms and nodded. Her toe was planted firmly into the ground and one heel ground firmly into her calf. "Everybody says we look alike, but I don't see it. She has no passion. She's just a dried up old hag."

Dodd watched Mary Beth's mother glance at her notes and call the next move. She wore an outfit similar to Mary Beth's, accented with small but expensive pieces of jewelry–a diamond ring and two diamond earrings. Her hair fell into place around the curves of her face and head, and she showed only the slightest traces of crows feet at the corners of her eyes. Only the thin but slightly loosening skin at her neck gave her age away.

"How do you ride without holding the reins?" Dodd asked.

"It's dressage," she explained. "You communicate with your horse through your body movements. It requires more skill but it gives you more control over your horse."

Marla saluted the judges and rode from the circle. The crowd applauded, with a lot more enthusiasm than they had for Mary Beth.

"Bitch," Mary Beth said. "I won two regional championships before she came along. Now the judges just want to fuck her."

Dodd didn't point out that the two judges in the trailer were women.

"Do men compete?"

Mary Beth laughed. "In the Olympics, yes. Tell that to the men in this town and they'll think it's queer. Our men go off to their offices and ranches every day so we can lead lives of leisure. If this was an event men put together, they'd ride into the rings with guns and shoot at each other until only one horse was left standing. Then they'd sell the horse and rider for stud rights."

"I missed you last night," Dodd said.

She turned her face up to his with her mouth screwed into a small circle, like a lock. "You don't own me," she said.

"I don't want to own you. I just said I missed you. You told me you wanted to see me last night, remember?"

This time she looked away toward her shoulder. Then down. "Something else came up. All right? Surely you don't think my life revolves around you."

Dodd knew where this was going. He'd been there plenty of times before. Something had changed; someone new entered the picture, Dodd had done or not done something that pissed her off since he last saw her. Something too unforgivable to discuss. Anything he said now, especially any question he might ask to illuminate the situation, would only drive the wedge more deeply between them.

"Give me a call when you want some company."

Mary Beth started to fidget. Even that little bit had been too much. "Shit, I left my cigarettes in my purse," she said. She began to dance, ever so slightly, on her toes. "You've got my number."

Actually, Dodd thought as she rushed away, he didn't. He picked up his plate and cup and tossed them into the nearest barrel.

"She does that to men," a woman said from behind him. Christ, Dodd thought, that's twice in fifteen minutes. He turned around to find Rhonda Mayfield standing at his shoulder. "Mary Beth, I mean. She always says her mother's an ice cube, but I've never seen her thaw for a man either." She wore blue jeans and a plaid western shirt with snaps, penny loafers and a ponytail.

Dodd felt awkward standing with this woman, knowing her sleeping arrangements better, perhaps, than she did. "Your daughter's a lovely rider."

Rhonda closed her hands in front of her. "She takes my breath away. I never had that grace with horses or men. She tames every beast she touches. And she's good with money too. I make twice as much and I couldn't afford to buy those outfits, much less stable that horse. I hope she has better luck with men than I have."

"Women these days would say you were pretty lucky not being hooked up with one."

"Not around here, Mr. Dodd. There are no women's libbers around here. I'm certainly no women's libber."

Dodd laughed. "Well, ma'am, I didn't mean to imply you were."

She stepped closer, and placed her hand tentatively onto the middle of his chest. "Are you sure I couldn't persuade you to have supper with me tomorrow night?"

"I think my other engagement just got broken, don't you?"

She blushed deeply. "I wouldn't presume to...."

Dodd put his finger on her lips. "I'd be delighted to have dinner."

She perked up, bringing her shoulders in. "Maybe you would dance with me when the music starts tonight?"

Dodd wondered what Rafferty would think about his dancing with the man's mistress at his own barbecue. What the hell, he told himself, if the man's fucking her daughter, he doesn't have a lot of room to complain.

Even as he thought those thoughts, Mal Rafferty seemed to appear beside them, almost emerging from the wood smoke and the darkening sunset. Rhonda blushed again. "Oh, excuse me." She dashed off before Dodd could say any thing.

Rafferty watched her rush off, puzzled by what her sudden departure. "Did you say something to offend her?"

"She begged me not hurt your kind and generous family, who kept her employed all these years. You've got the whole town convinced I'm one of those Dodds."

The sun seemed settled in for the night. Rafferty was illuminated only by the fire from the barbecue pit and the arc lamps bar-b-quing mosquitoes. In the pale light, he seemed more robust than in the daylight, his cheeks more flush and his skin brimming with color. "That's not any of my doing. But I was hoping you would join me in my office to discuss a business proposition."

"To negotiate how quickly can I get out of town?"

"I think we're seeing the same stripe down the center of the road." He pulled a pewter cigar case from his pocket and offered Dodd a stubby cigar. "Cohiba."

"Actually, I promised that old man I'd bring him another beer." Dodd nodded to Ellerd. "He wants to tell me stories about family I never had."

Rafferty's face turned darker than the surrounding shadows. He inserted the tip of his cigar into a pewter cutting tool. "Fifteen minutes to discuss a small investment with a potentially lucrative return."

"Fifteen minutes," Dodd said. "In half an hour." He didn't give Rafferty a chance to answer, slipping away and wedging his way through the crowd.

The riding contest seemed to be over. The spectators cleared out. Marla accepted a sizable trophy from the judges while Mary Beth stood fuming with a less than sizable trophy.

A half-ton pick up pulled a flatbed stage in front of the bleachers. A van painted with psychedelic horses tumbling over stars and smoke followed. Three men with shoulder-length hair and cowboy boots set up sound equipment while a fourth ran power cables to a generator beside the stable.

The band members barely missed tripping over Ellerd's father several times. He sat in his wheelchair a few feet from the grandstand. Dodd figured the son must have parked him there for the night, and no one in the band had figured out it would be easier to move him than to keep tripping over him.

Dodd sighed and walked to Ellerd's wheelchair. "You want a better seat, old timer?" Dodd asked. "These fellows can't seem to steer clear of you."

Ellerd tried to angle his neck to get a better look at Dodd. Unlike his son, Ellerd was bone thin, and he sat with a greasy, empty paper plate in his lap. His skin stretched tight across his skull as though someone had tucked a flap and stapled it behind his neck. His left nostril flared upward in a permanent sneer. His polyester shirt looked so old, Dodd thought it would fall away at the seams to reveal a skeleton underneath. "Who the hell are you? Where's my fat ingrate of a son?"

"He's lined up for chow."

"That's a polite way of putting it. I'm sure he's got his mouth wrapped around the end of a picnic table waiting for that hog wife of his to lift the other end and shovel it all down his throat. The farm don't turn a profit anymore, that boy eats it."

"Do you want me to move you or not?"

Ellerd waved his arms around. "Move me, leave me here what do you care? You ain't kin."

"Suit yourself," Dodd said, taking his hands from the grips.

"Well, maybe over by the keg," the old man said. "Maybe somebody'll take pity on me and spill some beer on my face so I can lick it off."

Dodd pushed the wheelchair toward the keg. "You're a sour old bastard. I don't think I ever heard a human being complain about so many things in the span of five minutes."

"You don't like the company, you can look for better... Wait," he put his hand on Dodd's wrist as Dodd began to walk away again. "I know you. You're Zack Dodd's boy. I told Will about you."

"Name's Dodd, Mr. Ellerd, but my father's name wasn't Zack."

"So you say, but I shot squirrel with those boys and I can see perfectly well you're one of 'em. You come back for it, ain't ya?"

"Would you like me to get you a beer?"

"It makes me piss," Ellerd sneered. "You gonna wheel me to a Port-A-Can too?"

Dodd considered the possibility that leaving the old man alone at the grandstand was too kind for him. He should have dropped him off at the land fill. "Ungrateful son-of-a-bitch too, aren't you?"

Ellerd's eye twitched like he was blinking away a bug. "Ungrateful? How'd you like sitting in a puddle of piss in a wheelchair? Son-of-a-bitch son of mine wouldn't clean it up. Smell like piss till Christmas. But we was talking about the flying saucer. You come back for it. Right? Now that it's safe and all."

The band powered up for their sound check. The guitar players hammered their strings. The drummer ran riffs across his snare and toms. He tightened the heads and ran the riffs again. The vocalist pulled on a jacket made from reptile skin and battered the audience with, "Check, mike check, one-two-three, check."

Dodd laughed. "You people are crazy, but you're the craziest, old man. Why would I come to this town to dig up a flying saucer? After all this time?"

"Because it was radioactive. That's why the government couldn't get it all. It was too radioactive for their suits. Something about a half-life. The flying saucer would kill you until all its radioactive rays went away."

"Who told you this?"

"Your uncle Zack, boy. Before that son-of-a-bitch sheriff shot him in the back."

"Now see, everyone else that tells me this story says Zack and the other brother got away."

The old man sloshed his tea in his lap. "Don't you believe it. The Meekers ambushed those boys. Shot Zel and Zack in the back. Only one got away was Zane and the Rangers shot him in the back later. You don't think they're hiding something when they have to shoot every body in the back?"

"And you think they're hiding a flying saucer?"

"Hell, yes, they're hiding a flying saucer. I don't know where it is, but it's out there, on the Dodd ranch."

The band stuck up Jambalaya. Dodd waited for the fiddle to cut in. Then he realized there wasn't a fiddle on the stage.

"How do you play Jambalaya without a fiddle?" he asked, not realizing he said it out loud.

"Ain't you heard a word I said?" the old man shouted over the music.

"I heard it all. About flying saucers and everybody getting shot in the back. You can't play Jambalaya without a fiddle. That's like playing Foggy Mountain Breakdown without a banjo."

Ellerd tugged his belt. "Well these boys went and done it didn't they? There it is. Jambalaya. They're playing it. No fiddle. Now're you listening to me or not?"

"Of course, I'm listening to you. How is it you know for sure there's a flying saucer on the Dodd ranch?"

Ellerd slammed his cup on the arm of his wheelchair. "I told you, goddam it. Cause your uncle Zack told me. It was a big secret. The government told him not to tell anybody."

"So why did he tell you?"

"I don't know. He just told me."

Dodd shook his head. "Let me get this straight. The government tells a guy to keep something absolutely secret so he immediately blabs it to you?"

"He didn't just come over blabbing about a secret flying saucer. He wanted to sell me the property cause they was having money troubles. They was barely making it as it was then the government ruined it for them. Tore up their farm, ruined their crop. Come harvest, they were going belly up."

Dodd stroked his chin, pretending to take the information in and seriously think about it. The band segued from Jambalaya to Rocky Top Tennessee, electric guitar, bass and drum in accompaniment. First a song you should never play without a fiddle and now one you should never play without a banjo. In spite of Dodd's misgivings, the crowd cheered.

Then again, he figured they would cheer at at a steel guitar rendition of Ave Maria considering how many empty kegs had already been rolled aside. Purple Haze on acoustic guitar.

"Sound like that's a motive to rob the bank isn't it? They were going belly up?"

The old man beat Dodd's arm with his fist.

"You don't get it. How were those boys going to rob a bank that was closed on Christmas Eve when they got no explosives, two squirrel guns and a pickup truck won't go better than forty miles an hour? And what the hell was Rafferty doing on his bank on Christmas Eve?"

"Counting his money?" Dodd suggested. He'd heard more conspiracy theories than he could count on both hands on the inside. He hated to admit it, but he loved being part of one, as stupid as it sounded.

"Fuck you," Ellerd said and looked at his lap.

Dodd put his hand on the old man's shoulder to reassure him. "Okay, I'm being an ass. But let me get this straight. Zack Dodd told you there was a flying saucer to get you to buy his farm?"

"Not get me. He wanted to sell me his farm. While he was trying to sell it, he just happened to bring it up."

"Would you have bought their farm without the flying saucer?"

"Hell, no," the old man said, leaning forward in his wheelchair as though Dodd had insulted him. "That was about as useless a piece of shit land as you can get. They could barely float on a good season."

Dodd patted him on the arm. "Seems to me you came up a sentence short when you bought that story."

The old man threw his cup at Dodd, spilling the last dregs of sugary tea into the grass. "I don't get you, young fellow," but by that time Dodd was wandering away. Since Rafferty wanted to see him in his office, he decided he might as well head that way now. Being a little early wouldn't hurt.

Dodd strolled past the revelers who danced and shouted to the music. He realized that the whole barbecue was laid out to keep people away from the Rafferty house. The port-a-cans actually stood between the keg line and the house, the riding ring was built at the far end of the clearing and the barbecue pit was half-a-football field further down.

Dodd found the gravel driveway even in the dim light of the evening. He followed it back to the house. He wasn't good at estimating square feet but he would have guessed from first sight that the Rafferty's could put the whole county up for the night.

The house was completely dark except for the lights on the verandah and those in the entry hall. Even the rich have to worry about their electric bill, Dodd figured.

He didn't know what the proper etiquette for entering the house for a meeting would be, so he walked onto the verandah and tried the doorknob. It was locked, but within seconds the door swept inward and Dodd found himself facing a bouncer wearing a sharkskin jacket, just a kid no older than twenty-two and sporting the long sideburns that, with the sole exception of this guy, hadn't been sported since the seventies.

"You heard of a door bell?" the bouncer said. His jacket shoulders stretched at the seams, but buttoned loosely at the waist. Dodd figured this kid took the Charles Atlas ads at the back of his comic books to heart. No one would be kicking sand in his face.

"You need to lose those sideburns," Dodd said. "People will think you're gay."

The bouncer placed his palm flat against Dodd's chest. "What's wrong with being happy?" He pronounced "being" with one syllable, like, "been." "Now turn around because the party's outside, bud." He pushed Dodd back toward the door.

Dodd blocked the door with his elbow. "Hold on there, bud." He spat "bud" out in precise imitation. "Rafferty asked me to meet him in his office."

"Bud" stiffened. "Mr. Rafferty don't ask nobody. He tells. And he didn't say nothing to me about no visitors." Again, "didn't" was collapsed to a single syllable, "dent."

Dodd pressed closer, his hand on the bouncer's chest. "Does he have to?"

The kid thought about it for a second, and for a second Dodd actually thought he would be stupid enough to let him through the door. But then Dodd saw the light flash, and the kid told him, "He does," and proceeded to push him back through the door.

"For God's sake let him in, Dylan," a woman's voice called. The bouncer stepped back to let Dodd through the door. Dodd had no problems recognizing her, Mary Beth's mother. "You can be nicer to guests, you know. Mal's a banker, not a gangster."

The woman had changed from her riding outfit into jeans and a man's work shirt with sleeves rolled to the elbows. Her feet were bare, the nails painted a deep crimson. Her fingernails were glossy but clear. Dodd wondered why women painted their toenails but not their fingers, but when he got one alone he was always too busy hitting on her to ask. She held her hand out, dangling at the wrist, for Dodd to take. A diamond bracelet dangled from the wrist as well and the diamond on her wedding ring could have dwarfed one of Dodd's molars. Her other hand held a martini glass frosted up from the bottom. Her voice was slightly frosted too, anesthetized by the alcohol. "I understand you, on the other hand, come from a family of thugs and gangsters."

She waved her free hand toward Dylan. "Go. Leave us alone."

Dylan shuffled back to the door, throwing his shoulders back and his chest out to show he was only obeying orders and not being pushed around by a lush.

Dodd took a second to examine the room. The size of it brought him up short. He imagined airline hangers smaller than this room. The room was absolutely bare except for a large buffet and an even larger gun rack on the west wall. Dodd studied the gun rack, which sported more than two-dozen hunting rifles, including a .450 Webley Nitro double barrel, a Rigby .500 caliber sidelock, and a .470 Purdy 12-bore side-by-side hammerless–none of which Dodd could imagine being used around Sweet Water Falls. At the bottom of the cabinet, settled into its plush velvet case, was a long barreled Smith and Wesson .38, chrome plated with pearl handles.

A small stage was recessed into the opposite wall, with curtains behind it. A single, crystal chandelier fell like an octopus from the ceiling, each arm slowly unfolding until it literally exploded into dozens and dozens of light.

Nothing in the room impressed him, however, except for Mary Beth's portrait, life size and displayed on the east wall in a gilded frame underneath a spot light casting a soft-focus glow across her neck and shoulders. She seemed to glide in clouds, the faintest of gossamer gowns doing little to hide the curves of her breasts, stomach and thighs.

"It's not my daughter," Mrs. Rafferty assured him, "It's me. She would never display such grace or class for portraiture. My daughter would drop her pants, flop on her bed, spread her legs and say, 'Snap that Polaroid. I'm in a hurry.'"

Dodd looked at the portrait again and then back at the woman. Sure enough she was the subject and not Mary Beth. But only the subtlest of differences betrayed her. Her hair had been slightly darker once, and her nose thinner, flaring out only slightly at the nostrils. But the body.... Dodd shook his head. Their bodies were ringers.

"It's a lovely portrait, ma'am," Dodd said.

"Not half so lovely as I am, don't you think?"

"I had a friend in prison who once told me never to come between a mother and a daughter. Both vent their wrath on you and end up closer friends than ever."

She laughed and pushed back a lock of hair dangling over his forehead. "Mr. Dodd, in a town this insulated, sometimes a mother and daughter have to share their toys. It's a fact of life. Why, I share Mal with his secretary and her daughter. You don't see them squabbling do you?"

"Maybe that's because that particular mother doesn't know about the daughter."

She opened her eyes in surprised, and let her fingertips brush against his shoulder. "You are very perceptive for a stranger."

"Most wives wouldn't take their husband's infidelities with so much grace."

"It's not fair to change the subject. Mal's job is not to be some stud pony in my pen. His job is to keep me rich. When he finally departs from this world, I want to remember him fondly for all the security he left me."

She glanced over his shoulder, "Ah, here's the dear man, now." Even as she said it, her eyes gave way to an alcoholic glaze.

"Were you talking about me, Elizabeth?" Rafferty asked, emerging from a dark corner of the room.

The glaze in her eyes turned into a permanent frost. "Why, Mal, when you're the only subject of interest in this town, what else is there to talk about?"

Rafferty seemed to glide across the ballroom floor. He leaned into her neck to give her the slightest nibble. "Is that so? I never knew you to be concerned about a man's success at work. I would have thought you didn't think about men at all, at least not outside the bedroom."

She touched the back of his hand with her finger. "Sometimes, we all are shaken from our reveries, dear."

Dodd cleared his throat. "Listen, if there's a more convenient time, I can always swing by later."

Rafferty laughed, his lips blood red in the light of the room. "Don't be so hasty. In fact I was tempted to comment how civil things had become. Younger men bring out the best in her." He adjusted the collar of his wife's shirt, to cover her neck just slightly. "Let's retire to my office."

Rafferty's hand waved ever so slightly as they walked away. To Dodd's surprise, a door he hadn't noticed simply opened in a far corner. They entered a dark corridor with solid oak walls and plush brown carpet. The hallway was dimly lit by a row of electric lanterns, each barely glowing.

Rafferty pulled open a massive door at the far end. Rafferty guided Dodd inside with a firm hand on his shoulder. A single neon desk lamp cast its faint light across the room.

The neon desk lamp made the room only barely more bright than the dimly lit hallway. It was turned away from the desk and toward the room, which was paneled with mahogany stained darkly and chocolate carpeting. The desk was also a dark-stained mahogany—a lodge-style executive desk, with an inlaid marble writing surface.

On the far wall stood a buffet underneath a portrait of Rafferty's father, a dour man, with a thin face, narrow neck and no hair. As best Dodd could tell, Rafferty took after his mother. The furniture was western style, red leather in dark wood. The walls were ornamented with two southwestern desert prints, ram horns, deer horns and a bear's head. A gun rack hung behind Rafferty's desk sporting a Winchester 76 lever action and a 1906 slide action rifle.

Rafferty steered Dodd to a seat in front of his desk. The only ornamentation included a simple digital clock, a pewter cigar clipper and a gold fountain pen.

"I guess you're not a morning person," Dodd said.

"What makes you say that?" Rafferty asked. He settled into a high-backed leather chair on the other side of the desk.

Dodd shifted his chair so he would be slightly out of the light. "A passing observation."

"A comedian, too."

That isn't how Dodd would have put it, but since he'd been accused of the same thing by principals and prison guards as well, he decided there might just be some truth to it. "You wanted to talk business?"

Rafferty leaned back in his chair and crossed his fingers across his chest. "I want my money back."

Dodd leaned back in the chair and propped his boots on Rafferty's desk. Rafferty squeezed his fingers together, but pretended not to notice. "You know, Mal, I'm getting tired of having the same conversation over and over again."

"Men say one thing and later change their minds."

Dodd rolled his eyes. "Well, if we're going to go all Zen, ducks swim in the water and then they get out. Why don't we talk about something useful?"

Rafferty opened his desk drawer and pulled out a bottle of whiskey. It had a white label, "Scottish Malt Distilleries," with a number stamped above the distilling date, 1945. "I don't drink," Dodd reminded him, wishing, only for a second, that he had postponed his sobriety until after this meeting.

"I'm not offering," Rafferty said. He pulled a hand cut crystal tumbler from the drawer and filled it with the pale red liquor. His eyes were lost in shadows, but Dodd thought he saw two red dots glaring back at him. "I'll give you a twenty-five percent finder's fee." He reached for the glass. Dodd dropped his feet to the floor and put his hand on top of Rafferty's.

"Thirty-five."

Rafferty slipped his drink from under Dodd's hand. "I thought you'd be reasonable."

Dodd laughed. "You're serious?"

Rafferty frowned. "Of course I am."

"You clearly didn't think this through. If I find half a million dollars, why should I give it up for a finder's fee?"

"Because it's my money. Thirty-five percent is more than generous."

"Not as much as a finder's fee of one hundred percent."

"Then you'd be a criminal."

Dodd drummed his fingers on the desk. "If I found half a million dollars, who would it belong to? Not you. The federal trust would've covered the stolen money twenty-five years ago. That makes it their money. So if I give it to you, I'd be helping you steal from the Federal Government."

"Maybe I'd call in the Feds, myself."

"Why? It's not your money. The feds could come after me, but then we have the problem of establishing ownership. If I find a half million dollars there's definitely a presumption that it was the stolen money. But then someone would have to come up with records of serial numbers, and other documents that may or may not exist any more. Even if I play nice and assume there really were serial numbers. By the time the bean counters found them, I'd be in Mexico laundering the money anyway. Maybe the Feds can prove I didn't earn the money, but they won't be able to prove where I got it. Besides, they'd spend that much money on extradition and trials."

"That scenario isn't likely to deter the Federal Government." Rafferty rolled his glass in his fingers, letting the light from his lamp skip across the surface like a sprite. "They'd come after you no matter what. So you can to return the money to them, or return it to me. Their finder's fee would be much less generous."

"Except that the minute I give it to you, I'm aiding and abetting fraud. I passed the bar exam, remember? If I'm going to be honest, I give it to them. If I look for the biggest payoff, well, my choice is obvious."

Rafferty shook his head sadly, as though Dodd had let him down completely. "You are a most disagreeable fellow."

Dodd uncorked the Scotch and filled Rafferty's glass to the rim, so that if he lifted it he couldn't avoid spilling it over the edge. "I'm not going back inside. The only question is whether I take the money and run, or play it safe. So you damn well better hope I don't find any money because I won't be giving it to you."

He stood up and offered his hand.

"We struck no bargain," Rafferty said.

"I just want you to know I offered you my hand. I'll see myself out." He crossed the room, and slipped through the door, closing it behind him. From this side, the corridor looked more like a tunnel disappearing into infinity than the hallway of a home, even a spacious one. He counted off his steps, looking to his left for some sign of the door that would get him into the ballroom, or at least another hallway.

About half way down, another corridor veered off. Dodd wondered if that was a new wing of the house. He stepped on something soft and leaned over to pick it up. He found himself holding a pair of women's panties. He sniffed them, recognizing Mary Beth's scent immediately. Musk and perfumed talcum.

He glanced down the new wing and saw a clothes trail on the carpet–jeans, riding pants, riding boots. The yellow English riding jacket outside one of the doors was the tip-off. He'd seen Mary Beth in that jacket when she rode her horse in the ring.

He put his ear to the door. He heard a man laugh and a woman drawl, "Why George, you must have exercised that thing while you were in Amarillo cause I swear it grew."

Dodd felt a finger tap on his shoulder. He turned around to find Dylan standing behind him.

"Did you just find me here, or were you sent to keep an eye on me?" Dodd asked.

"There's a door at the end of the hall, sir. You can walk straight back to the barbecue from there. Mr. Rafferty asked me to make sure you knew you were welcome to stay."

"Hell, son, I knew that. I just was waiting to hear it from you." He pushed himself away from the door and strolled casually down the hall, waving as he went.

The door he'd been leaning against opened. Dodd glanced over his shoulder and saw the back of Mary Beth's head sticking out into the hallway. Her elbow was thrust outward, as though she were holding a sheet around her. "Do you have a problem here, Dylan?"

"No, Miss Rafferty, I don't," he mumbled.

"Then don't be hanging outside my door and don't bring your goddam friends with you."

Her door slammed as Dodd turned the knob to step outside. He wondered how long it would take him to find his Mustang.

Chapter 21

Rafferty pushed the intercom button on his phone as soon as the red light flashed. "Yes, Dylan?"

"He's gone, Mr. Rafferty. Drove out just now. Didn't give me no trouble."

"Thank you, Dylan," Rafferty said, his voice filled with more disdain than thanks. He punched the disconnect button. Ralph sat in front of him, slouched in his chair, hands wrapped around what may well have been his tenth drink of the day, shaking and looking very gray. Joe Bob leaned against the filing cabinet, holding his drink with three fingers. Even in the dim light, he wore his mirrored shades.

"No more excuses, Joe Bob, I want to know who that bastard is." Rafferty said. His voice was flat, even, irritated.

Joe Bob shrugged. "I don't know who he is. Other than that his name really is Dodd Dodd."

Rafferty refreshed his drink. "I can't believe that in America, with computers everywhere you look, we can't identify one ex-convict."

"We don't have computers, Mal," Ralph reminded him.

"The council approved a purchase," Rafferty grumbled. "Last year."

Joe Bob laughed. “That money went to the racetrack campaign, where you wanted it. That’s one of the reasons we’re worried about this bastard, remember? Don’t want him poking his nose in the wrong books?”

Rafferty sat in silence, barely visible to the two men in front of the desk. The small lamp was adjusted outward to put Rafferty’s visitors in the light, not the other way around. “The race track isn’t the topic of discussion. The issue is Dodd and why we can’t prove who he is.”

“This is the best I could do, Mal,” Ralph said. “After the Rangers killed Zane Dodd in Llano his wife Elizabeth was destitute and, as you may recall, suffering from cancer. She turned the boy over to Social Services and checked into a state hospital. She died there in 1961. He ran away from a foster home when he was fourteen and that’s the last record of him. But the kid’s first name wasn’t Dodd. Hell, he didn’t have a first name. Zane wanted to name him Zelbert and Elizabeth refused, so he was just the Dodd kid.”

Rafferty threw his pen at Meeker’s head. Meeker just barely dodged it. “We know the story, Ralph. Joe Bob bounced the little bastard on his knee back when he was still trying to make folks think he was a nice guy. Dodd changed his name. Wouldn’t you if you were coming back to town and didn’t want people to know who you are?”

“If his name was Dodd Dodd when he went to jail, that means he was planning this years ago,” Rafferty said.

“I’d change my name just cause it was Zelbert,” Joe Bob chuckled. “Good thing they’re all dead cause they was sure bad at picking names.”

Ralph ignored his brother. “The point is, Mal, that if he was going to change his name, why not change his last name too? Why pick a name that would rub Dodd in our faces?”

“Because he’s fucking with us,” Joe Bob said. He made a move to perch on Rafferty’s desk, but Rafferty stopped him with a raised hand.

Joe Bob stood awkwardly. “Let’s just get rid of him. Folks’ll just think he blew town.”

Rafferty opened his desk drawer and removed an onyx cigar box, offering a stubby hand-wrapped Partegas to his partners. The men dutifully trimmed their cigars and lit them with the crystal lighter on Rafferty's desk.

"Just tell me what you found on Dodd Dodd." He turned the cigar toward Joe Bob.

"Two arrests, two convictions, one for DWI and assaulting a police officer, the other for armed robbery. The first arrest was in Sabine County and he was young, probably more mouthy than he is now. Coulda been a bullshit charge. You know how Johnny Law can be in that neck of the woods."

"Not really," Rafferty said.

"A real siege mentality," Ralph embellished. "They're almost inbred."

"Get on with it."

Joe Bob drew a thick cloud of smoke through his cigar and let it float to the ceiling. "Dodd says he's from Louisiana. Sabine's right there on the border. I checked with the parishes in the area and there is a couple of Dodd families."

Rafferty studied his drink, his cigar trailing smoke in a thin stream to the ceiling. "Go on."

"He did a year in county. After he got out, he moved to Houston where he went up for armed robbery. Huntsville this time. Only he got his law degree. Secured his own early release. Worked off his parole as a law clerk for the Houston public defenders' office. Passed the bar on his third try, the month he finished parole. Then they let him go."

Ralph nodded vigorously. He leaned across Rafferty's desk with the confidence of man holding a full house. "I told you the boy's on the level. You're just being paranoid."

Rafferty took Ralph's drink away. "I was talking to your brother, not you. You've had too much of this already."

Meeker withdrew, pulling himself back into his chair. "I was just contributing to the conversation."

"Nothing useful. You don't run this operation, Ralph, I do. You don't enforce this operation. Your brother does. What do you do? You run your little stores and buy your nickel and dime real estate and rubber stamp everything we tell you.

Understand?" He settled back into his chair, out of the light. "Why'd they let him go?"

"Just what he claims. He passed the Bar they gave him the sack. Seems there was a story in one of the Houston papers about how the city was planning to hire an ex-convict. His ass was gone in a month."

Rafferty drummed his fingers on the arm of his chair. He didn't look at either of the brothers, but stared at the back wall of the room as though calculating an impossible angle.

"How'd he end up here?"

"He was supposed to get a job in Santa Fe, but he got a little side tracked when my dipstick brother offered him a job." Both men stared accusingly at Ralph.

"I thought you wanted to keep an eye on him. I figured this would be the best way to do it."

Joe Bob opened his mouth to release a smoke ring. It floated above Ralph's head and, just for a moment, seemed about to move down around his neck. "Keep an eye on him for the night, you idiot. I didn't expect you to ask him to stay."

"You told him he had to stay to keep the kid out of jail."

Joe Bob curled his left lip. "No wonder you never win at poker. I was bluffing. I wanted him to leave the kid in jail and move on. Only a dim wit would move into town and agree to parent some snot nosed kid who robbed a store with a shotgun. Unless, of course, a dimmer wit offers him a cushy job doing next to nothing for twenty-five thousand a year."

"He's done a hell of a job. My office never looked so good."

Rafferty rolled his cigar between his fingers. "So what do we do with him?"

"I say nothing," Ralph insisted. "What can he find about his family? It's all buried. If he's here for the money, he's not going to start looking until he thinks we stopped watching. If he's on the level, I've got an administrative assistant to lift my workload."

Joe Bob laughed. He stretched his leg and shook it like a dog's. "You don't do any work now for free. You expect us to twiddle our thumbs while he digs up our money and runs off with it?"

Rafferty interrupted the Sheriff. "Actually, Joe Bob, your brother may be right for once. If Dodd knows we're watching, he'll lay low. Why risk digging up the money when there's good possibility we'll just take it from him? He probably thinks we plan to kill him."

"He'd have good reason to, wouldn't he?" Ralph pointed out.

"Now you're getting sentimental," Joe Bob said.

"The point, gentleman, as I believe Ralph so accurately put it, is that Dodd will start looking when he thinks we've given up. So let's wait him out."

Joe Bob leaned over Rafferty's desk, cigar pointing outward from his thick fingers. "I waited twenty-five years, Mal. I'm goddam tired of waiting. I can't spend my third of money I don't have. So I guess I don't vote for waiting no more."

"Don't forget," Ralph added, "there's more at stake than money."

Joe Bob and Rafferty exchanged puzzled glances, as though Ralph had moved the conversation to a different room without telling them. Then Joe Bob raised his eyebrows. "You think he'll find your flying saucer."

"Let's stay grounded in reality, Ralph," Rafferty said.

Ralph flushed. "It's there. Ask Joe Bob."

Rafferty rapped on the desk so hard the ashtray bobbled. "Let's stay on topic. Ralph says we back off and give Dodd room. Joe Bob?"

"I say lean on the fucker hard till he tells us everything he knows. Then dump him in the river with the other two."

Rafferty held his cigar in front of him and meditated. "You're not using your head, Joe Bob. For one thing, that was a purely rhetorical question. You were supposed to answer, 'Sure, Mal, whatever you think.'" The smoke rising from his cigar seemed to focus his thoughts, draw him to the edge of a steep drop and push him past.

"Dodd came at just the right time. We funneled a lot of taxpayer dollars to legalize gambling and push through our race track. Todd and Rayburn are making a fuss about our civic campaign. Sooner or later someone may want to look at the records. So we make the records point to Dodd. Who's more likely to embezzle county revenues? God fearing honest businessmen, or the ex-convict son of a murdering bank robber looking to get revenge?"

Joe Bob mashed his cigar into the ashtray, splitting the leaves into a hundred pieces. "I'm not giving up the goddam money."

Rafferty leaned back into his seat and blew a thick stream of smoke into Joe Bob's face. "We all have a vote on this, Joe Bob. Ralph proposed it, I vote with Ralph. It's decided. Wouldn't you agree, Ralph?" Before Ralph could open his mouth, he added, "Remembering what I just said about rhetorical questions, of course."

Ralph stared at the whiskey sitting just out of reach at Rafferty's elbow, almost as though he hoped he could dive into the glass and swim away to safety. "I think anything I said now would just be my lips flapping in the forest with nobody there to hear them."

Rafferty held his cigar at his teeth and considered his complaint. "You know what, Ralph? I think you're right." He placed his hands behind his head and stretched his feet under his desk. He didn't bother calling the meeting to a close.

Sunday Morning

Chapter 22

Sunday mornings were the mornings Dodd most enjoyed, mainly because he always dedicated Sundays to doing nothing—no errands; no obligations. If someone wanted him to help with anything on Sunday, Dodd always said he was too busy.

The sun spilled through the windows and into every corner of the kitchen; washing over dust, dust balls, spider webs, rat dirt and every other sign of sloth and resistance to order. This was Dodd's natural state, a celebration of anarchy cultivated by years inside. In public he could look as neat and polished as any lawyer with a Brooks Brothers suit and pearl-handled briefcase, but his soul thrived on disarray.

He toasted his toast in the frying pan, scrambled his eggs and scooped them out on top of the toast. He dipped his mug in the coffee pan and sat at the table with his breakfast and a Zane Gray novel.

Bobby poked his head around the door to his bedroom. "Goddam, are you up already? Hell, it's Sunday and the sun ain't overhead yet. What's wrong with you?"

"You and I going to tube the river," Dodd told him, without looking up from his book.

"Say what?"

"Don't talk Black unless you are Black, son. It's disrespectful to the brothers."

"There ain't no niggers around here."

"Now's as good a time to learn respect as any. You got any shorts or swimming trunks?"

"I might. Why?"

"I just told you. I got a couple of inner tubes from the store on my way home last night. Big mothers, perfect for a lazy water like the water in the gorge. I'm taking a thermos of coffee, but you can bring beer if you like."

Bobby's face twisted like he had sucked on lemon juice and salt water. "Why'd I want to go tubing?"

"I said you could bring some beer if you like. I didn't say a thing about not tubing if you like."

"I might as well be in jail," Bobby moaned. His shoulders collapsed and he fell against the doorframe dramatically. Dodd thought he would melt into a puddle of piss and self-pity any minute now.

"Easy to say when you're not in jail. Trust me, you'd rather be tubing."

They dressed in T-shirts and cutoffs and hopped into the Mustang. The two inflated truck tubes bulged out from his trunk, tied in with a rope.

The sky was already bleached as bone by the blistering morning sun. They drove on a path in the tall Johnson grass beat down by car bumpers, through a landscape of waist high grass and sparsely scattered mesquite trees that appeared to be stretching their sparse limbs for any brief breath of wind they could catch. Grasshoppers catapulted across the car, occasionally bashing into the windshield with the speed of an armor-piercing bullet.

Bobby tossed one leg across the window ledge, his foot brushing the passing grass. He slumped all the way down in his seat, his arms squeezing his chest so tight Dodd thought he might crush his ribs. "This is stupid," he said, then sighed, loudly, and screwed his face together like a squeezed pump.

Dodd drove toward the gorge and then angled south for three miles. He parked at a ledge with easy access to the riverbed and untied the rope. The trunk sprang open and Dodd told Bobby to grab his tire.

Bobby pulled the largest tire from the trunk and headed toward the ledge. Dodd used a piece of rope to tie his stainless steel thermos to the other. Just before Bobby stepped over the edge, Dodd called, "Where are you going?"

Bobby rolled his eyes. "Ain't that the river down there?"

Dodd bounced his tube on the ground and held Bobby's eyes until he knew he had his full attention. "That's where we're getting out." He pointed north. "About a mile and half that way's where we're getting in. If we hustle, it won't take more than half an hour."

Bobby choked. "You don't mean we're gonna walk all that way just to ride on top of a stupid river? Hell, wouldn't it make more sense to swim? Then we'd get all wet."

Dodd pulled a blade of grass from the ground and put it between his teeth. Bobby stood defiantly with his tube planted firmly in the grass as a though it were fortress he was challenging Dodd to storm.

"We either walk to where we're getting in, when we're not tired and before we have our fun, or walk from where we get out, when we are tired and we already had our fun."

He turned around and began walking before Bobby could answer. He didn't look back; he didn't need to. He knew Bobby would still be striking a defiant pose, convinced Dodd would return to negotiate. Dodd was on the other side of a small rise before Bobby came running up beside him, trying to keep the oversized tube tucked under his arm. He dropped it in place and demanded, "You were going to leave me there?"

"It's farther to the cabin than where we're going. You made the right decision."

He walked another forty yards before Bobby picked up his tube and rushed to catch up. Dodd walked another hundred yards. Bobby stopped and then shouted for directions to the cabin.

Dodd didn't look back; he simply pointed east.

"I can't find that," Bobby shouted.

Dodd turned to face him. Bobby's tube lay flat in the grass, Bobby planted one foot defiantly on the rim with both fists pasted firmly to his hips.

"You should've paid attention when I drove," Dodd called back.

He walked another forty yards with Bobby stonewalling. Finally Bobby rushed to catch up again. "I get it. This is some kind of initiation, right?"

Dodd spit out his grass blade and stopped over to pick another. "Nope."

Bobby kept up with him for the most part after that, but not without making a production of blowing hard, clearing his throat, slamming his tube down, stumbling, stomping and generally making as much noise as he possibly could to protest his unfair treatment.

Finally Bobby forced his way into Dodd's path, throwing the tube down as a challenge. "I know what you're planning to do. I ain't no dumb shit. But it ain't gonna work."

Dodd pulled the grass blade from his teeth and passed it to Bobby, who took it before he realized what he was holding. He dropped it like a match burned to the very bottom.

"I'm planning to have fun," Dodd said. "It appears to me that you're planning to continue bellyaching. You can bellyache or have fun. I'm going down the river all the same."

Bobby poked his finger in Dodd's chest. Dodd had seen guys do that on their first day in the yard, just before the lifer they thought they were threatening took them down. "You think you did me a favor keeping me out of jail? Well you're wrong, Dodd. I can handle the biggest nigger come gunning for me. Best get that straight right now."

Dodd raised his eyebrows. "Better not push my luck then." He hefted his tube over his shoulder and started walking again.

"It can't take much to make it in jail," Bobby shouted behind him. "You made it."

Dodd wondered to himself if he was like that at Bobby's age, when he was ready to drive back to Sabine County and show that Deputy just who he could and who he couldn't push around. Before the deputy spun him around, slammed his face into the roof of his cousin's car and snapped the cuffs on both hands with one twist of his wrist. None of which took the wind from him like the quick knee from behind to his balls.

Dodd took off again. Better to walk and listen to Bobby's whining than to listen to it standing still. In another minute, Bobby was back at his shoulder.

"How'd you make it in jail, Mr. You're-Not-So-Tough? Tell me that."

Dodd looked straight ahead. "Same way I kept you out of jail, son. I bluffed. The difference between us is, I was willing to have my bluff called and you weren't."

Bobby stopped again; Dodd kept walking. "What do you mean call my bluff?"

Dodd turned to face him. He bounced his tube in the grass, which was difficult considering the dense stalks and coarse, dry dirt. "You didn't just miss a trick, son, you missed all of them. You were too fucking scared to pull that trigger, which was a good thing because Meeker wanted any excuse to gun you down."

"That's not true," Bobby insisted, letting his tube roll flat in front of him.

"Even if you'd've gone for me I was ready to dive behind the aisle while you shot the store up. You had two shots with a ten-gauge bird gun. What's the worst that could happen? Might've taken the skin and half the muscle off my leg, if I was slower than I wanted to be and your shot wasn't as wild as I expected. But that piddly little birdshot wasn't getting through the shelf with all those cans to the rest of me. Then, after you shot both barrels, because that's exactly what a kid like you would do, I knew Meeker was going to empty his clip and it wasn't going to be into me."

"You can't know that."

"Doesn't matter, does it, Bobby? I called your bluff, and now we're both going to spend a nice day on the river, which is a hell of a lot better than my being laid up in the hospital and your being in the morgue."

Bobby picked up his tube and passed Dodd without a word. Dodd grabbed another blade of grass and let him keep the lead. They walked another half mile before Bobby asked, "So that's what you did in the pen? Call those big bucks' bluff?"

"They aren't bucks, Bobby. And they aren't niggers. They're men. And my strategy was to make friends with the meanest of the lot of them."

"Biggest one in there, huh?" Dodd could see Bobby's ears lift slightly, his first sign of interest all morning.

"No, he was the smallest. He was so small his brother called him Runt, and trust me, his brother was the only one who called him that. This guy was five-three. But when I got in, I heard stories about how he shanked three inmates who threatened him his first day. I knew I better get to be his friend."

"Man," Bobby shook his head. "I couldn't never make friends with no nigger."

Dodd reached over and slapped the back of Bobby's head. "Did they vacuum your brain before you started school? Or is this one of those towns where the whole point of education is not to get any?"

"I got held back twice," Bobby said. He said it with pride.

Dodd spotted a workable path down to the riverbed. They scrambled down the slope, doing their best not to trip over loose rocks. "This sure seems like a lotta work for fun, Dodd," Bobby told him.

"The only thing working today is your jaw," Dodd said. He threw his tube onto the water, turned around and hurled himself backside first into the tube. Ten feet downstream he grabbed a stray root to stop the tube. "Hurry up," he yelled to Bobby. "This water's faster than you think."

Bobby tried the same trick and landed butt down in the water. Dodd grabbed the tube as it rushed by. Bobby swam slowly over and Dodd coached him while he pulled himself through the tube, face first then knees up the middle to pull one ankle through at a time. Dodd released the tube and watched it speed away. Then he let go of the branch and chased Bobby downstream.

"This isn't so bad," Bobby said.

Dodd pulled his thermos out of the water. He unscrewed the cap and poured his coffee.

"That's a neat trick," Bobby said. "I bet I could a tied some beer cans in a net and brought them along. Let the water keep them cold."

"I offered."

"Well I couldn't figure out how to do it till I seed you just now."

Dodd didn't bother to point out that he could have asked.

"Say, Dodd," Bobby asked. "How come you're doing this anyway?"

Dodd leaned his head far back over the tube to dip it into the water. "Cause I like it."

"No, not the tubing. Staying here in town?"

"I don't know. A friend asked me to check it out. I didn't plan on staying."

"Why did you?"

"Ask yourself that. It's on your account I'm still here."

"That's not what Mr. Meeker thinks. He thinks you're looking for something. He's paying me to keep a eye on you. But I think it's more than he's letting on."

"Probably."

A solitary cloud crossed the sun, as rare in August as water in the desert. It drifted over long enough to lower the temperature one or two degrees. Dodd's damp skin felt deliciously chilled, even though he knew the temperature was still pushing one hundred. He closed his eyes and dipped his head back into the water. When he opened them the cloud was well past and the sun white enough to burn his eyes.

"Well don't that worry you when a man like Mr. Meeker gives you a job when he don't even know you? And then shows all that interest in you? Sure would make me wonder."

A hawk circled and dived to the west, no doubt closing in on a field mouse rendered senseless by the heat.

"He wants my flying saucer."

Bobby laughed. "Yeh, sure."

The hawk dove. For a moment, Dodd imagined Rafferty and the Meekers diving to snatch him from the river.

"Ask him. He thinks there's a flying saucer buried somewhere on that farm and that I know where it is."

Bobby pushed himself up in his tube to see Dodd better. "No shit? You mean there's really a flying saucer?" His tube almost capsized. Dodd grabbed the side to keep Bobby from tumbling over.

"No. But if there was, the last place it would visit would be a West Texas poke-in-a-hole like this one."

"Those ain't the stories. You being a Dodd and all. Not that I ever really believed 'em." Dodd was surprised by Bobby's interest.

"So if you already heard all that, why're you pestering me?"

"After a while you get kind of curious even if it sounds all stupid."

"Believe what you want to believe. That seems to be the favorite local pastime." Bobby looked disappointed, and Dodd wondered if he hadn't broken any trust they were building. If the kid wanted to believe in flying saucers, why pull his chain?

Bobby kept his peace for a few minutes. Dodd splashed water over his legs in a futile attempt to reduce the burn from the overwhelming sun.

The river took them around the bend and the island, past the rusting pick-up remains. Bobby craned his neck to see better. "'S'at the truck your uncles was shot to death in?"

"They weren't my uncles," Dodd snapped. He regretted being so sharp the instant he said it. Bobby was finally showing some interest in participating. He softened his tone. "According to local legend that's the truck."

Bobby pointed toward the truck, his eyes wide with excitement. "Shit, you can still see the blood on the rock."

"Your eyes must be better than mine," Dodd said.

Bobby rolled his eyes with exasperation. "Come on Dodd. What could be more cool? One big shootout. Going out in a blaze of glory. A half-million in a suitcase and bullets flying round your ears and shit. It'd be like Butch Cassidy and Sundance Kid."

Dodd sighed. He let his hand trail behind the tube, sending a long ripple upstream. "Keep thinking that way and you'll end up in jail yet. Or just like the Dodds." He paused, then stressed, "The other Dodds."

"Maybe one of them floated down the river right where we're floating now," Bobby rhapsodized. "Blood still pumping into the water. From farmer to bank robber to fish food in one day. Shit, people still talk about 'em twenty-five years later. That'd be a hell of a lot more far out than dying as some store clerk and nobody remembers who you are."

Dodd offered Bobby what was left of the coffee in his cup. Bobby waved it away. He drained it and reached for his thermos.

"Maybe you need a few more years to get perspective. When you're fish food you don't give a shit who remembers you or not. You might want to put off being fish food for a while."

"Jail sure straightened your ass out. It made you into a store clerk for sure."

Dodd screwed the cap back to his thermos. "Maybe I'd've been better off as a store clerk to start with."

They rounded another bend and the pickup was long ago out of sight. Dodd thought to himself that he might have enjoyed this more if he'd come alone.

"How'd you end up in jail anyway?" Bobby asked. "I mean what did they get you for?"

"Which time?"

Bobby started to push himself up in the tube then thought better of it. His eyes were wide, the whites like cream swallowing coffee. "You mean you went more than once?"

"I did a twelve month stretch in county before moving on to the big time."

"Well, both then."

Dodd stretched his head back into the water. He knew some folks loved to tell their life stories. Preacher had been good at that. For Dodd it was just a reminder of how stupid he'd been, which was far more stupid than anyone with any sense would want to admit to. "The first time was in Sabine County. Badassed cops there and me thinking I was a bigger bad ass. A cousin and a couple of his buddies were drinking and driving and he took a curve way too fast. County Sheriff pulls us over. The other guys, being local, they were smart. 'Yes sir' and 'no sir' the whole time he talked to us. Me, I figured this punk cop should give my cousin the fucking ticket so we could be on our way, and I told him so. Before I knew it he kicked the shit out of me, and dropped a couple of joints in my jacket pocket."

One of the finest moments in his life. Head slammed to the roof, arm twisted behind his back and no clue that any of it was coming. Too scared to put a thought in his head and still stupid enough to say, "You can't get away with this. This is fucking America."

Of course, it wasn't America; it was East Texas and he was from Louisiana. The cop elbowed his temple for using "fuck" and "America" in the same sentence. "Son," he said, "you don't have a clue what fucking is, but you're about to."

"I wanted everybody to know I was set up. My mother got a lawyer. He told me to hold my peace and he'd get me off with probation. I told him to get fucked, I'd been set up and beat up. He walked out; they charged me with DWI, resisting arrest, misdemeanor possession and contributing to the influence of minors. All of whom were older than me."

Dodd could see Bobby's eyes wide open and focused on him.

"'Resisting arrest?' I said. 'That's bullshit. I had the bruises, not him. And the sheriff dropped the joints on me. And how can you drive under the influence when you're in the back seat when the sheriff stops the car? If anyone should go to jail it's that fucking sheriff.' So they add charges for assaulting the arresting officer.

"My cousin testified that I did everything the sheriff accused me of. They dropped his ticket. I got twelve months. Shit food, no pay, backbreaking road work, and if I got too smart for my mouth, the guards roughed me up. I got too smart twice, and became a model prisoner after that. The brothers weren't so lucky. They were never allowed to become model prisoners."

"I smell bull shit," Bobby said, following his comment with a loud sniffing noise from his noise.

Dodd splashed water across Bobby's face.

"Smell what you think, kid. That's what happened."

Bobby raised his arms to shield him from the water. "I suppose you ended up in the State prison cause you bad mouthed a cop too."

Dodd tugged on the rope to his thermos so that the cap came out of the water and he could watch it trail behind him. "I deserved to go up that time. After I got out of county, I couldn't get a good job in Louisiana, but with the energy crisis and shit I figured I could hire on in Houston, working the oil rigs."

"Instead you robbed a liquor store, huh."

Bobby tried to hold on to his skeptical expression, but Dodd could see this was the part he was dying to hear.

"A gas station. When I got to Houston, I figured I could walk right into a job, but I was dead wrong. You had to know somebody or know somebody who knew somebody. I got a job as a fry cook at a Whataburger. A buck an hour; below minimum wage. I could barely pay my rent. So one night two work buddies came over with a couple of twelve packs and we got to complaining about how broke we were. Before I knew it we decided to hit some gas stations to get flush. Worked the plan out right there. Never occurred to us that a fry cook and two counter clerks weren't likely to win a Nobel Prize for brains even if we multiplied our IQs and squared the results. We figured we'd drive out to these small joints on the way to Anahuac cause it would be easy to get away before the county dogs came barking."

Bobby was transfixed. No bluffing this time. Dodd thought maybe, just maybe, he could see his own sad story coming.

"So what happened?"

"We got drunker and drunker, we made another beer run, and once we were in the car, my buddy, the guys name was Johnny Cates, says, 'What the hell, boys, let's do it.' Before I know it we're at his old man's house stealing two shot guns and a .44 Magnum. The luckiest thing I did was talking Johnny into leaving the ammo behind. Lucky for me, any way."

Bobby shook his head. "Why'd you do it at all?"

"I was drunk," Dodd reminded him. "Hell, I survived county. I figured felony prison time couldn't be any worse. I was wrong, of course. That's why I don't drink any more. Because the two most stupid things I ever did in my life I did while I was drunk."

Dodd pulled the thermos out to pour another cup of coffee. He balanced the cup on his chest and let the thermos fall back into the water. "We drove out I-10, past Katy, on the way up to Columbus. Drinking non-stop the whole way, getting our courage up. The others are asking me, 'You done time, right? Isn't all that bad is it?' And I'm telling them jail is a cakewalk, which was a bigger load of horse shit than the idea we could be good at armed robbery. They figure if I can do it, they can do it. Before you know it, facing jail time is a badge of honor for everyone in the car.

"So we find this mom and pop gas and grocery, looks like it's just about to close. Johnny goes in with the gun under his jacket and we slide the shotguns down the side of our trousers and walk in a couple of minutes later; shuffle into the first aisle by the door so old pops behind the counter can't see how stiff-legged we are."

"What happened next?" Bobby was grinning now. The kid was eating the story up as though he still thought it would have a happy ending just because Dodd was alive to tell it.

"Johnny takes a six and smokes to the counter and opens his jacket to pull that Magnum out. What we don't know is that the owner is a gun nut like Meeker. Before Johnny can get the gun past his waist band, the owner has a twenty gauge pump aimed at his stomach. So the other guy, Ray Gallagher, and I step up to the counter with our shotguns. It's a Mexican standoff, see, only none of us has a loaded gun. Then, for some reason, I don't know why, Johnny pulled the trigger on the Magnum. Just like that. We all heard the hammer click, and nothing happened. So the owner smiles, pumps the shotgun and blows Johnny all to pieces. Knocks him from the counter halfway down the center aisle, covered with broken glass, ketchup and blood."

Now Bobby's eyes were wide and round. "No shit? He killed him? In cold blood?" Dodd didn't answer, figuring that would speak for itself. Unfortunately, Bobby was more aroused than horrified. "What did you do?"

"What could I do? I dropped my shotgun and yelled, 'The guns ain't loaded. Nobody's is.' My English wasn't as good back then. But Ray doesn't drop his gun, he keeps it aimed at the old man, who pumps again and blows the right side of his head off. So now both Johnny and Ray are down and that son-of-a-bitch is aiming his shotgun at me. I yelled, 'I dropped my gun, mister.' That cold-eyed bastard said once I was dead he could claim he didn't know that and I swear to God he would have shot me too if his old lady hadn't talked him out of it. He even told her, 'Let me be, Martha. It'll be cleaner this way and fewer questions asked.'"

"So what do you do?"

"I got smart. I dropped to my knees and pissed in my pants and told that old bastard, 'Please don't shoot me. Just call the cops and I'll say you didn't know the guns wasn't loaded.' And that son-of-a-bitch was still going to shoot me, except that his wife said she'd divorce him if he did, tell the cops what really happened, and tell the IRS about how he was marking up real sales on the register tape as over rings. That got him to put the gun down."

Bobby shook his head, more in worship than in horror. "Shit. I bet you were scared shitless."

Dodd decided to get the real point of the story. The action sequences weren't having their intended effect. "I did eight years for that robbery and that old bastard never did a day for killing Johnny and Ray. He swore I never said the guns weren't loaded. But let me tell you, had I let those boys put ammunition in those guns we'd've all been dead, and I'll take Huntsville over dead any day."

Bobby whistled and said, "God damn. Nothing cool like that ever happens to me."

Dodd spotted the Mustang at the top of the ledge. He figured it was time to surrender. "This is where we get out." He flipped out of the tube, hooking it with one elbow and swimming to the bank with one arm. Bobby paddled to the side, grabbed a root and floundered to keep the tube from darting downstream.

The dirt and dry grass stuck to their feet and ankles as they climbed the ledge. Dodd noticed they were starting to sport a healthy pink glow. They had to grab at roots to keep from stumbling in the loose, dry soil but they made it to the top without covering themselves in dirt.

They stuffed their tubes into the trunk, and Dodd looped the rope through the lock. “Damn, that’s one exciting story,” Bobby said.

Dodd leaned against the roof with his elbow. “It isn’t meant to be exciting. It’s meant to scare you into staying at that shit job of yours and spending the rest of your days outside of a cell.”

They climbed into the Mustang and Bobby slammed his door behind him. “Yeh, but be honest with me. If you’d a told me this story when you were my age, would you’ve listened?”

Dodd turned the engine over and backed away from the ledge. He could barely resist smacking Bobby’s head so hard he would tumble through the window and into the tall grass.

Bobby shook his head, as though he finally understood something he’d been mulling over. For a moment, Dodd hoped his story had affected him just a tiny bit, but then he said, “You’re right about one thing. I’m glad we did our walking before we hit the river.”

Chapter 23

Dodd didn't tell Bobby the half of it. He still had nightmares, in full color, always starting with a close up of Johnny Cates, covered with broken glass, ketchup and soy sauce, pulling his hand away from his stomach and his intestines falling out, trying to say something to Dodd but not able to say it. A single tear rolled down one cheek and then he looked back down at his intestines, which he was holding in his hand, blood pouring out like water flooding a broken dam. Then his head simply fell forward and his hand fell into his lap and Dodd knew that was it.

Ray Gallager lay on the floor with half his head missing, a spray of blood and pieces of gray matter covering the Nacho Cheese Doritos display behind his body. A large piece of his skull somehow kept its balance on top of a Doritos bag, just beneath 99¢ price label. His gun hand was open and the shotgun rested six feet down the aisle, knocked away by the impact of the blast.

Dodd didn't know how he got to his knees but there he was, in a puddle that he only later realized was his own piss. Then he looked back at the counter and saw the shotgun aimed at him. Not just any shotgun, a twenty gauge pump action shotgun with the barrel sawed off and wrapped in duct tape. No more than four feet from his head.

An older woman behind the clerk, maybe in her fifties, stared at the man with the gun and shouted. "Stop it, Ray. You done killed two of them already."

The old man wasn't even shaking. His eyes looked lean and hard and focused on Dodd. "They was gonna kill us. Can't show no mercy to punks with guns."

Dodd dropped the shotgun to the floor, spinning it so that skipped like a rock for six or seven feet. "I told you it's not loaded. None of them are loaded."

The old man pumped again, and stepped even closer, leveling the barrel at Dodd's head. He felt like he had a load to dump down the back of his pants, but he was already embarrassed enough. He didn't want the cops to carry his body out with pants full of crap as well.

"I swear to God we just wanted your money. We never planned to hurt no one. Check the guns. They ain't loaded."

The woman lit a cigarette. Her hands shook visibly even as her husband stood there cold as stone. "You think the cops're stupid? You think they won't look for bullets in those guns."

The store clerk turned his head slightly and let a gob of tobacco juice fly onto the floor just inches from Dodd's knee. "That's my goddam point. Better for us if they're all dead and the cops think we didn't know those guns wasn't loaded. Way it stands now, my ass is neck deep in trouble."

Dodd began to cry, hating himself for crying, and still picturing the long steel tunnel of the shotgun barrel even when he closed his eyes. "Please, mister, I won't say nothing. Just don't kill me."

The woman saved Dodd. He sure didn't save himself crying and begging. The woman grabbed her ashtray and threw it at her husband, scattering ashes like they tumbled from an urn and hitting him in the hand so hard he almost dropped the shotgun. When the ashtray collided with the old man's hand Dodd knew the gun would go off and he was gone for sure. But it didn't.

"You limp-dicked bastard," the wife yelled. "Shoot that kid and I'll make it hell for you with the cops. I'll tell them every thing. How he begged for mercy and how you shot him anyway."

The old man dropped his shotgun to his side." Go right ahead. Your word against mine. Think they're gonna take the word of a badgering bitch like you that I should of left a long time ago?" Dodd didn't dare move even though the gun was aimed away.

"Then I'll call up that guy at the IRS that put you through the ringer last year. I'll tell him how you go back at the end of the night and add over rings to the register tape so you don't have to report all we made. Once you get those bastards on your back, they stay on it. You think about that before you try something with that kid."

Now the old man lifted his gun at the old woman. As soon as he did, Dodd ducked behind an aisle and out of the way, dropping his head between his knees and wrapping his fingers behind his neck the way they had taught him for air raid drills.

The old woman kept yelling. "Go ahead, shoot me you bastard. You think the cops'll think I was one of them robbers? No way. Kill me and I'll be done with you, you old fat bastard, and then they'll fry your ass till your nothing but a puddle of grease beneath the electric chair."

Dodd sat behind the aisle in his wet pants, with his head between his knees and his fingers behind his neck crying and telling God he would never do another bad thing again if this son-of-a-bitch didn't kill him, and listening to the couple yelling until he heard the sirens from the county deputies car and felt someone grab his wrists so they could slap the cuffs on.

"I was never so fucking glad to end up in jail," he said to Preacher, when he first told his story.

"Started getting smart that very day, didn't you?" Preacher said, bumming a cigarette off him. "Be getting some priorities."

They sat on a bench in the prison yard, shirts off, in the late July heat—Preacher chain smoking, Dodd feeding him cigarettes. They bunked one cell apart, and when it came to cigarettes, their relationship had become symbiotic. Preacher smoked, Dodd fed him the cigarettes.

According to Preacher it worked out for the best. None of the brothers would bum smokes off a white boy, none of the white boys would bum smokes off a white boy that loaned all his cigarettes to a nigger, and this way none of the brothers could bum cigarettes from Preacher. In fact, when Alvin sent Preacher a dozen cartons of Luckies in a care package, the cartons went right to Dodd.

"Bet looking at that shotgun scared the outlaw life right out a you," Preacher laughed.

"Scared the stupid out of me."

A guard crossed the prison wall on the far end of the compound and gave them both the evil eye. They moved slightly further apart so no one could accuse them of conspiring.

"Be getting ten years worth of wisdom during one quick piss, you might say."

"You might say. First time I got out of county, I had a hard time finding good work. A year on your record before you're even eighteen, people take a shorter look at what you can do and a longer look at what someone else can do. So I'm stuck as a fry cook, hell, a fry cook's assistant, figure I'm going nowhere soon. Drinking more than I should be. I figured quick cash was better than earning it. Now, I figure I'm paying the state by the hour for that one little job."

"I keep forgetting you be a white boy. Bloods don't talk like that. Talk to the bloods, it don't be their fault going in, won't be their fault going back in."

Dodd found a loose clump of dirt by his foot and worked at it with the toe of his shoe. "What are you going to do when you get out?"

"Be old, mother fucker, that's what I be doing. Be too old to fuck, too old to piss. Too old to do nothing besides drink and watch the TV. What you think I be doing when I get out?"

"Can't you work for your brother? He got you into this."

Preacher didn't even ask for a cigarette. He took the pack out of Dodd's pocket and fired one up.

"Naw, them Meeker brothers fucked his business pretty badly. He's got enough clients to get by now, but he ain't gonna be taking on no ex-con brothers out of charity."

"So level with me, Preacher. How did you end up in jail?"

They sat silently for a minute, staring across the yard at inmates exercising, running, playing cards or joking around. Dodd had tried for months to get Preacher to tell him how he got arrested but with no luck. Finally he said, "Look, you tell me the details of your arrest, maybe I could work out a brief on your case for my class."

"That law shit?"

"Yeh. That law shit." That law shit, of course, was his extension course in basic criminal law. "I figure I can make some kind of living as a lawyer when I get out. Good enough to pay the rent and keep me out of jail in the future." He leaned over to pick up a pebble and tossed it at Preacher's shoe. "Come on. Give the story up. Let's see what I can do with it."

But Preacher didn't give the story up, didn't give it up until a lazy November afternoon when the dye cut machine in the tool shop was down and the two of them had a rare moment of idle time in what was supposed to be their workday. Both Dodd and Preacher worked at dye cutting, a special skill that only the brighter and more trusted inmates worked. They had to earn their way into the Huntsville tool shop and a heavy equipment assignment where they could work without their shirts so that sweat soaked down their pants from the waistline. Most of the prisoners were glad to work laundry.

Preacher told Dodd that the only people who considered it a special privilege for an inmate to work the heavy machinery were the prison staff. It sure as hell didn't bring them any more money or earn them good behavior. But it did keep them in top physical shape. Preacher believed that avoiding violence was the best solution to any situation, but he believed in being prepared should anyone call his bluff.

When the dye cut machine broke down that afternoon, and the shop foreman realized it wasn't going back up soon, the guards posted Preacher and Dodd to a wooden bench on the far corner of the room where they could sit until the machine was fixed. As the guards and the foreman gathered around the machine, they kept glancing at Preacher and Dodd, eyes averted but clearly curious.

"Those mother fuckers think we sabotaged that machine to get out of working," Preacher mumbled.

"Why would they think that?" Dodd asked.

"Couple of missing stress pins, I would think."

Dodd smiled. He knew better than to inquire any further.

"How can you do this, day after day, knowing you have another fifteen years of this? I'm going stir crazy and I'm out next December."

"That's cause you gonna take parole."

"Of course I am."

Preacher laughed. When he laughed he dropped his jaw so low Dodd could count his missing teeth. Two from fights and one that fell out because he didn't trust the prison dentist. "Shit, man, do the five. Then, when you're out, you're clean. You can go anywhere. They can't keep track of you. Me, I'm doing the full sentence. No parole officer's gonna make me strip search, take no urine test for him."

"Three's enough for me, Preacher." He could see the man twitching in the dim light of the room. Preacher could make it through a shift without a cigarette when he was sweating away setting up the press. But when he had to sit still, he wanted a cigarette bad.

"Yeh, I guess the longer the sentence the shorter the years seem getting there."

"Why'd you do it, Preacher? Part of me can picture you as an armed robber, but part of me thinks you were too smart to do something like that."

"I be as dumb as you when I be your age," Preacher said. "I did it for Alvin, I guess. And the money. Course, it always be for the money, bro. They promised me good money, and I be just stupid enough to believe them."

"Who promised you good money?"

"Them Meekers. See that be the deal. They be running short on money they owed Rafferty. They planned to take that Dodd farm and build a Boondock Super Sized Department Store. Mars Discount Warehouse. Figured people be driving out from all the surrounding towns to drop they hard earned money in this big mother fucking discount store. Bigger than a Gibsons or a K-Mart even. Three stories, chock-full-o-shit for white people to piss away they money."

He pulled his right leg up and fiddled with his laces. His knee was almost even with his ear. It amazed Dodd that anyone could be that limber and that fidgety. Preacher couldn't sit still for a second. He was always scratching, stretching, fiddling with his laces.

"According to Alvin, the investors be running away and the Meekers be going belly up on a balloon payment if they don't come up with a hundred quick grand right away. Don't ask me what a balloon payment be, I just heard Alvin say it a bunch of times."

"How does their bad debt get you in jail?"

Preacher grinned, and scratched his ankle, pulling out a half a Lucky, cut straight through the center. He ran it under his nose, inhaling deeply, then slipped it back into his sock. Every morning he cut a Lucky in half and slipped one half in each sock for moments when he desperately needed a smoke. Sometimes, in the machine shop, when he wasn't allowed to smoke, he would pass the cigarette back and forth under his nose for a minute or two, until, as he said, he got his nerves back.

"Well, see, they planned for me to rob they stores and shit. Me and a buddy, Delroy Lean, we's to knock over the gas station and the two stores. Go in three times, come out, like we be a gang. Then we give back half the money, and they tell they insurance about them robberies and lies about how much we be stealing. Get it? Hiring us they gets half they money back and collect on even more insurance."

"You got set up, I imagine." Dodd watched as the foreman pulled two six-inch bolts from behind one of the plates. He showed them to the guards and they all looked Preacher's way.

Preacher pretended not to see anything. He sat with his back against the wall and pulled his heel up to the edge of the bench. "Well, see, I be stupid about that. Couldn't figure for the life of me why those white boys be so generous. Delroy, he say, 'Fuck it, Preacher. Take the mother fucking money and run."

"Before you go on with this, Preacher," Dodd interrupted him. "Did you West Texas niggers really say 'mother fucker' and 'this be that' all the time? Or did you pick that up from all the city niggers inside?"

Preacher lowered his feet to the floor, sat straight, and stared at Dodd. "Listen, peckerwood. You want to hear this story finally or you want to argue with the way I tell it?"

"I'm just pulling your chain, Preacher. Tell the story."

Preacher narrowed his eyes and stretched his neck toward Dodd. With anyone else it would have been the first step toward a fight only Preacher could win. Dodd knew Preacher was only playing with him. Even then the look could be menacing.

"Well don't be pulling my chain, cause I still a brother and you still a peckerwood. So where I be in the story? Oh yeh, on the last robbery, the Meeker's be waiting for us with they guns and they kill Delroy and lock me up. Only reason I ain't being dead too is cause I figured they plan about a minute before Delroy did, he being dead and all, and I runs like a mother fucker out of the store. Out in the open, I figured they still got me, but they can't shoot me. I know my goose is cooked one way or the other, I figure better it be cooking here in prison that in the hot dusty ground like Delroy."

Dodd noticed the foreman was holding something in his hand and the guards were discussing it. "I can see your thinking on that," he said.

Preacher snorted and leaned his head back against the wall. Dodd realized he was watching the conversation by the dye machine too. "Turns out they reported all they intend to report lost on the first robbery. Plus, they got lots of stuff to dump all over Alvin with, and he done them nothing but favors. So I figure, what the hell, I do the crime, I be doing the time. Least I ain't six feet under like old Delroy."

"That's it? Three counts of armed robbery and you're behind bars for life? Doesn't that seem a little extreme?" Even though the guards and foremen were all pointedly staring at them, Dodd kept his eyes focused on Preacher. He had already taught Dodd how to become invisible to people. They sat and talked as though nothing else were going on.

"Well that judge be a mother fucker himself. He be about as white as they come. Even his asshole be lily white. I figure those Meeker boys run the whole story past him before he ever gave his papers a look. I got me no favors in that trial, I tell you. Alvin, he kind of backed out of their affairs, figuring they be setting him up next. Them Meekers, they be making their payment that time, but it didn't do them no good. Could never attract enough investors to get that store up. A three-story K-Mart in the middle of the mother fucking desert. Can you imagine that?"

Dodd shook his head. He couldn't imagine anything like it. Businessmen with their money baffled him, how they always seemed to be willing to piss it away on the stupidest idea, and even drag investors down with them.

Both he and preacher glanced up to find the guards and the foreman standing over them. One of the guards held out two thick bolts.

"You boys know what these are?"

"I do," Preacher said. "That be a one inch plate bolt. Don't want any of them falling out of you machines or things could go real bad."

"How about you, Dodd? You seen this before."

"I'm sure I have, Petovsky, but I'd have to count all the bolts over there to figure out exactly which one it was."

The guard tucked the bolts into his waistband. "I catch you fucking with that dye cutting machine again and I'm going to stick you fucking hand in there."

Dodd felt certain the guards knew damn well only Preacher would have the balls to sabotage prison machinery. They still preferred warning Dodd. As they should.

"Clear as a bell, Petovsky," he said. "So when are you gonna get those bolts back in that machine so we can go to work?"

Petovsky watched over Dodd and Preacher every minute his attention wasn't demanded elsewhere. A bull-necked, red neck with shoulders even broader than most of the guards, he could never understand how a white prisoner and a black prisoner could get along so well. As a result he figured the two of them must be queer or really queer, which, by Petovsky's thinking, made the two of them just about the lowest kind of person you could be with the exception of a University of Texas graduate. Petovsky grew up in Bryan, under the shadow of Texas A&M. He wore maroon t-shirts under his uniform and called the prisoners "faggots and tea sips."

"You boys are going back to work right now," Petovsky told them, leading them to the maintenance closet and issuing mops and buckets.

"Goddam, Petovsky, I just saw some boys swabbing these floors not two hours ago," Dodd said.

Petovsky looked around, made sure no one was watching, unzipped his fly and pissed on the floor around their boots. He barely missed pissing on their boots. Then he wiggled his penis, tucked it inside his shorts, zipped his pants, and said, "Looks like they missed something."

Preacher mumbled, "Fuck you, mother fucker." Before Petovsky could ask what he said, Dodd said, "He said we'll be glad to, officer."

Dodd filled the buckets with industrial soap and hot water while Preacher groused. He didn't mind; it was the way Preacher was. He knew Preacher wasn't getting any time off for good behavior, and a week in solitary was almost a vacation for the man. "A whole week when I ain't breaking my back so I can work through my thoughts," he liked to tell Dodd. "What kind a punishment's that?"

They slapped their mops down onto the floor and Dodd tried to steer Preacher back to the subject. "So what happened?"

"What happened is some night that white ass mother fucker gonna find himself all alone on the ward and he ain't getting his ass back off it ever. Won't be me tending to business either. Meaner bloods than me want a piece of his bony white ass."

"I mean about the robbery."

"We was set up, white boy. That's the best way I can tell you."

"Or you could give me the details."

"Damn you be one nosy cracker. Deal be we rob his feed store first. Go in with shotguns; tell that boy behind the counter to hand over the dough. Meeker be there jawing with his clerk; be telling the boy to give up the dough cause nobody wants no trouble. We tie them up, drive away. Sheriff pretends to chase us; we all pull off at the old Dodd farm where nobody can see us and split up the money. Not a big take. Maybe a grand. We get five hundred. I don't see it was worth the effort, but old Joe Bob told me shut my mouth and it will get better."

He glanced over to see if Petovsky was looking, and when he realized the guard was out of sight, he stopped mopping and leaned on his mop with his hands folded over the handle.

"Next time we do the dry goods store. Same story, we got shotguns, only this time Meeker don't be showing up. Guy behind the counter's this new guy, real nervous. Heard about the last robbery. He pulls a gun on us. Delroy be ready to shoot him then and there but I talks him out of it. Say no fool white boy be worth us taking a fall. Now, all these years later, I figure the Meekers be giving him that gun figuring somebody gets killed in the shoot out, gives them an excuse for deadly force next time around. As it is I ask Joe Bob what's going on when we splits the money. He say, 'Damn fool kid. I told Ralph not to hire him.'"

Petovsky stepped around from behind the drill press and Preacher slid his hands down the mop handle and began to work on the floor like he'd never stopped to rest. Dodd, who had finished the floor anyway, shook his head. When the guard left, Dodd asked, "How much did you get that time?"

"Fifteen hundred. Seven fifty for us. Now I be thinking, this cracker's setting us up. Told Delroy this be the time to get out, we twelve hundred ahead. Delroy, he say, 'Naw, man. One last score likes they tells us. Then we be sitting pretty.' I call Alvin since he's got a stake in this too, ask what to do. He tell me, 'You don't trust them, bro, you do what you think best."

"Alvin said, 'You don't trust them "bro"'?"

"Seems that's what I heard myself say."

Dodd, who had already met Alvin when Alvin visited him to thank him for keeping his brother in cigarettes, knew Alvin called him "runt," but he let it slide.

"So you went in anyway."

"That's the day I learn the difference between a boy and a man. Boy do whatever other folks want him to do. Man listen to his gut and fuck the others. We be driving to that gas station for the last job, my guts be telling me get out of the car. We walk through that door, my guts be telling me, get in that car drive away. Leave Delroy to this business. But I still a boy, I still be stupid enough to think a man be sticking with the brothers even if the brothers be totally fucked up. But I walk through that door behind Delroy, see both those Meekers waiting, I say to myself, you been set up. Right there I became a man. I say, 'Let's go, Delroy.' He say, 'You fucking nuts?' I be through that door and even as I gets that door open I hear a gun shot and I know it ain't Delroy shooting no sheriff."

He stopped mopping again, and leaned across mop handle. He leaned his face to Dodd's conspiratorially. "Let me tell you. Outside I be fixing to get in that car? Drive off? For the first time in my life, my brain come to me. It say, 'You drive off nobody can see when they catch up to you. Here you be in the middle of the road with all these white folks watching.' I looks around and, sure enough, that's where I be. In the middle of the highway, folks coming out to see what those shots were. I drop that shotgun, get down on my knees with my hands up in the air? Soon as they bursts through the door I be yelling, 'I give up. Don't shoot.'"

He shook his head, checked to make sure Petovsky wasn't looking, and hawked a goober into a dark corner next to a drainpipe. "My lawyer tells me to plead. Says life is the best I can get, being a nigger and all, that's how he put it, especially one who stole more than a hundred thousand dollars. 'A hundred thousand dollars,' I yell back at him. 'You don't really think those white-faced, red necked mother fuckers ever had any hundred thousand in those tiny store safes in all the years they lived.' But that's when I saw how it be going down. Figured if life be the best I could get, sure as hell didn't want to find out what the worst be. So I pleaded just like he said. On my best behavior, I get out in thirty years. So what's my cut of twelve fifty? Six hundred dollars? Guess I be making about twenty dollars a year for that job. Only I ain't getting out in no thirty years."

For the rest of his sentence Dodd would always wonder about luck putting the two of them together. A third of Huntsville was filled with drug dealers who had thousands stashed away and would make thousands more when they got out doing the same thing that put them inside to start with. These guys would kill you if you looked at their dope wrong. Another third was filled with men convicted of sex-crimes and violent crimes—rapists, short-eyes, men who cut other men and women up just because they looked at them wrong. Then there were the guys like Preacher and Dodd, stupid schmucks who went into some store with a gun for a few hundred dollars, ended up cooling their heels with the rapists, murderers and drug dealers. Of all of those, the two dumbest fucks got put in cells next to each other, one who robbed a store because he was drunk and the other who robbed a store to do his brother a favor.

That thought made Dodd work hard to never be one of the dumb fucks again. He took correspondence courses and extension courses in law, so he could get out, pass the bar and help keep other dumb fucks out of jail.

Where did he end up instead? In Sweet Water Falls, working for the same two cold-hearted bastards who set up Preacher and maybe even the Dodds. Shit, he thought to himself as he floated on the river that Sunday morning listening to Bobby yammer and complain, you just can't quit being a dumb fuck.

Chapter 24

Rhonda Mayfield's pastel blue A-Frame sat back from the road by a good fifty yards, surrounded by mesquite trees, trim and freshly painted with scalloped shingles along the roof. The translucent curtains sported lilacs on white muslin and fluttered against her well-scrubbed screens in the slight evening breeze.

Dodd figured he should bring flowers and wine, but West Texas blue laws kept stores closed on Sunday. He looked for a bottle of wine at Meeker's station, figuring he could pay for it later, but the best he could find was Boone's Farm. That didn't strike him as the kind of wine to bring on a date. He finally let himself into the general store and left two dollars for a box of chocolates on the register.

Rhonda answered the door dressed in a T-shirt with no bra, and blue jeans. The fabric of her T-shirt flattened her breasts against her chest, showing the softest hint of nipple against the fabric. Her feet were bare. If it weren't for the faintest traces of crow's feet at the corners of her eyes, and the practiced alcoholic flush in her cheeks, Dodd would have thought she was pushing her late twenties.

She surveyed the chocolates and his suit, which he had brushed thoroughly before driving over. "I wasn't sure you'd come," she admitted, "and now I see you came with far more formal expectations that I had."

He handed her the chocolates. "You could invite me in."

He ducked under the low doorframe and entered her living room, which was the only room on the first floor. A loft extended half-way into the main room, and Dodd could see the blue quilted bedspread covering what seemed to be a waterbed. A long couch, which seemed to come straight from a modular furniture catalogue, separated the living area from the kitchen.

She opened the box and tasted one of the candies. "Do you bring chocolate to Miss Rafferty?" she asked.

"Our relationship never made it to the dinner stage. We went straight to the honeymoon."

"A gentleman shouldn't say things like that."

"I would think a gentleman in Sweet Water Falls is nothing more than a fantasy."

She blushed to a tint about half as red as the candy box. "I presume too much."

Her kitchen and the living area, like the bedspread and outside walls, were pastel blue, accented only by the colors of her knick-knacks: books, porcelain animals and wall hangings. The long couch and matching modular easy chairs were blue floral print. He saw no photographs.

The books and animals dovetailed each other on several hand-hewn bookcases. The books, all hard cover, seemed to have been issued in collections. Dodd recognized the Durant histories, a small set of blue complete Shakespeare plays, collections of Hemingway, Fitzgerald and Faulkner, French and Spanish novelists, each set defined by its distinctive leather-like cardboard cover—the Hemingways in leatherette blue, the French novelists in Baptist Bible red.

The animals ranged from deer to kittens to a bashful skunk with his tail wrapped under his legs and cheeks blushing. In fact every single one of the figurines could be described as bashful or playful, as though they leapt from the screen of some Disney movie and solidified on Rhonda's bookshelves. The wall hangings, perhaps to be expected, sported homespun mottos: "God guides baking hands" written in needlepoint in a circle around a brown needlepoint loaf of white bread, one slice falling away from the rest of the loaf with a hint of needlepoint steam floating away; "A woman's place is in control" underneath a crocheted caricature of a woman with enormous glasses sitting behind a large desk with a placard proclaiming, "Boss," beside her elbow; and Dodd's favorite, "Book readers are novel lovers," in counted cross stitch underneath the book "Moby Dick."

"Let me put these away so I don't eat them all at once," Rhonda said. She tiptoed into the kitchen and put them on a cabinet next to her cookbooks. Dodd had seen women in bare feet tiptoe in movies and wondered if it was a double-X chromosome thing, or something women did to create the illusion of height. Her jeans accentuated her ass, which was as firm and plump as a cantaloupe. Her legs were even longer than Mary Beth's; he just couldn't imagine Rhonda locking them behind his neck the way Mary Beth did.

Shame on yourself, Dodd, he told himself.

Rhonda stretched to take down two highball glasses. Her T-shirt pulled up from her jeans and pulled her breasts up with it. Dodd wondered if he shouldn't put the young beauties behind him and accept the virtues of maturity.

She cracked a half dozen ice cubes and dropped them into the two glasses along with Boodles and Canada Dry tonic. "I hope you like gin tonics."

"I thought we were having lemonade."

She padded back into the living area on the balls of her feet and held out his drink. "That's with dinner. This helps us get to dinner. I prefer to lubricate encounters with virtual strangers."

"I don't drink."

She wrinkled her tiny mouth as though she never heard any one say that before. "Mr. Dodd, you don't strike me as a Christian or a Mormon. And in this neck of the woods there isn't much to do besides drink or read the Bible." She blushed again. "Well, when you're by yourself, I mean."

"I do things I regret when I've been drinking."

"So do I, Mr. Dodd. So I drink more to forget about them." She put the glass down on one of her bookshelves and returned to the kitchen to pour lemonade. Dodd wondered how many gins she worked through waiting for him to come over.

He also wondered whether all the blue symbolized a light spirit and daylight, or if it was a sign of depression. Maybe he would know that had he gone to college.

Rhonda settled on her couch and tucked her ankles underneath her. "Hang your suit jacket on a chair," she told him. "You look like you're here to sell insurance."

He draped his jacket over a chair at the kitchen table then sat next to her on the couch. As soon as he settled in she swung her feet into his lap. "Do you give foot massages?"

He put his lemonade down, untouched, then took her right foot and began to rub the ball under her big toe. "You move fast, don't you?"

"At my age you have to move fast even if you aren't sure where you're going."

Dodd dropped his hands down to the arch of her foot and began to rub gently there.

"You look a lot like your uncle Zel. Anyone ever tell you that?"

"No, but that might be because I never had an uncle Zel."

"Oh, you did," she smiled, pulling a sip of her drink through a thin cocktail straw. "I've seen the pictures. Zel was as handsome as you; not quite so rugged. I guess prison weathers you more than an Army desk job. He wasn't quite put together straight, you know. My mother called him 'high strung.'"

Dodd dropped her foot into his lap, and stretched his arm down the back of her couch so that his finger almost touched her shoulder. "When you invited me to dinner, I didn't expect the conversation to move in this direction."

She sighed and looked at the ceiling. "My mother was in love with Zel. I think she would have left my father if the Meekers hadn't killed him. Didn't matter. The Meekers killed my father too. A few years later." She paused and looked at him expectantly. "But you knew that, I would guess."

"I'm sorry to hear that, but how could I possibly know?"

She smiled mysteriously, as though they shared a secret only she was aware of. "You're right. How would you? They said it was a hunting accident. The Meekers said that anyway. Mamma said they killed him because he found out about what really happened to Zack and Zel. But mamma'd been strange for quite a while by then and no one believed her."

She put down her empty glass, and took the gin and tonic she made for Dodd. "You sure you don't mind?"

"Why would I?"

She shrugged. "Of course not."

"Why did your mother think the Meekers murdered your father?"

"I found your uncle's pictures behind her bureau after my father died. Must have been half a dozen. There was even a Polaroid of her and Zel on a picnic in the gorge. She wore a fringed one piece suit that was popular back then; he had a narrow mustache and wore a Hawaiian shirt. The kind of shirt that would make men in Sweet Water Falls call him a faggot."

Dodd smiled and rubbed the meat between her toes. He figured she would take her own time and own path through the story, and hoped it would make sense when she finished.

"I made her tell me about it. At first I couldn't forgive her, sleeping around on my father, although she swore nothing really happened between them. But later, before she died, after I left my own husband and realized how hard it is to keep a good man in your life, I realized that they had something special and maybe she should have left my Daddy and run away with him. Before the Meekers killed them both. But everybody really thought he was crazy, with the flying saucer business and all, and mamma couldn't picture herself leaving my father for a crazy dirt farmer. Maybe that's why she went crazy herself."

She lifted her foot from Dodd's lap and wriggled her toes. He picked it up again and started rubbing around her ankle.

"And your father?"

"Mamma told me, after I found the pictures, that Daddy found them too. Just a month or so before he died. He was mad at first, then she told him what Zel gave her. That's when he realized the Meekers really did set up the Dodds. I asked mamma wasn't he mad anymore? She said my daddy was never mad when he smelled money. She thinks he tried to blackmail the Meekers and they took care of him."

Dodd reached over her foot and picked up his lemonade. He was surprised to find himself getting somewhat aroused.

"She gave the pieces to me, after Daddy died, asked me to get rid of them for her. Sure enough, the day after Daddy was buried, Joe Bob showed up looking for them."

Dodd put his lemonade down without having tried it and turned his attention to her left foot. "I'm missing something. Pieces of what?"

"The flying saucer, silly. I have three pieces. That's how daddy thought he could get money from the Meekers and that's what they killed him for. That's why they killed your family, don't you see?"

Dodd let her foot drop back into his lap and tried his best to keep from laughing.

She pulled her feet away and sat straight up, planting her feet on the throw rug. "It isn't funny. It's true. I'll show you." Her cheeks were flushed, whether from the irritation or gin Dodd couldn't be sure.

Dodd tried to keep a straight face. "Sure, I'd love to see them."

She disappeared up her stairs and returned five minutes later with three of the strangest items Dodd had ever seen. One was a long piece of marbleized plastic. He seen plastic toys marbleized like that, old ones from the forties and fifties. A series of characters unlike any alphabet he'd ever seen were carved into one side. A second piece was a long metal rod that could have served any purpose. The third piece was thick metal foil that lay flat against the table.

"You expect me to believe these were from a flying saucer?" Dodd said. This time he couldn't conceal his skepticism.

She wadded the foil and for a minute he thought she would hurl it in his face. Instead, she spread it flat against the table. "See how smooth it is even after I wad it up?"

"It's heavy gauge foil, four or five times as thick as the stuff in your kitchen. It's supposed to stay smooth."

"You don't want to believe." Her eyes turned downward, as did the corners of her tiny mouth. She had really expected him to buy this. "Zel swore to my mom this was a real flying saucer, just like the one at Roswell."

"You don't believe things because you want to, Rhonda. You believe because they make sense. Why would alien astronauts fly across the universe in a ship made from plastic and tin foil?"

"Because it's indestructible. Didn't you see how that piece just flattened back out?"

Dodd wadded it up himself, and flattened it back out across the table. Sure enough, most of the seams faded away. She watched him as though she expected him to confess he'd seen the light. Instead he asked, "If it's indestructible, how come you've just got a piece of it?"

She tucked her legs up under her knees again, cradling her glass with her fingers. "What do you mean?"

Dodd swept his hands over the pieces. "I mean, if this stuff is indestructible how come you have pieces of it instead of the whole thing?"

She shook her head and looked down at her glass. "You're not making sense."

Dodd thought it was a good thing Sweet Water Falls didn't a have televangelist on every channel or Rhonda wouldn't have any money left.

"Look, you told me yourself Zel Dodd was crazy. Now if a crazy man brought you pieces of something that was supposed to be indestructible, which means it can't be broken into pieces, wouldn't you have to say to yourself, 'This guy's a little crazy,' and not, 'Wow, these are pieces of a flying saucer?"

"Zel was in Army Intelligence."

"Was that before he went crazy or afterward?"

He noticed a tear running down her cheek, almost ready to tumble off into her gin and tonic. He leaned over and brushed the tear away with his finger. "I'm sorry. It's none of my business. Especially if this stuff got your daddy killed."

She started to cry some more, and he pulled her over onto his shoulder wrapping his arm around her. Dodd hated it when women did this, like what happened was his fault and not their gullibility.

Of course, he realized, he could have just said, "Wow, what do you know, pieces of a flying saucer," and dropped it at that. Arguing with women rarely accomplished something other than to make him feel like a shit.

"How about that dinner you promised? Sandwiches and coleslaw? You think it might be time to dip into that?"

She nodded her head, and pulled away from him. She stood up to straighten her T-shirt, which was angling her breasts slightly to one side. Then she straightened out her jeans. "Everything's in the fridge except for the bread. Do you mind getting it out while I go change?"

She didn't give Dodd a chance to answer, skirting upstairs almost before she finished her sentence. Dodd said, "Be glad to," to the air. He took his lemonade and wandered into her kitchen to set out the dinner items.

When he took the first sip he realized how fortunate his timing was, waiting until she was out of the room to try her lemonade. The first sip made him pucker so hard he thought he would suck his cheeks down his throat. He dumped half of it down the sink, added three spoons of sugar and filled the rest of the glass with water.

It didn't help. For some reason her lemonade was so tart it seemed to suck the water out of his body. He put the glass aside and set about setting out dinner.

In his life, Dodd never saw a refrigerator as organized as Rhonda's. Every item was sorted and stacked: dairy products, meats, condiments, and leftovers. The leftovers were labeled with felt-tip pen on masking tape. The masking tape was cut straight at each side, each strip equal length, nothing just ripped from the roll to get it on the package in a hurry. She hand-printed her letters in block letters, all capitols with larger capitols beginning each word, red felt tip for someone else's recipes, blue felt tip for hers. Or so Dodd guessed because the labels in blue all had names like "CHICKEN A LA RHONDA," "SWEET POTATOES WITH RHONDA SAUCE," "SPAGHETTI MAYFIELD."

Dodd found the ham neatly sliced on the rack beside a crisper full of iceberg lettuce, a jar of Dijon mustard and Hellman's mayonnaise. Beside the condiments stood a bowl of coleslaw that looked almost translucent, and beside that the pitcher of lemonade. He laid everything out on her counter, the fork and knife parallel to the ham, and opened the bread so the slices spilled out of the wrapper.

"How wonderful," she applauded him. He turned to bow and was taken off guard by her peasant blouse, and full Spanish skirt that flared outward at her knees. She complemented her outfit with a single pearl necklace and thong sandals that laced up past her ankles. She lifted the hem of her skirt and bowed. "How do I look?"

"Good enough to eat," Dodd said. "Only I'm not the big bad wolf."

She blushed. "Do you think your little friend would go through this much trouble for you?"

Dodd ignored her question and poured himself another glass of lemonade. He held out a glass to her and she shook her head. "Another gin tonic please."

Dodd shrugged and dosed the glass with Boodles, adding ice and tonic after. She suggested they dine on the porch. He carried the platter of meat and the bread out, while she arranged the coleslaw, drinks and condiments on a small picnic table looking onto a thick mesquite grove. The late afternoon sun angled its way through the trees, creating an effect like the stereoscope viewers Dodd played with as a kid.

He piled the ham on his bread, and scooped the slaw onto his plate. His mother taught him to always be gracious about food, even when he didn't like it. As a kid he thought she was crazy. As he got to know women better he was glad she taught him the lesson.

She slid onto the bench across from him, arranging her skirt casually and tucking it under her knees. "How do you like my coleslaw?" she asked, bumping his ankle with her toe.

"No mayonnaise," he said. "Not exactly something I'm used to."

"I use salad oil. Makes it less likely to spoil in the heat."

He made a production of shoveling in several mouthfuls while she watched, chewing and smiling to indicate how good he thought it was. To be honest, it was okay, but his mother raised him on Miracle Whip and he couldn't imagine slaw, or even a sandwich for that matter, without it.

She dropped a small slice of ham on a piece of bread, folded it over and left it on her plate. She picked at her salad, nudged his ankle again, and then he realized she was rubbing his leg with the side of her foot.

He swallowed and said, "Rhonda, I hate to break the mood of the evening here, but I was under the impression you were slightly attached."

She blushed and pulled her foot away, crossing her legs and sliding them inward beside the bench. "Whatever gave you that idea?"

"You and Rafferty. Body language is everything, and your body language the day we met was pretty protective of Mal, Jr. Not that he needed protection, mind you." He took another bite of his sandwich and waited for her to answer.

Instead of answering she stared at the sunset and blushed, sipping quietly on her gin and tonic.

"I didn't mean to pry," he apologized. "I just thought we should were being up front about who we're seeing and all. And you have to admit it's kind of ironic; you're doing the dad and I'm doing the daughter."

"You're a heartless bastard," she said finally, still staring at the sunset and making a point to not look at him.

"I learned my manners in jail." He folded her bread over her ham and offered it to her, but she wouldn't acknowledge the gesture. "Look at it from my side. From the minute I arrive in town, everyone's prying into my life. Are you related to these bank robbers? Are you sleeping with Mary Beth Rafferty? People cozying up to me like I'm out to get the Meekers and I'll share their swag when I do. Then, I just happen to point out that you seemed to be attached to Mal Rafferty, and you give me the cold shoulder."

She slipped her legs back under the table—knees together and ankles crossed under her bench—and looked down at her plate. "I'm not proud of it. I was flattered that the richest man in town was willing to risk his marriage for me. But when I fell in with Mal, things were rough. Marla's father just up and left me with a six-year-old after I worked to support the both of them. He figured he was going to be a country-western singer. I worked while he played thirty dollar a night gigs in every little poke hole in the area. Then this country band was in Lubbock one night looking for a back-up guitarist, and they just happened to hear George in a lounge. Well, he was never good enough to be his own act, but he was good enough to play for them."

She folded her hands in her laps and twiddled her fingers. "Of course, he was good enough for the band cause they weren't that good a band. Now he's a studio musician in Houston; makes just enough to get by as long as he doesn't have to send me child support. Now that Marla's working, it's too late anyway. Anyway, I was all messed up, and Mal was having problems with Beth, who makes her daughter look like a nun. But he always put me first, even offered to pay for marriage counseling to get me back together with that rat bastard husband of mine."

That didn't surprise Dodd. In his experience, men like Rafferty, who wanted to play the sidelines but keep their marriage intact, generally didn't want the married women they were sleeping with to get divorced. Once divorced, the women often expected the men to follow suit.

"Don't you get tired of a guy like Rafferty? Always on the make? Figure you'll end up playing third or fourth string when he sets his eyes on someone younger?"

From the way she stared at him, Dodd figured he crossed the line again. But after a few seconds she said, "You have Mal all wrong. He's been faithful to me all these years. I don't think he'd leave Beth for me, she's got the money hooks into him, but I know Mal comes to me when he needs affection."

Which told Dodd she knew nothing about Rafferty and Marla. He knew better than to press on this issue. In Dodd's experience, women in denial preferred to remain in denial until the facts are dropped undeniably in their lap. They do a good job of denying the facts even then.

"Of course, knowing Mal will never leave Beth doesn't exactly leave me in a good spot. She doesn't care where he sleeps as long as he stays out of her bed, but if she did decide to push it, just to make him dangle, Mal would have to cut me loose. That doesn't make my prospects for a happy home life look good."

"So you're thinking about giving Rafferty his walking papers?"

Now she looked him in the face. "No one's given me a reason to yet." She let her toes dance up the inside of his leg.

There it was. Dodd never knew a woman to come out and say what she wanted. It was their first rule of male/female relations. They always left hints and signs for men to interpret so they could claim the men took the signals wrong if things didn't go the way they wanted.

"I still don't see why the Meekers would kill your father over tin foil and plastic."

That caught her off guard. Her smile left and she took her foot away.

"How'd we get back to my father?"

"I've been thinking about it ever since you showed me that stuff. Let's look at the facts. If you didn't already believe there was a flying saucer buried in Sweet Water Falls, would you really believe that stuff came from a flying saucer?"

She shook her head. Her hair caught the wind and danced quietly in the diminishing sun. "But it was a flying saucer."

He reached over and covered her hands with his. "Be honest. If someone put those three pieces on your table and simply said, 'where do you think these came from?' would you think they came from a flying saucer?"

"I don't know."

But her eyes gave her real answer away.

"Sure you do. The last thing you would guess is a flying saucer. Then you have to ask yourself, if that saucer was powerful enough to blow indestructible tin foil into pieces, where's the scorching? I've seen metal after an explosion. It's not just in pieces; it's twisted and charred. And that plastic would have melted. If it can dry out and fossilize like that, it should've melted." He reached for his pocket. "Hell, let's get my lighter out and see what happens."

She stopped his hand then leaned back on her bench, agitated, trying to avoid thinking about it.

Dodd tried not to look like he'd won, or even made a point. "I've got this other problem. Who would kill someone over a flying saucer? Real or not? Especially under the circumstances we know for sure. If the Meekers had a flying saucer, and your father showed up with pieces to blackmail them, maybe they'd want to do him in. But they didn't have it. The whole town knows it. So that means they want it. Why kill him?"

She pulled back entirely. "I showed you those pieces so you'd admit you're Zel's nephew." A tear formed at the corner of her eye. "And maybe because I thought we might have a connection the way he and my mother did. But I didn't mean to turn this into a murder mystery."

Dodd took a bite from his sandwich and chewed it thoughtfully. "Ever since I've been here people keep throwing this Dodd shit at me, like some bone they want me to chew on. So I've been chewing, only it doesn't taste like bone. It tastes like shit."

"I really don't care to drag this out."

"Everyone says the Meekers killed the Dodds because they wanted their land. But the Dodds were desperate to keep up their payments. Zack was running hustles, like selling pieces of a UFO to cover their mortgage payment. So why stage a robbery and kill them if the land was going to default anyway?"

Rhonda actually took a bite of her slaw. She stirred with her fork, and then slipped then tiniest sliver of cabbage into her mouth to chew. "I don't follow."

"The farm was going to be repossessed. The Meekers could buy it for a song at auction. They didn't need to set the Dodds up."

"So you think your uncles really robbed the bank?"

Dodd shook his head. "They're not my uncles. But you have to ask yourself, if the Meekers killed the Dodds when they were going to get the land anyway, is it possible they set up the robbery too?"

She crossed her legs and leaned forward on her elbows. "You mean the Meekers robbed the bank?"

"Exactly. Who's more likely to rob a bank? A family with one brother off his rocker, another one a born hustler and a third with a wife and kid? A family who could barely afford a squirrel gun? Or did the Meekers, who had the guns, the tools, the motive and the connections to Rafferty?"

She slid her fingers up and down her highball glass. "What motive?"

Dodd finished off his lemonade. "The town council. Meeker wanted his property zoned commercial and the old council under mayor Mal, Sr. turned him down year after year after year. After the Dodd ambush, the sheriff ends up disgraced, the mayor dead and little Mal and the Meekers sieze control. That sounds like plenty of motive to me."

"But why would the Meekers need half a million? And why kill Mal's father?"

"It's something to think about isn't it?"

She continued to trace her fingers across the highball glass, thinking Dodd's version through. Her feet were under her bench now and her attention on the story. Then her eyes grew wide, reflecting just a trace of the magenta sunset.

"You think Mal had them rob the bank."

Dodd nodded. This would be the hardest part for her to buy, especially if she was sleeping with him.

"Mal would never...."

"Ask yourself, Rhonda. Who stood to gain the most with big Mal out of the way? And who was in the best position to carry off a robbery? And then there's your father. I can't see the Meekers killing your father over some trinkets that may or may not be a flying saucer. But if they thought your father's questions could bring the real story out? That would be a reason to kill him."

She shook her head. "I don't believe this." She swept to her feet, whisking both plates and glasses with her and backed into her kitchen.

Dodd followed her into the kitchen. She was already pushing the scraps into the trash with a fork. He leaned closer, making sure to keep his space to avoid spooking her.

"You remember the Rawlings brothers, the two Black fellows that robbed Ralph Meeker two or three times in the Sixties?"

She rinsed the plates off and stacked them on a towel on the sink counter, running the water through the glasses as well. She dropped the silverware into a tub of soapy water. Then she steered clear of him and into her living room. Dodd followed her and found her sitting on her couch, back straight, knees together, feet on the floor and hands wrapped around her knees. "Maybe. A little," she told him.

Dodd sat next to her, facing her, his arm draped across the back of the couch. "Preacher Rawlings and I knew each other. He told me the Meekers hired the two of them to rob their stores so they could collect the insurance. To make a payment on a loan they were about to default."

"So?"

"When I came to town and everyone started telling me these stories about the Dodds, I started thinking back to Preacher's story, about the Meekers robbing their own store to collect the insurance, and using two Black guys for patsies. Made me think, maybe they did this before. Maybe they knew the routine already. And if your father was sniffing around, talking about flying saucer parts and setting up the Dodds, they sure as hell would want him out of the way."

She scooted a foot or so further down the couch. "But Mal wouldn't help them if they killed his father."

Dodd kept an even expression. "I've been thinking about that too. What if Rafferty wanted his father dead? What if his father found out something Rafferty didn't want him to know? Like maybe he embezzled a half-million dollars of the bank's money? A fake hold-up would clear that problem up in a minute wouldn't it? The Meekers get the money they need, daddy's dead and insurance covers the losses."

She scooted even further down the couch, stiffening her back even more. "Mal wouldn't do that."

Dodd scooted down the couch beside her. He touched her hair. "You know Rafferty pretty well."

She stayed on the couch, looking away from him as she had outside. "I know him better than his wife does."

"Does his wife know he's fucking Marla?"

That got her attention. She pushed his hand away and pushed her back into the arm of her couch, drawing her legs up beneath her. "That's not true."

"I followed him to Fort Stockton Friday. He got there an hour and a half early. Marla left an hour later, half an hour before you arrived. Try showing up early sometime; see what happens."

She sighed and picked up her glass. Instead of sipping she held it up to the light to study the reflection through the glass. "I guess that explains how she can afford the dressage."

He reached to touch her hair again, but she pushed his hand away. "Why couldn't you just come over for company? Why bust up everything good in my life?"

"You can't tell me that you've worked for him all these years and haven't seen a single hint that the man's not squeaky clean. I know better, Rhonda. Everyone in this town genuflects to the man; even the Meekers. He gets that power from somewhere, and it isn't from running an honest small town bank."

She still wouldn't look at him, choosing to sit forward now, feet on the floor, rolling her glass between her fingers.

"Keep your eyes open. Will you at least do that?"

"Why?"

"You'll know when you see it. Then you can ignore it, use it to your advantage or clue me in. Either way's fine with me." He picked up the foil and the piece of plastic from the coffee table. "Mind if I borrow this?"

That got her attention. "What for?"

"To satisfy my curiosity. To see if I can find more pieces."

"I didn't think you believed in UFOs," she said,

"I don't. But it's a big world, and the Meekers are interested. I'll give them back."

She returned to her reverie, staring at her wall and rolling her glass in her fingers. He touched her shoulder. "I'm sorry I told you," he said. "Maybe I should have kept my mouth shut."

"That's all right." She still wouldn't look at him. Clearly it wasn't all right.

"I'll let myself out." He stood up, collected the pieces and walked to the door. To his surprise, she continued to sit on her couch. He turned around and leaned on his palm just inside her door. "You know, I came over with chocolates looking to sweet talk you, not to talk town business. You brought the whole thing up. When it turns out I'm right," he said, "and it also turns out that I'm not Zel's nephew, but a Dodd you never heard of before last week, I just want to know if this dating thing's still going to happen?"

She looked at him again, more curious than upset. "The door locks itself."

Chapter 25

Dodd pulled into Meeker's store for gas. He studied the sun while the pump ran, watching it hang at the rim of the horizon: a bright electric magenta halo casting a single streak about to be quenched by the deep blue night. Sunsets seem to take forever around here, he thought. The trip popped in the pump handle and he slipped it back in its cradle.

When he stepped into the store he saw Wetzel sitting behind the counter, eyes glued to a Hustler while two cigarettes burned in the ashtray on the counter. "Evening," Dodd said.

"Just getting gas or you gonna look around for awhile?" The kid didn't bother to look up from a two page spread featuring triple F cup breasts.

"Guess I'll look around," Dodd said, mildly surprised that the kid wasn't jumping to attention. Then again, considering the kid, he guessed he shouldn't be.

He grabbed a bag of Ruffles and a six-pack of RC from the cooler. At the counter he pulled out his wallet. Wetzel turned around the spread he'd been drooling over. "What a ya think of those? Talk about hooters, huh?"

Dodd wondered if Wetzel would have struck up the same conversation with a middle-aged grandmother coming home from church. "I like them bigger myself."

Wetzel gave him a constipated look. Then he got the joke and broke into a laugh. "Haw, haw, haw. Ain't seen you before, mister. You from around here?"

That explained why the kid didn't jump to attention. His short-term memory must expire before he blinked. "Visiting my cousin, Bill Todd."

"The car salesman?" He said it with total contempt.

"That's him." Dodd pulled a large Mars Bar from a candy display and added it to the six pack and chips.

"Well your dickwad cousin's behind on his payments to the bank. Might have to foreclose." Wetzel said it with the voice of God's authority.

"And you know this how?" Dodd asked.

"My old man. He holds the paper. He puts the word out, people stop buying cars. Your cousin'll have to sell his lot to the Meekers who can make money with it and bank dividends go up. Whadda you think of that? Your cousin better be nice to my old man."

Dodd pushed his food items and cash closer to Wetzel, wondering when he would shut up and start ringing up his items. "Who's your old man?"

"I can't believe your cousin never mentioned him. Double W Wetzel." He pronounced it "dubayah." "He's the real money in this town. Hell, he practically owns the bank. That's why I hold my executive position. Shit, I manage this whole operation. By myself. Even have help during the week."

"You think you can manage to ring me out while we're talking?" Dodd said, tapping his finger on one of the cola cans.

The kid slammed the Hustler closed and made a production of clearing his throat. He rolled his eyes, as if to say customers like Dodd were typical of the problems managers put up with. "This all you gonna buy?"

"Why? You make commission?"

Wetzel held the six pack in front of him to find the price even though a sign three feet high and only two feet away said they were $1.99 a six pack. He pecked the price onto the register one key at a time, spelling the price out with his lips. “On the guns,” he said, as he picked up the candy bar to search for the price.

“You make a commission on the guns?”

“Six percent.” He lipread the price on the candy bar and punched it into the register.

Dodd didn’t know what gave him the idea; it just came to him in a flash. “That’s a nice looking piece behind you,” he said, pointing to a Smith and Wesson automatic. “Can I check it out?”

Wetzel’s eyes lit up. “Sure.” He pulled a small key from the cash drawer. He slid the glass open and handed the automatic to Dodd.

“Is that a Magnum?” Dodd asked, pointing to a long-barreled chrome-plated Colt.

“Sure is,” Wetzel said. “You want to see that too?”

Dodd held his free hand out, and Wetzel slapped the handle into his palm. Dodd lowered the automatic to his side and extended the Colt to the end of his arm, looking through the sight. He pretended to pull the trigger and whispered, “Pow.”

“Pretty cool, eh?” Wetzel said.

He laid the automatic on the counter. “I’ll take it with two boxes of shells.” Wetzel pulled two boxes down from the gun case and stacked them beside the automatic. Dodd hefted the Magnum. “What does this take, forty-fours or forty-fives?”

“Forty-fours.” He started ringing up the gun and ammo. This time he didn’t even need to look for the price.

“You sure? This looks like a forty-five.”

Wetzel stopped keying the register and rolled his eyes. “I think I know a little more about hand guns that some guy in his Sunday suit.”

“I’d like to make sure,” Dodd said.

“You can take my word for it.”

Dodd started to push the automatic and bullets back. “Maybe I don’t need this after all.”

Wetzel threw up his hands. “All right. All right. Here why don’t you try them and see for yourself?” He reached back and grabbed a third box of shells from the cabinet, slamming them in front of Dodd.

Dodd popped out the cylinder and slipped three shells inside. "Son-of-a-bitch, you're right." He slammed the cylinder into place and pointed the gun at Wetzel. "Now give me all the money in the register, you stupid fuck."

Wetzel's jaw almost crashed into the counter. "What?"

"Give me the goddam money." He pulled back the hammer and shoved the barrel in Wetzel's gaping mouth.

Wetzel immediately pulled bills from every pocket in the drawer, handing them to Dodd with both fists. Dodd took the money and stuffed it into his pocket. "Call Meeker," he said.

The kid's jaw unlatched and dropped a few inches further. "Pick up the phone and call Meeker. Now."

The sweat started to pour from the kid's eyebrows. Dodd had seen sweat pour from a lot of places, but eyebrows was a first. "Who?"

"Your boss. Ralph Meeker. Pick up the phone and call him."

Dodd thought he would piss his pants. In fact, he was surprised he didn't. "I forgot the number."

"It's right there on the cash register." He resisted the urge to add "dumb shit, dip shit, dim wit" or any other number of well-deserved pejoratives.

Wetzel pulled the phone from under the counter, and dialed slowly, reading each number under his breath one-by-one. Dodd grabbed the receiver and tucked it under his chin.

Meeker's sleepy, drunken voice came on the line.

"It's Dodd. I'm at the gas station. Get Joe Bob and get out here. I just robbed your store. And the best part is, Weasel face gave me the gun and the bullets."

He let the phone back down in the receiver and smiled at the clerk, who was beginning to realize he was in more trouble than he could have imagined.

"You're that new manager, ain't you?" Wetzel swallowed.

Dodd kept the Magnum on him, not sure the kid wouldn't try something even more stupid, like escaping. "Can't say we weren't introduced."

"That was a long time ago," the kid squawked. "And I' ain't that good with faces."

"Maybe you need to brush up on your Dale Carnegie."

Wetzel's face made a blank slate look ornate. "I ain't queer."

Dodd almost shot him on the spot.

They waited together, in their awkward standoff, until Ralph Meeker slammed open the door, almost knocking it off its automatic closing rod. Joe Bob followed with an enormous but short man dressed in a Hawaiian shirt and chewing on a Dominican cigar. Dodd assumed he was about to meet oil magnate Dubayah Dubayah Wetzel.

Wetzel stormed past the counter and shoved his cigar and balding head under Dodd's nose, the top of his belly bumping Dodd's belt buckle. "You got a problem with my son?"

Dodd stepped back and brushed off his belt buckle. He decided the simplest approach might be best. "Yep."

Wetzel began to poke a finger thicker than a pork chop into Dodd's buckle. "Who the hell are you, anyway, let's you think you can fuck with my son?"

Dodd took the cigar from Wetzel's mouth and crushed it under his shoe. Then he grabbed the Magnum from the counter and aimed it at Wetzel's belt buckle. "I'm his fucking boss, that's who I am. I came in this evening and, not only did your son not recognize me, not only was he reading a pussy magazine and showing the pussy to his customers, not only did he treat me with absolute disrespect, but he loaded this handgun and gave it to me."

Wetzel stuck his fatty finger in the Magnum's barrel. "So?"

"So I think he's saying the kid's an idiot, which is something I've been telling you since the idiot was born," Joe Bob said. He leaned back against the counter, and smiled broadly. "By the way, you might want to take your finger out of that barrel because it's still loaded."

Wetzel senior jumped back as though he'd been stung. Ralph jumped between him and the barrel of the gun. "W.W., you said you'd let me handle this."

"Why'd you even call him, Ralph?" Joe Bob asked. "It won't change the fact that his kid's a total fuck up." He reached over the counter and grabbed a handful of cigars.

"Ralph, I thought you own this store." Dodd draped the gun over Ralph's shoulder and dropped it so that Ralph barely caught it with both hands. "Don't worry," he added, "the safety's on." Had Ralph been sober, he might have remembered that handguns don't have safeties, being the sheriff's brother and someone raised around guns. But Dodd figured he was too deep into his cups to think his gun facts through.

Wetzel poked his finger into Ralph's shoulder, almost pushing him out of the way. "And you keep out of this, Meeker. This is between me and this convict you hired to boss around my son."

Joe Bob laid his thick fingers on Wetzel's collar and pulled him back. "Goddam it, Ralph. I hate it when you force me to agree with Dodd. And W.W., as sheriff, not to mention Ralph's business partner, I have real problems with your son handing out free guns and bullets to people he doesn't even know."

"I knew who he was," Wally broke in. "He asked me to show him those guns, so I did. He's the boss."

Wetzel brushed Meekers hand away. "See there, Joe Bob. My son was just doing what he's told. There was no reason for me to even come here tonight."

"Actually," Dodd said, "you need to drive him home since I'm firing his ass."

"You can't do that," Wally said. "You're not my boss."

"Exactly," Wetzel said, puffing out his chest.

"He is the boy's boss," Joe Bob said, "so he can do that."

Ralph shook his head apologetically, "Technically, W.W., I'm afraid he is."

Wetzel grabbed Ralph buy the shirt, even though the man was holding a loaded Magnum between the two of them. "Then you hire him back."

Dodd retrieved the Magnum before one of them shot the other's testicle. He popped the chamber open and shook the bullets into his hand. "That's a bad idea, W.W, and let me tell you why."

"Hey, dad, he can't talk to you like that," Wally sulked.

Wetzel stepped back and studied Dodd from toe to head. He stuck his hand across the counter and into his son's face. Wally grabbed a Panatella from the cigar shelf and handed it over. "All right, Mr. convict. Why don't you tell me why it's a bad idea for Meeker to hire my son back?"

"Because your son's got a big mouth. He likes to tell people about your deals around town. Brag about the old man. When I came in tonight he was bragging to a customer that you and Mal Rafferty were bribing several legislators to get a race track built on the west side of town."

Wetzel turned a deep color of purple, biting his cigar in two. "He said what?"

"You heard me."

The Wetzel kid turned a deep purple. "No fucking way I said that, dad."

Wetzel reached across the counter and slapped him. "Watch your mouth."

Wetzel turned to Ralph. "You told an ex-convict about the race track?"

Ralph shook his head. "I haven't said a word, and you and I know damn well Mal and Joe Bob wouldn't discuss it. If Dodd heard about the race track, he heard it from your son."

"No fucking way," the kid repeated.

Dodd had never witnessed a man turn from red to purple to royal blue in one evening, but Wetzel turned so blue Dodd thought he would drop dead on the tile. He turned to his son who dropped below the counter and crouched while he said, "He's lying pop, I never said nothing and he told me he was that idiot Bill Todd that you hate's cousin."

Dodd snapped his fingers. "That's right. Your son also told me that you could discourage customers so Todd would default on his loan. Then Meeker here can buy the lot's paper. Do you really tell your business to your son, Double W?"

Wetzel spit all over the boy and the counter. "That's it. I've given you your last goddam chance." Dodd would never have believed a man that short and that fat could reach over a store counter and pull a hundred and fifty pound sack of shit across it.

Wetzel not only grabbed his son but he pulled him over the counter, knocking the snuff display and key chain rack to the floor.

Wetzel slapped his son half a dozen times while the boy pleaded his innocence, and then he carried him under his arm into the parking lot where he threw him into the car.

Joe Bob slipped beside Dodd as he watched Wetzel tear out of the parking lot. "What else did that kid tell you about the race track?"

"Nothing. He shut up as soon as I asked if he thought that was something everybody in town should know."

Joe Bob brushed off Dodd's shoulders. "That's smart thinking, son. Seems to me that's not the kind of thing a dip shit like Wetzel should be telling anyone."

"So it's true? You guys are trying to bring a race track to town?"

Joe Bob's hand stopped brushing. "I wouldn't know anything about that."

After Joe Bob left, Ralph stayed behind to help Dodd clean up the store. As Dodd slipped the Magnum and the bullets back into the gun rack, Ralph told him to lock up and go on home. Dodd watched Meeker pull out of the driveway and then turned out the lights and locked the store. When he climbed into his car, he slipped the automatic and a box of shells under his seat. All in all, he thought, not a bad way to end the evening.

Not a bad way to end the week.

Chapter 26

Dodd woke late Monday morning and decided to make do with a quick shower before throwing breakfast together. He pulled his last clean shirt out of his suitcase and realized he would need to get to a Laundromat. He brushed a day's worth of dust from his spare suit and realized he would need a dry cleaner too.

Bobby sloped into the kitchen and drooped into the other chair. "Bet you had a better evening than I had."

"Since I don't know what kind of evening you had, it would be hard to say."

"Some preacher fellows dropped by looking for you." Bobby announced and pulled a stack of publications from under the table. The stack was half a dozen magazines thick boasting titles like: "Liberals and False Gods: Baby Steps to Hell," and "Voting Democratic: Selling God to False Politics"

"You let them into the house?"

"It got a little boring with you off tomcatting around. There's no TV, so I needed some entertainment. There was two of them, one was a Bedrock Baptist and the other was a Bible Believing Bedrock Baptist and their mission was to make sure their two churches had more members than the false and deceiving Baptist church. Course half way through their speech they got to arguing. I thought one of them was going to cut the other one's eyes out with this little cross he had around his neck. The only thing that saved the other one was that he twisted it off with his free hand and started screaming about idle heathens, or heathen idles or some shit like that."

Dodd tossed the magazines into the bin with the food scraps. "Don't let them in again. Now, let's go open the store."

Bobby picked up the pieces of plastic and foil that Dodd left on the kitchen table the night before. "What's this?"

"Some junk I found behind the house."

Bobby looked at the plastic strip more carefully. "The plastic's got some kind of writing on it, but it ain't English."

"It's Navaho," Dodd said.

"Bull shit," Bobby said. He crumpled the foil together and watched it fold back out. "Cool. This is the flying saucer, ain't it?"

Dodd took the foil and the strip and carried them to the counter where he dropped them into a drawer. "Is this whole town crazy?"

"I knew you was bull shitting yesterday. You been hiding a flying saucer. Wetzel bet me five dollars that there's a UFO out here and I was dumb enough to take it."

Dodd closed the drawer with his hip and leaned against the counter. "Now think about what you just said. Wally Wetzel thinks there's a flying saucer on this property. Wouldn't that tell you there's probably no such thing?"

Bobby stood from his chair and tucked it under the table. He grinned from ear to ear. "Even an idiot can see a hole in the fucking road, Dodd. He may be a dimwit but all the other dim bulbs in this town say they saw the flying saucer too. We even heard of it over in Tanglewood. Now that stick you had there looked like it was in a fire or some kind a wreck and those marks sure looked alien to me."

Dodd shook his head and grabbed his car keys from the counter. "Christ, Bobby, now I'm not sure I can trust you by yourself in the store for the next couple of days."

"Why would I be by myself?"

Dodd draped his arm over Bobby's shoulders and steered him toward the door. "I was hoping to surprise you. Wally's looking for a new job."

Bobby jumped off the porch and jerked opened the passenger door. "No shit. So I'm gonna be the manager now?"

Dodd stood on the porch a few more seconds to enjoy the unusually chilly morning. It must have been at least seventy degrees. "Hell, no. I'm going to hire someone older to replace him."

At the store Bobby showed Dodd how to dip the gas tanks, clear out the register receipts for the previous day, turn on the neon lights and load the Slurpee machine and the three coffee brewers that Meeker wanted going full time.

"Wetzel taught you how to do all that?"

"Nah, I just watched him. It took him most of the day to get all this done. Does this mean I'm the assistant manager now?"

Dodd opened a cold RC and poured half the bottle down his throat. He was still parched from Rhonda Mayfield's lemonade the night before. He didn't see the need to answer Bobby's question a second time.

Bobby began to restock the cigarette rack. "Hell, I can do three times the job Wally did."

"So can a trained seal, kid. Meeker would blow his top if I hired you."

Bobby turned to face him, juggling a pack of Camels in and out of his right hand. "Why?"

"Maybe because you tried to rob his store last week?"

Bobby rolled his eyes. "You think he holds that against me?"

Dodd finished the Cola and tossed the can across the room to the garbage can by the far door. "I already have a replacement. You're lucky I'm leaving you on your own till then."

Bobby stuck his hand out over the counter. "Mr. Meeker says employees pay for all food and soft drinks. Are you going to pay or are you going to let me take inventory the way Wally did." He smiled broadly and held his hand out further.

Dodd peeled a dollar from his pocket and slapped it on the counter.

He parked in front of the town hall and walked to the Paris Cafe. The morning shift was already settling in to make sure they would have their tables at lunch.

He tried to dodge the five Right Reverends sitting at their usual table, but the Baptist Spears managed to make eye contact and rose halfway from his chair. "Brother Dodd, do you mind if we have a word with you?"

He spotted Del Rayburn and Bill Todd and waved. "Sorry, boys, I have a meeting scheduled." He hurried over to Todd's table. Rayburn stuck his finger out like a gun and said, "I heard you robbed the same store you saved. And the clerk even gave you the gun."

Tom Robbins, a farmer with property fifteen miles west of town, leaned over the back of his seat and said, "W.W.'s hot under the collar. Found out the only feller stupider than himself is his own son."

Dodd aimed a finger right back at them and drew up his chair beside Bill Todd, who was doing his best to ignore him. "What's the matter, Bill? Couldn't turn a simple repair into a sale for once?"

"Good will, boys" Todd said, with the most unconvincing smile. "I sell good will."

Dodd waved to Elna for coffee then patted him on the shoulder. "That's right, boys, think about the resale value of good will."

Rayburn slapped the table. "Bill, you been taken by every smart car buyer in town." He leaned toward Dodd and winked. "I got him to sell me a '77 pickup for the price of a '76 because he parked it on the wrong side of the lot. Got it paid off before the warranty expired." Dodd could barely understand him between the tobacco plug in his jaw, the snuff under his lip and the cigar in his teeth. "The best part was, all the major repairs showed up before the warranty expired too. Got me new headers, a new tranny and new bearings all around. Didn't cost me nothing. Bill here's the patron saint of car buyers."

Todd seemed to be the only one at the table not enjoying the conversation.

Before they could continue heaping onto his misery Elna the waitress slammed a white ceramic mug in front of Dodd and started to pour. He slipped his hand over it, causing the coffee to stream onto an already badly stained tablecloth. It was cool enough to feel good in the heat of the day. "Can I get this to go, hon? And maybe from a fresh pot that's still warm?"

She held the pot in front of her and rested her free wrist on her hip. The look she gave was nothing less than an evil eye. Dodd slipped a dollar onto the table. "Large black. Keep the change." She grabbed it before his fingers fell away and stormed back to the bar.

"I love this town," he said to Todd, who looked away.

"It does grow on you, doesn't it," Rayburn said.

While Elna fumbled under the counter for a paper cup, Mal Rafferty walked into the cafe. Rayburn mumbled under his breath, "Surprised to see him slumming."

Rafferty caught Dodd's eye and nodded toward the door.

"Excuse me, boys, I think I've been summoned," Dodd said, rising from his chair. He took the cup from Elna and followed Rafferty outside. Rafferty took a seat on the scrolled iron bench outside the cafe window and nodded for Dodd to join him.

"Wouldn't you rather meet in your office?"

Rafferty waited without saying a word and finally Dodd sat beside him. Rafferty laid both arms across the back of the bench and stared across the street. "Where did you really hear about the race track?"

Dodd smiled to himself. "Meeker left a letter from Wetzel on his desk for me to file. He probably forgot it was there."

Rafferty nodded again and shifted his gaze to the steeple of the Hard Shell Baptist Church. "How much do you know?"

"As a lawyer? Or as Meeker's manager?"

That caught Rafferty's attention. He finally looked into Dodd's eyes. "I'll let you decide."

"If I were his lawyer I wouldn't let me near that letter. It would be locked up in a fire proof safe at home. As his manager, I buried it in his files. I doubt even you could find it unless your secretary went through all his correspondence one page at a time with no other distractions."

Rafferty sucked his upper lip between his teeth and stared across the street again. "You could do a lot more for that race track than the Meekers could."

"I don't know, Mal. Folks around here seem to think Ralph is the town's brain trust. That's a hard billing to live up to."

Rafferty sighed. He clearly didn't like a Meeker being given more credit than him. "It's a small town, Dodd. Wouldn't take much to be the town's brain trust. And I promise you Ralph is not it. You, however, are young, reasonably ambitious, and, I hope, reasonably reasonable."

"Are you offering me a piece of the race track?"

"You couldn't afford a piece. I'm offering you sweat equity for two points the first year, and a half point every year after that. Just keep your mouth shut and run a few errands for me. Keep me informed of any correspondence that may cross Meeker's desk."

Dodd chewed the thought over for a moment. He studied the street. The few people passing by made sure not to notice the fact that he and Rafferty were having a conversation. They made it a point to look across the street. "I just finished parole and you want me to jump back into something illegal?"

Rafferty sighed and stretched his legs out into the sidewalk. "Your end will be on the up and up. I'll offer you a contract based on the contingency of legalized gambling. And since the Meekers and I are partners in this, any exchange of information is quite ethical. Does that reassure you?"

"Define point."

Rafferty's smile faded, ever so slightly. "A small piece of the action, son. One you don't want to miss out on. I'll spell out the terms in the contract. If you don't like it, don't sign."

"Didn't you want me out of town just the other night?"

Rafferty slipped his wrist off the bench and draped his fingers around Dodd's shoulder. He held Dodd's gaze. "I can't afford to have you running around loose in my pasture any more. I need you safely in my stable."

Dodd nodded his head and stared across the street, sucking his upper lip just as he watched Rafferty do. "As long as it's warm and there's plenty of hay, I can stay inside."

Rafferty stood and stretched without acknowledging Dodd. "Good. I'll have Rhonda send a contract over this afternoon."

Chapter 27

Ralph Meeker sputtered over his Beam and coffee. "You want me to hire a nigger to manage my store?"

Dodd placed his hand over Meeker's cup and eased it down onto the desk before he spilled it. "Not a nigger, Ralph. A retired accountant. A retired accountant who used to be your accountant, if you'll recall."

"Yeh, but he never worked in my office. So the good folks didn't have to look at him. Now, he'll be right out in the open. Handing white folks their change, touching their food wrappers. That won't go over too well."

"Jesus Christ, Ralph, times have changed. Folks are used to dealing with Black people."

"Not in this part of the country," Ralph insisted. "You see any niggers living in town? There's good reason for that."

"Just in the daytime, Ralph. Until we can find somebody to replace Wetzel."

Ralph was having none of it. "That nigger's brother robbed my stores. Why the hell should I give him the time of day? Before I know it, I'll let my guard down. He'll run off with my money, and I won't even know he did it." Ralph's neck began to seep red under his collar. Dodd wondered if maybe he wasn't pushing it slightly. "Why can't you do it? I hired you to manage, after all."

"If you want me to do it, I will. But that will keep me out of your other offices, and you'll be back to where you were before your hired me. Bobby can deal with the customers. Let Alvin manage."

Meeker poured his Beam and coffee into the trash and filled his cup with straight Beam. "You don't understand, Dodd. He might fuck me just to get even with me for sending his brother to jail."

"Why would he want to get even for sending his brother to jail. He held you up, didn't he? Don't you think Alvin knows his brother's guilty?"

Meeker held his mug up from the desk, rolling it between his palms, studying the rotation.

"It's not like you and Joe Bob gunned Preacher down the way you did the Dodds," Dodd added.

Meeker's mug almost slipped from his hand. He recovered before more than a drop could spill and swallowed about half the contents. His hand began to shake. "How do you even know Rawlings?"

"Huntsville. You don't think I heard his story about how you boys set him up? How you and Roy Lee blew away Delroy Lean? Wasn't that his name?"

Meeker began to stammer, the whiskey beginning to splash past the top of his mug. "Surely you don't believe anything that nigger told you in prison. You being a lawyer and all."

Dodd took the cup from Ralph's hands. "What I'm saying is that Alvin Rawlings didn't rob your store, his brother did. Why would Alvin want to settle a score over a legal arrest?"

Ralph snatched back his cup. He took another swallow and began to cough. For a moment Dodd thought he was going to have a stroke. Dodd leaned over and patted him on the back until the coughing fit ended.

Ralph studied Dodd through unfocused blue eyes. "I don't feel good about this."

"He's got to be better than Wally Wetzel, Ralph. Wetzel is too stupid to understand the operation, and he's a petty thief beside. He's always pilfering from your store. Besides, I promise to keep an eye on him."

"Why Rawlings?"

"Name one person who could do that job that you don't have to train, or isn't too stupid to trust with your store? Or both?"

"Maybe there are advantages to store managers who are too stupid to catch on. Maybe there are worse things an employee can do than pilfer."

Dodd eased Ralph's hands back to the desk. "I'll check the books and keep him honest, Ralph."

Ralph pushed away from his desk and stood up to stare out his window. "Maybe that's the problem. Maybe he already is honest and he may see things that will rekindle old grudges about his brother. Maybe his being an accountant isn't an advantage, if you catch my drift."

Dodd wondered how much caffeine and alcohol the man actually put away in a day. "You haven't been cooking the books have you, Ralph?"

Ralph's face turned as white as ash, the alcohol glow drained from his cheeks and nose. "No, I ain't saying that. Well, maybe not me. But maybe there's things in the books a nigger shouldn't be looking at."

"Or an auditor?"

Ralph nodded his head and eased himself back into the chair. He refilled his mug yet again.

"It wasn't me. Joe Bob and Mal have some scheme cooked up. I can't tell you what it is. But we've been underreporting store receipts for a while now."

Dodd shook his head with disappointment. "What are you telling me, Ralph? You're laundering money? That you boys're selling drugs in Sweet Water Falls? I have a hard time with that."

Meeker's face flushed deep red. "No. I would never sell drugs. I believe thrift and sobriety's good for me and it's good for the rest of the town as well."

Dodd leaned in, so that his nose was close to Meeker's. He caught the undeniable scent of a distillery. Meeker swallowed more than half of the contents of the mug, but his shakes only got worse. "I shouldn't be telling you this," Meeker confessed.

"About the race track you mean?"

Ralph leaned back in his chair and lost his grip on the mug. Dodd caught it before the rest of it splashed across his desk. "How did you know about the race track? I thought the Wetzel kid told you only his father and Rafferty were involved."

Dodd leaned across and patted his shoulder. "Relax, Ralph. Rafferty met with me at breakfast to cut me in. Offered points off the action over the first few years if I'd keep an eye on you and Joe Bob's end of things. Protect his interests in the enterprise, if you catch my drift."

"He wants you to spy on me?"

"I couldn't figure out why until you mentioned the exaggerated store receipts. Personally, I would never have told me, but now that you did, it's in the open. You boys are laundering the bribe money through your businesses."

Dodd opened Meeker's bottle and topped off his mug. "Let me guess. The cash comes through your hands and gets washed in the business transactions. Then it goes to willing legislators who will cast the vote to put gambling on the ballot. Of course, Rafferty wants to make sure you aren't playing footloose with the money yourself because it's mostly his money. Or else it's the bank's money and he's using you to make it disappear."

Ralph wouldn't touch the mug. "What's your interest in this?"

"I don't want to go back to jail. So I figure I better watch your ass, not Rafferty's. Because you're the fall guy if this goes in the shit hole."

Ralph shook his head, and put his fingers through the mug handle, still not ready to drink. "No, that would never happen. It's Joe Bob's and Mal's baby. I'm just sitting on the edges, letting them run the money past me."

Dodd laughed and stood. "That makes you the perfect patsy, Ralph. If I can see it, you should be able to. That's why I want Rawlings in the store. If the books need to be cooked, I want them cooked to our advantage. Do you see where I'm coming from?"

"Quite frankly, no."

Dodd laughed. "Jesus, Ralph. If you're going to be the patsy, you ought to be the one to profit the most as well."

Ralph breathed in deeply and drained the mug. He let his eyes focus, as best they were capable of focusing, before he answered. Dodd couldn't tell if he was trying to think or to keep from passing out, but he figured Meeker was so drunk by now he would never remember the details of their conversation. At best he would remember they were conspiring to save Ralph's ass. "Tell him to stay away from the customers. And you better check the books every goddam day yourself. And you both better keep your noses looking clean because if Mal even thinks we're going to double cross him he will drop us in cement bags in the deepest part of the river."

Dodd leaned across the desk and patted him on the shoulder. "Good thinking, Ralph. I knew I could count on you." Then he refilled Ralph's mug one last time and waltzed out of the office, blowing Mrs. Brazwell a kiss as he backed through the door.

Chapter 28

Mary Beth burst through the bank doors with all the force of a whirlwind. Dodd was double-checking the receipts for the afternoon deposits. Her speed, her direction, the purse swinging briskly from the strap over her shoulder and the tightly pursed lips that curled down above her chin suggested she was aiming straight for him and she wasn't looking for stimulating afternoon conversation.

She stepped up to his chest, her head butting his chin. She propped her hands on her hips to accuse him. "You were with that bitch last night."

"Excuse me?" Dodd said. He held his ground even as she tried to back him into the teller window.

"That bitch." She pointed toward her father's office. No one else in the bank, who consisted of two tellers, Marla Mayfield and a customer, looked with Mary Beth to the office. They stared at Dodd and the whirlwind that engulfed him.

Dodd pulled her aside by the elbow. "Aren't you being a little hasty to judge?" he said, trying to keep his voice down.

"What's there to judge?" Mary Beth shouted. Dodd put one hand over her mouth and held a finger to his lips to shush her.

"Then let's try some facts. Who exactly are you calling a bitch?"

He pulled his hand away. Mary Beth pursed her lips, pointed to Marla and said, "The little bitch's mother. The big bitch."

Marla, who so far had watched the exchange with mild bemusement, shoved her chair back and jumped to her feet. "Isn't that the pot calling the kettle black?"

Mary Beth turned on one heel and said, "The only kettle I see is the big fat one you sit on."

Rafferty's office door opened. Rhonda and Rafferty stepped through to see what was causing the commotion. At that point Dodd picked Mary Beth up by the waist, clapped his hand back over her mouth and escorted her out of the bank. "Excuse me, folks," he apologized.

Rafferty charged down the stairs. Rhonda hurled a withering glare in his direction. Dodd nodded politely and said, "Y'all can get back to work."

Once outside, Dodd set Mary Beth down on to the pavement and said, "You're a combative little thing, aren't you?"

She planted her legs firmly. "My daddy won't let you treat me like that."

"You think Mal likes you calling both the women he sleeps with bitches? In public?"

She lost her steam and stumbled back. "You know about that?"

Dodd guided her to a sidewalk bench and eased her onto the seat. "Wasn't hard to figure out. But that doesn't explain your problem with either Mrs. Mayfield or me." He sat down beside her, and draped his arm across the back of the bench.

"I want to know what you were doing with that slut last night."

Dodd gripped her chin with his free hand. "Let's get this straight, Mary Beth. As best I know that woman only slept with her husband and your old man. She sure hasn't slept with me. You, on the other hand, freely admit you'll turn down the bed sheets whenever it tickles your fancy. So who's the slut in this discussion?"

She pulled her chin free and looked away. "What's that supposed to mean?"

"It means she invited me over for sandwiches and lemonade and I accepted. No hanky panky. Besides, I got the feeling Saturday night that we weren't exactly obliged to keep up with each other about our comings and goings."

"What ever gave you that idea?"

Dodd laughed. He threw his head back and studied a hawk circling in on some distant prey. "You're the one who told me we have no lock on each other's affections. You're the one whose clothes were all over the hallway in your house. You're the one who rode the wild pony with some guy I don't know Saturday night."

"You're one to talk." She reached into her purse and took out a cigarette. She offered one to Dodd and he waved the pack away, knowing full well she hadn't forgotten he didn't smoke.

"For the last time, Mary Beth, I didn't sleep with Rhonda Mayfield. Why don't you ask her? Or does Daddy not like you fighting with his afternoon delight?"

She released a blast of thunderous gray smoke. "Watch how you talk around me. I'm still a lady."

"Does the lady have a sense of irony?"

She turned to look at him with an open and straight face. "You knew what kind of girl I was when you took up with me."

Dodd took her cigarette from between her fingers and crushed it out under his shoe. "This will kill you. And you're a fruitcake."

"I know this hotel in Fort Stockton. After you make your deposits tomorrow, we can drive over for dinner and the wild ride. I promise to keep you entertained till morning." She reached under his tie with her fingers and adjusted his knot. "You look sexy in a suit, by the way."

"A wild ride, you say."

"You'll need to iron this suit for a week."

Dodd stood, and dusted off his suit. "I think I can rearrange my schedule to fit that in."

Mary Beth left him with a look of satisfaction on her face. He wasn't sure whether the thought of their rendezvous satisfied her, or the fact that Rhonda Mayfield was watching them from inside the bank's front door.

Dodd waved to Rhonda and began to whistle as he walked to his car.

Chapter 29

At midnight Dodd heard Bobby calling his name. He sounded like he was fifty yards away, near the house. Dodd shoved his shovel straight into the dirt and answered, "Over here, by the light."

He lifted the Coleman lantern above his head. In a few seconds Bobby began to take shape in the diffuse light. Dodd waited for him to reach the pit, and put the lantern down.

"I figured it was you," Bobby said, kneeling down at the edge. He was dressed in his BVDs and Dodd's flip flops. "Especially when I woke up and your bedroom door was wide open and I could see this light through your bedroom window."

Dodd took his shovel up and began to dig again. "Sounds like you're ready for college."

"So what, exactly, are you doing?"

"I'm digging."

"In the middle of the night?"

Dodd leaned on his shovel. "It's a hell of a lot cooler now than in the daytime, isn't it?" He looked around him and realized he'd dug a decent pit, about three feet across and four feet deep, in little more than an hour. "I guess I'll call it quits for now."

Bobby offered Dodd his arm to help him scramble out of the hole. “How big is it gone to be?”

Dodd surveyed his work from ground level. “As big as it needs to be.” He picked up the shovel and the lantern. “I guess I’ll take a shower before I hit the hay.”

Bobby followed him. “Aren’t you going to tell me what it’s for?”

Dodd laughed. “Can’t you guess?”

“You know the Meekers want me to tell them every thing you do.”

Dodd held the lantern up to see Bobby’s face. “Well it’s hardly a secret is it? It’s going to get bigger too. Tell them whatever you want to tell them.” He doubled his pace. Bobby tripped over his flip flops trying to keep up with him.

Chapter 30

Tuesday morning he found Bill Todd, Del Rayburn and Will Gaylord sitting at the same table and trying not to look like they were sitting together. Todd drank his coffee and stared out the window to the street, Rayburn buried his head behind the paper, and Gaylord sat with his arm over the back of his chair, smoking and pretending to look at the special on the blackboard.

The only special Dodd had seen since his arrival was two eggs and ham with biscuits, gravy and coffee for three dollars—juice and onions extra, which seemed like it should be called the "normal" to him.

Dodd took a table on the other end of the room, a two-seater, the only table that wasn't occupied. He ordered black coffee and the special with juice.

"That's a buck fifty more," Elna said, her cigarette almost tumbling from her astonished mouth.

"I feel like juice today."

She poured his coffee and said, "As long as you're being the big spender, onions is only fifty cents more."

"Then you wouldn't kiss me," he said. He raised his cup to her. Todd nodded his head to Dodd, trying to get his attention.

Dodd waited until Elna waddled halfway across the room. He called after her, "Could you get me extra butter for those biscuits?"

"That'll be an extra quarter," she told him. He waved his hand to tell her go ahead. Four seventy-five. For breakfast. That was extravagant for Sweet Water Falls, a town where you ordered the specials and avoided the extras because that's what specials were for. Dodd knew Elna would probably have to slip out the back and run to the grocery store to buy the juice.

By now Todd had given up on nodding and was waving furiously. Gaylord was looking his way and hissing to get his attention. Dodd smiled and lifted his coffee in a toast. "Do you boys want to talk to me?" he called across the room.

Rayburn put his fingers to his lips and signaled for Dodd to join them, although Dodd was certain everybody in the room knew what they wanted. He picked up his cup and saucer and crossed the dining room to their table. The local grocer leaned toward him to whisper: "You ought a pay attention to what they tell you."

Todd lowered is voice and leaned in conspiratorially, "The boys and I have a proposition for you."

"Actually, I was going to bring the Mustang in for Tucker to adjust the fuel line. I have a date this evening and the fuel seems to be sluggish. And for some reason the timing's off."

Gaylord put his hand on Dodd's arm. "He'll have it this afternoon."

"I will not," Todd protested.

Dodd sipped his coffee. "That's okay, I'll just tell Ralph to pull your note."

Todd threw up his hands, "Okay, I'll have it ready by three. Now are you ready to listen to our proposition?"

"I've got all morning."

Todd huffed, "I'm not sure I want to discuss it anymore."

Gaylord leaned forward to initiate the conspiracy, ignoring Todd. "You might've noticed that folks around here are getting tired of the way Rafferty and the Meekers run things. They make the real money, we get the leftovers."

"I thought that's what free enterprise was all about. Handcuffing your competition so that you get the lion's share."

"Exactly," Rayburn said over a mouthful of eggs. "And we want to handcuff the competition."

Todd chimed in, "We want you to run for mayor. Local feelings run strong around here, and most folks think the Meekers set your family up. You'd be kind of a lightning rod in the election."

"And who would be sheriff and the justice of the peace?"

"We got that figured out," Gaylord said. "Todd's not making that much with his car lot anyway. So he can be JP. Del here did a six years as a deputy in Bexar County and another ten as a prison guard at Huntsville."

"Probably before you did time," Rayburn added, spearing another piece of diced ham with his fork.

"Wouldn't you think my doing time would hurt my chances?"

Todd broke in, still whispering, "See that's where you got popular sympathy. You'd a probably never done time if the Meekers hadn't killed off your family."

"I'm not one of those Dodds."

Gaylord shook his head. "Will you stick to the point here? The point is we think we can run you against the Gang of Three. All we need is your go-ahead."

"The Gang of Three?" Dodd asked.

Todd tried his best to squeeze a smile onto his face. "It's a joke, see. It's a play on the name of the Chinese..."

"He knows who the Gang of Five are, Bill," Gaylord said.

"Oh. You do?"

Todd stuffed half a biscuit in his mouth and waited for an answer. Dodd didn't have the heart to say anything. "It's a good joke."

Rayburn sopped his biscuit in the finger bowl of gravy beside his plate. "Let's be honest, Dodd, we'll do anything to get rid of those boys. We'd rather have you on our side than their side because things could get ugly."

Ugly like the keystone cops, Dodd thought. He noticed Elna bringing his plate from the kitchen on a tray that also held a six-ounce juice glass. "I know you boys have your own best interest at heart, but if I sell the Meekers out, how long do you think it will be before you begin to suspect I'll sell you out too?"

"Wait a minute..." Rayburn said.

"Gotta pass," Dodd said, rising from the table. "But I promise to keep out of your way, and I wish you the best of luck."

He returned to his table and waved as he sat down. The three men stared at him as though he'd dropped a bomb under their table. Dodd sipped his juice. It was Tang.

Chapter 31

Dodd found Joe Bob waiting in the mayor's office, sitting at his brother's desk with his feet draped over the calendar. He rolled a cigar between his thumb and index finger. "Waiting for a match?" Dodd asked.

Joe Bob didn't smile. He stared at his cigar while he spoke. "I understand my brother's new manager has been meeting with the town dissidents and riffraff about a coup-de-tat." He pronounced it "coupe" with a hard "t" to end the "tat."

Dodd removed his jacket and draped it across the coat rack behind the door. "People have long ears in this town. Was Elna on the phone to you when she wrote up my tab?"

"You didn't answer my question."

Dodd sat in one of the armchairs facing the desk. "You didn't ask a question." He leaned over the desk and took Joe Bob's cigar. "By the way, there's no smoking in the mayor's office."

Joe Bob grabbed it back, crushing it in his haste. "Since when?" He dropped the broken cigar into a wastebasket and brushed the loose tobacco off of his fingers.

"Since I became manager."

"I want to know about you and the malcontents."

"The boys asked me to run for mayor, and I said no."

"That's it?" Joe Bob tried to force him into a stare down as if his eyes were a polygraph.

That was it, but Joe Bob didn't seem to think so. So he decided to embellish. "I told them if they won, I'd be glad to be city manager. After all, I'd be silly to burn my bridges out of loyalty to you two. But I also said I wouldn't lift a finger till they won cause I sure as hell wasn't crossing my meal ticket."

Joe Bob cracked his knuckles."You're a punk, but you're an ignorant punk, so I'm gonna smarten you up right now. Then we won't have this conversation again."

He paused, as if waiting for Dodd to answer. Dodd raised his eyebrows and waited for Joe Bob to continue.

Finally, Joe Bob continued. "There's people with the skills to run a town and people what don't know shit. As of now you know one more thing than they know, and that's that you're one of those people what don't know shit. So people like you, who know they don't know shit, better remind your friends that they don't know shit either and y'all better leave the business of running this town to us. Capiche?" He pronounced it "cap-ee-chee."

"You sure get irritated easy, don't you, Joe Bob? You might want to see a doctor because all that stress could be giving you high blood pressure."

Joe Bob slammed his fist on the desk. "You just don't listen, do you?"

"Joe Bob, I already said I wasn't running against you. Now some people might say that only a stupid sack of shit would threaten somebody who's on his side. Or risk pissing him off enough to tell his enemies things he just found out that might throw an election their way. Not to mention bring a federal marshal and a Texas Ranger or two into the picture. And since we both know you're not a stupid sack of shit, then you might want to back off and not try to piss me off when I already told you I'm on your side."

Joe Bob continued to stare at Dodd for another minute or two, right over the the toe of his boot, which was still propped on the desk, as though he were using it for a gun sight. Finally, he said, "Well, all right. As long as we see eye-to-eye then I guess we don't have a problem."

Dodd lowered his legs and leaned back in his chair. "As long as we're seeing eye-to-eye, do you mind letting me have my desk back? I have work to do."

Joe Bob lowered his legs and rose from the chair. Given his immense weight, the chair seemed to rise several inches. "Oh, I doubt that. I think you're just fooling yourself about your value around here and any day now you're going to wake up and realize you got nothing going at all." He looked for another cigar in his pocket. "That is, if you wake up at all."

Chapter 32

During his drive to Fort Stockton with Mary Beth, Dodd found his attention sorely divided. The wind whipping past with the top down on the Mustang made him feel like a teenager again, with the open road before him and a fine girl beside him. The panorama of lace and fine pubic hair Mary Beth revealed by tucking her right ankle under her knee and leaning against the passenger door made him want to pull off the highway and dive head first into opportunity. Public decency laws and decorum be damned.

She wore a sunflower print skirt with a peasant blouse that scooped down to reveal the soft swell of her breasts. The blouse was semi-transparent, giving a hint of the slight pink of her brassiere, the same lacy pink she wore for panties. Her legs were bare except for sandals with thong straps that she wrapped up her ankles and tied mid-calf.

Even without Mary Beth in the passenger seat, Dodd felt on top of the world. He aired the engine out to ninety as soon as he knew it was oiled and able. He rested his left wrist over the steering wheel, his right wrist on Mary Beth's knee and listened to her voice and the wind droned past him, in perfect harmony with the highway and the distant horizon.

For the first half of the drive Mary Beth rattled on about her new investments, and the Arabian her father bought her the day before. She described how she braided his mane, how she was ordering a new hand-tooled saddle just to match his colors, and how she expected an eighteen percent gain on her newest batch of CDs within nine months.

Then, about halfway there, she pulled her right knee up under her chin and said, "You sure there's nothing between you and Rhonda Mayfield?" The wind threw her hair over the back seat, whipping and billowing in a small storm of its own.

"Not a damn thing. You're the only ride for me."

"I saw her look at you in the bank yesterday, and I don't think that's her version."

"The only things she and I shared were sour lemonade and sandwiches. Which she offered, I didn't ask."

"Well you're a man, and men are supposed to say that."

Dodd began to punch the buttons on his radio dial. "Don't they play anything but Hank Williams out here."

"That's Mel Tillis, honey. They don't even sound the same."

Dodd decided not to argue.

She leaned forward, tucking her hands between her legs and pouted, "So who do you like?"

"Elvis Costello. Kate Bush. Roxy Music. Last year I got into The Clash for when I want to bash my head in." She screwed up her face as though she never heard of them. Dodd realized there was a good chance she probably never had.

"You've been living on the wrong side of Texas," she said. "Country music is eternal, the same song sung over and over again, a million different ways."

Dodd wondered if he hadn't wandered into a county-western song himself. They passed the Old West Inn, the motel where he spied on Rafferty the week before, Mary Beth shouted, "What's wrong with there?"

"That's your old man's love nest, sweetheart. No way I'm taking you there."

She raised herself on her knees, hanging over the back seat and holding onto her hair. She never stopped pointing. "I want to do it there."

Dodd pulled her down in the seat. "No fucking way. He could be there right now."

She slipped back down, and crossed her legs, closing them off to him for the first time that afternoon. "That will make it all the more fun if we see him there."

"Not for me it won't," Dodd said, sensing that she really wanted Rhonda to see them together.

She leaned over and slipped her hand inside his leg. "I swear I'll make it worth your while."

He whipped the Mustang off the highway and into a convenience store parking lot, turning off the radio so he could be heard over the idling engine. "Goddam it, Mary Beth, this isn't a game. I love to fuck with you, but I sure as hell don't want to fuck with your old man."

She laid her head on his shoulder and pulled at his zipper. "I just want to see if he's there. If he is, we won't check in. If he's not, we will. How hard can that be?" She reached past his fly and began to massage.

Dodd swore under his breath and turned the car around. They cruised through the Old West parking lot, and when he was certain Rafferty was nowhere to be found, he pulled under the breezeway to check in.

"Haven't I seen you before?" the clerk asked.

"Probably," Dodd told him.

The clerk filled out a slip and then glanced outside. Mary Beth was on her knees in the passenger seat. "Do you know who that is?" he whistled.

Dodd dropped two twenties on the counter and signed the receipt. "Take a guess."

"It's...," the guy started, and then said, "Oh, I get it. I asked if you know who that is? I should guess that you do since you're with her."

"They've made managers out of less than you," Dodd said, adding another twenty to the counter. He collected the key. "If her old man pulls in, ring three times."

"Three times," the clerk said. "Sure thing. But won't he see the girl when you run for it?"

"Who said I'll be taking her with me?" Dodd replied. He wasn't smiling when he said it.

As soon as he pulled in front of the room, Mary Beth took the key from him and dashed into the room. Once inside, Dodd sat on the bed and began to undress. Mary Beth undressed as well, but in stages, a couple of items then glancing out the window before removing more. When she glanced through the curtain dressed in nothing but the panties she had tempted him with all afternoon, Dodd finally asked, "Who are you looking for? Your old man? Or one of your rivals for my affection?"

She dropped the curtain, and crawled on the bed with him, pushing him back into the mattress and rolling her tongue across his chest like a feather duster. "Nobody, silly."

"Then why do you keep looking out the window?"

"Because a cloudless day keeps me aroused." Then she pulled his pants off by the cuffs and, after doing the same with his boxers, she straddled him with her hips. "Looks like it aroused you too."

"That has nothing to do with the clouds in the sky," he told her, grabbing her by the neck and pulling her lips down to his. She responded by running her tongue across his teeth and then biting his bottom lip. He spanked her, and she giggled, "Ooh, mister tough guy." She slipped further down and ran her tongue around his nipples, his chest, his navel and then centered in on his somewhat indiscreet symbol of desire.

Not to be outdone, Dodd reached over her, and removed her panties, almost genuflecting to get into position to dive in on her as well, and they wrestled each other for position, her jaws locked on his cock, his tongue between her legs, rolling and thrashing until he found her on her palms and knees and he climbed behind her to ride the wild pony as hard and as far as he could take her. He thought he heard her neigh, but he was never completely sure. All he knew is that he held onto one breast with his hand as he rose with her hips which she shook every which way, tossing her head, tossing her hair, tossing her shoulders, until he exploded inside her and she arched her back and shook so hard his knees trembled with her.

She slipped away from him, slipped off the bed, grabbed a handful of Kleenex, and dabbed between her legs. "Sure do love that pill, don't you? Makes it a whole lot easier to get on with business." She wandered over to the window and pulled the curtains back. She glanced around the parking lot and said, "Let's go for a swim."

Dodd lifted himself up onto his wrists and said, "I didn't bring a suit."

She closed the curtain and giggled. "I don't see any kids. We can wear our skimpies."

"Wouldn't a shower do just as good?"

She dropped the wad of tissue into the waste can. "You have no spirit of adventure." She pulled on her panties and her bra, and tiptoed across the carpet to pull a towel from the bathroom. "This will cover me." She must have chosen a face towel because as small as she was, it barely covered her breasts and panties.

Dodd pulled on his boxers. "What the hell," he sighed. He grabbed a towel from the bathroom and wrapped it around his waist. In spite of his thirty-four waist, it barely made it around him. He had to tuck it carefully at the corner of his hip, and keep his fingers closed together to keep it from falling.

He followed her out to the pool and watched her drop her towel and skip onto the diving board. For all her attempts to hide her intentions, Dodd could tell she was scoping the parking lot.

She bounced to the edge of the board on the balls of her feet, and, when she balanced on the last inch of the board, she threw her arms back and her chest out in a magnificent stretch that pressed the shell of her nipples against the soft satin of her brassiere. Then she threw her hands above her head and dived into the water, not making a splash but slipping in, her shoulders disappearing into the blue. Her back glided into the tiny ripple. Dodd knew he would never again experience a moment so arousing in his life.

He dropped his own towel and slipped in the water with her. She broke the surface and began to tread water, pushing her hair from her eyes and again surveying the parking lot. Dodd swam out to meet her, slipping into place and treading water beside her. "You trying to make Rhonda jealous, or your old man kill me in a rage? The games are over nothing, Mary Beth. If you want me to stick around, I will. If you want me gone, I'll skidaddle."

"You are so lost to reality," she said, and pulled him with her to the side of the pool. She reached into his shorts and slipped him past her panty line and up inside of her. He followed through, balancing her against his hips, while she threw her elbows across the side of the pool and chewed on his shoulders.

He lost track of time, he lost track of himself, he lost track of everything but the rhythm of her hips and the clear blue water until her heard a voice say, "Look, mommy, they're wrestling."

Mary Beth's eyes popped wide and she pushed him away from her, sliding into the water and swimming to the shallow end. She stepped out on her toes and grabbed her towel to run to the room.

Dodd adjusted his shorts to let his cock drop back in, and looked up to see a woman in her twenties wearing Ray-Bans and a narrow pink bikini, her arm weighted down with silver and turquoise. Two young children, both under ten, stared at him. "You should pay more attention to what you're doing," she said, pulling a Virginia Slim from her slim gold purse and lighting it with a pewter lighter.

"I did, Ma'am. That's why I didn't see you."

She arched her eyebrows. "I can send them to the room if you have some unfinished business. I have the rest of the afternoon off myself."

"Aren't you afraid they might tell their dad?"

"He's in LA with his new bride-to-be. I'm not sure they'd have anything to tell them."

Dodd pulled himself out of the pool, and grabbed his towel. "We're on our honeymoon, so I think I'd better take care of my unfinished business with her."

"I guess my phone number wouldn't do you much good." She said, measuring him over the length of her cigarette.

Dodd wrapped the towel around his waist, and waved with a finger before sprinting down the sidewalk to catch up with Mary Beth. He heard the boy behind him say, "Why would he need your phone number, mommy? Is he going to clean the pool?"

"No, silly," the younger girl said. "Mommy wants to wrestle too. Isn't that right, mommy?"

Dodd didn't wait to hear the mother's reply, but pushed his way through the motel room door, which was slightly ajar. He found Mary Beth sitting on the edge of the bed, her wet underwear and towel lying in wrinkles on the floor.

He picked her wet things up and said, "Sorry about that."

She crossed her fingers and rested them on her knees, which she held tightly together as she bounced her toes up and down on the carpet. "No you're not. It's a great war story you can tell your drinking buddies till the day you die."

"What's the problem, Mary Beth? You've got something on your mind."

She continued to stare at her fingers, pushing her heels up and down from the carpet. "That woman's on my mind."

He slipped out of his own shorts and carried everything into the bathroom to hand over the shower curtain rod. Then he walked back into the room and sat on the spare bed across from her. "I guess I'm missing something here. I thought we came out to forget everybody else, have dinner and any other fun we have. Instead you spend the whole afternoon looking for ghosts."

"What did she really want?" She said, her eyes following the rhythm of her knees.

"She just came to the pool with her kids and found us already frothing the water."

She pushed herself off the bed, and dug one set of toes into the carpet, wrists on hips. "You know who I mean."

Dodd picked up his jacket, which was lying in a rumple on the spare bed, and straightened it to hang over the back of an armchair. "We're back to Rhonda?"

The memory of her, standing like a five-year-old in the middle of a pout, but with her breasts alert and her hair still wet, aroused him but he willed himself to not notice. He knew any signs of arousal on his part would be misinterpreted.

"Well, who else? She's fucking my father and now she wants to fuck you. It's just like her, getting to me through the men in my life."

Dodd picked his pants up and draped them carefully over his suit jacket. "Am I missing something? Last we talked, I am not the man in your life; at least not the only man. So what is bothering you?"

She slumped onto her bed, rumpled like her clothes. "She knows. She knows that if I fell for a guy it would be you."

"If you fell for a guy. That really makes me feel loved and appreciated, Mary Beth." He walked over to her, and then began to gather up her blouse, skirt and shoes.

"Leave those alone," she said.

"Fine," he said and dropped them into her lap. He sat beside her and put his arm around her. She slipped out of his embrace and walked to the dresser, dropping her clothes on the peeling walnut veneer.

Dodd spread his palms on the bedspread behind him, and leaned back, admiring the swell of her bottom as she stood in front of the dresser and crossed her ankles.

"Look, I told you the whole story yesterday. There is nothing between Rhonda and me. In fact, I told her the truth about your old man poking her daughter. She doesn't even want to talk to me anymore."

She tuned around and leaned against the dresser, her arm draped casually across her breasts as though she suddenly felt vulnerable in his presence. "You're kidding. She didn't know?"

"Do you think she really wanted to know?"

She picked up her blouse and lifted it above her head, letting it tumble into place down her arms and across her neck. "I'm having a hard time with this."

Dodd found himself having a hard time watching her stand there in a blouse with nothing on beneath. He felt his cock swelling in spite of his better judgment.

"Look, if you want to know the truth, the only reason she invited me over is because she had some pieces from a UFO she wanted to show me. Or what she thinks are pieces of a UFO. Her mother got them from one of the Dodd brothers, who, of course, is supposed to be my uncle."

She sat down on the bed beside him, still bottomless, and picked up her purse to fish for a cigarette. She held her lighter under her cigarette and puffed smoke from both sides of her mouth as she stoked the coal. Then she leaned back her head and released the smoke in multiple drifting layers. "I've heard a lot of bull shit from a lot of guys, Dodd, but that's about the best I've heard."

"She had three pieces. She was convinced I wanted to see them because, like everyone else, she's convinced I'm one of those Dodds."

Now she turned to stare at him, taking her hand and placing it in her lap. "Then it's true?"

"What, that I'm one of those Dodds or that there's a UFO?"

Her eyes were round, like a kid who had just seen Santa Claus standing in front of the fireplace, totally oblivious to the Sears and Roebucks price tag still dangling from the seam of the coat. "That there's a UFO."

Dodd suddenly wanted to laugh with the absurdity of the situation. A woman naked from the waist down, capable of sending men into erotic frenzy, sidetracked by ET trivia. "She thinks so. I wasn't exactly convinced; let's put it that way. It was a piece of metal, some tin foil and some melted plastic. Mirror pieces mostly."

She took her hand back and turned around on the bed to face him, tucking her ankles under her knees. "What's that supposed to mean?" Dodd wanted to dive right in to the damp triangle and change the subject back to something more tangible but held back.

"You know, stuff that reflects yourself back at you. If you believe in UFOs, then they could easily be parts of a UFO. If you don't believe in UFOs, there's no way in hell they could be."

Now she pulled her knees up under her chin, and wrapped a wrist around her ankles. "You didn't believe her." Something about the way she said it.

Dodd's erection was getting visible again so he stood up and walked into the bathroom to see if their underwear had dried. He didn't like the direction this conversation was taking. Like suddenly she stopped being a jealous woman demanding explanations, and had become someone fishing for information. If we were really going to play the game, let's play for the big score. "Not really. It did match some stuff I found on the farm, but I'm not convinced they're any more real than her pieces."

Her panties were reasonably dry so he took them down. The bra and boxers were still slightly damp so he left them behind. "Didn't you show them to anybody?" she called behind him. He stepped back into the room and tossed the panties to her.

"Didn't occur to me. Who would know anyway? I sure won't call the government. Once they get in your life, it's hard to get them out. Especially a jail-bird like me."

She slipped over to the edge of the bed and pulled her panties on as she sat in place, lifting her hips and wriggling to let them settle.

"You could show them to the sheriff."

"Joe Bob? Why would I do that?"

"He saw some of that UFO stuff when he was stationed in New Mexico after World War II. When the UFO crashed."

He sat down beside her, and ran his fingers down between her legs. "I'll think about it. The point is, Mary Beth, that nothing is going on between Rhonda and me."

She shook her head and released a thick cloud of smoke, like a geyser, straight out into the air. "Well, that doesn't matter. She's got plans for you. You keep away from her. Don't fuck things up between us."

She crossed over to the dresser again, crushing out her cigarette in the ashtray. Dodd followed her to the dresser and slipped his hand down the back of her panties. She leaned her neck back to kiss him and he reached around with his other hand to feel her breasts. She leaned back further to slip her tongue up his throat and he pulled her back onto the bed, her back to him and on top of them.

She turned around and slipped him into her, bracing her fingers on his shoulder as she rode him, eyes closed, tossing her head and humming to herself. Dodd let her ride him as far as she wanted, but he could sense they'd crossed a line and he couldn't say for sure where the line had been crossed. All he knew was that Mary Beth had left the room and this body on top of him was just going through the motions.

Chapter 33

Sunset brought no relief. After they left the motel room, Mary Beth grew more distant. They shared a mediocre dinner at a restaurant called the Hunter's Lodge. She had a Caesar's salad with pre-packaged croutons and white wine. His venison tasted like chicken, which is the last thing venison should taste like. She poked at her salad and polished off a bottle of wine, and he poked at his venison because he could barely cut through it.

He put up the roof for the drive back, and she leaned against the window to stare at the sky. The only dialogue came from commercials on the radio. He pulled up beside her truck in the bank parking lot.

"Spend the night with me," she said. She didn't look at him.

Dodd pulled her head across the seat and laid it on his shoulder. "That sounds more like regret than an invitation."

She pulled away and sat straight in her seat. "That's not fair."

Dodd sighed. "That means it's true."

She leaned kissed him on the lips. It felt like more of a wistful last taste than a desire to indulge. “You don’t need to get out.”

She crossed from his car to her truck in a single, fluid motion. She jammed her car into gear and pulled away, spraying the loose parking lot gravel across his car. He decided to head for home. He was always slow to recognize a last call.

As he approached his farm, he spotted some lights about fifty yards behind the house. He checked his watch; well after midnight. Too late for a party, he thought, at least in this town. He drove fifty yards past and around the next curve then he turned on the shoulder and headed back to town. He let himself into his office and called Alvin Rawlings.

“It’s after midnight, Dodd,” Alvin complained. “Wanda likes her whole nine hours.”

“They took the bait.”

“Oh crap, it would have to be tonight,” he complained. “I need at least a half hour.”

“I’ll give you forty-five minutes.”

Dodd killed twenty minutes playing solitaire with Ralph’s bourbon-stained and cigarette-singed deck. He placed one more phone call and let himself out of the office, making sure to leave the door unlocked. He took his time driving back, and doused his lights a quarter mile from the house. As he topped the hill leading to his property, he killed the engine and coasted into the yard.

From the back yard he could clearly make out two beams of light from the direction of his excavation the night before. He let the car roll to within five yards of the house, and then pulled up the brake.

He opened the car door as softly as he could and slipped out. He eased the door into place, not letting the latch click. He tiptoed into the house where he found Bobby sitting by the window, watching the light show outside.

“You told them,” he whispered as pulled up a chair.

“I said you were spending the night in Fort Stockton. They were busy at work when I got home.”

“You want to have some fun?”

Bobby shook his head. "If you're gonna go talk to them, I'd rather not be around. Don't want them to think I'm on your side."

Dodd rubbed the kid's head. "Bobby, there is no side to be on, but if you had to be on one, mine would no doubt be the wrong side." He glanced at his watch.

"Well, aren't you going to go confront them?" Bobby said. "They're wrecking your yard."

"Ten minutes," Dodd said. He remained at the window, checking his watch, until he reached the forty-five minute window he set with Rawlings. Then he stood up, stretched and said, "Show time."

He grabbed a half dozen of the stuffed green hefty garbage bags piling up behind the back door. He swung them over both shoulders, three bags per shoulder, and headed toward the dig.

A pickup and Meeker's patrol car sat a few yards from the pit. Two industrial strength Coleman lanterns lighted the dig.

The Meeker's laughter and the sound of dirt flying over the side covered the sound of his approach. Smoke from two cigars curled up from the pit. He stepped to the edge and shook his head. The Meekers stood at the bottom, leaning on shovels and watching three Black laborers who had dug another three feet down and tripled the size of the hole.

Dodd tossed the first three bags down into the hole. The bags glanced off Joe Bob's shoulders and landed at Ralph's feet.

"Hey, boys," he hailed them. "Thanks for the improvements. This should raise the value of the property by at least five hundred dollars."

The laborers stopped digging. They tried to shield their eyes from the lantern lights to make him out. Joe Bob stuttered, "What the fuck are you doing here?"

Dodd hefted the second batch of garbage bags and dropped them in. They landed on Joe Bob's boots. "I live here."

"You're supposed to be in Fort Stockton slipping it to the mayor's daughter," Ralph said. Joe Bob kicked him in the ankle.

"Well supposed to be and being are two different things, aren't they, Ralph? But I sure do appreciate your finishing my land fill for me."

Joe Bob threw his shovel into the dirt. "Land fill? What the hell do you mean, 'land fill?'"

Ralph wiped his face with his sleeve and began to grin.

"Didn't Bobby tell you I was digging a land fill? We got half-a-dozen bags of garbage behind the house already and no place to dispose of it. I figured it would be easier to bury it here than drive it to the dump."

Even as he finished his sentences the yard around them exploded with light. Two patrol cars rushed onto the property, slamming on their brakes and swerving into position at the edge of the hole. Carl Ray Hoskins jumped out of one, pumping the barrel of a twenty gauge shot gun, and another deputy Dodd didn't recognize dropped to his knees and aimed his shotgun over the hood of the car.

Hoskins rushed to the edge of the pit, shot gun aimed straight down to spray anybody hiding beneath the lip. He drew short when he saw Joe Bob staring back at him.

"Carl, what the fuck are you doing here?" Joe Bob growled, He let loose a dark gob that disappeared into the dirt.

"I got you covered, Carl Ray," the other deputy shouted from the safety of his car. Carl Ray held up his hand to shut him up.

Carl Ray lowered his shotgun. "We got a call, Joe Bob. Dodd here said some assholes was vandalizing your property and that we better get out here to break it up."

Ralph laughed and laid his shoulder on Joe Bob's shoulder. "That's pretty smart, Joe Bob. Getting us to dig his land fill for him."

Joe Bob spit again, barely missing Ralph's foot. "You ain't any fucking funnier than Dodd." Then he turned back to Carl Ray, who had been joined by his sheepish looking partner. "So tell me, Carl Ray. Who's in charge of the office now that you and Bobby Joe are out here aiming guns at me?"

"No one. Dodd said you'd want the full crew out here," Carl Ray stammered.

Bobby Joe nodded his head in unison. "That's the truth. I was there when he called, chief. Ask him. He's standing right beside you."

"I don't give a shit if he's standing neck deep in crap, whatever made you boys think that you should violate my standing order never to leave the office unmanned under any circumstances?"

Dodd put his hand on Joe Bob's shoulder. "I'm sorry, Joe Bob, I didn't know about those orders. I told them that I couldn't raise you on the phone, and I might need all the help possible."

Joe Bob threw his cigar into the dirt beside his shovel, and motioned for the three laborers to help lift him out of the hole. He struggled out as two of them scooped their hands for him to push off of them. Carl Ray and Bobby Joe strained to pull him up by his shoulders. Once he was standing on the surface, he brushed his shirt off and said, "You boys better get back to the fucking office now before I skin your asses alive."

Dodd helped Ralph climb out while Joe Bob chewed out his deputies. Bobby Joe returned to his car, but Carl Ray gave Dodd a hostile glare. "You better not fuck with me again, Dodd."

Dodd patted him on the shoulder. "It was a joke, Carl. I was just having some fun with your boss."

"Don't worry about, Joe Bob, boys." Ralph tossed in. "If he fires you, I'll make sure he hires you back."

Bobby Joe started his patrol car. He called out over the engine. "Sorry about this, Joe Bob. It won't happen again."

"That's what I call sucking up," Dodd said as the two cars pulled away. "That boy bucking for a promotion, you think? Maybe he even wants your job."

"Shut up," said Joe Bob. He scratched under his armpit then pulled another cigar from the plastic case in his pocket. "You tell that boy of yours this was gonna be a land fill?"

Dodd picked up one of the lanterns. "Who can recall a conversation in the middle of the night? Are you going to help me carry the rest of our trash down too, or are you just going to help out with the digging part?"

Ralph nodded his head and chuckled. "Joe Bob, cool off. We set ourselves up. We'll get him back some other time."

"You shut up too," Joe Bob growled. He took his cigar from his mouth and waved it under Dodd's nose. "You think you're so fucking smart, but you aren't. We're on top of you, boy, and we're gonna stay on top. Don't think any of this cutesy shit puts you in any better standing."

He ordered the laborers to carry the shovels and lamps to the pickup.

Ralph pulled his flask from his hip pocket. "Well I think it's funny. You'd think that sumbitch did all the digging himself, the way he's carrying on." He took a long pull. "Your old man had a sense of humor like that. In high school he used to send these love letters to Joe Bob, make him think one of the cheerleaders was so hot for him she'd put out on the first date. Joe Bob dated all the cheerleaders, spent wads of money, and got no pussy from any of them. Never once figured ole Zane was pulling his chain."

"Is that why Joe Bob killed him?" Dodd asked. "Because of a practical joke?" With the light departing to the pickup he could barely make out Ralph's face.

The smile dropped from Ralph's face. "You got a lot of queer ideas, son."

"He wasn't my father anyway," Dodd said.

Chapter 34

Joe Bob waited in ambush outside the Paris Café the next morning. He sat on the bench, trying to cross his legs, but could only get one ankle over a knee.

Dodd slipped next to him before he could say anything. "It's a great day to sit outside. Throw some exercise in and you might even start to feel better about yourself."

Joe Bob turned to face Dodd, causing the bench to shift against the sidewalk. "You and I gonna have a talk, boy."

Dodd checked his watch. "I'll be at my office in forty-five minutes. Call Mrs. Brazwell and tell her to pencil you in."

Joe Bob opened Dodd's jacket and shoved a cigar into the breast pocket. He dropped his volume by half. "Listen to me, you little worm shit son-of-a-bitch. You pushed this ole boy too far. You got that? I don't care that you're clear of parole so I can't yank you for a violation. You're still a fucking ex-con and in my town ex-cons belong behind bars."

Dodd knocked Meekers's hand away. "Sorry to interrupt you, Joe Bob. Especially since that's most likely the longest string of words you've ever put together. But look in the cafe window." He pointed toward the Paris window, where Todd's and Rayburn's faces were visible through the reflected sunlight and dust. "Those boys will probably be glad to testify in court that they saw you assault me on the sidewalk."

Joe Bob snorted. "Business and blood both run thick, son. You think Ralph would find for you in a law suit?"

"You think I'd be stupid enough to file in his jurisdiction? All I have to do is raise the ante on damages and the case moves to state courts."

"What makes you think I don't own that judge too?"

"I'll be glad to tell him you said that."

Meeker closed his eyes, pursed his lips together and kneaded his forehead with two meaty knuckles. He kneaded for twenty or thirty seconds. Finally he opened his eyes and said, "You've pushed me past the point where I'm willing to listen to my brother and Rafferty. I want you six feet under feeding the maggots like your old man and your fucking uncles. Understand?"

Dodd nodded carefully. "Hard to confuse that for an invitation to dinner."

"Then you get this clear. I want that money your family took. I know it's still here. You can't lie to me about that. There's no way your old man could have gotten away with it."

"They never found a body. So the story goes. Far as I know, he could be retired in Mexico."

"He's dead, Dodd. There's no lies between us anymore. You know as well as I do that his body floated down the Sweet Water, his blood running as free as his fuck-up brother. I put at least three loads of shot into him myself."

Dodd took the cigar from his pocket and unwrapped it. "That goes against the official version." He handed the wrapper to the sheriff.

"Then you know that I mean it when I tell you that you better get me that money. By Monday morning. If you don't, you're gonna go floating down the Sweet Water same as your family. Three loads of shot in your gut. Won't be no trial, cause no one'll ever find your body when it finally goes down. Now what do you think about that?"

"That scares the shit out of me, Joe Bob."

"It better." Joe Bob lit the cigar and turned to enter the Paris.

Dodd dropped his hand on Meeker's shoulder. "What if I really don't know where the money is, Joe Bob?"

Meeker brushed Dodd's hand away without looking at him. But Dodd could see his expression in the reflection in the café window. "You'll be just as dead. So I guess that ain't an option, is it?"

He pulled open the cafe door and barely squeezed through the frame. Dodd could see Rayburn nodding his head, indicating that he should join them for breakfast. But Dodd searched deep inside his gut for some sign of an appetite and failed to find any. He waved and walked to the courthouse.

Chapter 35

Alvin Rawlings waited for him in Ralph's office, sitting in one of the easy chairs, his legs crossed, as though this were a casual encounter. "I can't believe we're talking here."

Dodd settled in behind the desk and said, "We're discussing your job running Meeker's store. That's all."

Alvin ran a finger inside his shirt collar. "Shouldn't we be doing that at the store?"

"Relax, Alvin, the office isn't bugged. It's not Rafferty's style. He's too arrogant to believe the Meekers could plot against him."

"What about you?"

Dodd removed his jacket and draped it over the edge of the office chair. "You're too paranoid. These men aren't that powerful; they're not even that smart. But they don't understand that. They're small town, small-time operators with their fingers in a small pie that's big enough for three of them."

"That's easy to say for a guy that dropped a dime for armed robbery," Alvin answered. He reached inside his jacket pocket and removed a set of folded papers. He dropped them on the desk. "But you were right about their scam. Rafferty's using this racetrack to launder money all over the state, mostly in political contributions and lobbying expenses. If he gets the track, the backers will finance it and the county will float a bond to pay back every penny. If it doesn't, he still hid a boatload of money from the IRS."

Dodd browsed the papers–articles of incorporation, paperwork founding a political action committee, correspondence with the Governor and select legislators and Senators. He hoped Alvin would have had time to pull more documents when the deputies were out on the pit call the night before, but these painted a clear picture of the operation.

Rafferty's name showed up on nothing. The Meekers held all the liability. Rafferty's bank made the race track consolidation, headed by the Meekers, more than three million dollars in loans–loans that went directly back to Rafferty to distribute as he saw fit. If the track went through, everyone got rich. If the track went bust, the Meekers went under with it and Rafferty skated.

Dodd whistled. "That guy doesn't miss a trick."

Alvin pulled one of the documents out. "You really should look at this."

Dodd glanced through. It was an addendum incorporating him into the partnership and naming him the chief financial officer. Somehow his signature even appeared on the document. According to the addendum he, as Ralph's manager, received all funds and accepted liability for maintaining records and accountability.

"You signed that?" Alvin asked, his finger pushing the top of the page back down onto Dodd's desk.

"Of course not," Dodd said. "I would never sign this. They took my signature from some other document."

"That doesn't keep you clean when the shit falls."

"So what do you suggest?"

Alvin took the addendum from him, folded it and slipped it back into his pocket. "Every thing you have on the desk is a copy I made last night. Except for this. This is the original."

"You're going to make it disappear?" Dodd asked.

Alvin leaned forward and collected the rest of the papers. "I went you one better. I made a new copy, replaced all references to you with references to Rafferty, made a copy of that and copied Ralph Meeker's signature in its place. It wasn't that hard to find his signature in the town records."

Dodd scratched his chin and leaned back in his chair. "It's time to play hard ball then."

"You won't get anywhere waiting for them to make their moves. But I sure as hell wasn't suggesting hard ball."

"What then?"

"Get lost. Disappear. Beg that law firm in Santa Fe for your job. Let Rafferty and the Meekers gnaw on their own bones, don't give them your leg."

Dodd stood and looked out the window. He could see Joe Bob exchanging angry words with Carl Ray. "It's gone too far. I want to play the whole hand. I'm not leaving as long as these boys are around to run more scams."

Alvin stood as well, checking to make sure the documents were tucked firmly out of sight inside his jacket. "Then I'm going to the store. I just want to know. Are you really one of those Dodds or not?"

Dodd adjusted the blinds. "What do you think?"

"That's not an answer."

Dodd turned around. "It wasn't meant to be."

Alvin pulled a small black and white photo from his other pocket and dropped it onto the desk. "If you are Zane Dodd's kid, you might be interested in this. I slipped it off of the wall behind Meeker's desk."

Dodd picked it up and studied it. The photo was easily twenty-five years old, black and white and heavy on the contrast. Three figures stood around the gun cabinet in Rafferty's house. All three were armed with deer rifles. Rafferty had a long-barreled .38 slipped into his belt. They wore high brimmed cowboy hats, plaid shirts and jeans tucked into lizard skin boots.

"Help me out here," Dodd said.

"If you know anything at all about the bank robbery and the shit that went down with the Dodds afterwards, it will come to you."

Dodd studied the picture. It didn't even register when Rawlings left the room. Something about the picture knocked in the corner of his mind, but he couldn't figure out what it could be. He tried to picture the gun cabinet he's seen at Rafferty's. He could swear he'd seen every one of those guns locked in that cabinet on Saturday night.

He picked up his jacket, and draped it over the coat rack, brushing a couple of wrinkles out. He shook his head and decided to take a late breakfast. His appetite finally returned.

Joe Bob stood at the front door of the sheriff's office, still chewing out Carl Ray. Joe Bob tossed him an angry glare, but Dodd ignored it, trying to make a mental checklist of every thing he knew about the robbery.

As he pushed open the door to the Paris Cafe, it came to him, and suddenly every thing that happened on that killer Christmas Eve became clear—the robbery, the call to sheriff Hargess and the subsequent murders of the Dodd brothers. And he knew who could find the proof for him.

Chapter 36

Dodd created a dozen subtle plans for whisking Rhonda Mayfield aside and wrangling another dinner invitation. Unfortunately none seemed too subtle after a second consideration, and Dodd had learned after two tours of jail that plans fall to pieces far more often than they actually work.

So he sat around the Paris until eleven thirty, chatting up all the old boys. Todd and Rayburn introduced him to the other old boys who wanted to let him know that they might just support him should he run for mayor. Of course, they wouldn't be facing the Rafferty gang if Dodd ran, so it was easy for them to offer their support

Finally Dodd said, "For Christ's sake, y'all, I've only been in town two weeks and I'm an ex-con. Doesn't this strike you as a little hasty?"

Todd laughed and said, "You have a better chance of beating those boys than we do, and you sure as hell wear better suits than anybody else. Besides, you only held up a gas station. Those boys been holding up the whole damn town since they blew your uncles away."

Dodd examined the faces of his would be campaign committee—a used car salesman wearing a leisure suit that went out of style with Gerald Ford, a dry cleaner with chemical stains on his jacket cuffs, two ranchers who looked leaner than their livestock, a hay farmer and retired Hoover vacuum salesman. He began to wonder if he shouldn't take Alvin's advice, pack his bags and run.

At twelve-fifteen he took a Styrofoam coffee cup with him and parked on the sidewalk bench outside the bank. Rhonda spotted him as she emerged from the building and sat beside him with her knees straight in front of her and hands folded in her lap.

"You've been a busy boy," she said, shifting her hips so that they touched his leg ever so slightly. She didn't face him.

"In what way?" he said, peeling back the plastic lid to his coffee and offering her a sip.

She waved it away. "Aren't you afraid to be seen with me? At least by your little slut friend?"

"You mean Mary Beth?"

She turned her nose up in the air. "Who else in town fits that description?"

Dodd swallowed a quarter of his coffee and slid the lid back in place. "I wouldn't exactly say we're friends. I think it's pretty much about sex."

"Well, that makes things so much more acceptable."

"I thought you were mad at me anyway."

She shifted her hips again to snuggle even closer to his leg, but still refused to look at him.

"You should give a woman time to change her mind. Rather than running after the first bitch in heat, I mean."

"If you want to keep seeing me, tell me you want to keep seeing me and leave Mary Beth out of it."

For a moment he thought he'd been a tad too honest.

She sighed and opened her purse to look for her compact. "Does that mean you would have dinner with me again if I asked you?" She powdered the tip of her nose ever so slightly.

"Why don't you ask me to dinner, Rhonda, and see what I say?"

She touched touched-up a cheek. Finally she looked him in the eye. "Well would you have dinner with me?"

"How about tonight?"

"There's a restaurant in Ft. Stockton. The Cattle Haus. Right on the highway, but at the far end of town. Perhaps we could meet"

"Don't want Rafferty to find out we're having dinner?"

She put the compact back into her purse, placing it precisely at the bottom underneath her billfold and sunglasses. "I'm concluding my personal business with Mr. Rafferty. I just don't want him to think I'm doing it because of you. That wouldn't be good for either of us."

Dodd was tempted to ask if she ever thought about a romance out in the open but he simply nodded his head. "This Cattle Haus. Is it hard to find?"

"Look for the big horns and yodeling cowgirl."

She touched his knee ever so slightly with the tips of her fingernails and slipped away, back into the bank. He wondered, for a second, if he had reached a point where he was just looking for deeper quicksand to sink into.

Chapter 37

When Dodd dropped by the Real Estate Office later that afternoon he wasn't sure what kind of greeting to expect. He didn't see Ralph at the Paris, on the street or around town hall that morning, so there was a good chance Ralph was turning as cold a shoulder as his brother. He decided to make a personal visit to test the waters.

Mrs. Brazwell wouldn't even talk to him. She touched up her beehive with one finger, and pecked at her typewriter even though there was no paper in the roller. He found Ralph in front of his roll-top desk, even further into his Jim Beam than usual. The bottle sat open and almost empty beside his coffee mug, the cap just off to the side. Ralph sat with his hands in his lap, staring at his mug as though it were the object of zen meditation.

"Bad time?" Dodd asked.

Ralph didn't stir. "There's no time that isn't bad, which makes every time just as good."

Dodd settled into the armchair across from the desk. He sat forward, decided to make a show of respect rather than casual disregard. "I just thought you might be brooding about the stunt I pulled last night."

Meeker grinned, as though taking great pleasure just from the memory. "Joe Bob got what he deserved. Not like he did any work. Might as well be drinking at your place as drinking at mine."

Dodd poured the last inch of Beam into Meeker's coffee mug.

Meeker tipped the mug to Dodd in thanks. "Honest? The only reason I hired you was to piss those two son-of-a-bitches off. Doesn't matter that I'm the mayor and I own most of the businesses, both of them think they can run this town without me."

Dodd glanced out the window and spotted a roadrunner dancing in the dust, the second roadrunner he'd seen through that window that week. He wondered if roadrunners were West Texas omens.

"Can they?"

Meeker leaned forward, lowering his eyes and whispering, "Rafferty's assets are tied up in that bank and the loans he floats. If I decide to pull my money, it hurts him, see? And the rest of the town businesses are looking for a reason to bolt as well. They see me bolting; they'll do it. When Wetzel and his Permian Basin oil money buddies see the locals spook, they'll spook too. Then you got a money stampede. Get the picture?"

Dodd got the picture, he just figured the one Meeker painted in his head was closer to a Warhol print than realism. "What about the race track? I thought that was your sweetheart deal."

Meeker looked for one last sip in his mug, but it was already bone dry. "Ain't gonna be no race track. Haven't you figured that out? It's a money funnel. Just like the Mars Discount Warehouse. You ever hear of that one? 'Prices from another planet?' That was supposed to go on your daddy's farm, right after we dug up the flying saucer. We was gonna sell it to finance the warehouse, then build this aluminum copy, tell folks it was the real McCoy. They'd come see something from another planet then spend their money at our store.

"Course then we never found the flying saucer, and I find out I'm the only one thought there was a flying saucer to start with. Joe Bob and Mal were up to something else."

"Like looking for the stolen money?"

For the first time that afternoon, Meeker stopped to consider about what, exactly, he was saying to Dodd. He sobered, if only briefly, and studied Dodd carefully to gauge his reaction.

"Maybe," he said. "Maybe. But it seems to me you already know a lot of this."

Dodd tossed off a shrug. "Jesus, Ralph, it isn't as though everyone in town thinks I'm related to 'those Dodds.' And each time someone says I must be one of those Dodds, I get their version of what happened before, during and after the shootout at Sweet Water Gulch."

"What the hell is Sweet Water Gulch?" Ralph demanded.

Dodd leaned forward and traced a river across Meeker's desk. Then he pretended to fire both his index fingers like six guns, whispering "Pow, pow, pow." "It's my name for the western playing in everybody's head. Point is, sooner or later, I'm going to start putting pieces together."

Meeker pushed his mug away and leaned back in his chair. Dodd could hear the spring squeak. "And what have you put together?"

"Nothing that flatters the town council."

Ralph's eyes came back into focus, briefly. He struggled to keep them focused. It was a look Dodd rarely saw. "You didn't answer my question."

Dodd leaned his elbows on the desk and his chin on his knuckles. "I don't think the Dodds had the brains or the resources to rob that bank and you boys and Rafferty set those boys up."

For the first time Dodd noticed a real resemblance between the brothers. Ralph displayed the same blue-edged flint look that Dodd saw every day in the sheriff. "Joe Bob was right. You are pretty smart for an ex-con. Even one with a mail-order law degree."

Dodd leaned forward, placing his palms flat on the desk. "I worked hard for that law degree, Ralph. But what you got to ask yourself is this: Who's really out to get you here? Me, or Rafferty? More important, who's in a better position to double-cross you? Because you sure seem to think there's a double cross in play."

Meeker opened his desk drawer. When he didn't find another bottle, he slammed it shut with disgust. "I don't trust nobody. Not even you. Not until you tell me where to find the rest of that flying saucer."

Dodd wanted to laugh. Meeker hadn't hired him to set him up, or help Rafferty and his brother. He just wanted to get his hands on a flying saucer.

"So you're the one Bobby gave the pieces to."

"You know about that?"

"You think I wouldn't notice he took them?" This time he let himself laugh out loud. "Do you really think those are pieces of a flying saucer?"

Meeker's eyes opened wide, and his hands began to shake. He leaned across the desk and spoke softly. "You can't lie to me. I saw that funny writing on that stick. I just want to know where you found it."

"And I want to know why Rafferty's so damned eager to have me run point on his race track."

Meeker looked away this time, out the window. "Maybe he thinks you're the best man for the job."

"Maybe he wants a fall guy."

Meeker continued to look out the window. Dodd wondered if the roadrunner was still there, but he held his focus on Meeker. "What's the deal, Ralph? Are you setting me up the way you set up the Dodds?"

Meeker placed his cup in the bottom drawer. "I think maybe if you can show me where you found the flying saucer, maybe I can help you watch your back. I think maybe that's a deal that's in both our best interest."

Dodd pitched the empty bottle into the trashcan under Meeker's desk. "Then you better sober up and focus, Ralph, because if Rafferty and your brother catch any whiff that we struck a deal, they'll hang us both out to dry."

Chapter 38

Dodd entered the Cattle Haus with a half dozen roses he picked up that afternoon from Maple Thorndike, the florist. As far as Dodd knew, Maple was the only business owner who didn't socialize at the Paris on a daily basis. That might be because she was the only woman that owned a business in Sweet Water Falls.

Maple told him Mary Beth didn't like roses; she liked orchids (of which she just happened to have two or three on hand). Dodd was about to ask why she thought the roses were for Mary Beth and immediately realized that word might get back to Mary Beth that he bought flowers he didn't give her. Since they hadn't officially broken up, it didn't make too much sense to advertise that he might be moving on.

"Why don't you give me both?" he said.

He put the orchids in the Rafferty's mailbox with a note that said, "Sorry."

Ass sufficiently covered, he took the roses to Ft. Stockton.

The Cattle Haus was exactly where Rhonda described it, right down to the enormous plaster horns hanging over the highway from the parking lot. The sign itself was quite conservative, "Cattle Haus" painted in dark brown on beige with one of those woodcut lettering styles. Underneath it were the words: "German/Western Country Cooking." Any subtlety and taste were undermined by the bouncing neon cowgirl on the building that sang "Yodel-Layee-Haw" every thirty seconds.

Rhonda waited for him at the bar in a paisley summer dress with a narrow cloth belt. The dress dropped to her knees revealing her strong bare legs, which were accented by sandals with a narrow strap. She wore her hair pulled back into a ponytail and enough floral cologne that he noticed it from several feet away.

She moved her shopping bag style purse to the other side of her and then nodded to the maître d'. The image of a maître d' in blue jeans and a string tie with an Alpine hat didn't work for Dodd, but he figured he wasn't running the restaurant and the place did seem busy.

"I went ahead and placed a table," she told him, crossing her legs so that he could see a generous portion of her thigh. "The wait will probably be another fifteen or twenty minutes." She shifted her hem down to her knees.

"I came for the company more than the meal," he told her, handing her the flowers.

"You didn't have to do this," she told him.

"Just in case the evening ends like it did Sunday night, I want you to have these the next morning so you'll think more kindly of me."

The bartender sat a glass of water beside her gin and tonic. "They started to wilt quicker than I thought," he added. "I guess I should have looked for some in town."

"You can't expect men to think of such things. I'm surprised you even noticed," she said.

She dropped the stems into the glass, and leaned in to sniff them as they fanned around the lip. "Are you going to watch me arrange flowers or talk to me?" she asked, touching a stem here or there to nudge the roses into a more pleasing spray.

"I thought we were talking," he told her.

She turned into him so that their knees were touching. "I must apologize for the way I behaved toward you. Not just

Sunday night. My emotional life has been somewhat less than steady since you told me about Marla and Mal."

"No need to apologize. I can't imagine anyone being grateful for the news."

She placed her hand on his thigh. "It angered me, shamed me, and I thought that you were no gentleman for telling me. Later, I realized it is Mr. Rafferty who is not the gentleman to carry on with a mother and her own daughter, both of whom work for him."

"Are you sure you want to talk about this?"

She took her hand away from his leg and dropped both of them, clasped together, in her lap. "We have to clear the air if we're to become more intimate." Her cheeks turned the slightest shade of rose. "Or am I being too presumptuous?"

The maître d' appeared, menus tucked in his arm. He gestured toward a table. Dodd put his hand, ever so carefully, over hers. "Let's just have dinner," he said.

"Is this a polite brush off, Mr. Dodd?"

"I'm steering the boat into calmer waters," he told her.

The maître d' seated them at a booth directly under a large plastic lamp with Longhorns sweeping away to each side. A jukebox rested at one end of the table, and every title seemed to be by Patsy Kline or Conway Twitty. Rhonda ordered a cold roast dinner with stone ground German mustard, German potato salad and asparagus. Dodd ordered the T-Bone with sauerbraten and schnitzel.

The waiter offered him a wine list with three selections. He chose the Gallo Burgundy over the Lancer's Rosé and Blue Nun.

They treaded the calm waters until their dinner was served with polite chit-chat about town affairs and the people conducting them. When the meal arrived, Dodd poured a liberal portion of the burgundy into her glass, and she immediately steered the conversation back into the gale.

"Sooner or later you're going to have to confront our mutual attraction," she informed him.

He cut into his beef with his steak knife and dipped a small slice into the sweet and sour sauce. "I'm still somewhat entangled, Rhonda. And, so far as I know, you haven't ended your entanglements, either."

"Can't we become less entangled? Your amore is no more faithful than mine." She smiled as she speared a large yellow piece of potato with her fork, and cutting it in half. "Which should be no surprise considering the gene pool."

"I thought we were past this."

"Turnabout is fair play." She blushed and looked away as she slid the potato into her mouth.

Dodd put his fork and knife down and rested his wrists on her table. "Rhonda, Mary Beth and I match up because we have no future. You might say we scratch each other's itches when we're close enough to scratch. I can't help but feel you're looking to me for the permanence Rafferty will never offer."

She held her hands together in front of her plate and stared down at it, as though trying to determine the ingredients of her potato salad. "I was at the Old West Inn with Mal this afternoon. I was planning to call it off, but he took off for early for a meeting in town. So I went for a swim. I saw your back scratcher check into a room with one of Mal's ranch hands."

Dodd cleared his throat. "Rhonda, let's drop this subject."

She held up her hand to ward off his interruption, but she still wouldn't look at him. "Hold on, please. This woman was sitting by the pool with her two kids. Told me she saw Mary Beth there another day, but with a different guy. She's got plenty of people to scratch her back."

Dodd was tempted to point out that he was the other back scratcher, but he decided to keep his peace.

"I figured that out about as soon as I started seeing her, Rhonda. But let's be honest. If you haven't called it off with Rafferty, and I'm not ready to extract myself from Mary Beth, it could be difficult for us to arrange our own entanglement. And those two can be pretty spiteful if they even suspected. Which mine already does."

She sighed and sipped her wine. She dabbed the napkin at her lip. "I guess you're being kinder than most men. Most men would rent the room first and then deliver the good bye kiss."

"Sorry, Rhonda."

She pushed the asparagus spears to the edge of her plate one by one. They were the least appetizing things Dodd had ever seen, like lime green slugs that had died and gone to ground. They looked like they had been poured straight from a can onto the plate, nothing like the presentation on the menu.

"I practiced giving Mal his walking papers the entire drive from Sweet Water Falls. Get to the room, sit on the bed with my purse in my lap, and tell it to him straight. Don't fuck me anymore and you goddam well better quit fucking my daughter. But then he showed up, his stomach still flat and his hair thick and gray, and I thought to myself, 'If Mal isn't in my life, who is?'"

Dodd sipped his wine and waited for her to continue. She slipped her foot from her sandal and ran it under his pants leg.

"You aren't exactly a trade up," she added. "You know what I mean. But I couldn't imagine life without someone to spend time with. My courage gave way. You could help me with that."

He dipped his last piece of steak into the sauerbraten sauce and held it at the tip of his fork. That had to be the least romantic declaration of affection he'd ever heard.

"Rhonda, sometimes you have to disentangle yourself and stay that way. Get used to living on your own. See, then, a couple of years later, you fall in with someone cause you really want to, and not just to get disentangled from someone else."

She took her foot away. "You're a hard man to get close to, Mr. Dodd."

"That's because I really do like you, Rhonda. Mary Beth was just someone to get under the sheets with, and she sees me the same way."

She sighed again, and then pulled her purse out from under the table. Her entire demeanor changed. It was as though she'd put her hair up and dropped a pair of glasses on her nose. "After you mentioned those two black boys who did those robberies, I looked into some of the bank records."

"You mean Preacher Rawlings and Delroy Lean?"

She nodded and pulled a set of computer printouts from her purse, passing the wide, green and white striped paper across the table. She even seemed to sit straighter, more rigid. As though she were behind an office desk, with a pencil behind her ear and a calculator only inches from her hand. "You were right, something funny went on. I circled the important entries."

Dodd straightened and glanced through the numbers, but they meant nothing to him. "I'm a lawyer, not an accountant. Maybe you could interpret."

"First tell me what you know."

"The Meekers hired Preacher and Delroy to rob their stores. The boys took a few hundred each time but the Meekers reported huge losses."

Rhonda nodded. She cut a spear of asparagus, but it was more like mashing. The asparagus turned to mush under her fork. She pushed it aside, and returned to her narrative. "They were losing money hand over fist on a discount warehouse and the ground hadn't been broken. Everyone in town remembers the plans because they had architectural drawings and blueprints on display at Ralph's office. He and Mal loved to drag potential investors over to see it."

"This was the one with the fake flying saucer outside." Dodd could almost picture it. A three story department store rising from the dust bowl of the Dodd farm, surrounded by rusted out Ranchero and El Camino pickups, loose shopping carts drifting way with the tumbleweeds in the gravel parking lot and a large flying saucer rising from the roof, made from two burned out spotlight reflectors, bolted together and painted bright silver.

"Exactly. But they couldn't land any deals with investors because no one in the their right minds believed a shopping center way out here in Sweet Water Falls could make a go of it, much less a stand alone three-story department store. Fort Stockton didn't even have a strip mall at that time. Gibson's was about as big a discount store as you got, and Fort Stockton already had one of those. So the Meekers reported total losses on the robberies well in excess of three hundred thousand dollars."

Dodd tapped his finger on the printout. "How do these figures contradict that?"

She gently pushed his hand aside with hers, laying her finger on a column labeled "deposits." But she left her hand flush with his, so they touched ever so slightly.

"Before the robberies started, they stopped making their daily deposits and went to weekly deposits. That built up the amount of cash on hand. So they would have had a lot more lying around than a few hundred dollars. But their reported losses were well in excess of what they usually would have deposited anyway. The weeks they were robbed they claimed to have twenty-to-thirty times as much money in their stores as their usual take."

She held her fork in front of her, aiming it toward Dodd, to make her point. "Now, if it happened once, it wouldn't be suspicious. Somehow your friend Preacher and his partner could have known they were going to have an abnormally large cash flow on a certain day and timed the robbery ahead of the deposit."

"But not as often as it happened."

Rhonda smiled and moved her hand over his. "Exactly. To have them routinely hit those stores during a time when their deposits were so extraordinarily out of line, well, the fact would at least have raised questions from the auditors reviewing their claims."

"But someone made sure the auditors didn't ask the question."

She patted his hand and smiled. "Exactly. Mal helped them prepare the paper work and change the figures." She pulled a set of sheets from the bottom and spread them out on top. "Mal doctored their financial statements so that the insurance would pay without question. He overestimated daily and annual income to reflect the amounts they claimed were stolen. The Meekers completely cleared their debts."

Dodd nodded to make it clear he followed. It was pretty much what he expected to hear. He also knew the answer to his next question, but he chose to ask anyway. "And they owed the money to...?"

"Mal." She finally took a bite of asparagus. She delicately placed her napkin to her mouth and returned it to her plate. This surprised him no more than her answer. Even had she not let the green slime grow cold, it hardly qualified as asparagus even when it arrived.

And now for the real question. The one he knew she wouldn't see coming. The one that would answer the real question. "How far back do the bank records go?"

The question took her off guard. She sat back in her seat and took a moment to consider. "I don't know. We computerized the bank in the early seventies. Mal put a lot of money into installing our mainframe. We were one of the first small banks in the southwest to convert."

Dodd tapped his fingers on the table, on top of the printout. "But before the computers? Say the late forties? Do you still have records from the forties?"

She seemed genuinely puzzled by the question. She laid her fork on the table and rearranged the silverware. The fact that he was asking bothered her. "Of course. But they're filed and in storage. I doubt anyone's looked at them for years. Why?"

"I was wondering what the books in the forties would show."

She put her hand to her mouth. "You mean when the Dodds robbed the bank?" She rubbed her forehead as she pursued the thought. "I don't know how I would find an excuse to look. Mal really likes to keep an eye on us every minute of the day."

"Not when he's fucking your daughter, he doesn't."

Dodd let the phrase drop onto the table and roll between them until it halted from its own loss of momentum. Rhonda looked at him for several seconds, not sure how to answer. Finally she said, "Actually, that would be the perfect time to look. I'll work late and look through them tomorrow."

She took his hand. "Are you sure you want to keep this just business?"

To be truthful, he didn't. But he was entangled in so many different ways with so many different people he didn't see how he would emerge intact. At least in this one instance, he had to limit exactly how entangled he would get.

He placed his hand over hers. "Rhonda, you remember that scene in the bank with Mary Beth the other day? All the yelling and accusations?"

She blushed and looked down at her plate. "That was awkward wasn't it? It set the office talking for half an hour."

He leaned closer and touched her cheek, forcing her to look him in the eye. "Now imagine what would happen if both of them thought we were seeing each other and it turned out we really were." He held her gaze for a long minute, long enough for the though to sink in.

"Oh my," she said. "That could be no end of trouble. In fact, it might not end well at all."

Chapter 39

Joe Bob must developed a taste for ambush because the next morning Dodd found him standing at the window in Ralph's office, hands crossed behind his back like George Scott in the movie "Patton" and studying the two town squad cars parked outside.

"You know, Joe Bob," Dodd said, "when I was growing up I never imagined seeing your face first thing in the morning every day of my life."

Joe Bob turned to face him. He spoke around his cigar. "I don't take kindly to wise asses in the morning myself."

Dodd sat at Ralph's desk and opened the stack of papers Mrs. Brazwell had left the afternoon before. Joe Bob opened his mouth to speak and Dodd held up his hand. Then, as he had seen Rafferty do, he proceeded to scan each page line by line and initial it at the bottom. Finally, when he reached the bottom of the stack he leaned back in the chair and said, "Let's get down to business."

Joe Bob remained at attention, but his face had turned beet red and his jaw was locked rigidly around the cigar. It took him a moment to unlock it. "I want to know how you're coming with the money," he finally said.

Dodd opened some correspondence on the desk and signed Ralph's name without even reading it. He tore open another letter, but looked to Joe Bob before reading it. "You gave me until Monday."

"I thought you'd get to work instead of sniffing in Rafferty's bushes."

Dodd swiveled the chair to face the sheriff directly. "What's that supposed to mean?"

"It means when I give you till Monday I expect you to be out on your farm land digging for cash instead of taking Rafferty's real estate to dinner."

"That's what you call women around here? 'Real estate?'"

Joe Bob finally took his hands from behind his back and pulled the cigar from his mouth. He dropped a large clump of ash on the carpet. "We call 'em what's appropriate to call 'em and Rafferty already holds the title to that gal."

Dodd tapped his pen on the desk. "So by right of succession he also owns the title to Marla Mayfield as well."

"He owns the whole fucking town. Everything but what Ralph and I own."

Dodd perused the open letter in his hand. "I take it you had me followed," he said as he read.

"He keeps tabs on what he owns. Good thing you just had dinner or Rafferty would have had you skinned alive. You can fuck his daughter all you want, just don't stray onto his preserve. He sent me here to tell you that. I came here to tell you to keep focused until you get me that money cause I don't want you skinned alive before we finish our deal. Got me?"

Dodd dropped the letter to the desk, leaned back in his seat and threw his hands behind his head. "I've been thinking about that deal, Joe Bob. I keep thinking if the Dodds really stole all that money, someone would have turned it up by now."

"You can't steer me off course, son."

Dodd held his finger up to shush him. "Bear with me. See, I also keep asking myself how three farmers managed to break into a secure bank on Christmas eve, disable the alarm systems, and get away with five hundred thousand dollars."

"What makes you think they disabled the alarm system?"

"Well, as I understand the story, you and Ralph tried to get Sheriff Hargess out of a Christmas party and he wouldn't come. I can't imagine that would happen with the alarms going off."

Joe Bob's neck swelled every so slightly, like a balloon just at the point of bursting. "Well there are things about that robbery that's nobody's business to know. But you ought to stop and think about what happened to the rest of your family before you push too hard."

Dodd nodded his head, and opened a letter from a widow asking the Town Council to pass a resolution to organize a search party for her lost cat Peppy. "When I get you the money on Monday, will you really care about what I did in the meantime?"

Joe Bob stuffed his cigar back in his mouth and grinned. "No. And when you're dead will you wish you got off your ass and dug for treasure instead of rustling the mayor's property?"

Dodd handed the letter to Joe Bob. "I think this really belongs in your inbox. You being in charge of search parties and all." Joe Bob took it without realizing what he was looking at. Dodd sat back in his seat again. "So I guess the question is which you want more. Me dead or your money. I'm betting on money, but if you're too stupid to see which is in your best interest then I guess I'm shit out of luck."

Joe Bob looked at the letter, then wadded it up and threw it on the floor. "Then I guess you're shit out of luck, boy."

Dodd didn't even look at the wad of paper. He opened his desk drawer and stuck his hand inside. "Of course, I guess the question is also which Mal Rafferty wants more, me dead or his money. And if I end up dead before he gets his money you may be shit out of luck too." He removed his hand from the drawer and aimed it at Joe Bob, cocked like a pistol. "So maybe you better settle for the money." He pulled the trigger on his finger, hoping Joe Bob, for once, got the message.

Chapter 40

Dodd cruised through rest of the morning in low gear, trying to sort out the angles in his head. He wanted to hold on to Rhonda because she had a line on Rafferty that he needed to access, but the more he relied on her, the more likely she was to expect romance in return. Now that Rafferty knew the two of them had dinner together, things were bound to get more dicey.

He couldn't figure out who could have tipped off Rafferty until he walked into the Paris for lunch to see Mary Beth, dressed in a plaid shirt and blue jeans, sitting at the counter with the same threadbare, long-legged cowpoke he'd caught a glimpse of in her bedroom on Saturday night.

The cowpoke wore the same color plaid shirt and the same fade in his jeans as Mary Beth. Both sat swinging legs to show off their snakeskin boots, a pack of hundred millimeter cigarettes sticking out of each one's shirt pocket–hers Virginia Slims, his Benson and Hedges.

Dodd tipped his hat to her, said, "Misery loves company, doesn't it?" and sat down beside Del Rayburn. He picked up the menu and studied it even though he already know all six items by heart.

Mary Beth, for her part, turned her head away without acknowledging him, took a long drag on her Virginia Slim and started talking to the cowpoke as though she hadn't even seen him.

When Dodd left the Paris after lunch, however, he found her sitting on the hood of an early seventies Chevy Pickup. The truck's engine pumped out the slightest trail gray exhaust. Her cowpoke friend sat behind the wheel looking halfway bored and just a little bit embarrassed.

She pushed herself off the hood and crossed the sidewalk in two steps. "What were you doing with that middle-aged bitch last night?"

"Having dinner."

"Yeh right," she said, pulling a cigarette from the pack in her shirt pocket and popping it into her mouth like popcorn.

Dodd took it away from her and said, "You should never smoke in anger, and it really was only dinner, for Chrissake."

She snatched the cigarette back and pulled a lighter from her hip pocket in the same motion. "Once is dinner. Twice is an invitation to fuck. You can't fool me, Dodd."

Dodd glanced over at the cowpoke. He had pulled his hat over his eyes and slumped further down into his seat. Dodd wondered which of the two of them was the more embarrassed by all this. Then the light flashed.

"You two planned on dinner at the Cattle Haus but you saw our cars there," Dodd said.

Mary Beth held her cigarette into the flame, and refused to answer.

"Or you walked in and spotted us and left," Dodd added. "That's how Rafferty knows we had dinner together. You told him."

"What makes you think I was in Fort Stockton with Jack?"

"You were in Fort Stockton with somebody because Rhonda saw you and a cowboy at the Old West Inn where she was shacking up with your father yesterday afternoon. Did you drag your friend there to get the old man's attention again?"

Mary Beth stamped her foot. “That bitch. Can’t be discreet about anything. What right does she have telling people who she saw me with?”

Dodd grabbed her under the arm and lifted her to her toes. He shoved his face into hers. “Listen, sweetheart, Rhonda didn’t tell your old man anything about you and your cowboy and you two were getting at it all afternoon. But you did tell your old man about Rhonda and me, and we weren’t doing anything at all. So you may just have cut off that poor woman’s gravy train over nothing.”

Her face turned scarlet and she yanked her cigarette from her mouth. “Oh, yeh?”

“She found out your old man was fucking her daughter. She was upset and she asked me to ask you what you thought she should do, you being Rafferty’s daughter and all. That’s how much she respects your opinion. Only I didn’t get a chance because you blew the whistle on everybody.”

Mary Beth seemed to fade into her boots.

“Really?”

“Really. Rhonda didn’t want to cause a scandal, she didn’t want to cross your mom, and she didn’t know how she could break things off with your old man without Marla finding out as well. She figured you might have some ideas but she was afraid to ask you herself.”

Mary Beth studied the tip of her cigarette. “I feel like such a shit. And now daddy thinks you two are stepping out on him.”

“What do you intend to do about it?”

She shook her head. “Well I’m not going to see you anymore, that’s for damn sure. And I guess she won’t be seeing daddy anymore either. Tough luck for both of you, I guess.” She smiled at him, pitched her cigarette off the corner and climbed into the passenger side of the cab. “Enjoy your life without me,” she called as the driver put the car into gear and pulled away.

Chapter 41

Dodd ran by Meeker's Corner Store to pick up the deposits. Alvin told Bobby to check the levels on the gas pumps. Bobby, who was pricing and stocking groceries said, "Mr. Rawlings, you just had me do that this morning."

Both of them looked to Dodd to intervene and Dodd said, "Can you at least pretend to check the gas levels again?"

Bobby dropped his pricing gun and took the fuel rod from behind the counter. "Shit, if I got to stand out there in the heat I might as well be doing something."

"Kid developing an attitude problem?" Dodd asked when the door closed behind Bobby.

Alvin leaned over the counter on his elbows, clasping his hands in front of him. "Kid's developing a black boss problem. Folks in the town been telling him he should appeal the sentence. Kid robs the owner of the fucking store, gets off with probation, and when he has to work for a nigger, the good white folk think he's being mistreated."

Dodd took a Snickers bar from the candy rack. "What's really on your mind?"

Alvin lowered his voice even though there were no customers in the store to hear them. "Sheriff dropped by. Told me that you and he had a deal that comes due Monday. Told me I might want to be out of town when that happens. Might want to be out of town quicker than that, if I got his drift."

Dodd took a bite of the Snickers and chewed for a second. "Did you? Get his drift, I mean?"

Rawlings held out his hand, and Dodd pulled a dollar out of his pocket to pay for the candy. "It was a big drift, Dodd. Bigger than the fucking river. Of course I got his drift. He's going to kill us both the way he did Delroy and the Dodds. The other Dodds."

"The Rangers killed one of them, not Joe Bob," Dodd reminded him.

Rawlings punched the cash button on the register with the back of his fist and popped the register drawer open. "Jesus, Dodd, quit worrying about the facts and take a look at the big picture."

Dodd leaned over the register and took the dollar from Rawling's fingers. "If you aren't going to ring it up, don't expect me to pay you, Alvin. Now trust me, Joe Bob wants that money too bad to make any serious moves before he's sure I don't have it. So we're safe until Monday."

"What are we going to do Monday?"

Dodd handed him the candy bar with only the single bite missing. "Would you throw that away for me?" he said. "And don't worry about Monday because everything will be over this weekend. I promise."

"A white man's promise don't mean a whole lot to someone like me," Alvin called to Dodd as he pushed his way through the door.

Dodd found Bobby outside, waiting with the gas pole. "Can I go back inside now?" he asked.

"Go ahead."

He held the pole across Dodd's chest. "What kind of deal you got working, Dodd? You got him nervous as hell."

"I did time with his brother, son. Just doing a favor for an old friend."

Bobby stepped back and let Dodd pass. Then he called out, "Don't do any of those favors for me, okay?"

Chapter 42

Dodd waited until dark to drive to Rhonda's. He didn't want Rafferty or anyone who might talk to Rafferty to see them together. When he approached her house, he wondered if she were thinking along the same lines.

The house looked as though she weren't home at all. The shades were drawn; he only saw a single light through a back window. Her car sat outside her house, pulled in from the road, as though she might have left with someone else.

If Rhonda was home, she didn't want anyone to know. Maybe not even him. Which made him think she might be scared.

He walked back to his Mustang and drove to the Stickett Inn. He wasn't quite sure why he was taking so many precautions, but he could feel the hair on the back of his neck standing. He ordered a cup of coffee and sat in a back booth. He waited fifteen minutes, wandered to the bathroom, and then wandered through the door leading into the hotel side of the restaurant.

Once he slipped out the back door, it was a five minute walk to Rhonda's, in shadows, on her poorly lit street. Even then he decided against ringing her front door bell. He walked around back and rapped knuckles on her back door. She pulled back the kitchen curtain ever so slightly to see who he was.

Had he not been expecting her to look out, he would never have noticed her. He held his finger to his lips, and waited for her to unlatch the door.

She pulled the dead bolt and cracked the door just enough for him to slip through. Even then she didn't turn on her lights.

"You're spooked," he said.

She led him into her living room by his arm, and sat him down on the couch, sitting beside him and leaning her face into his shoulder. His shoulder muffled her words. "I couldn't break up with him again. I just didn't have the words. But then I noticed Marla taking off early and him busting at the bit to take off after her. So I went through the old files. I knew he had played with numbers here and there, but I never expected what I found."

She leaned across him to lift a sheaf of Xeroxed papers, copies from old ledger books. "Besides," she added, "he was angry with me himself."

"Did we just skip through three different plot lines?" Dodd asked. He took the materials from her and spread them on her coffee table.

"He found out we had dinner last night. It was hard to break up with him when he wanted to know why I was carrying on with you. Couldn't convince him otherwise. He already thinks you're the ghost of Zane Dodd back to haunt him."

"I need some light if you want me to look at these," he told her. She sighed dramatically and reached across him to turn on her lamp. She circled behind him, and leaned her chin over his shoulder.

Dodd fumbled through the pages trying to figure out what he was looking at. The entries were handwritten, the copies gray and he wasn't clear what the numbers meant.

"Can you help me with this?"

"I'd recommend you find an accountant to look at them. Maybe that colored man you hired for your store. He used to keep the Meeker's books. The bottom line is, the Dodd brothers didn't take five hundred thousand dollars because most of it was already gone."

He turned one of the pages at a forty-degree angle, trying to follow a series of numbers she had circled. "Mal was embezzling money from his own bank?"

She lifted his hand up with her own hand to bring the figures closer to his face. "No question about it. Only it wasn't his bank at the time. Now read the memo at the back."

Dodd flipped to the last page and found a hand-written note from Rafferty, Sr., to his son: "We need to discuss the Bakersfield accounts tomorrow. Client has some concerns."

"That's where the money was taken from?"

Rhonda shook her head. "It's more complicated than that. He actually shuffled money between dozens of accounts to cover his tracks. Mal never took more than ten thousand from any of them. But if Mal's father had problems with one of the accounts, he was bound to find them with the others sooner or later. There was only one account exception."

"Can I guess?"

Rhonda leaned her chin on his shoulder and holding back the punch line for one more second. "His real victims and partners in crime. The Meekers. He manipulated the money to show a flush account balance for each reporting period, but in the end he actually soaked them for more than fifty thousand. Better yet, any audit would make them look culpable. Now on the day that memo was written, Mal had begun to move the money again. If his father found the discrepancies in the Bakersfield account, he probably was able to follow the thread straight to the Meeker's account."

Dodd whistled. "So Rafferty was embezzling from the Meekers the whole time."

"Once I found this I reran an audit of the books twenty years later. Same story. The Meekers may have set up your friend in prison, but their cash flow problems started at the bank itself. Since 1953 Mal Rafferty cleaned a quarter million out of their accounts and they still haven't figured it out."

"Why didn't Rafferty destroy this memo?" Dodd wondered, holding Rafferty Sr.'s memo away from him as though the answer would come into focus. He felt her hand slip over his other hand.

"It's not incriminating if you think the bank was robbed by three farmers in a pick-up. All told Mal embezzled three hundred thousand dollars. He reported half a million missing, and the FDIC settled up. The embezzled dollars are back in place, Mal is two hundred thousand richer and nobody is the wiser. Mr. Rafferty is happy, Mal's back in good standing."

"Only the old man gets killed."

"I thought about that, and that's the part of the story that doesn't fit. If the Dodds robbed the bank, then it makes sense that the old man tried to stop them and got killed. But if Mal was just covering his tracks, how did his father get killed? So I'm thinking maybe Mal was embezzling the money, and when the Dodds robbed the bank, Mal included the amount he embezzled in his report to the FDIC."

"Or he shot his old man himself, and the Dodd's never got a penny. If the Dodds even robbed the bank at all. Maybe Rafferty offered them a loan, tossed them a few thousand, and when they left he sicced the Meekers on them."

She pulled away. "I can't believe that."

Dodd folded the papers and tucked them into his back pocket, wishing the bulge was less visible. He would have to have Alvin look at them right away. "If he set up three dumb farmers to get slaughtered by Joe Bob and Ralph Meeker in the canyon, he was perfectly capable of pulling the trigger on his father."

She fell back onto her knees behind the couch and stared up at him. "I just can't believe Mal would do that," she repeated, the pitch of her voice slightly higher, as though repeating it several different ways would make it more real.

"You don't have to. I can."

She put her finger to her lips and stared at the rug beneath the chair. "I should have left him today. I'll call him tomorrow and break it off. Let Beth hear. She needs to know what her husband's up to anyway."

Dodd said nothing. She leaned her face against his shoulder. He draped his arm across her shoulder. She threw her arms around his neck, stretching up kiss him. “Not now,” he pushed her away, “We need to keep clear heads.”

“My head is clear,” she told him, grabbing his arm and pulling him toward the stairs to her loft. “And the time to get things straight is now.”

In her bed, she climbed on top of him, ripping his shirt open and biting his chest, his shoulder and then his neck. He pushed himself up to protest but she pushed him back into the bed, locked her mouth on his, and rode him with the fury of a mare in a tornado. After they both came, and he let his leg dangle off the side if the bed, and she collapsed shaking across his chest, he thought about stories of Pecos Bill and Widowmaker that he heard as a kid. Then she covered his mouth with her mouth and they rode off into the whirlwind again.

Chapter 43

Dodd walked to Ralph Meeker's house from Rhonda's at four thirty in the morning, knowing he would find his boss hungover but as close to sobriety as he would ever be. He walked because he though Joe Bob might already be up and about and would spot his Mustang from one of his black second-story windows. He only made one stop, at his car, to reach under the driver's seat for the papers he'd already stashed there.

Meeker's house was the next-to-last structure on a street called Town Council Lane, a wide street that veered southwest from the highway before curving back east, sloping downhill and emptying into Rafferty's estate. It stood back from the road in a grove of mesquite, a ranch-style with split log railing surrounding the yard. Dodd could see Joe Bob's house at the top of the hill, where the road curved back eastward—a two story fortress with no windows on the first floor and painted battleship gray with black trim.

Dodd entered Meeker's property through the woods at the back of the house, climbing over the fence and slipping up to his back door. He rapped against the glass with the soft part of his fist, hoping that Ralph wouldn't be too out of it to hear him.

He rapped consistently for ten or fifteen minutes when he finally saw a light switch on in the hall. The kitchen curtains were up and Dodd saw Ralph turn a corner into the kitchen, still tying his robe and squinting in the light. When he reached the back door he pushed back the curtain and said, "Jesus Christ, is that you Dodd?"

"I need to talk to you."

But Ralph chose to talk through window. "What the hell are you doing? It's not even five in the morning."

Dodd pulled the paperwork from his pocket and flattened it against the window. "I have some numbers you really need to see. This won't wait."

Ralph muttered obscenities under his breath while he pulled back the bolt lock and let Dodd through. He turned on the kitchen lights and said, "This better be good."

Dodd spread the papers out across Meeker's table. "No, Ralph. This isn't even close to good."

"Give me a second to adjust," Ralph said, turning to his cabinet and pulling down a bottle of Jack Daniels.

"Put it up, Ralph," Dodd said, taking the bottle from his fist and returning it to the cabinet. "For once we're going to have a conversation without all that whiskey fogging your brain."

Ralph took the bottle back and cut the foil around the lid with a paring knife. "I don't need this to fog my mind, I need to cut through the crap to clear it."

Dodd put his hand on top of Meeker's. "Look, Ralph, you're a drunk and that's your own business, but you're drinking too much right now and you need to stay sober for two minutes."

Ralph shook his head and sat compliantly in front of the paper work. Dodd returned the bottle to the cupboard one last time and then put some hot water on to boil for coffee.

Meeker shuffled absent-mindedly through the papers as though not entirely sure what he was looking at. "You know I'm not good with the books, son," he muttered. "That's why I let you hire Rawlings. So why are you showing these to me?"

"Don't bullshit me, Ralph. Those figures document a trail of malfeasance that goes back to the forties, and you and your brother are at the center of it."

Ralph held up one of the computer printouts as though it were a soiled diaper. "I don't play with numbers, I tell you. If there's any foolishness here it's Rafferty's foolishness."

Dodd was counting on the fact that Ralph didn't want to focus on the numbers, and counting doubly on the fact that Meeker was desperate to get rid of him so he could get to his first drink of the morning.

The pot whistled. Dodd found two chipped ceramic mugs and poured the boiling water over Taster's Choice crystals so congealed they barely dissolved in the steaming water. He stirred the brew and carried the cups to the table.

"You should have been paying attention because Rafferty's using his race track proposal to launder money from the IRS. The best part is, he's named you as the front man." Dodd pulled a copy of Rawling's forgery of the transfer document. The one with Meeker's name where Dodd's should have been. He laid it in front of Meeker's mug. "If the Feds come looking, yours is the first door they'll knock on."

Meeker lifted the paper from the table and read it. Then he read it again. Then he wadded it up and tossed it against the wall, underneath a hunting calendar with the picture of a mallard flying across a lake. "That rat bastard," he shouted. "That wasn't supposed to be my name on that." Then he realized whose name was supposed to be there and shut up.

Dodd let it pass as though he didn't notice. "He put your name on a lot of things. For instance, did you know that the big robbery back in forty nine covered a shortfall of deposits to your account." He tapped his finger on the Xeroxed figures from the old ledgers, knowing Ralph was too distressed to actually look at them. "If these figures came to light, it would make you and Joe Bob look like embezzlers. Like you set the Dodds up and then killed them to cover-up your own shady dealings."

Ralph's face turned gray. His hands started to shake. "That's not true. None of it,"

"It doesn't matter, Ralph. What matters is what's on the paper." Dodd retrieved the paper with Meeker's forged signature, and spread it back out in front of him. "I have documents from the forties, the seventies and the eighties and the paper trail leads to you two and you two alone."

Meeker laid his arms across the papers and his head on his forearms. "What am I going to do?" His words were barely audible.

"Man up, for Christ's sake. Stack the deck in your favor. Half the businessmen in Sweet Water Falls want to run your brother and Rafferty out of town, and if you go with them no one's going to cry. But if you turn the tables, let Rafferty and Joe Bob sink, they'll probably let you stay on as mayor, run your businesses as you please. It's your call."

Ralph didn't even look up, muttering into the paperwork. "They're the only friends I've got."

"Just two days ago you told me you didn't trust either one. Make a choice, Ralph, but make the right one. Do you go down with Joe Bob and Rafferty, knowing they'll be pointing their fingers at you, or do you point the finger first and save your ass?"

Finally Meeker looked up from the table, his eyes red and eroded. "I hate making hard decisions."

Dodd took Meeker's cup and tossed the coffee down the sink. "Jesus, Ralph, you hate making any decision. Put off this one and there's nothing I can do to save you."

Meeker sighed. "If I sell them out, you'll make sure I'm still mayor?"

"Do you honestly think any one else wants the job after the mess you made?"

He was shaking so badly now Dodd thought the papers would fall off the table and onto the floor. "What do I do?"

"Give me all your paperwork. Anything to point the paper trail back to Rafferty. Even the stuff you buried about Preacher Rawlings and Delroy Lean."

Meeker stared at him, adding the consequences up in his mind. "I'll do it on one condition, and only one condition."

"You're not in a position to bargain."

Meeker swept the papers off his kitchen table and slammed his fist down. "Neither are you. I may be Mal's fall guy, but you're the one he's gunning for, and Joe Bob's itching to pull the trigger. So take my deal or don't, but if we're gonna get into bed together there's only one way to do it."

"What do you want, Ralph?"

Dodd didn't need to ask, but he wanted Meeker to say it.

"The UFO. If you don't show it to me, we both go down together and I don't give a shit what happens to you. I'm too fucking old to care, Dodd. Are you?"

Dodd pretended to think it over. As though there was anything to consider. Finally he sighed. Dramatically. As though he was about to let a great load off his chest. "I'll show it to you tonight."

Meeker slumped back in his chair and let his breath out. "So it's really there."

Dodd smiled. "Has been all along."

Chapter 44

Dodd made an appointment with Rafferty for ten-thirty that morning. He arrived at the bank at ten-fifteen, dressed in jeans and boots, carrying a thick manila envelope. Before he left the ranch he made sure to scuff up the boots even more than usual, add a few scratches to the leather.

On the way to the bank, he stopped at the feed store, opened a bag of fertilizer and stuck the toe of his left boot in it. Fred Waspergas watched from behind the counter. "What the hell is that about?"

Dodd tossed him a five, and said. "I have business at the bank. Can you dispose of the rest of it for me?" Waspergas said he would be glad to.

He entered Rafferty's office unannounced, dropped the envelope on Rafferty's desk, then dropped into the chair across from him. Rafferty sniffed the air distastefully and studied Dodd as though he'd brought a dead rat into the room. He curled his nose, opened the envelope and spilled the contents onto his blotter. "What's this?" he demanded, waiving his hand across the documents.

"You're the money honcho, not me. Ralph Meeker showed them to me; asked me to give him a legal opinion. Hinted around that I should watch my back." He leaned across the desk and lowered his voice, as though sharing a confidence. "I think he's planning to sell you out."

Rafferty leaned his elbows on his desk and rested his chin on his crossed fingers. As he leaned closer, he caught a stronger whiff of Dodd's boot. He stared hard into Dodd's eyes, as though studying him over cards at poker. "Why are you telling me this?"

Dodd leaned back in the leather chair and crossed his legs. The shit on his boot continued to annoy Rafferty nose, but he tried, once again, to pretend he didn't notice. "It's pretty clear who butters the bread and which side it's buttered on. I'd like to keep my bread buttered."

Rafferty held his breath and wriggled his fingers, his chin still resting on his knuckles. "And what do you propose?"

Dodd waved his hand, fingers flying, as though whisking a fly away. "Go after the Meekers. You keep good records, probably better than they do. Surely you have plenty on them. Something that won't also implicate you."

Rafferty scowled, as though he had just been insulted. "Do you think I'm a moron?"

Dodd leaned back in his chair. "No, I think you're planning to sell them out already. I just want to make sure my back is covered."

The two men stared at each other, silently. Then Rafferty relaxed and leaned back in his own chair. "I can't think of anything that could possibly help you."

Dodd draped his left leg on Rafferty's desk the toe of his boot pointed upward, crossed the other leg over his ankle and pulled a piece of wood and his pocket knife from his pants. He began to whittle a stake. "When I was in prison," Dodd said, "I became good friends with a man named Rawlings. He always hinted around to me that he was sent up for some scam the Meekers ran. That might provide fuel for the fire." The wood scraps fell onto Rafferty's carpet but Dodd ignored them.

Rafferty winced, forced a smile, trying his best to ignore the shit on the toe of Dodd's boot, and crossed his fingers in front of him. "There were some robberies a few years back. Two niggers involved, one of them was, in fact, the Rawlings boy. Come to think of it, there were some questions raised that were never answered."

"For instance?"

"When Rawlings was arrested, there was no money on him. His partner didn't have the money either. Yet the Meekers collected the insurance. It's possible that they kept the money and reported it stolen anyway."

"Someone should run an audit. Someone you can trust."

"My secretary could do that. She'll do anything I ask and keep it confidential." He smiled. "But you know all about her ability to keep secrets."

Dodd stood up. He put the stake back in his pocket and leaned across the desk to shake Rafferty's hand. "Good. I'll be waiting for her delivery."

Rafferty took a tissue from his desk and leaned across to clean the edge in case any of the fertilizer from Dodd's boot transferred. "You know, up until now, I really thought you had Dodd blood in you. But now I know. They never had your smarts in their gene pool."

Dodd turned from the door, his hand still on the knob. "I'm not sure how to take that."

Rafferty handed the tissue to Dodd. "I thought you came to town with some stupid plan to get revenge. But you figured out the angles instead. They were easy marks, but you could be useful." He took a cigar from his drawer and rolled it lovingly between his fingers. "Or dead. Depending on how you play this. Please throw that away outside the bank."

"I'll play useful," Dodd said. He dropped the tissue to the floor and smiled.

Chapter 45

Dodd took fewer than three steps from the bank entrance before he spotted one of the right reverends, the baldest one—with five o'clock shadow already pronounced at eleven in the morning—heading straight toward him, determined to tackle him and share the good news.

Dodd spun around to duck back into the bank and bumped right into Joe Bob's chest, already stained with sweat in the early morning. Joe Bob shoved his finger in Dodd's face. "You and I gonna talk again."

Dodd sidestepped him. "Actually Joe Bob, I think the minister here, St. Matthew isn't it?" He turned to acknowledge the balding man who caught up with them, "I think the minister had my attention first."

"St. John actually," the man said, "and I have been trying to get Mr. Dodd's attention for over a week now, sheriff, to share with him the message of Christ and his kingdom to come."

"Fuck off, preacher," Joe Bob said, grabbing Dodd just under his shoulder.

The Right Reverend St. John stepped back and blushed. “Really, sheriff, there is no call for language like that from a man who God appointed over his people.”

Joe Bob leaned his face into the minister’s and said, “Fuck off or I’ll close you down for a dozen health and building code violations. With four other churches on this street alone, ain’t nobody gonna miss yours.”

St. John gripped his Bible with both hands and stepped away hastily. “Yes, I see. Well, go with God, brothers. Mr. Dodd, I hope to have a chat with you soon.”

St. John headed away as quickly as he could, and Joe Bob slammed Dodd into the wall. He twisted Dodd’s collar so hard it pinched the back of his neck. “I saw you at Ralph's house this morning. I want to know what you and that alcoholic dip shit are planning.”

Dodd wedged his hand between them and pushed Joe Bob back. Joe Bob didn’t release the pressure on his collar. “Ralph got drunk, smashed a bottle. Thought he was bleeding everywhere. Turned out to be ketchup. He wasn’t even cut.”

“Bull shit.” He lifted Dodd from the sidewalk.

“Ask Ralph. If he’s even sober enough to remember.”

Joe Bob released the pressure and stepped away from Dodd. “You’ve got two days to deliver that money.”

Dodd brushed his shirt off, finally able to breathe more comfortably. “You’ll have it tomorrow.”

Joe Bob leaned in, the coal of his cigar almost singing Dodd’s nose. “And if I don’t?”

Dodd held his hand in a solemn pledge. “I’ll run for it.”

Joe Bob bit off the end of the cigar and spit it next to Dodd’s boot tip. “Son, there ain’t no where you can go where I won’t find you and fuck you. You’re asshole will be so big you’ll shit as soon as you eat. You believe me?”

Dodd took the cigar from the sheriff’s mouth and ground it into the sidewalk. “Joe Bob, if this goes south, I’m sure the size of my asshole will be the least of my worries.”

Friday Night

Chapter 46

The town council met every Friday night of the year except the Friday night before the barbecue. The Friday night tradition began with Rafferty's grandfather, the founder of the town and the Sweet Water Bank, and continued through three generations of Rafferty's family and town councils.

The council met in Rafferty's home office, not the town hall. Rhonda Mayfield, as had the secretaries who preceded her, made a buffet of Johnny Walker Blue, Cuban cigars, potato salad and cold sandwiches, which she laid out against the far wall before leaving. Every Saturday morning she returned to clean away the remains, a duty for which she was not compensated.

Rafferty arrived first, as he always did, slightly after seven in the evening. He made himself the first of three sandwiches he ate at every meeting, poured the first of his three double Scotches. He set up the tape recorder to record every word uttered, something else he did at every meeting and which neither Joe Bob nor Ralph knew. Then he turned on the lamp and turned it to face away from him and shine in the eyes of anyone facing his desk.

Once finished, he settled back in his chair, trimmed the first of his cigars, lit it with a match and waited for his sparring partners to arrive.

Joe Bob arrived, as he always did, at seven-twenty. He piled four helpings of beef on his sandwich and lathered the Miracle Whip across the bread. Then he filled a highball glass with Scotch and nothing else, taking his seat beside the window so the lamp wouldn't be glaring directly in his eyes and so he could count the stars when the meeting drifted to details he cared nothing about. He lit his own cigar and held it between his thumb and forefinger, letting the ash fall into the carpet.

Neither man spoke until Ralph arrived fifteen minutes late, as he always did, made his own sandwich and spilled the Miracle Whip on the buffet, as he always did, reached under the cart for an unopened bottle of Johnny Walker, as he always did, and sat down, trying to balance sandwich, glass and bottle at the same time.

Since he hoarded the bottle, Rafferty made sure Rhonda reserved the still choice, but less premium, Johnny Walker Black for his consumption. He didn't seem to notice. She probably could have given him Early Times and he wouldn't have noticed.

Ralph settled into a chair next to the buffet, under the picture of Rafferty's dour faced father, where he balanced the sandwich on one knee and the bottle on the other. The shaking in both knees made it likely that one or the other would topple over, but somehow he managed to hold onto both.

Rafferty called the meeting to order. By this time the smoke from his and Joe Bob's cigars drifted across the room, crisscrossing the room like fine lace. "The only issue on the agenda is Dodd. He's becoming a serious impediment."

"I like the boy," Ralph said. The other two glared at him and he shut up.

"Well, you're too fucking drunk to see what he's been up to," Joe Bob growled.

"I don't see your problem, Joe Bob. It's Mal's daughter he's fucking."

"He told me he's part nigger." Joe Bob said. He spat it out, like a wad of of tobacco he had chewed too long.

Ralph took a long pull from his bottle. "Sounds like he's fucking with you, too."

Joe Bob's face turned dark. "He hired a nigger to run your store."

Ralph put the bottle back on his knee. He had drained it well past the neck in a single swallow. He bit into his sandwich. "Sounds like he's doing a good job of fucking with you." He could barely keep the food in his mouth as he spoke.

"Let's keep the meeting professional," Rafferty interrupted. "Ralph, did you know he threatened to expose our involvement in the race track?"

"That's not what he told me," Ralph said. He rose from his seat, almost dropping everything. Then he gathered his composure and his booty and settle back down. "Why would he want to do that?"

"Because he's playing us for patsies. He thinks he can set us against each other."

"How'd he go about doing that, Mal?" Joe Bob interjected.

Rafferty cleared his throat and leaned back into his chair. The light outside was fading, leaving the only light the lone lamp on his desk, completely his face in shadows. "He can't. But why put up with it? Frankly, I've looked at the books, and the race track's becoming a liability. Let it burn and burn Dodd with it."

"No," Ralph cried out. "He promised to show me the UFO."

Joe Bob bit the end of a new cigar and spit it into the waste basket. "There ain't no flying saucer, Ralph. He's fucking with you."

Rafferty raised his hand to silence them. "Ralph, if Dodd blows the whistle on us, or persuades one of us to blow the whistle on the others, we'll be in such deep shit that we won't dig our way out until we're toothless and dickless. He has to go."

Ralph seemed to shrink in the chair. He took another drink. "How?"

"By any means necessary." He pointed his cigar at Joe Bob. "Can you do it?"

Joe Bob grinned as he lit his cigar. He let the match burn to his fingers then, still grinning, shook it out. "It's done as we speak."

"Make sure the paperwork's on the body. Can you do that?"

Joe Bob rolled his cigar between his fingers. "I can handle it."

Rafferty doused his cigar in the scotch. A waste of a good cigar in better liquor, but what better way to symbolize his determination. "That's it. The meeting's adjourned. And gentlemen, I want this finished tonight."

Ralph stood, dropping his sandwich and bottle to the floor. He didn't even notice the liquor soaking into his boot. "Not tonight, Mal."

Joe Bob rolled his eyes. Rafferty said, "Don't worry, Rhonda will get that in the morning." He turned to Ralph. "Why can't we do this tonight?"

"I told you. He's gonna show me the UFO."

Joe Bob almost snorted his drink through his nose. "And I told you, you dim wit. There ain't no flying saucer."

Ralph held his hands in front of him as though he were actually grasping his prize trophy. They were trembling so hard he would have fumbled it had he had it in his possession. "No, he found it. I've got pieces. At home. He's gonna show me the whole thing tonight."

Rafferty laid his palms on the desk and leaned across it. The skepticism laced his voice. "Where?"

"I'm not telling," Ralph said. He lifted his boot, realizing it was wet, and kneeled to retrieve the bottle before all the scotch drained into the carpet.

Joe Bob threw up his hands. "How about we kill him first thing in the morning then?"

"Thank you," Ralph said from his knees. He grabbed the bottle. There were still a couple of swallows remaining. The sandwich was a sodden mess. "That will allow me to finish my business." He scrambled to his feet and stumbled out of the room, clutching the bottle to his chest.

"Maybe we'll kill both of you," Joe Bob muttered once he was gone.

"Do you think Dodd found it?" Rafferty asked.

"There ain't no UFO, Mal."

"The money."

Joe Bob pulled on his cigar and let the smoke spiral from his mouth to the ceiling. "He must have found something. Don't matter to me. He's a dead man either way."

Chapter 47

While the town council plotted Dodd's murder, Rhonda drove to his house to deliver yet another stack of documents. She found Dodd and Bobby waiting for her on the porch. He smiled as he glanced through the contents.

The sun hovered above the hills, lush and purple, diffused by a wash of magenta. It was as though the fire and orange that swept across the horizon only moments before had suddenly sighed with relief and chilled out. The cicadas were out in full force, singing in their high-pitched ratcheting frenzy. What little breeze would come out in the day blew across the fields now, carrying mostly dust from land that had long ago forgotten how to be fertile.

"Can I go now?" Bobby asked.

Dodd tossed him the car keys. Bobby caught them underhanded. "Do what you got to do, kid."

"Thanks," Bobby said. "You're a decent guy." He leaped over the door and into the driver's seat, revved the engine and tore off, spraying gravel across the side of the house. Dodd covered his eyes with his hand.

Rhonda kneeled next to him and wound her fingers through the fingers of his free hand. She was dressed in a sleeveless shirt and jeans, her hair pulled back in a pony tail and tied with a pale blue ribbon. “You are a pretty decent guy.”

“But will you tell me that in the morning?” Dodd was still in his jeans, but had changed into a heavy duty work shirt. He made sure to clean the fertilizer from his boot before she arrived.

She looked across the wide yard to the last purple shades of sunset settling over the gorge. The Mustang was just a distant speck on the highway. She squeezed his arm and pulled herself close. “So what do you intend to do now?

“Nothing,” he said. He wrapped his arm around his shoulder. “Whatever they have on the agenda, it’s their move.”

She stitched her fingers through his. He thought he felt her hands shaking. “Be careful. Those guys are dangerous.”

”Too bad I swore off drinking,” he said.

“Too bad you swore off guns.”

Chapter 48

Ralph's truck pulled into the dirt lot behind Dodd's house slightly after ten-thirty. He knocked quietly at the back door. Dodd answered wearing his blue jeans but nothing else, as though he wasn't sure Ralph would even show.

"I gave up on you. Thought you had your arms wrapped around the bottle for the rest of the night."

Ralph held his hand against the door frame to control his shaking. Dodd didn't turn the light on, but he could see the gun under Meeker's shirt by the way the moonlight silhouetted his body.

"It ain't easy to sell out friends and family."

"Give me the gun," Dodd said. "The aliens are all dead by now." He held his hand through the door. Ralph stared at the ground, trying to think up a good excuse and finally reached behind his back to remove the gun. Dodd took it by the barrel and slipped it into his back pack then stepped back from the door. "Let me get some clothes on."

Dodd drove Ralph's truck to the gorge. He wore jeans with a jeans shirt and hiking boots. He tossed his back pack in the bed of the truck. His last experience in the gorge taught him to be prepared for the trail. Ralph, who had probably been drinking during his cub scout pack meetings, wore ostrich boots and boot pants with a western sport shirt. Dodd could picture Ralph twisting an ankle and having to carry him most of the way.

The moon was high in the sky and three quarters full, the night clear enough to light their way. Dodd felt like he was driving in a negative print of the countryside during the day.

Ralph put his hand on Dodd's forearm, his shakes almost out of control. Even at night, in his air conditioned cab, he was sweating. "Did you really find it? Is it really there?"

Dodd stopped for two cows who wandered onto the trail. "Calm down, Ralph. You'll have a stroke before you ever get to see it."

Ralph leaned his head into the window. "I can't believe you actually found it. I always knew it was there. No one could fool me. It had to be there." He kept it up the entire drive. Dodd didn't know which was more likely to drive him crazy, Ralph's blathering or the blare of Mel Tillis cutting in and out on his AM radio.

When they reached the gorge, Dodd parked parallel to the ledge and led Ralph down the embankment the way Mary Beth showed him. He held Ralph's arm to keep him from sliding down the rocky slope and breaking a leg.

They walked slowly, glacially, in short steps, partially because the old man had a hard time navigating the terrain in the shadows and partially because he would have had a hard time navigating even if he was sober. Every five minutes or so they stopped so Ralph could catch his breath and complain about the rocks and steep grade of the trail. It didn't help that every hoot of an owl or screech of a night hawk spooked Ralph and he had to stop and put his hand to his chest. Nor did it help that when trees blocked their path, Ralph would bat at the branches as though they were attacking him.

"For Chrissake, Ralph, it isn't that difficult. Didn't you do this as a kid?"

"When I was a kid I didn't carry all this weight," Ralph complained. "And my knees were't swelled with arthritis."

"Bet you whined a lot," Dodd said.

They crossed the island and passed the pickup, which looked lonely and skeletal in the moonlight. Delight and rapture swept Ralph's face. "I know where we are," he shouted. He scampered over to the truck and ran his hands across what remained of the fenders.

"You ought to," Dodd reminded him, "You killed two men down here."

Ralph allowed Dodd to drag him away. "I ain't seen that in twenty-five years," he said. "Maybe longer." His finger pointed back in the truck's direction.

"Fine," Dodd said. "You can come back and worship tomorrow." He dragged Ralph into the river and back onto the bank, into a thicket of mesquite trees, past another twist of the river and around two more turns of the gorge. Finally, they stood under an overhang that shot eight feet out from the rim and over the water. Dodd reached into his pack to retrieve a road flare.

"What's that for?" Meeker asked.

"I can barely find this place in the daylight," Dodd explained.

"What place?" Ralph asked, stretching his neck to find an opening or trail.

Dodd struck the fuse against the flare's cap. Ralph watched as the orange yellow sparks arced into the night sky. Dodd dropped the cap and tossed his pack over his free shoulder. He grabbed Ralph by the elbow, yanking him behind a wall of ivy and into a cave that was completely indiscernible from the woods.

Ralph was wonderstruck by the gypsum sparkling in the light of the flare. What would have been completely black suddenly glistened pink, blue, yellow and white, dancing in the sparks. "In all my days I never dreamed of such a thing," Ralph said. They stood in a narrow tunnel so long the flare's light seemed to be sucked into blackness.

"Hard to imagine isn't it?" Dodd added. "It goes back about a quarter mile, downhill the whole way. All that digging you boys did, but you never dreamed it was down here waiting the whole time."

Ralph stopped to catch his breath, holding his hand to his chest. "You mean?"

"What do you think I mean? Where do you think Zane hid while his brothers floated down the river? Did you think he actually made it out of the canyon?"

"So we searched the gorge and he was holed up here the whole time?" Ralph spun around to comprehend what he was seeing.

"The official story was that two of them got away," Dodd added. "But we both know that's bullshit isn't it?" Ralph didn't answer. He simply stared at the sparks from the flare.

"Let's get on with it." Dodd gripped him under the shoulder. He led Ralph down the tunnel. The incline grew steeper as they descended, making it more and more difficult to keep a steady pace, and though it didn't seem possible, the tunnel seemed to grow even darker the further they descended. After ten minutes they were stepping sideways, sliding as much as stepping, gravel and dust scattering with them.

The passage hooked to the left after five hundred yards and the passageway became even rockier. Dodd had to lift Ralph to keep him from stumbling over some of the larger ones, which didn't help when Ralph sidestepped into yet another rock and stumbled anyway. It didn't take long for Ralph to suggest that a drink might steady his nerves. "Sorry, Ralph," he said. "It's the one thing I didn't think to pack."

A twist to the right, another few hundred yards and finally, when it seemed that Ralph might run out of breath entirely and collapse from hyperventilation, the passage opened into a chamber as long and wide as a football field.

The flare died just seconds after they emerged from the tunnel. They saw a brief reflection of a dry wall cave, and then blackness.

"I hope you have another flare," Ralph said.

Dodd fumbled in his backpack and pulled out a table lantern. He switched it on, and the white light illuminated the center of the room. He left the lantern in the center of the floor, and a second ten feet away, then placed placed twelve flares at key points around the wall, setting each one off to fill the room with light.

The cave was disjointed and rocky. An earthquake thousands, perhaps millions of years before had dislodged mammoth boulders, then trapped them between the shifting walls. The rock strata looked as though they were sliced open in one blow with a gigantic axe. Gray, brown, black, quartz reflected from the flares. A giant fissure ripped through the ceiling, a large section six feet lower than the other. The same with the floor where half was sunken in the center. Giant jagged pieces of rock pushed out from the walls at odd angles. Small fissures tore through the walls.

The cave lacked the stalactites and stalagmites caused by eons of erosion and water dripping usually found in most caves. The walls were lined with loose rocks which had been collected and piled by the Dodds years before.

Ralph's eyes fell on the pile of wreckage as soon as Dodd set off the last flare. The pieces lay arranged against the farthest wall, under an outcropping. "Oh my," he gasped, and ran to the pile, his shakes gone until he touched the first piece.

"This is just like I imagined." He pulled out a long, fused rod with hieroglyphics embossed the length of it. He ran his fingers down the long pole, and then peered down one end of it like sighting down a gun barrel. "This must be a cross beam. Just think. This came to us from the stars, son. From the stars themselves."

Dodd leaned against the wall and waited while Ralph took inventory, laying the pieces out, trying to fit them together, flattening the thin metal on the cave floor, even tracing two of the hieroglyphs in the dust.

"How many millions of miles do you think they traveled to get here, only to explode over a little canyon in Texas?" he asked.

"I couldn't say, Ralph." He crossed his arms, as though the discovery were no more newsworthy than a handful of arrowheads or buffalo nickels.

"How can you not be excited?" Ralph demanded. He showed Dodd a balsa wood sprocket. He held it gently in front of him as though it were a newborn he was presenting to his family for the first time. "This stuff was made from star dust." His eyes were wide open with wonder, even if they were unable to focus clearly.

"He's not excited because he knows it's a fake," Joe Bob's voice boomed across the cavern.

Dodd looked over his shoulder. Rafferty, Joe Bob and Bobby stood just inside the tunnel opening. Rafferty carried two large leather satchels. Alvin stood behind them, his hands behind his back as though handcuffed.

Dodd kicked the dirt as though caught in the act. "What did he do, Alvin? Arrest you?"

Joe Bob hooked his thumbs behind his belt buckle. "Just holding him for questioning. In case you don't cooperate."

The sprocket tumbled from Ralph's fingers and into the dirt. "Joe Bob? How'd you get here?"

"It wasn't hard to follow you. You were too damn drunk to walk," Rafferty said. It was said with a sneer, his upper lip curled with derision.

Joe Bob put his arm around Bobby's shoulder. "I gave the kid here a radio, and he called as soon as you showed up at Dodd's farm. Mal and I were sitting in the cruiser sharing some Beam. We thought we'd wander over and crash the party."

"Thanks, kid," Dodd said.

"They made me an offer I couldn't refuse." Bobby shrugged. He refused to look Dodd in the eye.

Joe Bob tussled the boy's hair. "Hell, he was already into larceny. Might as well have him doing it for us."

Alvin leaned against the cave wall, his face down and his neck sagging.

"You can unlock his cuffs, Joe Bob," Dodd demanded. "I'm not going anywhere."

"I'm okay, Dodd," Alvin answered. "I don't think we ought a be pushing things right now."

As he spoke, Ralph reached down into his neatly arranged pieces and pulled up the long beam with the hieroglyphics. "Joe Bob, you're wrong. It's here. Just like I thought it was. A real UFO."

Joe Bob spit a wad of tobacco onto the floor. Rafferty laughed."Are you going to tell him, Joe Bob, or keep fucking with his head?"

Joe Bob readjusted his belt buckle. "You tell him, Dodd. You're the one who brought him here."

"Tell me what?" Ralph said, glancing back and forth between the two. He clutched his precious pieces as though they would disappear should he drop them. "It's all right here. What's there to tell?"

"It's a surveillance balloon," Dodd said. "Designed by Army Intelligence to detect atomic explosions from Soviets nuclear testing. The Army knew the Reds were trying to build their own bomb months after the war ended, they just didn't know when they'd get one. So they started floating balloons in '47."

"How stupid do you think I am?" Ralph said, "The weather balloon story was a cover-up." He held the cross beam in his hand as though it were a sacramental object. His hands began to shake, his entire body began to shake, whether overwhelmed by awe or withdrawal it was difficult to tell. "It didn't work at Roswell either. Your uncle Zel was there. He was Army Intelligence. He told me the whole story."

Dodd stepped away from the wall. He made a production of holding his hands in surrender for Joe Bob and Rafferty. "Well, Zel was always a little loopy, wasn't he? Yes, the weather balloon story was a cover up. To cover up a spy balloon. The UFO story was a happy accident. Between the UFO and the weather balloon story the Army had their bases covered."

He walked over and took the cross beam from Ralph's fingers. "Do you really believe aliens would travel the galaxy in ship made of wood and plastic?" He snapped it between his fingers, shattering it into several pieces. "Especially one this flimsy?" He let the pieces tumble to the cavern floor.

"Your see, with two versions, your average Joe would think it was a balloon and all you gullible crackers would think it was aliens. No one would suspect we were spying on the Russians. Of course, Joe Bob knew that all along. Didn't you, Joe Bob? Because you were at Roswell, too."

"Glad to hear you finally admit you're one of those Dodds," Joe Bob said, letting another wad drop into the dirt beside him.

Rafferty interrupted the conversation by dropping the satchels onto the floor of the cave. "You really are nuts, Ralph. I'm surprised you didn't bankrupt us. We could've made millions, but you just had to find your space ship."

He turned to Dodd and propped his foot on one of the satchels. "Did you know he wanted to build a theme park?" He pointed at Ralph as though he were accusing a rapist or serial killer. "Wanted to call it Spaceland. Can you believe it? I kept telling him, Ralph, there is no land in space, but he didn't get it."

A tear formed at the corner of Ralph's eye and trailed down his cheek. "Zel swore there was no secret project."

Rafferty knelt beside the satchel and removed two pick axes and shovels, laying them neatly on the ground beside the bag. He used one of the shovels to stand back up, leaning against it to wipe the dust off the knees of his trousers. "Honestly, Ralph, you'd think the human race would be extinct by now, people like you are so dumb. Why would you believe the government when it says there's no secret project, but call them liars when it says there's no aliens?"

Ralph picked up one of the surviving pieces of cross beam. He ran his fingers across the lettering. "What about this writing? It can't be from this earth."

Dodd tried not to laugh. He tried very hard. But Ralph looked like a kid who had just been told there was no Santa Claus. Albeit a kid also suffering from the early stages of alcohol withdrawal. The fact that Joe Bob wasn't even trying to hide his sarcastic, if not outright malicious smirk, was the only thing that kept him from busting a gut.

"Zel dreamed up covert ops for the Army," he said. He took the cross beam and ran his fingers down the lettering. "This was called an encryption deception. They started with Navajo and then altered the basic characters. The plan was to lose several balloons to the Russians. The Soviets would waste years trying to decode characters that had no meaning to start with."

Ralph dropped the plastic into the dirt and pushed himself up. "How do you know that? The code stuff?"

Joe Bob shook his head derisively. "Where do you think, dimwit? His last name's Dodd."

Dodd picked up his pack and dusted it off. "Zel told my dad. Before he went totally over the deep end." He pointed to Joe Bob with the cross beam. "Your brother tortured you with the flying saucer the same way he tortured Zel. Being the spiteful bastard that he is."

Rafferty rested his right foot on the blade of the shovel and leaned across the handle. "Goddam it, Joe Bob. Just tell him so we can get on with this."

Joe Bob let a sly grin crawl across his face and let a gob of tobacco fly onto the cave floor. "Aw, hell, might as well let the cat out of the bag. I drove in the convoy that delivered all them boxes to Wright Patterson. Got Zel drunk one night, us being old friends and all, and he admitted he was in charge of floating them balloons. Even Major Marcel didn't know and he was the base's intelligence liaison. Hell, he didn't even know Zel was Intelligence. No one did. Thought he was dispatch officer."

One of the flares went out. Rafferty reached into his duffel bag for another half dozen. He handed them to Bobby to put out before the others flares burned through.

"Zel was one fucked up kid," Joe Bob said. "Little piss ant if you ask me, but he told me he dreamed up all kinds of shit for OSS during the war. If you could believe him. Which I didn't particularly, him being a Dodd and all." He ground the toe of his boot into the gob of tobacco to illustrate.

"Little fuck swore this was gonna be his best job. Told me the Army was afraid Congress might cut back funding, what with the war over and all those brainwashed voters and pinko sympathizers in government. So Zel decided to kill a bunch a birds with one stone." Joe Bob held up fingers to count. "Listen for atomic tests, see if they could get past our own radar, fool the fucking Rooskies, even blow up a balloon to see if our own numnutzes will find those made up letters and think it was a Red spy balloon."

"It was actually pretty smart," Dodd explained. "He figured Congress would hear about the Soviet spy balloon and increase Army Intelligence funding. He never dreamed that the base intelligence liaison would dream up alien invaders instead of Russian spooks."

Joe Bob laughed from his throat, a tobacco gurgle, and spit yet another wad onto the cave floor. Dodd couldn't look at the disgusting little mound piling up beside him. "That's exactly right. But for the brass it works out better. Now they got people afraid of big red men and little green men. They can see those Congressional dollars stacking up."

He pulled his gun from his belt, opened and spun the cylinder. "So I run across Zel in a bar, him crying in his beer over how the Army really stuck it to Marcel and it was all his fault. Zel being such a sensitive fuck and all. Hell, every one knew he was queer, but he was too important for the Army to admit it. So I feed him six or seven scotches, and Zel pours his poor queer heart out. That's when I told him I was one of the drivers on the Wright Patterson Convoy. Told him I took a look inside those boxes myself."

Ralph's face was ghostly white in the light of the flares, but Dodd noticed the slightest trace of hope suddenly gleam in his eye. Like one ember falling out from a pike of long dead coals on a winter morning. "So you saw them. You saw the aliens."

"Get on with it, Joe Bob. Tell him what you did find," Rafferty prodded. He kicked at the shovel head with his boot, clearly impatient to end the story and start digging.

"Balloon parts," Joe Bob said. It wasn't so much a statement so much as a proclamation, the climax to a grand narrative. Joe Bob even held his hands out as though addressing a theater audience, his pistol dangling by his trigger finger, as though anticipating thunderous applause before launching into his denouement. "Recognized 'em right away."

Dodd added. "Which is what you told Zel."

"Hell no. I told him I saw bodies. About four feet tall. And wouldn't you know it? The kid had dreamed up so many double and triple crosses he convinced himself the government used his weather balloon story to keep him out of the loop about the aliens. He went half nuts thinking they wanted to prove he was queer. Started looking behind every cabinet and corner for the little traps they set for him. Two months later he went Section 8 and they sent him home."

"When the second balloon crashed here, and Zel told everyone about the UFO, you knew what it really was," Dodd said.

"You bet. But I let him babble on."

Ralph pushed himself from the floor. He was barely able to stand, but managed to stay upright, "Why did you torture that boy? You pestered and beat up on him since he was old enough to chew on your ankle. What did he ever do to you?"

Joe Bob crossed the cavern to Ralph in three steps. He held the barrel under Ralph's chin and shouted, "He was a smart-mouth, smart-assed, panty-wasted pip squeak and I should a beat him to death when he was three years old. But you wouldn't let me."

Rafferty kicked over the shovel and followed him across the cavern. He pulled Joe Bob's arm to his side. "Goddam it, Joe Bob. Focus on why we're here."

Joe Bob swung around, yanking his arm free and pointing the gun at Rafferty's belly. "Don't fucking order me around. I can kick the shit out of both of you any day."

Rafferty put both hands over his wrist, and lowered the gun again. He turned to face Alvin. "You, nigger boy," he barked. "Tell Joe Bob what you told me when he was in his office talking to his deputies?"

Alvin turned his back to them and pretended to study the cave wall, as though he hadn't heard Rafferty calling to him. Only then did Dodd realize that Joe Bob had handcuffed his arms halfway up his back.

"Speak up, goddam it," Rafferty yelled. Even in the low light, his face was clearly flushed.

Alvin turned to face them slowly, only he didn't face them. He looked downward, into the dirt, doing his best imitation of a servile negro. "I just said Dodd might know where that satchel is what holds that stolen money. That's all I said. 'Might.' I didn't no way say necessarily does."

This time Joe Bob raised his gun toward Dodd. Rafferty turned with him. Their faces were dark, their eyes hidden in shadows, but their intentions clear. "Well, that settles it," Joe Bob said. "I'm calling in our deal, Dodd. Where's the money?"

"And if I don't give it to you," Dodd said, "are you going to kill me like you killed Zack and Zel?"

Ralph cleared his throat.

Rafferty said, "Joe Bob, you'd better be careful what you say," but Joe Bob refused to listen.

"Goddam right," Joe Bob said. He worked on the wad in his cheek with extra zeal and spit it across the cavern to land just inches from Dodd's boot. "I popped that crazy fucker Zel in his truck, and shot your uncle Zack in the back while he was swimming upriver. My only regret is that I didn't pop your old man too. Had to wait till some Ranger in Llano to shoot him in the back."

"Enough of this," Rafferty demanded. "Show us the money, Dodd."

Dodd casually bit off on a piece of thumbnail and spit it to the floor. "What money?"

Rafferty crossed back to the satchels and grabbed a shovel. He brandished it with one hand blade facing Dodd. "The money your family stole."

Dodd scratched the back of his head as though he didn't have a clue in the world what Rafferty could mean. "You sure are one cold customer to carry a joke this far."

Rafferty stared at him with empty eyes, as though he was talking to a stone wall.

"The joke being that Ralph and Joe Bob think they're gonna be rich and you know damn well there never was any money."

"Now you're talking pure nonsense." Rafferty remained perfectly still. His lips didn't even seem to move.

Dodd didn't flinch. "They have no idea you're planning to kill me as soon as the money doesn't turn up."

Not another word was spoken. Ralph and Joe Bob exchanged glances, not sure what they were hearing. It didn't take Joe Bob more than a second to realize whatever he was hearing, he didn't like it. His eyebrows raised, if only slightly. "Now wait a minute," he said.

Dodd turned suddenly and dived toward a small outcrop at the foot of the far wall. Before anyone could react he reached under to pull out a torn and dusty leather bag. He tossed the bag to Joe Bob. It spiraled several times before dropping into the dirt at Joe Bob's feet. Joe Bob kneeled to search the bag. His knees cracked with his extreme weight and the stress on his knees showed on his face. Everyone leaned an inch closer to see what Joe Bob would pull out; everyone, that is, but Dodd and Rafferty.

"You bastard," Joe Bob yelled, "there ain't more than twenty thousand in here." He removed a slim pack of hundred dollar bills, still wrapped in the bank wrapper. He held the bills out for everyone to see, and then let the pack fall from his fingers onto the cave floor.

Dodd dashed across the floor and leaned over to pick the bills up. He dusted them off and slipped them into his pocket. Joe Bob raised his gun to bring it down on Dodd's head, but Dodd grabbed his wrist and took the revolver.

"How much money did you really think there was, Joe Bob?" he said. He aimed the gun at Joe Bob, pulling back the hammer with his thumb.

Joe Bob leaned back with his hands up. He studied Dodd through hooded eyes, looking for his move but wary of his own gun. "Five hundred thousand dollars. That's how much your uncles stole."

Dodd released the hammer and slipped Joe Bob's gun into its holster. He laid his hand on Joe Bob's shoulder and leaned in confidentially. "Who told you that? Rafferty? How dumb are you, Joe Bob? Who in this town was more likely to steal half a million dollars? Redneck farmers, or your old buddy, Mal?"

Joe Bob stared at him defiantly while Rafferty cleared his throat and looked down at the bag of tools by his feet. Ralph looked back and forth between Rafferty and his brother. Finally Joe Bob asked, slowly, with a long drawl, "What do you mean?"

"Come on, Joe Bob. How could three peckerwood farmers who couldn't even float a loan break into the bank, break into the vault, shoot the old man and get away without tripping any alarms?"

Joe Bob looked back down at the empty bag. Dodd raised to one knee, his hand still on Joe Bob's shoulder. "That's the key, Joe Bob," he said, almost sympathetically. "If they tripped the alarms, Hargess would have been charging down to the bank in his own cruiser instead of sipping toddies at a Christmas party. So how are three peckerwood farm boys going to pull that off, Joe Bob? Can you tell me?"

"Zel planned it," Rafferty said, backing away toward the tunnel. "You said yourself. He was a whiz kid."

Dodd choked to keep from laughing out loud. He jumped to his feet and into Rafferty's face. "How long have you been waiting to tell that story, Mal?" He circled behind him and spoke over his shoulder. "Thinking how to explain why three farmers were smart enough to get past your bank security if someone questioned you too closely?"

Rafferty turned away, not wanting to catch Dodd's glare. He glanced over to Joe Bob and Ralph for support, but they didn't appear to be very supportive at the moment. Bobby and Alvin managed to slip out together and creep back to the cave wall, just a few feet from the same tunnel where Rafferty was headed.

Dodd continued, shadowing him. "Zel was an addled fuck-up by then. But that doesn't matter, does it? Even if he did still have the wherewithal to cook up a bank robbery, where did they get the tools? How did they open the vault? Or did they? I've read the reports, and there's no mention of the vault even being opened. It's like they walked through the walls. Like the 4-D man. Remember that movie? They walked through the walls and took five hundred thousand dollars, but only left twenty thousand behind. In that satchel."

Dodd could see Joe Bob had put together most of the story by now. But he still had one question. He held up his hand. "Okay. Then where did they get that twenty thousand, Dodd? It didn't fall from the sky."

Dodd pulled out some papers he had folded in his hip pocket. "These are Xeroxes of the originals my father left. He told me I might find some use for them some day." He handed them to Joe Bob.

Rafferty suddenly moved to the left, but Joe Bob dropped his hand onto his gun and said, "Wait a minute, Mal." He struggled to his feet and pulled his lighter from his pocket to read through the papers. His face grew darker as he got to the second page.

Rafferty started to move again and Dodd said, "I wouldn't do that, Mal. He's pretty fast on the draw."

By now Rawlings and Bobby had slipped to within a couple of feet of the tunnel. Ralph demanded, "Would somebody explain what's going on?"

"Don't you remember, Ralph?" Dodd told him. "The three of you planned the whole thing. How you were going to rip off half a million dollars, blame it on the Dodds and boot Hargess and the town council in the process? So Rafferty called the Dodds on Christmas Eve, said he'd refinance for twenty thousand if they'd give you three acres."

Ralph dropped to his knees. He looked to Rafferty, then Joe Bob then realized what the papers were that Joe Bob was looking at.

"Only Rafferty would destroy the loan papers, cry robbery, you and Joe Bob would ambush them. You'd kill them, report the entire half million missing. Who's going to question Mal, when his old man's lying dead on the floor and there are three convenient bodies to take the blame? When the Feds paid the bank, you guys kept the half million. Wasn't that the plan, Joe Bob?"

Joe Bob torched the papers with his lighter and dropped them into the dirt. He drew his gun, holding it loosely to the side. His eyes followed both Dodd and Rafferty, as though he were unsure which to shoot. Ralph looked from Dodd to Joe Bob to Rafferty, even more lost in confusion.

"It was," Joe Bob admitted. He returned his lighter to his pocket and spit the entire wad of tobacco onto the floor. "But for a hundred thousand, not no half a million. And there was nothing said about the old man dying." He reached into his shirt pocket for a cigar. "Then Mal told us the fuckers pulled a fast one and actually did rob him. Since they killed his old man, I figured the plan backfired and they got away with five times as much."

He took his lighter out and fired it. He held it in front of his cigar and stared at Rafferty over the flame. The hand with his gun was rock steady at his side. "But the more I think about it, the more I think Mal gave them the twenty thousand for the mortgage and kept the rest for himself. Let the poor fuckers drive away wishing themselves a merry Christmas."

"That's preposterous," Rafferty said. "They killed my father. And why would the government pay us for the losses if the money wasn't really missing?"

"Oh that's easy. You doctored the books," Joe Bob said. He snapped the lighter shut, stormed over to Rafferty and stuck the gun under his nose. Between the gun and the cigar smoke, Rafferty looked like he was ready to choke. "Or had you embezzled the damn money already, you skunk?"

"You realize he's wants us to double cross each other," Rafferty said. He could barely get the words out. Sweat began to pour over his collar. "He has all the money. He just wants you to think he doesn't."

Ralph pulled at Joe Bob's arm. "Joe Bob, they did kill the old man."

"Did they?" Dodd asked.

All three of them turned to look at Dodd. He began to cluck his tongue. "Brothers. You two should have known better," Dodd scolded them. "The old man was killed with a long-barreled .38 revolver. My family only carried squirrel guns. But Rafferty has that very revolver in his gun case. In fact I've even seen a picture with you three boys together and he's holding that gun."

He reached into his back pack. "Oh wait. I have it right here." He walked calmly over to Joe Bob and balanced it on the gun barrel. Joe Bob ripped it from his fingers. Ralph ran up to see it.

"You've had that gun since we were kids," Ralph said, almost tearing the picture apart in his trembling fingers. "We used to shoot rabbits and squirrels with it." He dropped the picture.

"You son-of-a-bitch. You weren't fucking the farmers, you were fucking us."

Dodd stepped away carefully, his hands in front of him, fingers spread wide. "Rafferty used you and my family to get his old man out of the way and take over the town. If you two weren't always convinced you could outdo each other, you would have seen what he was up to all along."

The three men sized each other up, stepping back and circling each other, Joe Bob with his gun to his side, the other two opening and closing their fists. "Of course, it isn't as though y'all haven't been ripping each other off ever since," Dodd said circling back to his pack. "Rafferty's been investing your funds without telling you, Ralph's been playing with the money from the race track, and Joe Bob's been moving capital out of the family business for years to finance oil investments. You boys have been stealing each other blind for twenty-five years and not one of you is smart enough to catch on."

Joe Bob stepped back and aimed the gun at Dodd. His neck was purple, his face was black. "You really are a son-of-a-bitch."

"Joe Bob? You've been stealing from me?" Ralph demanded. His shakes had gotten so bad Dodd thought he might drop to his knees.

"Alvin and Rhonda Mayfield took a look through the books for me," Dodd said. "I have copies of everything in my backpack if you want to look." He picked it up and tossed it to Ralph's feet. Ralph dropped to his knees and reached inside.

"He's lying, Ralph," Joe Bob said, dropping his gun to his side. "I never borrowed more than a couple of thousand and I paid it back both times. I just didn't know how to tell you I needed the money."

Ralph stood up, one hand holding the bag, the other hand still inside. "You lied about a lot of other things it appears to me."

As he Ralph spoke, Rafferty dropped to the floor and rolled over to his satchels. He rose to his feet with the .38. Without hesitating he shot Joe Bob in the shoulder, and then, as the sheriff spun around, shot him in the chest, and finally, as he fell, in the back. Joe Bob fell onto his face, his gun skittering off to the side.

Bobby and Alvin disappeared into the tunnel.

"You didn't have to shoot him," Ralph said.

"Looks like I did," Rafferty said and raised the .38 to fire at Ralph. Before he could pull the trigger, two shots barked and Rafferty clutched his shoulder with his free hand. As he dropped to his knees, Meeker pulled his hand from the backpack, clutching the .45 automatic Dodd had stolen from the store. He aimed it directly at Rafferty. "You are one mean son-of-a-bitch, Mal Rafferty, you know that?"

Rafferty opened his mouth and tried to lift the gun one last time. Meeker squeezed his own trigger six times. Four of the bullets missed, but one hit Rafferty in his chest and one hit his neck, driving him backward against a boulder that had ripped its way through the floor millennia before.

Alvin and Bobby Wayne stuck their heads out of the tunnel to see if the shooting was over. Alvin let out a low whistle. "We got a first class white boy shit storm."

Ralph dropped the gun into the dirt and surveyed the casualties. A single tear streaked down his cheek. "I'm in a lot of trouble, Dodd."

"Don't worry, Ralph," Dodd said. "You're not as bad off as they are." He nodded to the two bodies.

Joe Bob lay face down in the debris, his face buried in his hat and his boots turned toe inward. His gun was still in his fingers, pointed outward as though he could still take a shot. Rafferty was sprawled against the rock, eyes wide open, possibly still breathing but not for long. His neck was open from his ear to his shoulder. The bullet that hit his chest had taken out the upper part of his shoulder, hardly fatal but making it impossible for him to shoot. Blood trickled from his mouth and his gun hand dangled uselessly at his side, the gun several feet from his reach. His foot spasmed uncontrollably.

"And you've got me as your lawyer. If I can get Preacher Rawlings out of jail, I can probably keep you out too."

Ralph's eyes widened. As drunk as he might have been earlier, he was cold sober now.

Bobby Wayne walked up to Dodd, his mouth wide open. "Wow, Mr. Dodd. You didn't do nothing. They all killed each other and you ain't got a scratch on you."

Alvin said, "It wasn't that hard. These boys been itching to kill each other for thirty years. They only been itching to kill Dodd for a week or two." He walked up to study Rafferty's body. Then he studied Ralph. "Jesus Christ, old man. You never had a steady hand in your life. How'd you put two bullets in that bastard?"

Ralph shook his head in disbelief. Dodd reached under his arm to lift him up. He managed to stand without stumbling. "I would say adrenaline trumped alcohol," Dodd said. He dusted the dirt from Ralph's clothes. "Besides, from what I heard, Ralph was a better shot drunk than Rafferty was sober. Lucky for all of us."

Dodd took the twenty thousand from his pocket and passed it to Alvin. "Bobby earned some of that. It'll give him some capital to get on his feet. But it's up to you, Alvin. The paperwork on Preacher is in the car like I promised. Ready to file."

"That's it?" Bobby asked. His pupils were wide and he bounced on the balls of his feet, tracing little circles in the dirt. "That's all there is to it? Those guys are dead, Dodd. They would a killed all of us."

Alvin counted out five thousand and handed them to Bobby. "Keep your mouth shut, son. Keep your job, spend the money slow, and don't let the IRS see you spend it."

Bobby stared at the money as though it would disappear if he blinked. Finally he rolled it as tight as he could and stuffed it far down in his jeans pocket. "Aren't you gonna keep any, Dodd?" he asked.

"It's got my family's blood on it, son," Dodd said. "Besides, if I really want it, I've got a new job as mayor."

He took Ralph by the arm, and steered him toward the tunnel. Ralph followed in a daze, staring at the ceiling as though seeing the cavern for the first time. The flares were starting to die one-by-one and shadows were shutting down the cave to them. Alvin leaned over to pick up the back pack and satchels. "Leave everything for the state troopers to sort through," Dodd told him. "They aren't going anywhere."

Chapter 49

Dodd could imagine the US Marshal John Pepper's distress at the interrogation, if it could be called an interrogation. With Dodd serving as both witness and counsel for the defense the Marshal could do little more than sit with all four witnesses and try to figure out what really transpired in the cave.

They sat crowded in Joe Bob's office, around Joe Bob's desk, Pepper underneath the dusty photo of Dwight Eisenhower. Pepper had his notepad and tape recorder laid out before him and the five men were facing a box of biscuits and styrofoam cups of the best coffee Hazel could muster from the Paris (which, in Dodd's opinion, was still terrible).

"Let me get this straight." Pepper was trying to sum up a story line that even Dodd knew didn't add up. He rattled his pen on the table in a 6/8 paradiddle. "The four of you and Sheriff Meeker were in the cave looking for proof that Marion Rafferty, and not the Dodds, was responsible for the bank robbery of 1949. Rafferty found you, already certain you were going public with this race track deal. Then, when he found out you were going to prove he robbed the bank, he shot the sheriff. Fearing for everyone's life, the mayor here shot Rafferty? Is that your story?"

Peppers stood six feet six in his boots, but most of his height was in his torso, which towered over the table. His stomach creeped over the desk edge. He wore a wide-brimmed felt hat—even when he sat—and a navy blue sharkskin Western suit, one of the off-sized suits so common to barrel-chested men, with a fifty-four chest and forty inch waist. He wore his pants at his hips because they were narrower than his waist. Dodd thought Peppers would look a lot like the Meekers in another thirty years, once the Marshals put him out to pasture and he gave up on his waistline.

"That's it, Marshal," Dodd said. Alvin and Bobby Wayne nodded their heads in agreement, perhaps a touch too eagerly. The Marshall cleared his throat and stared at Ralph, who was staring at his twiddling thumbs rather than paying attention to the proceedings.

"I'd really like to hear it from the mayor," Peppers insisted. He made a constant chewing motion with his jaw, even though he had nothing in his mouth to chew.

Ralph still didn't look up from his thumbs. "Marshal, the entire evening was spent in an alcoholic haze. If it wasn't for the testimony of my dear friends at the table with me, I couldn't have told you whether I shot that rat bastard out of self-defense, sheer malice, or, for that matter, shot him at all."

Peppers clucked his tongue and stared back at Dodd. "And you swear that the mayor had no idea the gun was in your back pack."

"None whatsoever," Dodd swore, not wanting to add that he fully expected Ralph to find the gun when he looked inside. Which is why he put it there when he took it from him to start with.

"And why, again, did you have the gun? If you weren't expecting trouble, I mean."

"Snakes and rats," Dodd said.

"And bats," Alvin added.

"No shit," Bobby said, shivering. "Have you ever been in a cave?"

"And why was the sheriff armed?" Peppers asked.

"Joe Bob didn't go any where without his gun," Ralph said, his voice rising like a tea kettle. "He used to tell me he'd hang them on the bed post when he was in bed with some young woman and come while he was gazing at the gold-inlaid pearl handles. Joe Bob was like that."

"Why did you have the papers with you?" Peppers asked Dodd. "That seems like an odd thing to carry into a cave."

"I didn't want Rafferty to find them," Dodd said. "I thought it best to keep them with me. When I was in town I would keep them tucked under the driver's seat. I thought about leaving them in my car last night, but at the last minute I had a second thoughts. A hunch. You know, I just had this impulse to take them with me." He offered Peppers a biscuit, but Peppers declined. Dodd pushed aside several biscuits to look for some butter in the box, but found none.

Bobby, taking that as a cue, grabbed three biscuits for himself. Alvin slapped his hand and he put two back.

Peppers pushed his chair back from the table and sighed. "You found nothing in the cave that shed any more light on the robbery itself?"

"All we found was that weather balloon," Dodd said.

Alvin broke in. "But the records speak for themselves, Marshal. Rafferty called the Dodd family in to sign loan papers on Christmas Eve, shot his father and blamed the robbery on them. Had the Meekers killed all the Dodds, people would have assumed they buried the money somewhere. Had they been arrested, nobody would believe them anyway. I think it's admirable that the sheriff and his brother were willing to put their lives on the line to rectify that old wrong."

Peppers pushed his hat back and touched a bead of sweat from his forehead. It was in that moment that Dodd realized Peppers was bald. "Well, I don't mind saying that I smell some bullshit here. Not a little bit of bullshit, mind you, but a big steaming pile of bullshit drawing flies from here to Pecos. But I'm not sure it's worth poking my boot in it. This guy was a snake oil salesman and probably a grade A skull fucker.

"So, until I turn up any evidence to the contrary, I'm going to let you boys go, and I'm going to drop charges against the mayor on the condition that he doesn't run for re-election. Change his mind, I may stick my nose into this case a little deeper. You understand?" He held Ralph in a glare so cold it brought the temperature down several degrees.

Ralph nodded his head without a word. Alvin clinched his jaw in a silent victory cheer.

He turned to Dodd and pulled out another folder. "As to you, who the hell are you? According to your parole papers your name is Dodd Dodd Dodd, but I have an earlier driver's license with just the name Dodd."

Dodd blushed slightly. "That's a long story, Marshal. You see, my daddy wanted to name me Zelbert and my mother, God bless her, put her foot down. But daddy being unwilling to accept a name without Zel in it chose not to give me a name, so I was just Dodd until I went to Huntsville where an administrator insisted I had to have three names. So he put Dodd in all three blanks."

Peppers jaw stopped. "That makes no sense whatsoever."

"God bless the State of Texas," Dodd added.

Every one stood but Ralph. "I don't think Ralph has any inclination to run for mayor, Marshall." Dodd said. "He told me he planned to retire when he interviewed me for the job."

"Been planning it for quite some time now," Ralph mumbled.

"Do you mind if I talk to my client alone?" Dodd asked.

Peppers resettled his hat and shook his head. "You two are free to do whatever you want." Bobby held his hand over the biscuits and looked at Alvin. Alvin nodded and grabbed a handful along with a couple of napkins. Peppers held the door open for Alvin and Bobby to pass through, and then passed through behind them, still shaking his head.

He cast one last look at the gun cabinet. "You ask me, there are too damn many guns in this town."

Dodd sat across from Ralph, waiting for him to say something. Ralph placed his palms face down on the table and stared at the backs of his hands. The Saturday morning sunlight danced through the room, dust motes dancing in the yellow beams. Ralph was sober for the first time since Dodd had seen him, thanks to a night in jail waiting for the Marshall to arrive. Dodd wondered how long it would take for serious signs of withdrawal to set in.

"So it's just Dodd," Ralph said.

"Just Dodd," Dodd insisted.

They sat in silence for a few more minutes. "You could of pinned it all on me," Ralph finally said. "You had enough on me to tie me in with it."

"With Rafferty and Joe Bob dead, I didn't see any need. Besides, you were the only one who saw the humor in my garbage pit." He handed Ralph a biscuit. Ralph pushed it away.

"Jesus, Ralph, you need to eat. Nothing but booze and it will eat your stomach away."

"How long have you known about that cave?"

Dodd bit into a biscuit. Without the usual dripping melting butter at the diner to lather over it, it was almost too dry to swallow. He spit it back out onto the napkin. "Since I was a kid. Zel found it when they were little, and they always kept it secret. When he found the balloon he figured the Army would take it away, so he hid the pieces there."

Ralph finally looked up. "For God's sake why?"

"Because he really believed it was a flying saucer. That's how bad Joe Bob fucked him up. Joe Bob had him convinced the Army used his covert ops to cover up a real alien crash and section eight him at the same time."

Ralph clinched his fingers to keep his hands from shaking. The blood vessels in his eyes ran like rivers. "And there never was a UFO?"

"There are lots of them, Ralph. People see them every day. It kind of goes with the name. But these turned out to be balloons."

"So when Joe Bob and I ambushed the truck and killed Zel, your father and Zack ran and hid in the cave."

Dodd drummed his fingers on the desk. It didn't matter how often people faced the facts, they never wanted to see them. It was like looking in the mirror at the boil on your face and convincing yourself you just had a slight blemish.

"Zack never made it. You buried him somewhere."

Ralph blew through his lips as though blowing through a trumpet with no mouthpiece. "Joe Bob must have done that," he finally mumbled. He began to fidget. Finally he pushed himself out of his chair and walking over to the window. The sky was bone white again, another August day preparing to bake the ground rock hard and dirt dry. "Why'd your dad leave the money? It could have bought you all new identities. Got you started on a better life."

"He figured if he got caught with the money people would never believe he was innocent. Told my mom where it was if I ever made it back this far."

Ralph continued to look through the window, although he had to hold onto the frame to keep steady. "That's why you were passing through town."

Dodd considered another swallow of coffee and pitched the cup into the trash bin instead. He leaned across the desk to gather the rest of the cups. He noticed Carl Ray and Bobby Joe standing outside the door, peering in, as though they were fifth graders waiting for the principal. "It was a coin toss. Truth is, I had decided to move on when I noticed the leak in my fuel line. I figured the money would be rotted away after all these years. Then when you asked me to stay, I couldn't resist."

Ralph turned his back to the window and leaned against the wall. He closed his eyes for a moment, as though trying to settle his stomach. "I been thinking. People who really believe in UFOs would see that stuff in the cave and still believe it was a UFO. Especially if we advertised it that way. We could glue that cross beam back together; hell, just make a new one. Open up a UFO museum outside the ranch, put those pieces on display." He waved his arm dismissively. "Let the experts call them fakes, weather balloons, it really don't matter. All the better that they do. People'd pay five bucks a head just to see for themselves."

Dodd felt like leaping across the desk and slapping what was left of the liquor out of Ralph's system. "You can't be serious."

"Let me have those pieces, I'll make you full partner in everything I own. There was no one to leave the business to but Joe Bob. Hate to see the IRS liquidate when I'm worm food. You and me go in on this one last venture–Spaceworld –and you get it all when I croak. You run for mayor and, hell, son, what more could any American ask for?"

Dodd rapped his knuckles on the desk. "Bad idea, Ralph."

Ralph dropped into Joe Bob's chair and crossed his fingers as though in prayer. "You want the Feds to get my money? Son, you could of left me for dead in that cave. You and me. Partners for life." He stuck his hand across the desk.

Carl Ray and Bobby Joe couldn't wait any longer. Like overgrown puppies they decided Ralph's gesture was meant for them and pushed their way through the door at the same time. Carl Ray pushed his way in front of the desk first. He stood there, with his hat in both hands semi-respectfully in front of his belt buckle. Bobby Joe tried to step beside him, but Carl shuffled in front of him each time.

"Ralph, you need to make it clear which one of us is gonna be sheriff now that Joe Bob's gone, no disrespect," Carl Ray said, almost as a single word. "We gotta get our ducks in a row before this town falls apart."

Ralph's neck turned red and the color quickly spread to the top of his head. He slammed his fist on the desk. "Goddam it, boys, ain't neither one of you got enough brains between you to be sheriff, so count yourselves lucky to keep your jobs when I do appoint someone until the next election."

Bobby Joe finally slipped under Carl Ray's arm and said, "Come on, Joe Bob, who's gonna come to town just until the next election?"

This time Ralph pushed himself to his feet, and, in his best imitation of Joe Bob, he shoved his nose directly into Bobby Joe's. "Get the fuck outta this office or I'll appoint Dodd right here on the spot and let him deal with you."

With a chorus of obsequious "yes, sir"s and "absolutely"s, the two of them trampled over each other to escape the office. Within a matter of seconds, the office was quiet again and Ralph and Dodd faced off across the desk. Ralph extended his hand.

"A smart guy like you, hell, you'll own everything in town before you know it."

Dodd walked the door and then stood in the frame, leaning his shoulder against the jam. "Ralph, it may not be a town I'm interested in owning."

Chapter 50

As best Dodd could tell, the entire town turned out for the funeral at First Baptist Church and half the surrounding county as well. They didn't necessarily come to mourn the loss of their banker, so much as to enjoy the spectacle surrounding the biggest bloodbath since the Dodd ambush in Sweet Water Canyon.

Dodd and Rhonda sat in the last pew, allowing him to see everything. The church was too small for the number of people present, but, with twenty pews, it boasted the largest of the many contentious congregations in town. Rhonda dressed in black and cried more visibly than the widow or daughter, occasionally pushing aside her veil to dab her eyes with Dodd's handkerchief. Everyone stopped at their pew to shake Dodd's hand and tell him they always knew the Meekers had set up his family.

A man Dodd didn't recognize, dressed in a thousand dollar suit and three hundred dollar shoes, escorted Elizabeth and Mary Beth to the front pew. Elizabeth was dressed in a black chiffon dress that would be equally appropriate at a cocktail party, especially with the double strand of black pearls accenting the gentle thrust of her bosom. Mary Beth wore a navy cocktail dress, not even bothering with double entendre.

"Bitches," Rhonda whispered under her breath.

"Jesus, Rhonda, how can you be grieving that son-of-a-bitch," Dodd whispered back. "If he made it out of that cave he would have made your life hell."

"He gave me nice presents," she whispered back and then broke out into more tears and blew her nose in his handkerchief. "Besides, how do you know I'm not crying for Joe Bob?"

Joe Bob's casket stood head to head with Rafferty's—Rafferty's made of polished bronze with hand carved rails, Meeker's a plain casket with no adornments. Joe Bob's widow sat in front of the casket, a plain woman dressed in a plain black dress. She seemed only a little more upset than Elizabeth Rafferty. Both caskets were closed, lest the curious lean in to count the bullet holes.

Ralph sat across the aisle from Elizabeth and Mary Beth, his head rolling into his shoulder, clearly unaware of the proceedings around him. Dodd figured his moments in the sunlight of sobriety lasted as long as the walk from the jail to his car, where he kept a spare bottle of Beam under the passenger seat.

The right reverend Malachai Spears conducted the service, having won the rights to the funeral by the size of his small congregation. He led the mourners in a hymn, and then opened his eulogy with the words, "The town of Sweet Water Falls has lost two of its finest citizens and Christians." Nonplused by the chuckles that passed involuntarily through the audience, he painted a picture of Mal Rafferty and Joe Bob Meeker as saints of God who would march proudly through the gates of heaven. "Mal always gave him a sizable yearly donation to keep him from coming around the business or his house to witness," Rhonda whispered. "Never stopped him from coming to mine."

After the service, the mourners passed by the caskets, sang one more hymn about God welcoming the faithful into heaven, and most of them managed to keep a straight face. Dodd led Rhonda outside, her hand tucked through his elbow.

Bill Todd, Del Rayburn and Jaspar Huggins almost tackled him as they passed through the door. All three were giggling and Dodd was pretty sure Todd and Rayburn had been drinking. Rayburn was dressed in a forest green double-breasted suit, and Todd wore tan slacks and penny loafers. Todd draped his arms around Dodd's shoulder. "I hear you and Meeker are partners now. Things sure worked out for you."

Rhonda squeezed his elbow reassuringly.

"He offered. I was there when he made the offer," Dodd said. "Doesn't make us partners."

"Well, one thing's for damn sure," Rayburn snorted, throwing his right hand out to punch Dodd in the shoulder. "The road's clear for you to run for mayor."

"Who woulda thought?" Huggins smiled. The lift of his lip revealed a missing tooth. Somehow it spoiled the effect of his neatly pressed blue suit.

The five right reverends burst through the door, Bibles open and all arguing at once about the scriptural accuracy of Spear's eulogy. When they bumped into Dodd, Spears held up his hand to silence all of them, and said, "Mr. Dodd, you have managed to slip past us for two weeks now, but it's time we had a talk."

Dodd glanced at his watch. "Gee, sorry, preachers. But I have to be in Sante Fe tomorrow morning, so its time for me to head back to the farm house."

"You're leaving?" Rhonda said, her face turning visibly white, even under her veil. Her shoulders seemed to collapse a little.

"You're joking, aren't you," Todd said, slapping him on the back.

"I was supposed to take a job at a law firm two weeks ago," Dodd said, placing his hand over Rhonda's and squeezing. "I talked to them on the phone last night and they said the job's still open if I can get there by tomorrow. I really don't have much choice in the matter, fellows."

"I thought you and Meeker was gonna open up a UFO museum," Rayburn said. "I thought you was gonna run for mayor." He wiped his forehead with his sleeve. The sun was already set to broiling, and the polyester in his suit wasn't helping.

"Do you people honestly believe I would do business with one of the men who murdered my family? Or stick around the town that didn't even question their story?" Dodd turned to Rhonda. "Let me take you home now." Her eyes were moist and she nodded her head.

"Mr. Dodd," the Right Reverend Spears interjected, "your soul is more important than your time table."

"Jesus, Dodd," Todd said, "ain't no one else around here who could run for mayor and get away with it."

Even as they flung their protests toward him, Dodd led Rhonda another step down and onto the sidewalk. Mary Beth pulled up beside them in a Pink Cadillac Seville Convertible, dealer plates still in place.

Dodd stepped off the curb. Mary Beth powered down her window with a single finger on the electric switch. A cold blast of refrigerated air slapped him in the face. He leaned his elbow across the roof. "The insurance settlement came quickly didn't it?" Dodd said.

Mary Beth lit a cigarette with a gold plated, hand-carved lighter. The cigarette fit snugly into an ivory holder. "I just wanted to tell you I don't think we should see each other any more," she told him, letting a cloud of smoke from her cigarette fly in his direction.

"I thought we already agreed on that, Mary Beth."

She glanced at the rearview and touched up her lipstick with her little finger. "Do you honestly think I would be interested in the man who killed my father?"

"I didn't kill your father," Dodd said.

"It's all in the details, isn't it?"

He stepped back from the door and surveyed the length of the car. "Mary Beth, I hate to say it, but you aren't exactly grieving as far as I can tell."

"Well," she said, releasing an elegant smoke ring that drifted out over the hood of the car, "how upset do you expect me to be? He did kill my grandfather after all.

"I loved my grandad," she added, managing a tear at the corner of her eye.

"The grandfather who died before you were born?"

"All the more reason for me to cherish his memory."

She pushed the window button and the smoked glass slid back into place. Then she pulled away from the curb, almost brushing Dodd back and peeled out down the highway.

As he watched the car disappear he felt someone tugging at his elbow. He turned to see Joe Bobb's widow standing next to him. The veins in her nose made it clear she spent more time drinking than mourning. "I never intended for this to happen, ma'am," he said with as much sincerity as he could muster. A little more sincerity, he felt, than the condolences of most of the other folks in town.

"Don't be sorry," she told him. "Those two had half the meanness and twice the greed in Texas between the two of them. I'm surprised they didn't shoot each other in the back years ago. I just thought they'd take his no account brother with them."

He drove Rhonda back to her place. Dodd draped his jacket over his sofa and let her make lemonade. She brought his glass in from the kitchen, sweating in the morning heat and slight breeze from the overhead fan and her open window. Then she kicked off her shoes and tucked her legs underneath her on the couch.

"Do you really have to go?"

Dodd sipped and nodded his head. It was no sweeter than the last time. "I have a real job in a real city."

"I thought we had something," she said. She kept her eyes down, as though she didn't want see otherwise in his.

"We do. But do we have enough to keep me here?" He looked for a magazine to keep from leaving a ring on her coffee table. She seemed like the kind of woman who might hold that against him far longer than the brush off.

"You really are a cold-hearted bastard, aren't you?" she accused him, but gently, less in anger than disappointment.

He leaned across the couch and touched her knee reassuringly. "I'm an ex-con and a lawyer. What did you expect?"

She glanced up suddenly. "I could come with you."

Jesus Christ, he realized, she's serious. "Am I inviting you?"

"I don't have a life here anymore," she said. She tucked her feet under her legs and leaned forward eagerly.

Dodd backed away. "There are lots of places you can move to. You don't have to follow me."

She slid across the couch, and nestled her head on his shoulder. "One last time then, for the road?" She ran her hand down his chest and let it linger on his belt buckle.

He stopped her hand. "This wouldn't make it easier, Rhonda."

She jumped off her couch and tossed a throw pillow at his head. "Then go ahead and get out of town, you bastard. I hope I never do see you again."

She stormed into the kitchen. Dodd watched her leave. "I just meant a goodbye kiss and your phone number might be less awkward."

Chapter 51

After Dodd packed his bags and closed down the house, he left the keys under the porch. Bobby would stay with Alvin and Wanda until his probation was up, which didn't make Wanda happy. On the other hand she couldn't really argue when Dodd reminded her he'd just given them fifteen thousand and filed the paperwork for Preacher's release. Ralph's sworn statement and the documents about the robberies would have him out of Huntsville by the end of the week.

He threw his luggage in his Mustang, and, rather than heading North to New Mexico, struck out West to Fort Stockton. He pulled into the Old West Inn and parked in front of the same room where Rafferty trysted with Rhonda and Marla.

The door opened as soon as he turned the ignition off, and Elizabeth Rafferty stuck her head through the door, wrapping one leg around the frame and beckoning him with her finger.

He jumped over the door of his Mustang, not worrying about his loose luggage in the back seat, and rushed into the hotel room, unbuttoning his shirt with each step.

Elizabeth slammed the door behind him. Stark naked, she dropped to her knees, and pulled his pants past his hips without loosening his belt or opening his fly. The minute she kissed his cock it shot straight out in front of him. "You've been waiting to play," she laughed. Then she stood, wrapped one arm around his neck, and wrapped her legs around his waist, and guided his way into her with her free hand.

Even as they began to push against each other, she managed to spin him around so fast they he fell backward on top of the bed, and she rode him there, biting his neck, his nipples and his earlobe, laughing and giggling and squeezing his thighs with her knees.

After they both came, she jumped off him laughing, and pulled him with her into the shower, where they soaped each other down and kissed and caressed and slid each other fingers into every place of their bodies fingers could go.

"I'm mad at you, you know," she said, soaping his chest with a bar and her hands, tweaking his nipples and running the soap down his stomach.

"For sleeping with your daughter?" Dodd asked.

She dropped the soap, and bent down on her knees to retrieve it, reaching up to soap his cock and balls once she found it again. "No, silly. She's a tramp. She doesn't count. She has no class. Did you know she bought a condo in Dallas yesterday? Over the phone? She already packed up her things; only stayed for the funeral."

"Where are you moving to, Elizabeth?" he asked, massaging her wet hair with his fingers.

She stood up and traced her fingers down his breastbone, down his stomach, and even further on. "I made the down payment on a villa in Provence months ago. But that's not the point. The point is her father's not even in the ground and she's already going through the insurance money. Do you know how hard it was not to come visit you with you being so close? It was difficult indeed."

She dropped to her knees and took him into her mouth, once hand flat against the shower wall, the other hand gripping the shower curtain. He let her bring him to the point of coming and then he pulled her up, backed her into the shower wall and plunged inside her again.

Later, he lay on the bed wrapped in a towel. She sat naked at the foot of the bed, drying her hair. "You did a marvelous job," she said. "I didn't think you'd actually kill him, but it was well worth losing controlling interest in the bank just to see that double-dealing cooze hound dead."

"I didn't kill him, Elizabeth. Ralph did."

She leaned across the bed, pulled the towel away and thumped him on the cock with a fingernail. "Details, details. Although I am a bit miffed you never told me you really were Zane's son."

"You could have asked. When you asked my boss to introduce us at his Christmas party."

She pulled away from him and began to dry her hair. "Actually, you look just like your father. I thought that if you really were his kid, you would jump at the chance to kill Mal."

"I didn't kill him, Elizabeth."

She turned off the blow dryer and laid it on the bed stand. "Posh. We both got what we wanted. The means hardly matter, do they? I had my cake and ate it too." She crawled across the bed like a cat, settled against his chest and began to purr. "I had my attorney draw up the papers. Do you want to look at them?"

Dodd nodded his head. "Sure."

She climbed off the bed, gracefully, like a dancer, and tiptoed to a small leather attaché case on the dresser. She popped the latch with a quick movement of both hands, and within seconds settled in on top of him, wriggling her hips and handing him the papers at the same time.

He scanned the pages while she wiggled and leaned over to blow in his ear. "How can you concentrate when I'm trying so hard to distract you, darling?" she said.

"Nothing is more erotic than reading briefs while a woman grinds her hips into your waist," he told her.

"We drew them up exactly the way you asked. The first set gives you power-of-attorney over our shares of the bank for the next year. Then second set transfers ownership to you six-months at a time over the next four years as compensation for legal representation and managing the bank. If at any time you advise us to sell the shares to another owner, we split the profits on a sliding scale based on how many shares you actually own."

He flipped through the second document. "I asked for controlling interest, Elizabeth. Not a fifty-one percent share, just forty. That gives me enough clout but raises fewer suspicions."

She pushed the papers aside and leaned in to nibble his neck. "Dodd, you don't want all those headaches. And you're hardly in a position to challenge me. I mean, we don't want another investigation into my husband's death, do we?"

"I didn't kill him," he reminded her.

"Of course not, darling," she purred in his ear, and reached between his legs with her hand. Satisfied that he was ready once again, she pushed him into her at the same time as she pushed his papers down on the bed.

Night fell. They signed the papers, and then she dressed herself in a pale white cocktail dress with two diamond earrings and white satin pumps.

"How does it feel to own a piece of Sweet Water Falls?" she cooed from where she sat in front of the dresser. Dodd checked the signatures on the documents and then folded them to fit in his pocket.

"All I own is shares in the bank, Elizabeth and I'll probably sell those."

"I thought poor old addle-brained Ralph offered you controlling interest in his businesses. For a few scraps of metal no less."

"This is the last I'm going to see you, isn't it?" he said, sitting in the chair beside the window and watching her apply her make up.

She dabbed her lipstick with a tissue. "And poor Rhonda Mayfield. I heard she filled up a shopping cart with gin bottles after your visit this afternoon. She really thought you were going to be her knight in shining armor."

Dodd poured ice water from the ice bucket on the dresser. "Be kind, Elizabeth. And I'm not even going to ask why, much less how you were keeping tabs on the poor woman. That doesn't answer my question, this is the last time I'm going to see you, isn't it."

She turned around in her chair, and crossed her knees as she faced him. "Why, darling, whatever gave you that idea?"

"Let's just say that some things don't change from mother to daughter."

She smiled and turned back to the mirror to powder her nose. "Darling, let's just say this deal gives you a solid future, but I couldn't let you run my life."

Dodd set the glass down. He leaned against the dresser and leaned his face in to hers. "I don't want to control your life or run the town. I want the forty percent you promised me. Jesus, Elizabeth, it isn't as though your bank holdings come close to your total wealth now that Mal's gone."

She picked up her brush, then paused. "It's true, Mal was very good at making money, even if his ethics were questionable. But if we were seen together, it might raise questions about the circumstances of his death."

He lay his head flat against the mirror and closed his eyes.

"Darling, did I hurt your feelings?" she said. "I didn't mean to. You understood this wouldn't work over the long haul. I just think that means we shouldn't carry it any further than this."

She rose from her chair and touched his forehead gently. "You're a very understanding man. I'd kiss you if it wouldn't muss my lipstick. And if you ever do come through Provence, please ring me, because I enjoyed all our little afternoons as much as you did."

Dodd heard a car pull up outside. She fastened her valise and attaché. "Would you be a dear and carry my bags to the cab?"

Dodd didn't even bother to ask how the timing had been so perfect. He carried her luggage to the cab and loaded it into the trunk. She pecked his cheek. "Lovers come and go, darling. Business deals last a lifetime. If you learn that, you're on your way." She slid into the back seat of the cab and closed the door behind her, not even looking back as the cab pulled from the lot.

When the taillights disappeared, Dodd sighed and returned to the room to finish dressing. He lifted Elizabeth's papers and struck a match to the lower left edge. He dropped them into the trashcan to burn. Then he examined the papers she had signed, the ones he had switched, transferring forty percent of the stock on the terms they originally agreed to, and selling him her remaining shares in the Sweet Water Bank out of dividends accrued during the term of the contract. The papers that also gave him power of attorney over all other properties mortgaged or financed through the bank, which included her house as well.

Given the circumstances, Elizabeth was in no better position to challenge the new documents than he would have been to challenge her amended ones. He just paid closer attention to the details. Besides, she still had assets and accounts worth four times the value of her Sweet Water shares, and properties tucked away in a dozen Texas and offshore banks. All Elizabeth really thought about was the next party on her agenda anyway.

And Mary Beth? Well, Mary Beth might have to suck up to her mother for a few more years until her trust fund kicked in, but Dodd didn't find the thought of it all that sad.

He spread them out beside the partnership agreement he signed with Meeker just after he left Rhonda's, and sighed again. He really did own the whole damn town, even the farm where Ralph would build his UFO museum. He would have to rethink the name Spaceworld, but that could come later.

He owned everything but the Paris Cafe, Todd's used car dealership and the dry cleaner. Originally he had planned to sell cheap and walk away, bringing in out-of-town investors who would ruin Sweet Water Falls the same way they ruined every other small town they got their grips on.

But, as he looked at the papers again, he found it much harder to do than he expected.

Chapter 52

Rhonda woke with the first crack of dawn, although she could hardly call it waking when she spent most of the night sleepless and crying. And, if she cared to admit it, working through most of a pint of gin. She tiptoed to the bathroom and studied her face in the mirror, cursing herself that she'd let one more man make it so red and splotchy.

She spent half an hour in the shower, letting the water wash away her mixed feelings toward Rafferty and Dodd. Especially Dodd. When she finally thought she could face the day, and the bank, and her two-timing betraying bitch daughter Marla, she stepped out, dried off and spent a good twenty minutes creating a new face from powder, mascara, eye liner, blush and foundation.

She chose her best power suit for the day. The bank would be in turmoil as Elizabeth prepared to take over operations or transfer ownership. She really hoped Elizabeth would sell. She couldn't imagine having to work with Mal's wife on a daily basis.

She brewed a cup of peppermint tea and microwaved a muffin for her breakfast, deciding to finish it as she drove to work. She threw her purse over her shoulder, took in a lungful of air and opened the door while balancing the mug and muffin with her free hand.

When she saw Dodd asleep on her porch, legs stretched out into her garden and head rolling against the house, she almost dropped everything. "What the hell are you doing here?" she demanded.

"I came by so late I didn't want to wake you," he said, stretching and rubbing his eyes. He looked to her to help pull him up, and then, realizing she was occupied, he pushed himself up and dusted off his pants.

"We need to talk," he said, with his usual disarming smile. This morning it not only failed to disarm her, it brought out defenses she never knew she had.

"I have to get to work," she told him, pulling the door shut behind her.

He took her breakfast from her and leaned into her, speaking directly into her ear in a soft voice, "Call in and tell them you'll be late."

She pressed her back into the wall trying to slide free. "I can't. We'll be attending to transfers of ownership today. I need to be there."

He threw his palm up against the wall to bar her way. "The boss won't mind."

She ducked under his arm and trotted quickly to the car. She made it to the driver's door and deposited her breakfast on the roof while she fumbled for the keys in her purse. He followed her, grinning, like a faithful puppy you want to kick. "Fine," she said. "How would you know the boss won't mind?"

Dodd pulled the papers out of his jacket pocket and waved them in front of her. "Because I'm the boss. Elizabeth Dodd signed over controlling interest last night."

Rhonda dropped her keys into the purse and snatched the papers from him. "How did you pull this off?"

"I met her at a party in Houston two years ago. We became friends...."

"You fucked her too?" She was surprised she managed to get the words out of her mouth.

"When I lost my job, she thought my presence in Sweet Water Falls might work to her advantage. She was hoping to get the goods to divorce her husband. As it turned out, things worked out even better than she hoped."

"I'll bet." She took the papers from his hand and skimmed through them. When she got to his agreement with Meeker, she held it up and asked, "What's this?"

"I went ahead and took Meeker up on his offer."

"Even his stupid UFO Museum?"

"We break ground in January. I have to float a loan or two, but since I own the bank it shouldn't be hard. We invited several investigators to look at the pieces, but we're only inviting the respectable ones after the flying saucer crazies have picked them over and publicized them in all their fanzines. To get the word rolling you understand. Meeker even wants to start rumors that Rafferty had Zack and Zel killed to cover up their knowledge of the UFO cover up in Roswell. He thinks we can make this into the biggest circus in flying saucer history, and that in ten years half the people in America will believe the government covered everything up."

She rolled the contracts into a tube and banged the roof of her car with frustration. Finally she took a deep breath and asked, "What changed your mind?"

Dodd took the papers from her and leaned into her, pressing her into the car. "You're right. I'm a cold bastard. I thought you might thaw me out."

She wrapped her fingers behind his neck and pulled him in to kiss her. "I called you a cold-hearted bastard."

He kissed her back, "Is there a difference?"

She leaned her head away. "You never told me whether you fucked Liz Rafferty."

He put his hands behind her neck and leaned in closer. "You told me you never wanted to see me again."

She slipped underneath him and pulled way, leaning against her car with her hand over her breast. "There's fucking a woman, and fucking a woman, and that means you still haven't answered my question. Besides, I said I hoped I didn't see you again, not that I didn't want to see you again. There's a difference."

Dodd leaned his elbow on the roof of her car. "And the difference is?"

"I hope I never see you again because you're a cold-hearted bastard, and you're all wrong for me. But I want to see you again because I'm in love with you."

He nodded his head. "So you're glad I'm staying."

She took her hand from her breast and pushed it against his, leaning flat against him and stretching her neck to kiss him again. "So now that you own the town, do you plan to run for mayor?"

He circled her waist with his arms and said, "No. I thought you should run."

She stepped back and laughed. "Me?"

"It's bad to mix politics and money. I'd think folks would have learned that by now."

She tapped a fingernail against her teeth for a second, crossing one foot behind her ankle. He wanted to pick her up right their and carry her to the bedroom. But as he leaned over to kiss her again, she held him back with the flat of her hand.

"Wait a minute, buster. Maybe we shouldn't mix business with pleasure either."

He laughed and stepped back. "You're kidding?"

She kept her hand against his chest. Clouds crossed the August sun and he felt the temperature drop by a degree or two. A roadrunner touched down in the road to look for grubs. She could tell he wanted her right then more than anything he'd wanted in his life. Her hand pressed harder against his chest. Then she pushed away and touched up her hair.

"I've seen the light, Dodd," she told him. "This town needs a woman's touch a lot more than it needs a star struck lover."

From her rearview, she could him standing in her driveway as she pulled away for work. She waved. He was a big boy. He'd know how to find her.

Thanks to my wife Carol who puts up with my shit everyday, including proofreading this book. And to my mother, who put up with my shit until I left home and who will be really embarrassed when she reads some of the scenes in this book.

Additional thanks to Jamie Campbell, author of *Four Days*, who volunteered to proofread for the print-on-demand edition after reviewing the e-book.

Phillip T. Stephens is a mythological character who evolved from a spin-off cult of the Church of the Subgenius called Our Lady of the Lady of the Lord of the Subtransgender in the late 1970s. In Subtransgender mythology Stephens was Bob Dobbs sidekick who dreamed of surpassing Dodds as the universe's top salesman. In order to do so, he sold the Xists on plans to convert the earth to transgender only condos, which would, in essence, put a kibosh on the entire Subgenius sales pitch. Needless to say this subjected Stephens to the wrath of Bob who short sold all of Stephens' shares in America Online, causing the recession of 2000 and reducing Stephens into a clone of Pewee Herman. Many followers believe Stephens can now be seen as Jim Parsons on the Big Bang Theory with no awareness of who he truly is, but they are, of course, completely misguided.

Needless to say, the Church of the Subgenius in no way acknowledges Our Lady of the Lady of the Lord of the Subtransgender.

His wife Carol patiently waits for him to start behaving like a normal human being and devotes most of her time to patient babysitting and Austin Siamese Rescue.

Follow Phillip @stephens_pt

Also by Phillip T. Stephens

Raising Hell

A clueless optimist ruins a perfectly good hell.

Pity poor Lucifer. He rules hell with a vice grip. Demons and damned scatter at the sound of his footsteps. The Supreme Butt In hasn't pestered him in eons. Lucifer's future looks perfect, pitch black, until an administrative error sticks him with an innocent soul–an overweight optimist who calls himself Pilgrim and who believes he must be in hell to do good.

Lucifer never considers sending him back. He orders his subordinates to torture, degrade and humiliate Pilgrim until he promises to become evil if only it will ease the pain. Unfortunately, Pilgrim makes the best of the worst possible experiences. Always polite and well-mannered, he makes Pollyanna seem like a prophet of doom. Even worse, the damned start catching on, and set about making hell into the most enjoyable place of everlasting torment they can.

Lucifer can't let Pilgrim continue to wreak happiness, but he can't send him back untainted, either. When God arrives with a deadline for Pilgrim's return, he enlists fellow fallen angels Screwtape, Azazel and the gender morphing Mephistopheles in a plot to corrupt Pilgrim's soul before the deadline expires.

The Worst Noel

Hark the televangels sing...

Lucifer sends the only innocent soul in hell to save a small town church in Bedford Falls and its century-old Christmas pageant. But Pilgrim knows that if Lucifer wants the church saved, it can't be good. When a televangelist declares on FOX News that ground zero for the War on Christmas is Bedford Falls the church becomes national news.

Pilgrim befriends Elwood Wilson, descendent of the late Elwood P. Dowd, and George Bailey Jr., the church's pastor, to save the church. But they face what seems to be a losing battle against televangelists, megachurches and even the Governor of Texas, who have decided that the only thing to stop Chrismageddon is a Hal-lelujahpaloozah with rock bands and an all-star cast on national TV.

A holiday novelette from the author of Raising Hell in the tradition of *It's a Wonderful Life*, only this devil will never earn his horns.